WESTERMEAD

Also by
Scott Thomas

Cobwebs and Whispers

Shadows of Flesh

**The Sea of Flesh and Ash
(with Jeffrey Thomas)**

WESTERMEAD

Scott Thomas

"The Woman Who Cried Birds" originally appeared in
Penny Dreadful #12, Wynter

Published by Raw Dog Screaming Press
Hyattsville, MD

First Paperback Edition

Cover image: Jules-Joseph Lefebvre
Book design: Jennifer Barnes

Printed in the United States of America

ISBN: 1-933293-08-X

Library of Congress Control Number: 2005902916

www.rawdogscreaming.com

For Mama

Contents

✿ Spring ✿

Churn

The first month of the Westermead calendar expresses well the duality that wrestles and blends throughout the cycle of the seasons. The final throes of winter play harsh across the bleak earth, only to recede at the strengthening sun's insistence. This is the month when the sky and the sea share vastness, greyness and turbulence. Cold rains hammer the coasts and fields blur to mud as temperatures venture higher. On Plough Morn, at mid-month, there are rituals and celebrations across the land, to mark the Spring's rebirth and ensure fertility in the days ahead. Clouds churn menacingly as this month begins, as the life-force within soil-snug seeds churns, and the month comes to an end.

Seedstir

One rediscovers their winter-numbed senses this month. The pulse of life has quickened—it hums in the flight of bees and pounds in the hooves of pasture-bound herds. The hills are green, the meadows proud with their declarations of wildflowers. The sun's warmth urges gorse to gold and foals to shed the shaggy coats that winter had woven. The air is a delightful clutter of bird song as the nose revels in plum blossom and primrose. Eager branches purse their bud-lips, anxious to kiss the sun-drenched sky.

Greensurge

The rain is sweet and nourishing, the days gentle and warm. Vigor glows yellow-green from crowding vegetation. Sheep indulge. Farmers hasten their sowing. One can now gather the blond of broom and the fragrant white of hawthorn. Villagers in the Midlands celebrate Wreathe Feast, when all the pregnant women are given gifts, and their bellies are festooned with rings of flowers.

The Green Boy

TWO HALF-GROWN girls fluttered past the slow-footed woman, a breeze of giggles and skirts and perfume. Off they went, along the path and up the hill. Linnie Mossgrove trudged along with her staff, one hand soothing across the pout of her belly.

"Shhh, rest still, my small and kicking one," she cooed down at the bulge. "You can feel it, can't you?"

The rhythmic thumping seemed to come from the ground, as well as the air. It grew closer as she mounted the hill. The hem of her skirt was dark with mud, her hair like a mad spill of wind and her soles ached…still, she had reached the source of the drumming.

The villagers were gathered on the edge of a field, delighted and hardy in the unobstructed breeze. The land stretched far, all stubbled and hard, the scars of a previous harvest healed by winter's white ointment. A spell woman stood like fluttering ink in her garb of black, her tangled red hair crowding her face to shadows.

Linnie moved unnoticed to the outer edge of the revelers, smiling wearily. There were kegs of ale and tables of food and bored horses loitering. Old men with tankards abrim and black smiles cheered and joked. Children frolicked underfoot. Village women of all ages had amassed alongside the field, their collective whispers like a humming hive.

The focus of the assemblage was a row of men—naked but for rounded wicker cones fleshed in purple moss known as bruise fur which covered their faces and heads. They walked slowly, shoulder to shoulder, up, then down the length of the field, all the while pounding at the earth with long staves. They worked to set the earth's pulse thrumming, to waken the spirits of the soil.

The spell woman went about her business of chanting and sprinkling herbs, and rattling strings of bells. Her feet also drummed the hard ground.

The audience of women took great delight in admiring the charms of the

13

village men who comprised the stave-team. They made a game of trying to identify the men by their bodies alone.

"Ooow, I want that one!" a woman exclaimed, pointing.

"My, my, he's like a horse!" another replied.

"That's my Broondy, you lumps of lard, no mistake about it," another bragged.

Linnie Mossgrove stood back, hugging herself. She was not inclined to go down to where the others had gathered in their fidgety glee. She was solemn, her eyes a shy brown, her hair as dark as fresh-turned soil, her mouth a timid pout. She stroked her swollen belly and shivered in the breeze.

The month of Churn was a stormy thing, when winds howled grey and rain stabbed cold. The ground was stiff and ravaged in places, quick to mud in the first warm days. Linnie recalled the time she had met her husband, two years back, on Plough Morn. It had actually snowed! But today was not so bad, and might brink on warm were it not for the breeze. Merciful sunlight oozed out from behind that sky of far-flung shale.

She took in the guisers as they passed—inscrutable creatures, looking out through the skull-sockets of their purple helmets. There was a touch of guilt and the taunt of yearning as she eyed their flexing limbs. Heavy staffs set the earth beneath her pulsing, and the child within her squirmed.

The ritual continued. Two great and rippling bulls were yoked to a plough with the stave-team following. The animals' horns were bedecked with ribbons of green, their wide necks strung with bells. The leader of the staffers, his cone peaked with a spurt of fresh-plucked snowdrop flowers, clenched the handles…the initial thrust of the ploughshare broke the crust of earth and cheers went up from the crowd. A single furrow was cut down the center of the field; the spell woman danced along with a plump skin flask pouring blood from last Noovum's meat slaughter into the jagged fissure.

It was done. The folk took to celebrating; some of the staffmen chose to remain in "costume" as they mingled. Quite often young people paired off and slipped away for private rites of fertility. The feasting, fraternizing, music and dance would go on well into the night.

At last some of the villagers took notice of Linnie. They embraced her, saw to it that she was well fed and inquired as to the progress of her pregnancy.

"Ohh, he's a restless one," she reported, smiling, "growing impatient with his situation. He's terribly strong."

They were pleased. "You're sure it's a boy, then?"

"The spell woman thinks so."

"Ahhh, and she's never wrong!" another woman exclaimed. "She was right about my four."

An old woman, hunched with "the creak," hobbled over as Linnie departed her previous acquaintances. "Linnie, lass—it should've been you out there stirring them fields to life!"

Linnie grinned. "Why, hello, Old Mag!"

A crooked finger wagged in her face. "You've the touch to make things grow, lassie. Remember when my herbs were plagued, how you came and did your fancy tricks to make 'em well? And when Humber Clanside's turnip patch had them awful bugs hauntin' it? You took care of that right good, too!"

"I'm not a magic woman, Mag, I just try and try and put my heart into it is all. I speak to the earth with my heart, and she listens."

"Well, it ain't just collected bits of knowledge, that's a certainty, you've got that special something."

"I thank you for your words; you're kind."

Two young boys watched from behind the wall of tables and kegs. Old Mag hobbled away and Linnie stood looking out across the field.

"It's Widow Mossgrove," one boy noted in a hush.

"No it isn't, she's too fat."

"She's with child, you dung-head!"

"Ohh, right."

"I've heard," the first whispered, "that a strange white rodent comes to her bed at night and brings her gifts…"

                          ℧   ℧   ℧

The earth was warm beneath Linnie's knees as she knelt in the tangled womb of her garden. All around her Spring was about its subtle miracle. Buds like wind-stiff nipples pouted from long-barren branches. Fragile sprouts breached the soil's dry crust and unfolded their first shy leaves. The unruly snares of rose briar, along the fence to her right, were greening nicely. Violets peeked out from behind a burst of broad upright fronds.

Gentle hands probed and worked the soil. It was cool as it clotted between her fingers—the scent dark and rich. The texture was loamy where she had worked in sand. There were secret forests of roots and the clammy pink spasms of worms disturbed. Many marvelous little creatures dwelled in that hidden world—ants, beetles, quick spiders and centipedes like ambery chains.

With hoe and spade a spot was cleared, and the woman, at peace with this place, hummed as she worked. Bees spun about through the sweet plant fumes as she lifted a small ceramic pot and carefully worked loose the dying plant within.

"You poor thing." She gently shook off the excess dirt from the roots. It was a mothcandle, a smallish plant with greyish flowers, which, as the name implied, resembled moths. The flowers were doubly curious in that they only opened at night, and gave off a spectral glow. The village baker had given the plant to her after a bout of poor luck with it. The fellow had become quite flustered with the thing, for no matter what he tried, it would not bloom.

The plant was ill, its roots weak, stems near-brittle, leaves wilting and yellowed about their tips. Linnie examined it closely before lowering it into the hole she'd made. She closed her eyes as she worked the soil in around the base of the thing, her fingers swirling in the moist darkness until the earth seemed to hum.

"Nannie…" Linnie called softly.

Her fingers moved slowly, gracefully, emphatically.

"Nannie Blossom…where are you?"

The mothcandle sagged as if weary of this new place, stunned, even having been removed from that strangling clay pot.

"Nannie Blossom, come help, come help. As my love nourishes you, dear friend, then come help me heal this sorry little plant."

Beneath the soil, where her hands were immersed, Linnie felt something lick at her fingers, a worm perhaps, then something else… It was like a warm electric breeze surging in circles about the root ball of the mothcandle. It seemed to flow right through her hands.

"That's right, Nannie, do your dance. Spin and dance, my little friend."

🌀 🌀 🌀

The hamlet of Barrowloam was a farming community not twenty miles from the western coast of Westermead. When the month of Seedstir came the hills plumped green and sprawls of gorse blazed blond. Languid herds took to their grazing pastures as fields were ploughed to chocolate-brown and seeded. Sun-drunk blossoms crowded the bases of humble crofts.

Linnie sat alongside Reedly Grimledge, the village magistrate, as his coach creaked and jounced along the path to his house. The Kingdom official was a thin man with tousled grey hair and a horsey smile. His jokes were quick and tart and his laughter all snorts and coughs. He had Linnie pealing jubilantly the whole trip.

"Ahh, here we are!" Reedly announced. They came to a stop by a handsome two story building of stone—a rarity in that its roof was tiled in slate. On either side of the broad wooden door stood a lamp post coiled in ivy. Directly in front of these was a small ringed pool with a large stone vase rising from its center.

Reedly helped Linnie down. "Here we go. Right then, it's over here." He led her over to the pool.

"Mister Grimledge, would it have not been proper to ask the spell woman to tend to this matter?" the ever-humble Linnie inquired.

Reedly snickered mischievously. "Oh, I'm afraid I couldn't do that. She still hasn't forgiven me for that joke I played on her last Balance-Tide. Do you remember? I hid some sheep dung in a—oh, never mind! Come look at this poor wretch."

Linnie stepped up on the stone rim, which encircled the pool, and peered down at the plant inside the vase. It was a gullrose, so named because of the long beak-like thorns on the stems and the feathery white of its blooms. It was partly folded upon itself; some of the stems were snapped.

"Something crushed it, you said?"

17

"Ah, yes, I failed to elaborate. You may remember a few nights back—three, no, four, wait, three, yes, that's it. Three nights back we had a most vigorous storm. You recall?"

"Mm hm."

"Well, I heard reports from the coast, from most reliable sources I might add, that it rained hares as well as water."

"No...you're joking!"

"I'm not. Dozens of the buggers came down, washed up on the shore as well. Fishermen collected them and piled 'em like cairns. Dreadful, I know. They sold a good many of them to the butcher."

"Really?"

"Right. Anyway, as the storm moved inland some of these unfortunate beasts fell about my property. And, of all places, one landed smack on my favorite gullrose! Such a shame, too, it was budding up so well."

"You're not fooling, are you?"

"Dear Linnie, look at the thing, it's been hit with a hare!"

She laughed.

"I wouldn't joke about a thing such as that. The sky does rain strange objects on occasion. When I was a boy in Shropegrove it rained newts. I was lying out at picnic, dozing in fact, with my blasted mouth open and...blah!"

Linnie laughed until her baby kicked. "Now you've got him in an uproar."

"He's angry because you don't believe my story about the raining rabbits."

"All right then, I believe you. Now, I'd best get to work before I chuckle myself dizzy and fall in the pool."

Linnie tied some of the bent stems to splints and pinched off some buds so that the plant could conserve enough strength to heal itself. She sprinkled a blend of powdered nutrients onto the soil and watered them in. Finally she swirled her fingers lightly through the upper layer of mulch.

"Come, Nannie, come, help me do my bidding," she whispered.

The soil grew warm.

"Nannie Blossom, hear my call, come swift, come now."

Tingles of electric fur traced across her submerged fingertips.

Reedly came out of the house as she was washing her hands in the pool.
"Done so soon, are we, Linnie?"

"Yes, sir. Your gullrose will be fine now."

"Oh, splendid, splendid! Do tell me you'll stay for a meal, I can't send you off without showing my appreciation."

"I'll gladly stay if you like."

"Oh, splendid! We're having roasted rabbit."

❧ ❧ ❧

Linnie peeled back the bedcovers and slid beneath them. The weighty swell of her belly made even so mundane an action as this a task. She chuckled at her own gracelessness. As she sat there in the middle of that cool expanse of sheets her smile turned to pout.

She thought of those rippling men she had watched on Plough Morn, their healthy limbs all farm-work muscled, their backs strong and hind quarters taut. How comforting it would have been just to have such a body lying beside her again.

"Well, I'm not alone, am I?" she said, patting her belly. "We have each other, don't we, small one? Soon you'll be out, and won't that be fine? I'll take such good care of you, I promise."

The solitary candle by the bed lit the solitary tear on her cheek.

"What times we'll have. I'll teach you to garden, and to sing, and we'll play foolhardy games and picnic. I'll take you to visit your dear father's grave, and tell you how brave he was, going off to the North War, like he did."

She leaned over and blew out the rushlight before curling fetal on her side, her palms pressed to the warm passenger within.

"I hope you never have to go off to some awful war," she whispered. "Perhaps you'll be a man of peace and gentleness, content to make life grow from the earth, rather than cause others to be put into it. But your father was a good man, mind you, and he thought what he did was right. I don't know, but I loved him."

She hovered on the brink of sleep, listening to the chirping night. And before her awareness could give way to dreams, there came a sound.

Something was moving on the floor at the foot of the bed. A soft scrabbling, then the weight on the mattress edge. She raised her head and looked.

Soft bluish light shone; at first she did not know what it was, but she recognized what was holding it.

"Ahhh, Nannie Blossom, what have you brought me?"

She was a slinky thing with vaporous white hair, her face long and pointed, her ears with serrated edges like leaves, her eyes like two drops of emerald. She was standing upright on her haunches at the bed's edge. She held out a tiny moth-shaped flower, which glowed pale blue.

Linnie reached down and took the flower. "Oh, it's lovely! I must go see!"

Nannie sprang off the bed and ran towards the door, vanishing into the darkness. Linnie lit her candle and walked through the cottage, out to the sprawling garden, all crowded with shadowy vegetation.

There amidst the other plants stood the mothcandle, its gentle winged flowers spread in luminous glory.

"We did it, Nannie, we did it!"

Two small green eyes smiled out of the black mesh of plants, blinked, then were gone.

                ℰ   ℰ   ℰ

The two little girls fluttered past, all giggles and sun-bright skirts. They charged along the lane with baskets swinging, leaving behind the furrowed fields and the white stone house beyond. They reached the orchard, its blooms stark against the hills so green—great fragrant torches of pink.

"Wait for me, you silly things!" Linnie called.

The daughters of the farmer who had invited her out to "treat" his trees turned briefly, smiled, then dashed on, unhindered.

Linnie wagged her head. Kellen and Dreeny were bundles of gleeful disorder, there was no doubting that, but they cheered her nonetheless. She trudged along with her staff and basket of tools.

She was breathless when at last she caught up to them, yet they were all set to climb the apple trees. The baskets contained small plump-bellied figurines made of baked dough. Linnie and the girls had soaked them in honey and fastened bright ribbons to their heads. Each spring these dough dollies were hung in the orchard to draw the fertile spirits forth.

"I shall climb to the highest branch, on the prettiest tree, to hang mine," Kellen, who was seven, announced.

"Not too high," Linnie cautioned.

"But I can climb so well, miss, you should see. I'm like a squirrel."

"I'll take your word for it, Kellen."

Linnie picked out a dollie and admired the play of sunlight on its sticky gold flesh. She walked over to one of the trees, whose arms were low and gnarled, and with ceremonial concentration, hung the thing.

Kellen's assessment of her own climbing prowess was only slightly exaggerated. She made swiftly up one of the trees, festooning its blossom-softened limbs with dangling dollies. At first Dreeny was content to put hers on the lower boughs, but her older sister's nimble progress urged her to climb as well.

Dreeny scrabbled up one of the smaller trees. It was a none too graceful display. Her long skirt was burdensome; fortunately she had thought to loop the ribbon of the dollie around her neck like a pendant. It stuck to the front of her dress.

"Look, Kellen, look, Miss Linnie, I can hang mine high, too!"

Linnie smiled and applauded. "Good show, Dreeny!"

Dreeny, inspired by this attention, dared higher.

"Careful now, you're not a bird," Linnie called.

"I'm like a squirrel, just as Kellen is."

Dreeny was beyond the halfway point, and though this was barely ten feet up, the ground appeared to be quite distant. She leaned against the trunk of the tree and decided it was high enough. Time to hang her dollie.

"Now where can I put you?"

Something made a sudden crunching noise. Looking down she noticed that the plump belly of her dough figure had been raggedly bitten away.

"What...hey! Look, Miss Linnie, there's an apple up here!"

Linnie looked up from her basket. "An apple in Seedstir? That's not possible, Dreeny. There won't be fruit 'til summer."

"There's an apple, I tell you. A fat green one."

Linnie thought for a moment. By the time she pulled out her spade and started to run over, Dreeny had leaned closer to the dangling green orb, which had opened two glassy black eyes and a crooked mouth as well. It whispered something—she leaned close. The apple's smile became an enraged snarl, the jaggy teeth like sharp brown seeds.

"Aaaiiieeeee! My ear, my ear! It's got my ear!"

"Oh no! Dreeny!" Linnie charged, her belly heaving. The malicious little nature spirit known as a snap-apple was growling and shaking like a dog with a toy, tearing at the poor girl's ear. Dreeny grasped at a branch and tried to tug herself free.

Kellen shrieked and slid down from her perch. Linnie turned to her and pointed in the direction of the farm. "Get your father—hurry!"

The sight of blood on her white dress caused Dreeny's panic to accelerate. The apple-creature yanked at her, squinting in fury.

"Help, Miss Linnie! Help me!"

Adrenaline hoisted Linnie into the tree. She grabbed at the branches, fresh blossoms squishing, startled bees spinning. She dodged the little girl's kicking legs and struggled to position herself within striking range of the snap-apple.

"It hurts, my ear—ooowwwww!"

"Let her go!" Linnie shouted, swinging with her spade.

A shrill cry echoed across the orchard as the creature caught the sharp end of the spade. It released the child's ear, screwing up its features in a hideous grimace of pain; its stem broke free from the tree and it fell to the ground with a moist thump. Linnie went tumbling after it.

She grunted as she crashed through the branches which blurred past in greys and pinks. She landed on her side in the snap-apple's sour juices.

Dreeny slid down the trunk of the tree and bent over the woman. "Miss Linnie, are you all right?"

Linnie raised herself up on her elbow and tried to smile. "I, I think I'm well."

❧   ❧   ❧

The moon was a plump and chalky disc, her light an eerie pale blue about the garden floor. Vines and leaves and branches entwined, some ill-defined, some shadow-etched. A figure knelt rocking upon the cool earth, her palms warm on her stretched abdomen. She gazed at the ghostly blooms of the mothcandle plant—they seemed to hover in the night.

"Oh, you grow so impatient, small one," Linnie spoke a strained whisper. "You'll wait no more; this night you will be born."

The pains came, like heavy boots kicking from inside. She swooned, fell back, plants hissing across her arms, rustling as she sprawled gasping on her back. She screamed, convulsed, sweated. The hours that followed were the longest of her life. She watched the moon ride slowly across the sky, toward the west.

At last it breached from between her trembling legs, a small and glistening thing, bluish in the cast of the mothcandle. Linnie strained, sitting partly forward, guiding it out with slick palms. Its head was rounded, the eyes puffy squints, the mouth drooping and silent. Its belly was linked to her by a fleshy vine. She cut this with her spade.

"Cry," Linnie demanded.

It was all the way out now, the tiny limbs slack and dangling.

"Cry! Please cry!"

She shook it, the head lolled listlessly.

"Breathe, blast it! Breathe!" She burst into sobs, cradling her dead child, rocking there in the midst of her garden. All about her were the rich dewy plants she had reared and nurtured.

❧   ❧   ❧

Embalmed with numbness, Linnie staggered into her dark cottage and climbed onto the bed, still clutching the lifeless boy. Her skirt was wet with tears and birth-spillage, her face muscles ached from grimacing. She leaned against her pillow and stared at the wall.

Woe laced darkly through the chambers of her soul. She felt as if she were drowning in some great void. Such emptiness—an emptiness bigger than the pain.

The blankets at the edge of the bed jerked as something tugged itself up. A strange white serpentine rodent stood peering at her with dark green eyes. It held something in its tiny hands, a small dark object, like a nut. Nannie Blossom lay the thing down, blinked up at Linnie, then turned and sprang from the bed, vanishing into the shadows.

Linnie reached down and picked the gift up. It was a deep glossy green, plump and soft—some kind of a seed.

       ☙   ☙   ☙

The cobbled streets outside the window of the convalescent home were filled with the clatter of passing carriages. An old frail man with unruly white hair sat in a great wicker chair, his wrinkles stark in the morning glare. A plump young female attendant sat holding his breakfast tray, listening as he prattled on.

An older woman of higher rank came in. She smiled pleasantly at the retired magistrate. "Good morning, Mr. Grimledge, how are we this bright morn?"

"Spry as a squirrel, and feisty as a badger."

"Ah, that's good. I see you're entertaining our new girl with your stories of the country." She turned to the attendant. "Did he tell you about the time it rained newts?"

"Oh, yes," the young woman replied, "and hares too."

"Very nice. Well, don't let me disturb you. Carry on, Mr. Grimledge." The ward matron smiled again and winked at her co-worker before leaving. They both knew the poor old gent was mad.

"At any rate," Reedly Grimledge said, adjusting his frail weight in his chair, "I became concerned about Linnie, not having heard from her in some time, and knowing how far along she'd been. I'd been afraid she'd plop the bloody runt out the day I brought her over to help my gullrose. Naturally I took it upon myself to investigate."

24

The attendant nodded politely. She could easily imagine more strenuous jobs than listening to this old man's entertaining tales.

"I rode out to her place in the morning, but received no answer when I knocked on her door. I was alarmed at this, so I ventured inside. It was very still, yet the place seemed to be in order. I expected to find her napping, but the bed was bare, except for the sweet green bloom of a fortweed plant."

"Oh, I smelled one once," the woman said, "lovely!"

"Mm. Well, I remembered how the villagers used to say that some type of spirit brought her presents, sometimes flowers from exotic lands, or pretty things which were difficult to identify, things not native to Westermead. Later on I was to learn that the child was born dead, and that this spirit-thing brought her a strange seed which she placed in the child's mouth, before burying him in her garden…"

The woman leaned closer. "That's most curious. Did you ever find her?"

"Oh yes. I finished searching the cottage and went out into the garden. You've never seen such a garden! It was like a dense nest of leaves and blooms, crowding about the back of the croft. A marvel of textures and scents and colors. I could hear a soft singing coming from in there, so I sneaked over and peered out from my cover of vegetation.

"It was the oddest thing I've ever seen. There was Linnie, kneeling, smiling down at this little green boy. He was as much a plant as human, blending at the waist into dense roots. His arms were plump little things, the fingers much like mushroom growths. His head was shiny and green, and his ears looked like leaves.

"It was a delightful scene—they both seemed so happy. She held his little hands and sang to him and he smiled up at her, his green eyes glinting merrily. I can see it so clearly in my mind, after all these years."

The attendant grinned and patted the old man's wrinkled hand. His eyes glazed teary and he smiled foolishly. Poor old thing, she thought, of course he was mad.

Calling the Water

The following are folk-magic "recipes" for summoning precipitation, collected in the southern district of Westermead.

To Conjure Rain—*from Mother Nanty, Neebotton.*
Form a small dolly of sourgrass strands, lick four spider-tears (dew drops) from a web, then kiss the effigy about the waste. Go to where there is running water and cast the doll in, calling, "Sky blue, sky of mirth—shed thy tears to quench the earth!"

To Cause Rain—*Superstition, origin unknown, believed in many of the southern villages.*
Wet cabbage leaves laid on the naked belly of a sleeping woman will ensure morning showers. If the sleeper wakens, however, the day will be dry.

To Raise a Storm at Sea—*from Spellwoman Blind Lympton, South-haunt.*
Tie grey gull feathers to the tail of a black cat and cause it to run through bracken or heather.

To Make Hail (to blast an enemy's fields)—*from a manuscript belonging to Black Mally, found buried at Scorch Hill, Kilmnook.*
At dusk, bury a dead man's finger pointing in the direction of victim's land. Drink a mixture of goat milk, skullberries and ground sweet bark until the bladder is full. Urinate while running around the buried finger in a right-wise circle. Hail and wind will soon come.

To Make Snow—*passed down from a Spellwoman known as The Spinster, Weendell.*
Fill a vat with cool water and drown a white bird in it. Sprinkle a mixture of

chalk dust and powdered pansy blooms over this. Sleep with the dead bird under your pillow. The bird's spirit will become a cloud and its cold tears will fall. In the morning the ground will be white.

Four Bronze Sisters

ONE

The little dark-haired girl sat atop a grassy rampart, arms folded, rocking slowly as she sang, "Who walks soft amid the weeds? Whose flesh is mist, and sleeps with seeds?"

It was a local song she had taken a liking to. She came here often to sit, sing and look down at the curious stones of the Giant's Sleep. No one knew much about the place, not even the village spellman. Some felt it had been a fort, others said it was the ruin of an ancient ceremonial center.

From her high perch, Melly could gaze down on the great outline of a recumbent man, comprised of high stone walls. There was a wide hole in the center of the head-area—the opening ringed with chunks of milky-grey quartz, and it spoke echoey splashes when rocks were dropped in.

"Whose soft words exhale no breath? Whose touch is chill, whose home is death?"

Seven year old Melly was able to see things that others could not. Many a time she had spied the shades of those who had frequented this place long before. She had seen them moving about through the stone wall limbs of the structure below, or gliding sleepily about the steep encircling slopes.

She rose and began walking across the top of the innermost rampart. She observed the massive figure calmly. It seemed she had more success in seeing *them* if she allowed herself to grow relaxed, or better yet, drowsy. Recently she had seen two women in hazy shrouds drift down one of the leg-corridors, vanishing into the foot. Another time a boy with a gaunt face had climbed spindly-armed out from the mouth-well. He'd seemed to take notice of her and scurried back down, out of view.

The extreme slant of the earthwork surrounding the stone man forced Melly to run in descent. Spent dandelions broke into ghost-sparks at her swift trespass. The great feet of the figure grew bigger, nearer, the wall rising higher until it stood four times her height.

Melly followed the wall—now abstracted by its closeness, and not at all resembling a man. There was a spot along the left side, in the region of the hip, where some stones had tumbled loose and a person could crawl through. Melly ducked beneath the crude arch, into the body of the giant.

The air inside, even on a warm day in the spring month of Greensurge, seemed damp and chill. The girl moved quietly across the verdant floor; the main body of the figure opened wide. The sky above was overcast and pale—birds never flew over this place.

Several years back, an old man from the village had come here to try and re-seal the hole in the wall. He was convinced that the Giant's Sleep was a prison for ghosts, and that the inmates were apt to escape. He tried to move the fallen stones back in place, but, by doing so, accidentally loosened others, which fell on him, crushing him. Ironic.

"Would anyone like to show themselves?" Melly cooed. "I mean you no ill will."

She crossed the long chest-region. The walls on either side curved in where they formed the neck, almost making a separate room of the head area. The well-like hole with its encircling teeth of smoky quartz was now visible. Melly walked between the walls of the neck, onto the flat face of the giant.

Turning to look right, Melly saw the image of a man sitting against the wall, his head hanging down, his baggy grey shirt soaked red with blood, three white arrows protruding. She gasped and took a step back. The man looked up.

The figure was more distinct than the other spirits she had encountered here. The angle of the wall which he was propped against had prevented her from seeing him from up on the rampart, or perhaps he had just materialized. In either case, she had never been so close to one before.

"Can you speak?" Melly asked.

He was in his middle thirties, mustached, balding, the hair dark and disheveled across the ears. Deep-set doleful eyes peered out from his sweaty pallor.

"You are a ghost, aren't you?" Melly cocked her head.

He gave a trembling smirk and whispered, "Soon…"

"Oh, my! Oh, my!" No wonder he looked less ethereal than the others—he was a solid living man. Or dying man. "Oh, how terrible, you are badly hurt! I shall fetch my father; I'll bring help!"

The man coughed, squinted, the three white arrows quivered. He shook his head. "No—don't."

Melly turned on her heel and darted off. "I'll return swiftly!"

❦ ❦ ❦

Clooster Eastworth led the way on his pounding gelding. His son Bollin and daughter Melly followed on another horse, leading a spare mount by a rope. They crossed the solid green moat-waves of the enclosing earthwork and rode down to the high-walled exterior of the giant outline.

The tall gangly man dismounted and pulled a rolled blanket off the back of his beast. "Hurry, now," he called to the children.

The trio climbed over the scattered stones where the wall had crumbled and ducked through the opening. They made their way quickly across the length of chest grass, through the neck and into the head enclosure.

Melly half expected the man to be gone, yet there he sat, propped against the stones, head sagging, his chest red-wet. She walked up to him and prodded his shoulder. "Sir? I'm back, as I said. Sir?"

He moaned.

Bollin stared at the gory figure, those bone-white arrows jutting. "Father, should we pull these out?"

Clooster Eastworth approached the man. "I think it best that we wait until we're home. We'll let the spellman do that—I fear I'd cause more damage in trying to remove them myself."

The wounded fellow looked up, his eyes glazed. "Go away," he whispered.

Clooster bent closer. "Here then, not to worry, mister—we'll tend to you all right."

The farmer unraveled the blanket roll to fashion a stretcher. He motioned his son closer. "Be very gentle, son…"

30

The wounded man reached a jittery hand down to his side and brought up a stout flintlock pistol. He waved it from side to side, as if shooing away insects. "Get away," he demanded weakly. "Let me be!"

The would-be rescuers stumbled back.

"Whoa!" Clooster exclaimed. "Easy! Easy! We mean no harm!"

"Go. Go away, please..."

The man's eyes rolled up and his head flopped to one side. The hand with the gun dropped to the ground. Clooster sprang close and swatted the pistol away. "Now, Bollin—be quick!"

While her father and brother wrapped the stranger, readying him for transport, Melly picked up the flintlock and looked it over. She clicked it at the ground. "It was empty," she noted.

☯ ☯ ☯

Greyheather was one of several small farming communities edging a formation of small lakes known as The Paw. The ruggedness of the land, there in the north-eastern heights of Westermead, demanded hardiness from its inhabitants. The abundance of stones was so great as to dictate the nature of the people's lives—their activities and lore were woven about them like mortar. They farmed where the stones allowed, fashioned their homes with the materials provided and even built their legends out of them. Stones were great for building legends.

Four of these villages shared one spellman. Marrow Water was a tall spindly man with an angular stretch of face, his snowy hair drawn back into a ponytail. He moved briskly through the corridor in his long black robe, led by a woman in a bloody apron.

"He's awake," the woman said.

The hall opened up into separate side compartments. The air was thick with decay and moans. The injured and dying were ranked in these side rooms, where Marrow and his assistants tended the patients of Heal Home.

A single window allowed wan light into the room at the end of the hall. There were only five beds here—two were empty, one held an obese limbless man who gibbered softly at the ceiling; another contained an old woman who had been horrendously burnt in an encounter with a Summer Man spirit, and the last bed, snug in its corner shadows, held the newcomer.

When Marrow Water walked in he saw Melly Eastworth with her back flattened against a wall, gaping in horror at the stranger. Her father and brother stood alongside the bed, next to the attending woman who had just removed the last of the three white arrows. This final arrow had not been serious, while the expertise of Water himself had been needed to remove the projectiles from the man's chest. The attendant applied an herb paste and bandages to the man's hip.

The stranger was mumbling, "Gone—gone… Where is—gone…"

He felt the bandages on his chest where the arrows had been; his eyes widened, incredulous. "The arrows—where are the arrows? What have ya done?"

He sat up abruptly. The attending woman tried to ease him back. "Here, here, easy."

Marrow Water took the man by the shoulders and gently pushed him back onto the pillows. His tone was ever even, his manner soothing. "Rest yourself, good man, you've had an ordeal for yourself."

"What have you done with my arrows?"

"*Your* arrows? They're right here." The spellman held up the three projectiles; even in the weak light the white shafts gleamed. "Curious, I've never encountered this type of wood before—do you know what it is?"

The stranger put his palms over his face and groaned.

Water held one of the arrows out to Clooster. "Have you seen wood of this sort before? It's beautiful."

"I haven't."

The stranger raised his head. "It's wood from a gullbirch tree; it grows only on a small island off the western coast."

Clooster's son Bollin stood back, observing. He touched his father's arm. "Do you think he would have harmed us had his pistol been loaded?"

Clooster turned, his reply a hush. "No, son, he was delirious."

The spellman placed a hand on the injured fellow's head, smoothing the sweat from his brow. "Who did this to you, young fellow? Who shot those things into you?"

"It doesn't matter now," the man moaned. He dragged one of the pillows over his face and gave himself to sobs.

The obese limbless man in the next bed began shrieking, like some strange terrified bird. He was convulsing, his great bulk jiggling, the bed creaking, his eyes flicking erratically.

"Through the wall," the ogre rasped, "Through the bloody wall!"

TWO

The wagon jostled as it followed the painful twists of an ancient stone wall. A great tract of grazing land rippled green, the sky a heavy clutter of whale-grey wool. The pasture was haphazardly studded with rocks ranging in size from pebbles to boulders, as if some great hand had snatched one of the mountains out of the north and shattered it in a fit of temper. The vehicle labored along, creaking in protest.

The spellman waved when he spotted Clooster Eastworth leaning on a musket, monitoring a modest herd of cattle. Clooster started over to greet him, noticing that the stranger they had rescued several weeks before was seated in the cargo bed. "Hello there, Marrow Water, thank you for coming."

The wagon stopped and Water climbed down from the driver's seat. He smiled pleasantly. Clooster turned to acknowledge the passenger. "Good day, sir, are you healing well? Forgive me for not recalling your name..."

The man had a woeful look, no doubt due to the strain of his injuries. "Maple Rue is my name, and yes, I'm mending, thank you," he said, his voice gentle and low. He thought for a moment and added, "I fear I failed previously to acknowledge the goodness of your deed, I mean, in helping me. I am grateful for your concern."

"I only did as any decent sort would. My girl Melly's the one worthy of praise, having acted as quick as she did, alerting us to your predicament and all."

Clooster gestured toward a jagged outcrop of bedrock where his dark-haired daughter sat, watching them. Maple glanced over and met her strange gaze. The girl looked away abruptly.

The spellman took a sack out of the wagon and headed over to one of the cows. He examined it, tapping here and there with his fingers, checking the color of the tongue, the lips and teeth. "A bit of a pest problem, eh, Clooster?"

Clooster took the older robed gent by the arm and led him behind the jutting wedge of rock where Melly sat. One of the dead cows lay on its side, the carcass withered and dry. A plate-sized circular hole puckered from the belly. There seemed to be movement inside.

"There's one of the bastards now!" Clooster exclaimed, his angry expression accentuating the weathered quality of his features.

A glossy grey ferret-sized insect with a segmented body poked up out of the cow's side. It looked about with bulbous black eyes, emitting a series of rasps and clicks. The farmer aimed his musket and fired, blasting the thing into syrup and chunks.

"There, you rancid parasite!"

Maple Rue had struggled out of the back of the wagon and hobbled over with the help of a crutch. His bright white shirt concealed the tight wrap of bandages about his chest. He bent down to examine something.

"Sweet bugs," Rue noted. "One of nature's clever lies." He reached down and plucked what appeared to be a pretty golden mushroom sprinkled with beads of glossy black. "The egg sack has a taste no bovine beast can resist. Ahh, an ingenious design. And these little black eggs grow in the belly, and hatch, and feast. Poor innocent cows..." Maple's mournful stare was on the egg sack while his thoughts traveled to some dark internal land of pain.

"Bloody pests," Clooster grumbled. "We squash those sacks when we find them. We've had quite the abundance of 'em this season, such as I've never seen, I might add. It's hard enough for a man to make a living in these parts without these buggers about."

Marrow Water put a hand on the farmer's shoulder. "Well, my friend, we'll tend your beasts without further delay."

The spellman spent the next couple of hours distributing ambery beads of dry sap to the cows (which they eagerly ate) and painting magical symbols on their sides. He was finishing up when Clooster's son Bollin came riding up on a horse.

"Father! Father!" the boy panted, "I rode over to the Nultys' farm—something awful—there's blood, and..."

The boy sagged against the neck of his mount and sobbed. Maple Rue lurched to his feet and glared toward the south. Melly eyed him intensely and shuddered.

☙ ☙ ☙

The house stood on a modest hill with a grin of pear trees along one side. The misty grey of distant mountains lay beyond, and beyond that reared a menace of dark clouds. The lawn was dappled blond with buttercups, dandelion and broom, and red where some of the human inhabitants had been disassembled.

Clooster, Melly and Bollin arrived on horseback several minutes before the spellman and Maple Rue came in the wagon. The farmer had jammed a ball down the throat of his heavy musket, and readied a fresh charge of powder. He stood gawking at the house.

"It's enough to give a man chills," he breathed.

The door was gone, the windows were all shattered, there were holes in the stone walls where none should've been. A dead horse was sprawled on the thatched roof. There were gruesome patches of red where blood had strewn and streamed.

Marrow Water followed Clooster into the building. Maple and the children stood outside listening to their gasps of horror from within. Melly looked over at Maple—he was leaning forward on his crutch, muttering softly to himself, his eyes glossed damp.

When the men came back outside, they were pale and drawn.

"Bodies?" Maple asked.

"No," Marrow responded quietly, "hair, fingers, teeth, a few limbs here and there."

The bodies of Mr. and Mrs. Nulty and their three daughters were not to be found.

35

Clooster studied the spellman. "What do you make of such a thing, Marrow Water?"

"I have heard tales, from villages to the south, of occurrences such as this. There were several a few months back, in Killingrove and Lennet. Before that, this past winter, there were others further south."

"What could have done this? Surely not a man?"

"Most certainly not, I should hope to think."

Clooster handed his musket to his son and started back toward the building. "Let's see if there's a ladder about, I want to get that poor animal down from the roof."

The spellman went after him.

Maple Rue turned to Melly, taking her by the shoulders, twisting her around to face him. He knelt down and peered into her dark eyes with his own.

"You fear me, lass..."

She nodded.

"Why? What do you know?"

She shook her head.

"Were you there when they pulled those three white arrows out of me?"

She nodded.

"What did you see?"

She gulped, then said, "A large dark thing—it climbed out of you..."

"Where did it go?"

"Through the wall."

THREE

Old Rootman Rue and his mare wobbled across the narrow wooden bridge which led to the strange windowless building. Worried boards above the sable stillness of the moat. The structure loomed before the rider—circular, stone, with a sallow cone of rush-thatch. Dusk pursued them silently from the east.

He had made good progress in traveling back toward his home town in the south of Westermead when he learned of this place. They called it the

Four Bronze Sisters—where one could speak with the dead. Immediately he had set out, back to the north-eastern region he had so recently left behind. There was something he had to know...

Now his tired old horse carried him the last few feet across the bridge, a sheathed longbow and the three spare gullbirch arrows hanging alongside the saddle. They passed under a high arch, into a stony maw where other horses were tethered. Rootman dismounted and continued into the main chamber, closing a heavy wooden door behind him.

The room was large, round, with four opposing recessed chambers, like small hallways. There was a great chimney of stone reaching from the center of the floor to the thatched ceiling. Four fireplaces faced out from the thing, these and a few wall-mounted candles providing the only light. At the end of each of the halls, facing their respective fireplaces, were four impassive-faced masks of bronze, poking out from the walls.

Rootman hesitated, his aged bulk trembling. He observed two shawl-webbed women who stood in one of the sub-compartments, only half-hearing the weepy whispers of their interchange with the departed. Slowly he made his way toward one of the vacant cells.

The candles were of the rushlight variety—the piths of rushes having been soaked in melted fat. They sputtered, thickening the air with unpleasant smoke. Rootman scowled as he passed one, venturing into a vacant booth.

The mask was on eye-level, its dull bronze skin smeared mournfully with shadow. Indifferent. It resembled a female. The eyes were open, black. Behind the wall, behind each mask, looking out through those eyes, stood a person, female or male, who served as an intermediary between the dead and the visitor. The identities of the mediums remained undisclosed to those who came here.

Rootman felt awkward standing there, gazing at the metal face.

"There's someone you wish to speak with?" came a solemn voice. It sounded to be an old woman.

Rootman nodded. "Ah, yes."

"What is this person's name?"

"Maple. Maple Rue."

Silence. Jittery reflections of light fingered the mask. Now breathing strained as the medium behind the wall pressed her face deeper into the mask.

"I'm not finding him," the voice came. "How long has he been dead?"

"A few weeks."

A cough. "Wait—yes, yes, he is here…"

Rootman caught the glint of an eye through one of the mask holes.

The next voice was familiar to the old man, though distant in a way, watery. "I'm here, Uncle Rootman."

"Oh, Maple—it is you! Tell me, my lad, are you well, now? Are you at peace?"

"Yes, splendid peace, such as I've not known previously. I am ever grateful to you."

Rootman smiled, almost reached up to touch the mask. "I'm glad, so very glad. It was so difficult to do what I did to you."

"You released me."

"I did, yes. And the twin…it is done with?"

"Yes, trapped in my dead body. It will kill no more."

Rootman sighed. "Now I can rest. I needed to know."

"Do you still have arrows, Uncle?"

"I do, lad. Three."

"Ahhh. There's no need to trouble yourself with them henceforth. Pay me a final favor and I will appear to you one last time, dear Uncle."

"What favor can I do?"

"Break them. Toss them into the moat. A gesture to help you put this whole troubling thing behind. Could you do that?"

"Of course, Maple."

"I thank you."

When the spirit left the body of the medium, the old woman collapsed against the wall in a faint, and slid quietly to the floor.

❧   ❧   ❧

The smooth white shafts of the gullbirch arrows were resilient and strong. Rootman had to strain with all his strength to snap them. He carried the pieces out of the horse stable and stood on the bank of the moat. They plopped one by one into the sullen liquid.

Rootman stood waiting, his hands shoved into his vest pockets. Dusk had crowded most of the light from the sky and the air was somewhat chill. He heard the horses behind him shifting about, snorting.

Something whisked across the back of one of the man's calves. Now the other—the light, tracking sensation closed and exerted pressure. He winced.

"Ahh!"

Rootman turned. Something large was hunched down behind him. It was dark, yet strangely amorphous, more like a shadow than a solid form. It yanked his ankles out from under him and swung him up off the ground, slamming him against the side of the building.

The man cried out. He thumped on the earth. Hot ripples of pain tore through his back and his hair felt wet. He crawled toward the moat, panting. His fingers hooked in the grooves between the boards of the narrow bridge. He pulled himself along, as if climbing a horizontal ladder.

Heavy steps pounded on the wood behind him. Sharp swipes at the backs of his legs. It grabbed the collar of his vest and jerked him upright, then something like a damp sack slid over the top of his skull, down over his face. His entire head was engulfed, something like teeth clamping on his throat.

The thing thrashed its head like a dog with a toy. Rootman's body flung free and landed in grass. It spat his head into the moat.

FOUR

Maple did not need a map of Westermead to know that the "Twin" was heading north. He had seen the line of destruction progressing that way, more or less in a straight line. But Greyheather was close to the northern extreme of the continent—it could not travel much higher before reaching the sea, and what then? Would it work its way down again, form a great grisly circle leaving hundreds dead? There seemed no logical reason for the northern advancement, but then again the creature chose its victims randomly and might not require reasonable motivation for any of its actions.

A map of the local region was spread out across his bed in the cramped room where he was staying at Heal Home. He was now healthy enough to help around the place doing cooking, cleaning, feeding patients and the like. He told the spellman Marrow Water that he would like to stay on for a while to repay him for the care he had been given. In actuality he was remaining in the area to track down the Twin.

The spellman and others about the place seemed content to believe the stories he had given them concerning his past. He had told them that he had been a fisherman down south who had gotten into some trouble with a band of pirates. He blamed these nonexistent villains for pursuing him to these parts, and for firing the arrows into him and leaving him for dead. The story was not a total fabrication, for he had done some fishing work for a time, among other temporary jobs here and there, during those times when he could keep the Twin under control.

He had secured the three gullbirch arrows from Marrow Water—that was the most important thing. He had also retrieved his pistol. He would need some flints, powder and balls for it, though. One of the regular workers had assured him that he could supply such things.

The man leaned intently over the map, marking the places where the Twin had most recently struck. He drew a line connecting these, upward, stopping at the Nultys' famous farm which he and the others had found in ruin. A finger traced up beyond that to the next potential stop—the nearest northerly buildings belonged to Clooster Eastworth.

       ᘓ   ᘓ   ᘓ

Night leaned in across the rumpled lay of fields. Winding lanes cut through these, bordered by high mortarless walls, the road aflood with shadow. Occasional boulders and outcrops of bedrock appeared like shapeless creatures, hunched and waiting, watching as the creaky wagon passed.

The breeze was the smell of spring creeping in the dark—those scents that had waited a year to waft. The quiet spices of growth and stir. One could almost hear roots groaning through the soil, vines snaking across beetle-festooned stones, grass rising green in a whispering tide and the moist unfolding of leaves like wings, awakened from larval sleep.

Maple leaned forward, looking out over the rippling backs of the horse team. High walls coursed past, the spaces between the stones like erratic rivulets of dark liquid. The stones filed by, their pitted textures forming twisted faces in his tear-heavy eyes. An even more hideous mosaic of faces streamed red through his memory, a constellation of horror-wide eyes staring.

"Faster," he urged the horses, "faster!"

The stone house stood on a rise overlooking an irregular girth of pastureland. Even with the barn and small outbuildings close by, Clooster Eastworth's place seemed lonely there beneath the night sky with so much open space surrounding. Maple reined his horses still, the borrowed wagon stopping before the sound of hooves could alert those inside.

His chest burned from the arrow wounds as he climbed down. He tucked the arrows, which had made those wounds, under his belt, took lantern and crutch and hobbled closer to the buildings. A breeze came up from the fields, heavy with the scent of cow dung.

He did not know exactly what he would do if the Twin actually made an appearance, but he knew it was his duty to be there. He considered warning Eastworth about the possible danger, but decided not to. It was his business to deal with. If *he* could not stop the monster, no one could.

It was as long a night as he had ever known. Hours after those inside were safe in bed, tucked snugly into their dreams, he carried out his vigil, circling the cluster of buildings. His sad eyes peered out across the undulating acres, paying close attention to the sporadic misshapen boulders, in case some terrible form skulked out from behind them...

Maple felt the weight of a hand on his shoulder and his eyes went wide. A large dark form lumbered by, a silhouette against the morning sky—its deep lowing rumbled through his guts. His eyes flicked from the steer to the figure standing beside him; it was Clooster Eastworth.

"My good fellow," Clooster inquired, "are you well?"

Maple groaned, grinning nervously. He had fallen asleep propped against the outside of the house. "I, I am fine. Thank you. I came to pay visit last night, not, ahh, not realizing it was so late. There were no lights in your windows, and not wanting to be a source of disturbance, I chose not to wake you. I was tired, though, so I sat to rest a bit before heading back—apparently I rested a bit too well." He gave a deep chuckle.

"Bah, you should have knocked. You'll be a mass of aches, having slept out in the dewy air. Come in and we'll replenish you with a hearty breakfast."

The farmer helped the man up as the boy Bollin continued herding the cattle out to graze. The little dark-haired girl stared silently as the guest was brought in. He smiled gently at her and she nodded.

"You remember Mr. Rue, Melly."

"Yes, Father."

"Would you be so good as to provide a meal for him, then? He looks like he could do with a good feeding."

"Yes, Father."

Clooster bade him sit at a long wooden table that seemed to divide the main room of the house into sections. Half the space was a sitting area where twin high-backed settles faced a wide stone fireplace. The other half of the room served as a kitchen, the walls dangling blackened utensils and use-worn ceramic plates and pitchers. The few pewter mugs the family could afford were reverently placed on a shelf alongside a jug of sloe-spirits. There was another large fireplace, this one set with oven compartments and a rotary spit. The room was warm from previous cooking, and it smelled inviting.

"I see you still have those," observed Clooster, pointing at the three white arrows tucked under Maple's black belt.

"Why, yes. They are the finest arrows I've ever encountered. I thought I might get myself a bow and do some hunting. I understand there is some challenging game about these parts..." He fingered the goose feather fins on one of the things.

Clooster took down two of the pewter mugs (guests had to be impressed properly) and poured some tea made from dried raspberry leaves. "There is some game, but I'll not lie and tell you there's plenty. These are rugged parts, and the beasts are suitably rugged as well. If it's challenge you like, then you'll not be displeased. My father used to take me up to a rocky bit of valley we called Jeb Coffin's Dwindle to hunt boar. I saw a man nearly killed one time there. You'd best be a good shot with them—they can take an arrow or two and not lose a bit of their fightin' steam."

Maple Rue chuckled grimly. "I don't think I'm quite up to a foe so fierce as all that. I'm not fully mended yet. Besides, without a bow I'm not likely to be hunting anything."

Melly moved about preparing the meal, occasionally glancing over at Maple. Her eyes, dark as elderberries, seemed to probe him. There was a melancholy air about him, reminiscent of her own.

"Unless I'm mistaken," Clooster said, "I have an old bow lying about somewhere. It's just a short bow, mind you, but not a bad bit of work. I haven't used the blasted thing since I was able to afford my wheel-lock. You're welcome to it, if I can find it."

"You're more than generous, Clooster."

Before long Maple found himself sitting over a delicious morning feast. There was cheese—pale and soft, rolled in oatmeal and tartseed, and warm buttermilk bread guarding treasures of toasted walnut. There was a bowl of steamy oat porridge glazed amber with maple syrup, and, finally, a thick bacon and egg pie—the browned crust blurring to gold, the top all scattered with onions and meat.

"Ahh, this is a delight as I've not known in too long a time," Maple breathed enthusiastically. Melly stood fumbling the edge of her apron and smiled shyly at him. His eyes glinted at her, and she saw that there was a sweetness in them. "Such a young lass, too, to be cooking so…"

It had not struck him before that there was no mother about, and that the girl was the sole bearer of kitchen responsibilities. He looked at Clooster, who appeared to be aware of his guest's realization. The farmer returned a rueful smile.

"You are a fine family," Maple told him, his eyes damp, "I am envious."

43

FIVE

"Good shot!"

Melly smiled and lowered the bow. Maple handed her another arrow. She hooked the taut linen string in the rear notch, raised the bow and pulled back.

"Stretch a bit more, that's it…"

The arrow swooshed and struck the upright block of hay.

"A fine shot, indeed!" Maple proclaimed.

"Thank you, Mr. Rue. I think I rather enjoy this."

"With a little more practice you'll be as good an archer as you are a cook."

"I should like that awfully well. Though I wouldn't care to hunt my own food, mind you. I'm not one to hurt animals, you know. Animals are so pleasant."

"Ahh, of course," Rue said, slinging an arm around her shoulders. "It's best you never know what it feels like to kill something."

It was warm and bright. They were beside the long stone barn, the green herd-flecked pasture sweeping off behind them. Maple took the bow and examined it pensively. It was nicely crafted, made of polished yew.

Melly studied him. "I wonder, Mr. Rue, if I'm strange."

"Strange? Why?"

Melly was very serious for a child her age, her eyes deep, the dark hair framing her face in long somber drapes. She thought for a moment before replying. "Well, as much as I would dread killing something, even a fly, I myself am not afraid to die."

"You're not?"

She shook her head. "Are you?"

Maple worried the bow with his hands. He gave an embarrassed grin. "I guess I am."

"There's no need to, though. Dying isn't the end of a person."

"Why do you say?"

"Because I can see the dead sometimes. As I saw that dark thing that came out of you. It was different, though. Was it dead?"

"I don't know, Melly."

"It killed the Nultys, didn't it?"

Maple strung the last arrow, aimed and sent it deep into the bale of hay. The girl was watching him intently.

"I believe it did kill them, Melly," Maple admitted.

"I don't know..." the girl kicked at the ground. "Perhaps when I'm old like you I'll be afraid to die as well."

Maple chuckled, "Old, you say? I'm not yet forty years, I'll have you know."

"Well, you're losing your hair..."

"So? Here—look!" He plucked one from her head. "So are you."

She laughed and rubbed at her scalp. "That's not at all fair, Mr. Rue."

Melly went over and pulled free the arrows and brought them back to her friend. He insisted that she try again. This time all three struck the target.

"I suppose you've noticed that I don't have a mother," Melly said.

Maple grew morose. He nodded.

Melly remained nonchalant. "Is your mother dead, too?"

"Yes. She died when I was quite young." He squatted down beside her, holding his crutch like a staff. "I don't remember much about her, only that she was beautiful and that she would beat my brother and me with sticks. In fact," he looked off into the distance, "he died at her hands."

"That's dreadful."

He gave a grim smile. "Yes."

"We still talk to my mother," Melly cheerfully announced.

"You do? Talk, you say? How?"

"There's a place we go to every week—the Four Bronze Sisters. People go there to speak with the dead."

Maple Rue squinted, turned to gaze at the three white arrows protruding from the hay target. "Do you know how to get to this place, Melly?"

"Of course."

☙   ☙   ☙

"Melly! Clooster Eastworth called. "Melly!"

He stood in front of the barn looking out at the rock-strewn fields. The afternoon sun angled down, tucking clumps of shadow into grassy hollows, the grass defined in such a way as to resemble a rich carpet of moss.

"Maple Rue?" No reply came. Again he ventured alongside the structure to where they had been practicing with the bow and arrows and still there was no sign of them. He jogged around the long building and looked over to where the wagon had stood—it was gone. There was, however, a long stick stuck in the ground with something white fluttering from it.

Half-alarmed, the tall gangly farmer hurried over and snatched the piece of parchment that had been impaled on the stick. It read:

Dear Clooster,

    Do not worry, Melly is with me and no harm shall befall her. I needed her to direct me to the Four Bronze Sisters. Unfortunately I do not have time to explain things properly. Do you recall when we found the tragic wreck of the Nulty farm and Marrow Water described other similar occurrences he had heard mention of? I am the monster that did those things.

The paper began to rattle in the farmer's hands, his eyes climbed rapidly across the words...

    More accurately, I was the vehicle a terrifying agent acted through. I can not explain how it came to be in me, but the Twin, as I came to know it, empowered me with frightful, inhuman strength, and compelled me to kill and destroy. I fought it futilely, until at last I secured the assistance of my uncle, and the three gullbirch arrows. The wood of the gullbirch tree is magic, you see.

    The arrows were all that could stop the creature, by trapping it in my body. When the arrows were removed, it was as if a cork were removed, releasing the dark spirit to roam free. I have devised a plan to stop it.

    I am going to the Four Bronze Sisters to have one of the mediums call the thing. In order for me to trap it, I must urge it to go into a human body. You will no doubt think me mad and evil for what I will do, and I am sickened by the mere thought, but is it not better that one innocent die so that countless potential victims live? Once the Twin is inside the medium, I will kill that person with my arrows, thus sealing the Twin inside, where it will no longer be able to unleash its vile tantrums.

*I am truly thankful for the concern and kindness you have shown me,
but you see, you should have let me die.*

Maple Rue

Clooster looked up, crumpling the paper and muttered, "He's mad..."
He ran for the house to fetch his musket.

SIX

At first sight the building seemed small, hunched there beneath the amethyst
dome of dusk. Closer. The reins trembled in Maple Rue's hands, and the
horses seemed reluctant to advance. Closer. It was a circular stone building,
larger now, windowless. Bats squirmed out from the shaggy thatch roof and
flickered above the moat where a mist of tiny flies purged up from the sullen
water. Closer.

The wagon came to a stop in front of the narrow wood-plank bridge that
spanned the moat. Maple did not think it looked wide enough to accommodate
the vehicle safely. He helped Melly down from the driver's perch and
wrapped the grey blanket he had taken from the Clooster home about himself,
fashioning a hooded cloak. He had plenty of room inside to conceal his pistol,
the bow and the three white arrows. He left the crutch behind.

The bridge creaked as they moved across, into the dark stable foyer. They
came to a wide wooden door and Maple looked down, stroking the back of
Melly's head. "Listen well, lass—once the spirit I seek has been called into the
medium I want you to run out here to the wagon. If the building starts
breaking, or something like that, ride off. Can you manage a wagon all right?"

"I think so."

"Good. Come..."

The door opened upon a wide circular room where four recessed areas
faced a central multi-fireplaced chimney. A mask of bronze stared
inscrutably from each of these depressions, dizzy candlelight stippling their
forged features.

Maple shuffled along in his disguise, ducking into the nearest of the mask-booths. Melly followed. She nodded politely to a young couple who turned to look out from one of the other hollows.

The mask was eerie, longish, the lips thin, the eyes open so that the medium could look out. Though it appeared to be hanging there, the rim of the thing was embedded in the wall.

"Hello," Maple whispered.

"Good evening, sir," a polite wisp of voice came. The voice was rather young, though Maple could not tell if it was a woman's or a man's.

"I wonder if you might help me—I wish my dealings to be handled by the oldest medium among you. Who might that be?"

"Opposite of here..." the mask spoke.

Maple and Melly crossed the floor, which was comprised of massive plates of smooth slate. Watery ghost-laughter flowed from one of the far mask chambers. Mounted candles hissed and sputtered, flicking their snake-tongue sparks.

They neared the new mask, its bronze flesh mottled and shifting where reflected flame and shadow struggled. Maple squinted into the dark eyes, at the glint of the pupils beyond.

"Whom do you wish to contact?" an old woman's voice rasped.

"My..." Maple paused. "My twin."

The mask sighed. "Twin, twin," the woman mumbled to herself.

Maple's arms worked under his cloak. He gripped the bow, fitted an arrow, readied to jerk it up, to fire through the eye-opening...

"Twin," the woman repeated, "Yes, I think it is near..."

The wood was slick in Maple's grasp, his body poised taut and humming.

"Ohhh, it is coming...yes—strong, it is..."

Maple swallowed. He glanced down at Melly, who looked up at him with sad eyes. She saw a tear glass down his cheek.

A loud crash!

"Maple Rue!" a voice fired.

He turned to see Clooster Eastworth, the door to the great room kicked wide, a musket's accusing stare.

"Stop, Maple!"

Maple snarled, "Don't interfere!"

"You're mad—there is no monster."

The young couple in the other booth peeked out.

"You're wrong!" Rue barked.

Clooster strode into the room, taking deadly aim, his face flushed dark. Maple spun around; an arm shot out from beneath his cloak, grabbing Melly from behind and wedging the barrel of his pistol under her chin. The girl gasped.

"Get back, Clooster—I must finish this!"

The farmer froze, reluctantly lowered his weapon. "Careful, man, please..."

Maple bent close to Melly and whispered, "Don't worry, I won't harm you."

The hooded man then turned to the mask and demanded, "Continue. Call the Twin..."

Maple peered into the eyes of the mask; he saw the eyes inside it roll white. A guttural groan rumbled through the floor and the stones of the wall seemed to swell. Maple took a step back, eyes wide. The wall burst outward in a dusty shambles, chunks tumbling, the bronze mask flung clanking. The medium was sprawled, dazed.

Melly spun in time to see a large dark thing lurch through the opening and vanish into Maple Rue. She screamed.

Clooster hollered, "Melly, move!"

He brought his gun up, cocked the mechanism.

Melly spread her arms out and stood in front of her friend. "No, father!"

Maple shoved the girl aside and stabbed his pistol out, firing. Smoke flashed thunder-close. Clooster shrieked as a ball punched red through his thigh. He grasped the spurting pain and went down, his own weapon dropping.

Maple staggered back, releasing the empty pistol. The bow had fallen, the arrows scattered across the rubble from the shattered wall. He scooped one up.

"Must hurry—" Maple groaned. "It's in me!"

Twitching hands fumbled; he turned the arrow so that the sharp tip pressed against his stomach. With a grunt and a jerk he drove it in. He gasped and fell back onto the stones.

Melly stood numb, gawking, watching as a great shadowy torso strained away from Maple's body, wide arms flailing like boughs in a tempest. She could hear it roaring as it struggled to pull away, then wrapped huge hands around the shaft and tried to tug it out.

Maple groped until he had another of the gullbirch rods in hand. He jammed it in alongside the first and howled in pain.

Clooster dragged himself over to his felled gun, smearing blood on the cool slate. He grabbed the weapon and managed to sit up. He took aim as Maple Rue jolted into a standing position.

"Melly," Maple gasped, "the bow…"

The girl stared at the monster as it rocked, the face of vague and grimacing pits. She crouched suddenly, grabbing the bow.

Boom! The musket's recoil knocked Clooster back—the shot struck Maple in the side, hammering him against the edge of the broken wall. A thick starfish of red spread across his white shirt. Maple grabbed at one of the arrows protruding from his midsection, struggling to keep the Twin from withdrawing it.

"Mel-ly," he gurgled.

The girl strung the last white arrow, aimed and released it. It blurred white with a hiss and sank deeply into her friend's chest. The man sagged back against the wall and slid down—the black thing deflated, recoiling back into him like a mist.

"Good…shot," the man whispered.

Maple Rue sat propped against the stone wall with three white arrows poking out from the red ruin of his shirt. His eyes closed slowly and he smiled as he died.

Lore of Northern Stones

The northern extreme of Westermead is a place of moody beauty. Mystery abounds amidst the bleak moors and in the mists of the rugged coast. Ancient monuments of stone, raised thousands of years back, add to the eerie charm. The locals embrace these stones with both fondness and fear, and pass along tongue-worn tales about them…

The Singing Rock at Candlecheese

A single upright pillar of unhewn stone stands in a field in the tiny hamlet of Candlecheese. People travel for miles to come and listen to the lilting feminine voice that comes from the twelve-foot granite slab. Though the words sung are in an archaic language — ancient beyond interpretation — the tones and melodies are mesmerizingly pleasant. In Noovum gifts of nuts and fruit are left at its base. Some claim that on the day when the North War began, the singing ceased and the stone shrieked piteously for several hours.

Storm Man's Bite

A solemn circle of nine granite standing stones rises from the beach grass overlooking the cove at Greynoose. Legend maintains that long ago a violent ocean storm moved in from the north. Fishermen, hastily dragging their boats ashore, watched as the blurry figure of a gigantic man appeared. He seemed to be trudging through the water, far away, near the horizon. As the rains intensified, the vision was lost, but over the next few days, giant teeth began washing up on the beach. Each tooth was as tall as a man, and weighed a ton or more. To commemorate the sighting of the giant, the fisherman built a circle with the teeth, which have since turned to stone. So the story goes…

The Widow's Stone

The moors outside of Lennet are pocked with abandoned tin mines, but few know of the moss-saddened mass of the Widow's Stone. The squat table-like rock sits at the western side of a heather-strewn expanse. The top surface is riddled with pock-holes where rain collects. Anyone who drinks "widow's tears" from these markings is lost to irreversible melancholia and destined to suicide.

The Peeper

In Spring, barren women in the village of Strawbridge loop bright ribbons and garlands of strung flowers around the stoic nine-foot standing stone which looms sentry-like in a field behind a farmer's cottage. It is believed that such rituals will make them fertile. The stone takes on a quietly ominous role in Winter, when the fields are snug in snow—it wanders. There are never any markings in the snow surrounding where the thing stood, no tracks or signs of dragging, only the bare spot it previously occupied. One morning it was discovered standing in the middle of a barn some three miles south. The natives faithfully returned it to its rightful spot. Others claim it sneaks into the village at night to stare through the windows of unsuspecting folk.

They say that if a virgin dreams of the stone, she will become pregnant within the year, and that an old woman who dreams of the Peeper will die within the year.

Finch Crimm's Shadow

Finch Crimm was the son of a Spellman who lived on the outskirts of Greyheather. He went mad after taking a bite out of a snap-apple and vanished at the age of twelve, not to be heard from for many years. Finch Crimm, now an adult, lived near the fishing village of Coalthurst and spent much of his time scouring the shoreline for the raw fish and seaweed which he relied on for food.

He told fishermen that he was in search of "the dream that scorches men's minds and leaves them hungry for the darker places." He cast strange spells using bits of information he had learned from his father when young. They say he could blast a hole in the side of a boat by simply clapping his hands.

One night, he stood on a high cliff overlooking an expanse of flat stone that sloped down to the sea. The folk tale claims he leapt high into the air and grabbed the full moon in his teeth. The moon fell down, crushing him into the floor of stone below the cliff, before bouncing back up into the sky.

To this day, there remains the deep depression of a sprawled man, there at the ocean's edge. The man-shaped pit goes deep into the bedrock, never deviating in shape—deeper than anyone on a rope has yet dared to measure. Some feel the pit is bottomless, or leads into a spectral realm beyond this. On quiet nights when the full moon frosts the calm sea, a patient ear can hear the strange, sardonic laughter of Finch Crimm echoing up from the endless man-shaped hole.

Summer

Sunpeak

The days are long for work and mirth. Solstice celebrations rage. The first thunderstorms come, occasionally breeding mischievous balls of light known as Chuckle Skulls, which burn erratic trails through the fields, laughing as they go. Warm glades coddle their foxglove in secret. Knolls pout clover-pink, as dale and fen brag furze and foxgrass. The woods are dense with heat and leaves, and restless with game. The first hay falls to blade.

Growsurge

Now the air drags heavy and damp as the sun presses down without mercy. Natives are wary of high temperatures which can invite the dreaded Summer Men spirits, should they rage too high. Long haired Northern cattle steep in streams where frenzied flies bullet. Spellwomen dance to ward off draught, so that gardens might feast on moisture. The morning bares skies of haze and rust; it is best not to travel on moth-storm nights. One might find it fit to picnic or wander lazily on breeze-tempted afternoons. There is nettle to dread and fortweed to rob.

Gusstar

The corn is tall and golding, the marshlands swollen with meadow-sweet. Songfull thrush dine on the bloody berries of rowan trees. Wild herbs are gathered for spells. The long season of harvesting begins; hungry sickles feast on hay. The moors splay purple with heather, and goldenrod spreads unchallenged. The days tilt sooner toward darkness.

The Frost Mare

ONE

It began when a certain missive arrived at the offices of Beech and Purdy in Narrow Heights, Bellingtower. A clerk rushed the letter up to the main rooms and paused in the doorway. He took a brief visual assessment of the letter, noting the urgent script and the address; it was from the magistrate of Drowning Tin, a small wind-washed island off the southern coast of Westermead.

The clerk's employers were in the midst of an animated conversation with a rather fetching young lady, who, it turns out, was a wealthy widow. Mrs. Peebly, having inherited her husbands' publishing house, was considering taking on the bestiary the two documentalists were compiling.

"You should have seen it," Beech, a plump fellow with short bristly blond hair and round spectacles, said. "It was a ghastly thing with eyes the red of rowan berries and teeth like—"

"Daggers!" Purdy interjected.

Beech frowned over at his partner. "I was about to say that."

"Right. Sorry. Anyway...the teeth were like daggers and the noise it made was—"

"Deafening," Beech said, squinting over at Purdy. "I fear to think what should have become of our ears if it hadn't been for that beeswax."

The clerk watched, smirking as the two men competed for the woman's attention. Mrs. Peebly pivoted from one to the other with wide eyes, captivated by their tale.

Beech paced across the room and without interrupting the rhythm of his speech, snatched the letter from the clerk. "The strange and nauseating stench was overwhelming as the thing charged toward our trench..."

Purdy was taller and on the lean side, moderately handsome, despite a largish nose, his dark hair combed back into a knot. Never without his clay pipe, his expression was studied nonchalance. "I dread to think of the trauma such an encounter might have impacted upon one, let's say, less familiar with fantastic beasts. For the creature roared into the air, passing over our dugout before we could even get a shot at it."

Mrs. Peebly flinched at the sound of the envelope ripping open. Beech gazed over at Purdy and said, "That's when you fainted."

Purdy snapped upright. "Fainted! I did no such thing! I, I tripped."

Beech chuckled. "Well, it must have been quite a fall, for you were cold on the ground a good five minutes."

"I beg to differ!"

Mrs. Peebly smiled, embarrassed, and glanced down into her wine glass. "What became of the monster?" she asked.

"Gone into the night," Beech cooed, grinning triumphantly.

"All but for the scorched paw prints left on the moor," Purdy added.

Mrs. Peebly put a hand to her chest and sighed. "My, gentlemen, that is a thrilling story!"

She looked to Beech, who was so engrossed in the letter he had unfolded that he appeared not to have heard her. She watched his expression go from one of severe intensity to that of boyish delight. He looked up slowly, plucked off his glasses and announced, "The Frost Mare has returned."

🌀   🌀   🌀

The charming Widow Peebly was the last thing on Dover Beech's mind as he and his partner made their way down to the public house on Twelve Spires Lane. It had showered earlier but now the sun, having nudged free of the cloud cover, turned the slick cobblestones to bronze.

They took tea by a window overlooking the stagnant structures of Bellingtower's business district. The place was a frequent haunt of Purdy and Beech at this time of day. It was no accident that they would dine there just after the bustle of business types had departed. Awaiting his repast, Fin Purdy gazed out, puffing his pipe, recalling how delightful Mrs. Peebly had looked. Beech was busy wrestling with a map.

"We could take a carriage from Grey Bride to Wingle," Beech was muttering, largely to himself. "From there it's a skip and a half to Shellings Port. We could catch a boat there..."

"Right," Purdy said, obligatorily. He eyed the serving woman as she set down plates and cups.

"Your food'll just be a moment," the woman said.

"Splendid." Purdy smiled.

Beech was leaning his nose into his map, squinting, twisting the crinkled paper this way and that. He barely took notice when the servant returned with his buttered dandelion greens and rye cakes.

Fin Purdy restrained the smile of fondness he experienced watching his friend lose himself to his passion. He set aside his pipe and had at his meal of pork dumplings.

"Most intriguing," Beech concluded, stuffing the map back into the pocket of his jacket. "Twenty years have passed since this Frost Mare was about."

"I fear I'm not terribly familiar with the case, Dover," Purdy admitted, "and I've no doubt you'll take great delight in rectifying that situation."

"That I will," Beech said, leaning forward, rubbing his pudgy hands together. "Drowning Tin is a rugged little place, as you know, in turn populated by a rugged lot; tinners mostly—back then, at least. There are only three proper villages, and scattered farms for those hardy enough to rear crops from the stony soil. Well, in the summer of twenty years ago, pirates were using the island's eastern shore as a base to launch raids from. They could monitor the trade ships coming to and going from the mainland and orchestrate their activities accordingly. It was a bloody situation, I take it, the thieves being a ruthless lot. So, the King sent in the military to squash the scoundrels."

Purdy sat back, chewing.

"It was some months later that the unusual occurrences began. There were strange symbols discovered in the farm fields; the crops, in the midst of summer warmth and fruitfulness, being flattened by concentrated doses of killing frost. Then came the sightings. A farmer observed a ghostly creature one evening as he headed home across his pastures. He described a skeletal birch-white beast that traveled on all fours, as a dog would, the body being like that of a fleshless human, with a long whip of a tail, the disproportionate head like that of a horse with blank skull eyes."

Purdy shuddered.

"This creature came up from the south with a frightful swiftness and proceeded to dash about his property, carving patterns through his barley with its icy countenance. Then it simply headed off into the dusk. There were similar sightings reported. The group of soldiers stationed there were put on alert; one of their lot had been killed by the thing. Two others were set upon while patrolling. They were dreadfully shaken by the encounter, and slightly injured as well. Seems the beast knocked them down with its front limbs and wagged its great toothy face at them. They suffered severe frostbite where the paws, or hands, or hooves, whatever it has, had pinned their chests."

"It actually killed someone?" Purdy pushed the remains of his meal away and fired his pipe.

"Just two, or so it's believed. Besides the soldier, there was a girl. A farmer's daughter, unless I recall incorrectly. She was never found, yet it was assumed the Frost Mare, as it had been dubbed, got her."

Purdy wore a sour expression. He watched the mist from his pipe swirling past the windows which the lowering sun had changed to amber.

"The incidents stopped as abruptly as they began," Beech reported, "and the thing had not been seen since, until now."

"So it's verifiably been spotted?"

"Mmm, yes. A young couple was out strolling on the moor in the vicinity of some abandoned tin mines, which had been shunned since the creature first made its presence known. The Mare had been seen in the area several times, and people have steered clear of the place since."

"Until this couple, that is?"

"Precisely. They say it was running along a ridge, a bony luminous thing with an emaciated body and a large horsey head. Fortunately it kept its distance."

"There've been no attacks this time?"

"Not yet. The magistrate of Drowning Tin was familiar with my writings, having seen my work on water serpents, and thought it best to summon us."

Purdy gazed off through the window, brow knit and pipe clenched. "I wonder where it came from, this Frost Mare. Most of our critters have a long body of lore attached to them, yet this one appeared quite sporadically."

"And vanished with the same abruptness. Now it's come back, for some reason or other. After twenty years…" Beech said, turning to the sunny window, which set his spectacles on fire.

ᘓ   ᘓ   ᘓ

Purdy and Beech spent the next morning committed to research. Fin passed the hours in the Bellingtower City Library back-tracking through years' worth of documents to see if he could find any mention of a creature like the Frost Mare predating its visit of two decades back. There were musty tomes in shadowy aisles, misted with the pumping of his pipe.

Drowning Tin had its share of mysterious spirits and creatures (and what part of Westermead didn't?), but there was no mention of anything similar to the Mare. Next, he checked writings from the other islands dotting Westermead's coast to see if they had any comparable beasts. He found one story about a ghostly steed on the tiny stump of stone known as Grundle's Fang. But that creature was tall and black, not the crouched, sprinting mare-like thing of Drowning Tin.

The man was equally unsuccessful in finding information about the soldier whom the creature had killed. That information would be entombed at the King's Hall of Records in the military library, but there would not be time to dance the political steps necessary to gain access.

The only thing of interest that Purdy did observe was a young woman in a billowy white summer dress seeking books on medicinal herbs. Being the gentleman he was, he escorted her to the proper aisle.

Dover Beech had taken his shay outside of the great grey city to visit an old woman in Stormbroom on Wester. The woman was an expert on the stars and such. Beech sought to find if there were any occurrences in the sky, like planets aligning or rare conditions concerning moon and sun activity, which might have acted as a trigger for the Mare. Something that happened at twenty-year intervals, perhaps. The woman could think of nothing.

Beech and Purdy met that afternoon at their table in the public house on Twelve Spires. They discussed final plans, for in the morning they would set off on their adventure.

While sitting back, digesting, each in that pensive anticipatory silence they experienced when on the verge of a potentially hazardous embarkment, they were approached by a man in a plum-colored jacket and knickers. He had recognized the plump, bespectacled, late-thirtyish fellow with the close-cropped hair.

"You're that chap who's always running off here and there after monsters, aren't you?"

Beech looked up at the tall well-dressed stranger and straightened. "Correct, sir, and you're—?"

"Burlt Moorwood. I run a firearms manufacturing house here in the city."

"Ahhh, very good. How may I help you?"

"Oh, no way, really, it's only that I recognized you just now, having read of you in this or that periodical. You were pictured in one."

Beech grinned. "I remember. Not too good a sketch, I gather."

"So, you're still chasing ghosties and other nasties?"

Purdy looked over at his partner's dissolving grin. He didn't care for the man's tone.

"We're undertaking a new case come morning, as a matter of fact," Beech said coolly.

The man scowled. "I find it rather silly that grown men have nothing better to do than—"

"Excuse me." Beech straightened further. "You, sir, produce weapons; we document the natural world. Everyone has a vocation. Ours is no less legitimate than the next. We are presently compiling a book which documents our findings of lore and fact concerning the varied beasts, material and otherwise, which populate our good Westermead. We're historians of the mystical, if you will. Perhaps it distresses you to think that there are fantastic creatures about..."

"It's nonsense, Mr. Beech. Rubbish."

"Mr. Moorwood, the material world and the magical are as interconnected as veins and arteries. You have obviously spent too much time in the city."

"And you have spent too much time sitting on your fat brain."

Purdy shot up from his seat, face flushed, chin jutting. "I beg your pardon! You're insulting my friend!"

Moorwood raised his clenched hands. "Let's see your fists then, mister!"

When Purdy came to he was on the floor, his head propped up by Beech.

"Ohhh, my blasted gourd. What happened?"

"You fainted," Beech explained matter-of-factly.

"I did not! I, I tripped on the chair legs."

"As you wish."

"What of Moorwood?"

"He was off as soon as you hit the boards, the bastard. I believe he was embarrassed," said Beech.

"A jolly good thing he left when he did. If I'd gotten my hands on him I'd have shown him what for!"

☙ ☙ ☙

Hours had passed since the last carriage clattered past Dover Beech's flat. His dog, Chalker, a spindly white thing, was curled in a corner, watching him pace the bedchamber clutching a mug of warm buttered mead. The man's eyes were smaller minus the spectacles, smaller yet when squeezed in thought.

The packing had been completed hours before. Besides a bundle of clothing, he would be taking his spyglass, a book full of blank parchment, writing quills, ink and a small protective charm-sack the spellwoman at Neebotton had given him. There was also the long slender form of his wheel-lock pistol, a graceful thing of polished walnut with a steel ball at the butt of the grip. Beech looked upon the thing with fondness and resentment. Though he admired the weapon's look and even took pleasure in the way the weight rested in hand, he regretted the times he had been forced to use it.

"One more," Beech said, pouring mead from the warm pot on his bed-table, "to drown any nasty dreams."

  ℃ ℃ ℃

The scent of roses stole in on a summer breeze as Purdy worked at filling the heavy wooden trunk that sat open on his bed. He packed with a keen sense of economy, whistling patiently. Clothing, medical supplies, drinking skins, sketch books, compass, pistol and spare pipe all fit together in the cedar-scented box.

"That should do it," Purdy concluded, shutting the lid.

"That should do it," a squeaky voice mimicked from within a cage which rested on a nearby table.

The man grinned over at the plump grey echo toad; bland eyes like juniper berries gazed back. "Time for us to be off to sleep, Mr. Chub."

"Time to sleep, time to sleep."

Purdy lowered the trunk to the floor and changed into his sleeping gown.

"In morning you'll be going to visit with auntie," Purdy told his companion as he draped a cloth over the dome of bars. "You'll like that, won't you? She spoils you without shame!"

"Auntie, auntie."

Purdy mumbled to himself, "You'll probably be twice your size when I get you back. If I ever come back, that is. We're after a rough one this time…"

The man breathed in the whispers of the garden, blew out the candles, climbed into bed and settled.

"You fainted," a voice from the toad's cage squawked in the darkness, "you fainted!"

Purdy stared upward and growled, "Beech, you wretch, I'll strangle you!"

TWO

The Lazy Arrow was a creaking old thing, rolling wearily as greybeards slapped against her hull. Beech stood at the bow, staring; the Tarnic spread wide beneath a shale-welted sky. Purdy sat on his trunk of supplies, scowling, pale, clutching his midsection. He gazed back at the fading docks of Shellings Port.

The captain, a hunched leathery old fellow, approached his passengers. A tempest of surf-colored hair framed his gaunt face. Though the sky was bloated with clouds he squinted as if it were bright noon.

"Are ya comfortable, lads?" the captain asked.

Purdy groaned, triggering a wicked laugh from the man. "I'm a sailor, lad, dry land makes me dizzy."

"Is this thing safe?"

The captain frowned. "Patches have held this long…I'd wager we'll see you to Drowning Tin all right."

"How nice."

Beech turned, grinning. "Is firewood all you deliver to the island, Captain?" he asked.

"That's right. Their peat supply ran out years back. Too windy and rugged for prosperous tree-growth out there; a wonder they squeeze crops out the bleedin' rock. They're a mad lot to stay, says I, but so long as it fills me pockets with coins I'll bring their blasted wood."

"You're a pragmatic fellow," Beech noted.

"And what is it brings you two fancy city gents out to this lonely bit of dung?"

"I'm beginning to wonder myself," Purdy moaned.

Beech straightened. "We're investigating the Frost Mare."

"Ahhh, a queer thing, that Mare. The lads of me crew heard talk of that when we was out last. A frightful creature as I take it. We'll unload our wood and be off quick, thank you. I can do without meeting the thing."

Beech was all boyish smiles, riding the waves of his adrenaline as the Tarnic's rocked the Arrow.

"Best of luck to ya, then," the captain said, squinting. He turned to head back to his duties, wagging his skull and muttering, "Madmen. Everywhere I go, madmen."

Although it was several days into the month of Sunpeak, the air was chill. Dover wore a sepia-colored gabardine and vest over his white shirt. A tricorne capped his head. He fished his spyglass from his deepest pocket and aimed it out across the bow.

Drowning Tin squatted amidst the haze of the southern horizon.

      ❧   ❧   ❧

Harsh centuries had sculpted the green and grey of that lonely place. Hardy gulls knew its outcroppings and hollows, watching with black-lacquered eyes for the small green crabs which staggered over pebbled beaches. They swooped above the crawling foam, foam the white of frost, melting between the scales of stone, pooling where the rot of dead fish mingled with brine. Gods with bony hands had built that place.

The Lazy Arrow snuggled up against a salt-bleached dock where fishermen's boats mocked the grey water with their bright paint. The Captain took to gesturing and shouting orders, his scruffy team bustling. Villagers waited with mules and wagons and curious looks for the city men. Those two passengers struggled their luggage onto the wharf and stood a moment to reacquaint themselves with the virtue of balance.

Dover drummed his fingers on his belly, taking in the view. It was, from this vantage point, a treeless place; rugged was the word that rang foremost in his mind. There was grass wherever the abundant juttings of rock allowed. A single path led up to where stone buildings hugged a high plateau. Dover thought he had never seen the sky look so big. How merciful that the rumpled mass of milk and pewter did not sweep those foolish little structures into the sea.

"Charming place," Purdy said distastefully.

"Desolate, in a romantic sense of the word. A fine breeding ground for mystery," Dover offered.

"My thoughts exactly."

An arthritic cart came down the long trail, stopping at the edge of the dock. The pilot was a hunched old gent with a bald head and a frothy beard of rust. He smiled at the strangers and waved them over.

"Welcome, welcome, my boys. I'm Stoonian Fernwing, magistrate of this illustrious bit of rock and moss. Welcome to Drowning Tin."

Purdy gave Dover a whisper and nudge. "Now there's a man with commanding presence."

"Shh!"

The Kingdom official gestured to his vehicle, "You'll excuse me if I keep seated while you fellows load your belongings...I've a bit of the creak in my knees."

"Of course." Dover, ever the diplomat, smiled. He and his companion hefted their trunks onto the cart, then climbed up themselves.

"All set, then. Hold on, the path's a bit lumpy."

"This whole island looks lumpy," Purdy noted.

"Ahh, she is at that. I'm awfully pleased that you two have come all this way to help us. I hope it's no inconvenience."

Dover elbowed Purdy before the man could open his mouth and replied, "Not at all. We live for this sort of thing. I only hope we can be of some assistance."

"Oh, I'm sure, a pair of quick-minded gents like you...Oh, my missus has gotten our spare room all in proper order for you. I hope you'll find it a likable enough space."

"Oh, glorious," Purdy lamented, turning to his partner, "I get to listen to you snore."

"No worse than that fat toad of yours."

"Speaking of my fat toad, have you been teaching him new phrases again?"

Dover made innocent eyes behind his round spectacles. "What? Me?"

The buildings comprising the village of Gull Hill were huddled together against the wind. They were modest assemblages of stone with roofs of slate, rather than thatch. There was a potter's shack, a blacksmith shop, a boatmaker and a tavern called Ghost Oak. The magistrate's house was a quaint thing squatting in a nest of restless briar and air sweet with nipple-pink blooms.

The inner compartments were cozy enough. Low beams bearded with clumps of drying herbs, pots and cooking implements like an exploded suit of armor cluttering the wall near the cooking hearth. The scented ghosts of countless meals rose warm from the broad planks of the floor, exhumed by the trampling boots of strangers.

Mrs. Fernwing was a pleasant, round little woman who insisted on shoveling food into her guests. Purdy noted her girth, patted his friend's gut and hushedly observed, "Chubbiness loves company."

Purdy, however, did not decline a bowl of steamy pear porridge or plump fenberry scones served with rose-petal tea.

After their invigorating repast, the three men gathered around a map of Drowning Tin.

"That's where that young couple spotted it," old Fernwing said.

"The dots suggest tin mines, yes?" Dover asked.

"Right. Long abandoned mines. Over here," a finger rasped across the yellowed parchment, "is where the soldier was found dead, twenty years back."

Purdy spoke. "Were you here then, Magistrate?"

"Oh, no. Me and the missus been here just these past ten."

"I see."

Dover leaned back, removed his specs and rubbed at his eyes. "We'll want to speak with some of the long term natives, as well as the young couple who recently spied the thing."

Purdy nodded, adding, "What of the parents of that girl, the one who vanished the other time?"

"Her mother's still alive," Fernwing stated.

"Right then." Dover clapped his hands. "We'll just gather the necessary equipment and get on with it. Might we trouble you to introduce us to these good folks, Magistrate?"

☙ ☙ ☙

"Am I disturbing you?"

"No, not at all," Purdy's muffled voice came from beneath a pillow.

"Then why," Dover Beech asked, "do you have a pillow over your face? Some archaic ritual of self-beautification, perhaps?"

68

"No. Because you have a blasted candle blazing!"

Dover chuckled. "Ah, so I *am* disturbing you."

"Your powers of observation never cease to amaze me. Are you going to write all night?"

"I fear I'm having trouble hearing you, Fin. Can you breathe under there?"

Purdy tugged the pillow away and snarled, "I said, are you going to write all bloody night?"

"Not all night. Don't get your horsies in a trot, my friend. Next you'll be telling me I'm taking more than my share of the blanket."

Purdy gazed mournfully at the beamed ceiling and muttered, "I'm having a nightmare and I'm not yet asleep."

"You must forgive me; I'm terribly enthusiastic, you know, and liable to pace all night—and we can't have that—unless I put some of the day to paper, to purge my restless mind, if you will. Perhaps a warm buttered mead would soothe me."

Purdy rolled over onto his side, pulling the pillow back over his head. "Good night, Dover."

"Good night, Fin."

🙥 🙥 🙥

Dover could hear the moth-colored waves whispering up the shore, out there in the distant darkness. His back was against his pillow, his pillow against the stone wall, his face leaning close to the parchment. His script, in the faint glow of a lone sputtering candle, resembled fragments of black lace.

He wrote:

"Any doubts which might have reared concerning the integrity of the witnesses were eradicated upon meeting them. Drent Jemming and Pelly Whittle were neither mad nor pranksters; indeed, I found them to be cut of earnest cloth. The young man is apprentice blacksmith to Gull Hill, the timid wraith of a lass is a fisher's daughter.

"They led us out to examine the spot where they had seen the Frost Mare. The island, it turns out, does have trees, though sorry-looking things they are, both twisted and stunted. There were sporadic signs of summer to

69

brighten our way along the lonely trackways; blushing pastures of clover, crimson splashes of poppy and occasional clusters of wild herbs, seemingly nourished by the shadows of innumerable boulders and outcroppings of rock.

"The region where the actual sighting had taken place was a bland bit of earth. We were in something of a hollow, grassy mounds sweeping up, half-obscuring the sky. One had the sensation of being in a maze. There were granite formations like figures cowled and huddled. Even the grass seemed grey. The openings of abandoned tin mines were plentiful, like the eye sockets of great skulls, as it were, some choked with tattered vines.

"Drent pointed to the ridge where the creature had appeared and described it precisely as the magistrate had in his letter. The thing he had seen was quadrupedal, the body like that of a skeletal human, the massive head horse-like with shadowy hollows for eyes. The girl defined it as having glowed faintly, much like a full moon behind translucent clouds.

"We scaled the ridge in search of prints, but found none. No visible evidence remained. Perhaps this was a ghost of the seemingly corporeal thing which had pinned soldiers to the ground and wagged its hideous grin twenty years previous.

"Our two guides seemed ill at ease all the while we occupied the vicinity of the mines. With hardly any prodding on my part, I was able to ascertain that the villagers, as a whole, were dreadfully frightened, now that the mysterious beast was again roaming the countryside. It had been a year since the island's only spellwoman died, and her absence, I gather, compounded the air of apprehension.

"Mothers were keeping their children from wandering, livestock was only permitted to graze the closest pastures and few natives were venturing outside after dark. I myself would be less than truthful were I to say here that I was not unsettled being out in the wilds of Drowning Tin, enclosed within those alien ramparts of grass and stone amidst the vacant mines.

"It was inevitable that one of us would suggest the possibility that the creature we were investigating might be watching us, that very moment, from within the cool throat of one of the mines. It was Purdy who did the honors, shuddering as the thought left his lips. I laughed nervously. It was not an unreasonable concept. A creature, were it so inclined, might dwell long undetected in that network of dark forsaken tunnels.

"I saw my friend's face drain when I suggested that we would, at some point, need take on the task of exploring the caverns. I was quick to admit, however, that I was not yet prepared for such an adventure and he seemed relieved by my suggestion that we continue gathering whatever information possible, before going to such extreme measures.

"The young lass, all the while hugging herself, with eyes darting nervously each time a breeze swept through the shadows, asked just what we intended to do once we found the Frost Mare. Purdy and I looked to each other and shrugged."

THREE

Dover Beech watched the cat watching the wasp. The insect made its way down the handle of a scythe, which leaned against the side of a stone chicken house. The cat stared with wide grape-green eyes, back legs coiling like springs beneath its crouching form. The wasp was beautiful, and unbeknownst to the creature stalking it, dangerous.

"Don't," the man whispered, fearing for each creature.

The cat edged closer, a black puddle pouring through the grass, whiskers flattening against the sides of its face. The oblivious wasp moved lower along the curved wood, wings like rime glinting in the morning sun.

The cat pounced. Dover thrust an arm out, nudging the wasp with a finger. An angry hum as the insect spun off through the warm air. The cat composed itself, gave a flick of the tail and sauntered off.

"Can I help you?"

Beech looked up into the face of an old woman, her long faded hair blending into the drained white of her shawl. Her eyes were the pale blue of a forgotten summer sky, the fading tattoos of her youth.

"Good morning, good woman. Allow me to introduce myself. I am Dover Beech; perhaps you heard that I—"

The woman turned before the sentence was complete, scuffing back toward her house, kicking through a protesting moat of chickens. He had seen pain flash in her eyes.

"Mrs. Squill," Beech called, following, "please, might I beg a moment of your time?'

She had reached the door, a bony hand grasped the handle. "I don't want to talk to anyone. Be gone from my farm," the back of her head said.

"But I've come far, all the way from Bellingtower; I've come to help."

"You're twenty years too late to help me, sir. Now please be gone." A thin wrist rose to wipe something from her face.

Beech reached into his gabardine and pulled out a large silvery coin. He stepped closer, holding it in front of the woman's face.

"A whole fifty moon piece?"

"It's yours. You don't even have to say another word. It's my way of apologizing for coming onto your property and causing you distress."

"A whole fifty moon," the woman repeated. She took the coin in her trembling fingers and turned her mournful eyes on the man. "What do ya want to know?"

Beech felt a brief internal grin. He could be crafty when conditions called for it. He felt guilty, though, looking into the wrinkled face where pain had strewn its webs of flesh.

"I'm trying to find the Mare and stop it, if need be, so that no one else meets the fate your poor daughter did, twenty years back."

Mrs. Squill worried the coin, glancing out at the slopes of surrounding pasture. She nodded. "All the way from Bellingtower, you say? What brings a fancy man of your sort to this sorry rock?"

Beech smiled, his plump face warm with kindness. "I'm a madman, some might think. I study strange creatures, like our Mare. Like a cat drawn to wasps."

   ↄ ↄ ↄ

The room was shadowy, low-beamed, dusty. Straw-woven animals hung on the wall and dangled from rafters. Horses, goats, cats, even a bird with frayed wings, grey from the ash and smoke of the fireplace.

"I make them," Mrs. Squill stated, "keeps my fingers loose."

"They're charming. You're alone here?"

"I wouldn't say that." She jerked a thumb at a large white cat which sat on the table's edge, studying the man as he ate from a plate of boiled prawns and dandelion greens.

"How many do you have?"

"Twelve. That's White One. She can predict storms."

Beech looked into the noble creature's pale green eyes. "I've no doubt," he remarked.

The woman dipped a bit of prawn in melted butter and offered it to the beast.

"Tell me about your daughter. Her name was Pleasance, I believe."

"Yes. She was like a cat in her way. Too curious for her own good. Always wandering where shadows fed, tempting the steepest cliffs. Too much breeze in her veins, I used to tell her father. But she was a sweet girl, Mr. Dover. She had the loveliest hair, long and full and gold as Gusstar straw."

"Blue eyes like a summer sky?"

The old woman smiled. "Oh, yes. She…" The woman paused; an untouched door was about to be sprung—her tongue retreated from the key-hole. "She was too alive for this bland place."

"Might I trouble you to recall the night she…disappeared, as it were?"

A heavy sigh. "She was a restless creature, Mr. Dover, and, her being restless like that, was prone to trouble. She was up to something that night, something her father and I disapproved of."

"Like?"

"Well, that was back when pirates was using Drowning Tin as a base for raids…"

"Correct."

"And there was all these pretty soldier lads about the island, come to have at the raiders. Well, our local girls had never seen the likes of them, with their uniforms and swords and all. Pleasance was like a crow about shiny things, and she had a mighty fancy for one of them spiffy soldier lads. Ahh, she tried to hide it, but a mother knows. A mother knows."

Dover nodded, biting into a prawn.

"She was sneakin' off at night on her white mare, to meet him. That's what she did that last night. She sneaked off after all the lights was out. And she never came back and we never found her."

Beech's eyes brightened behind his spectacles. "The soldier they found dead…that was him!"

The woman looked down, hiding her blurry eyes. She nodded.

"The Mare killed him and she vanished?" Dover looked at his food pensively and said, half to himself, "What did it do with her body?"

"We found her horse wandering. It had blood on it, from no wound of its own. I'd venture to say that monster ate her. Why else was there nothin' to bury?"

"What manner of damage was inflicted on the soldier? Did it freeze him?"

The woman kept her eyes downcast. She fidgeted with the moon coin. "I'm not sure. He was dead, that's all I know. It's all I want to know."

Dover was silent for a moment. He sat looking at the snowy cat which returned his gaze unblinkingly. "Tell me, Mrs. Squill, where is this spot where the soldier's body was discovered?"

"Turtle's Heap. It's a hill out on the western side of the island, not far from where them soldiers was camped."

"I think I should like to see the place."

"There's nothing to see now, Mr. Beech, just some twisty birches and grass and sky. Lots and lots of sky."

❧ ❧ ❧

Thorns of salty wind had pocked the solemn granite marker which read; Pleasance Squill. Beech stood above the slab, lost in thought. Purdy was squatting nearby, a sketch book open on a knee, a deft hand wielding a drawing stick. He captured the monument with graceful ashy streaks.

"What's that you're clutching, Dover?" Purdy mumbled around his pipe.

Beech seemed to awaken. He turned, holding up a tiny horse, tightly woven of faded straw. It still smelled faintly of the secret herbs sewn into the belly.

74

"A good luck charm. It belonged to the Squill girl. Her mother gave it to me. She forgot to take it with her that night…"

Purdy nodded. "Are you quite all right, my friend? You're not your usual jolly acerbic self."

"Acerbic? I beg your pardon? When am I ever acerbic?"

"To me? Quite often."

Beech grinned, pocketing the charm. He walked over and observed his partner's sketch. "Quite good," he remarked. "So what did you learn from the locals?"

"There's a lovely plump young thing who helps tend the tavern where I took lunch."

"How delightful. What did you learn about the Frost Mare?"

"Oh, that. Well, I spoke with a number of folks. They are a rugged lot, but tolerable. Something quaintly barbaric about them."

"And the Frost Mare?"

"Well," Purdy sighed. "I talked with an old gent whose farm had been visited by it, twenty years ago. He told me about the frosty patterns it blasted through his corn. I had him sketch it, but he couldn't recall it properly."

"Let me see!"

Purdy fished out the parchment and Beech snatched it. The man had drawn a semi-circular design, one side split into subtle lobes. There were vague scribbles in the center.

"What's that stuff in the middle?"

"He never knew really, I'm sorry to report. Curious villagers had trampled the blasted thing, pardon the pun."

"Is it a symbol of some sort?"

"I don't know, Dover. Neither did he. He did know the name of that lass at the tavern, though. Lilly," he let the name melt buttery on his tongue.

Beech rolled his eyes. "Incorrigible."

❧ ❧ ❧

The tavern was called Ghost Oak because of the natural marking on the great plank door which resembled a mournful face. Inside a fiddler was perched on a table edge, the squeaky instrument playing high and fast. Many of the chairs and tables had been pushed aside to make room for the dancers who thumped and reeled. The air was warm with ale and pipe smoke and a touch of the bonfire roaring outside. The villagers had gathered for The Reaper's Dance to honor the first hay crop.

Dover occupied a table with the magistrate Fernwing and his wife. They sat smiling at Purdy as he spun past with a plump young woman, her cheeks dappled with nutmeg freckles and her brown hair slashing like a horse tail in mid-canter. Beech could not help but notice the impressive bosom pounding under her dress. He turned to the magistrate and said, "Could you tell me how to find Turtle Heap?"

"I could, if you'd like, my boy. You don't mean to go there tonight, do you?"

"No, in morning."

Purdy whirled past again, grinning and winking. He mouthed to Dover: Don't wait up for me tonight!

Dover chuckled. Good to see a little breeze in the veins of his friend. Some of the dancers clutched bundles of straw, preserved from last year's harvest—these would be cast on the bonfire after the dance. The charming plump girl had stuffed a bunch between Purdy's teeth. He glanced over and wiggled his brows.

Beech slouched in his seat, ale sitting heavy in his belly. He took out the worn little charm. A horse. He looked at Mr. Fernwing. "The Squill girl's horse was a white mare, wasn't it?"

"That's what I'm told. I gather it was in a sorry state when they found it. They say it was numb, like, up until it died."

Dover was pensive.

"Does that mean something, my boy?"

"Can't say I know."

Purdy, panting and sweaty, his white shirt's sleeves curled back, stumbled over dragging his partner with him. He scooped up Dover's ale and gulped.

"Dover, meet Lilly. Lilly, this is Dover."

The lass giggled and smiled.

"Hello, Lilly. No broken bones, yet, Fin?"

"Bah! I could dance all night, amongst other things…"

The girl giggled, grabbing his mug of ale away, slurping from it.

Dover sat blinking as the liquid drooled down onto her chest.

"Isn't she a charmer, Dover?" Purdy asked, smiling foolishly.

"I was just going to say."

The door swung open with a bang and a disheveled young man leapt in. "The Frost Mare! The Frost Mare's here!"

Dover lurched from his seat as a white form dashed into the room. A gleaming horse skull smiled as the disguised figure holding it spun around beneath a fluttering sheet.

"Blast the Mare!" someone shouted drunkenly.

"Blast the Mare!" the cry went up.

Dancers converged on the figure masquerading as the monster and with collective fear venting, they swatted at it with their bundles of straw.

"Blast the Mare! Blast the Mare!"

Dover sank back into his seat trembling and grabbed what was left of his ale. His heart was galloping in his chest.

FOUR

"Mrs. Squill was right," Beech muttered.

"What's that?" Fernwing asked.

"There's nothing to see, really." The man drummed restless fingers on his belly and looked out across a bleak expanse of moorland. Several spindly birch trees clawed at the dusty shroud of the sky.

Dover looked at the grass, trying to imagine what horror had occurred where he now stood, twenty years back. Had the young couple seen the ghastly bony figure charging across the moor? Where had the dead soldier lain? Where had it taken the girl?

"Tell me, Magistrate. When did the Mare first make its presence known? Was it the crop destruction?"

"No, not at all. I've always heard it was the attack, here. That was the first of it. The first crop freezing, to my knowledge, wasn't 'til several days later."

"Do you know of any lore concerning this place? Turtle's Heap, I mean. Any mystical tales about it? Perhaps some volatile forces dwell in this mound and the couple's meetings here disturbed it, or certain, shall we say, intimate activities triggered it in an unknowing ritual, if you will."

"There's nothing I've heard, Mr. Beech, 'cept the hill looks like a turtle."

"A pity we're not chasing after a Frost Turtle, might prove a less agile subject of study."

The magistrate chuckled. "Yes, I should say it would at that!"

Beech knelt to feel the ground for abnormalities, then he examined the trees, looking for frost burns, wondering if blood had marred the chipped white bark.

"Look here!"

Fernwing hurried over.

Dover's finger rested below a carving of a heart.

"The young lovers' mark," the old man breathed softly.

Beech looked up, his little eyes gleaming. "What's that in the middle? Some type of symbol. What is that?"

"I can't say as I know, Mr. Beech."

Dover fumbled for his parchment and drawing nub. He pictured the sketch that Purdy had shown him depicting the markings the Frost Mare had left, the rough circle with a subtle split, like the twin parts of a heart, and the scribbles in the center. He wondered if the birch-scribed image of an upward pointing dagger with wings for a handguard had been carved into that field before curious onlookers trampled it.

"Ahh, I recognize that now," Fernwing proclaimed. "I seen it on that soldier's grave in the Sleeping Yard. Exact same thing, without the heart around it, of course, that's why I didn't recognize it right off."

Beech looked up, perplexed. "Why would this creature run about carving some dead soldier's insignia into people's crops?"

"Not just that dead soldier's symbol, Mr. Beech, that was the emblem of the whole seventh cavalry—the ones that came to do away wit them pirates."

There were various clay containers set up on the table. One was filled with salt. Another contained a mixture of crushed sage and fortweed. Yet another held grave-dirt and dove feathers. The boyish pleasantness of Dover Beech's face was replaced with darker, intense features. With ceremonial precision he would place a musket ball in each container, then whisper something over it before filling his pouch.

Mrs. Fernwing observed. "What're these supposed to do?"

"Purifying agents, Mrs. Fernwing. Others are for spirit banishing."

"Supposing they don't work on it, Mr. Beech?"

"Then bury me someplace pretty, good lady. And don't put me near him!"

Purdy smiled back. His hands were folded behind his head, against the dark knot of hair. "Bury me outside a brothel," he chirped.

"Oh, Mr. Purdy, for shame…"

"Oops, just kidding. Really, though, Dover, our hostess brings up a certain point of some substantial weight, might I add. If indeed our blessed projectiles do not deter the monster, what recourse do we have?"

"We could always faint and make it think we're dead. You'd be good at that, Finny."

Purdy scowled. "Bastard."

There were three sketches spread out on Fin's end of the table. One was the sketch the old farmer had done of the crop damage. Another was the heart and symbol Dover had copied from the tree at Turtle's Heap and the third was one he had just done from the soldier's grave at the Sleeping Yard showing a dagger with wings.

"So, Dover, what do you make of it all?"

Beech whispered to one of the musket balls, wrapped it in a bit of cloth and stuffed it away. "I wish I had information concerning those pirates the soldiers slaughtered back when. I wonder if some of them, maybe one survivor, even, might have somehow conjured this creature to wreak vengeance on the Seventh Cavalry. It killed one of the soldiers and injured others.

Perhaps that's why it chooses to scribe their mark into the fields. But all the pirates are dead, to our knowledge, and the military are not noted for being cooperative in such matters."

"Mm. Right. Then of course it could simply be, as you speculated, that this one soldier and his passionate meetings with the local lass disturbed something at that hill and...I've got it!"

Dover looked down the table at his broadly smiling companion. "Do tell."

"I just solved this one, thank you! Yes, I do believe I have!"

"Well, spit it out, man, don't let it moulder in your mouth."

"Turtle's Heap. There must have been something dwelling in it, some sort of elemental hill spirit, as you've suggested. Well, along came these two silly lovesick humans, humping away on its good green grass. If that weren't enough, they go and desecrate one of the trees by carving the heart and dagger. That, my friend, is what I think fired the thing's temper. It's no coincidence that the first appearance of our beastie was at that hill. They disturbed it, it popped out and killed them, then went on to mock the symbol by plastering it elsewhere."

Beech worried a hand over his bristly scalp. "It does sound reasonable, Fin."

"Plausible. And, you'll recall that the thing has not killed anyone since the two lovers. Sure it gave a fright to those other trooper boys, knocking 'em down and all, but it didn't kill them. Why, you ask? Because they were not the ones to disrupt it."

"So it menaced them, perhaps as a warning," Beech said. "And it warned the villagers by freezing the heart shape and insignia in their fields. Fin, you may be onto something."

Mrs. Fernwing stood up, clapping her meaty hands together. "Oh, you two are wonderful! Absolutely wonderful!"

Both men stood stiffly and bowed.

It was drizzling the following morning when the two bestiary documentalists, mounted on borrowed horses, ventured along twisting trails, across wind-haunted moors to the plump green bulk of Turtle's Heap.

Besides their personal firearms, they had borrowed a number of muskets from the village, each loaded with Beech's specially seasoned projectiles.

"Who's going to carve and who's going to sit by with a musket?" Purdy asked reluctantly.

"Well," Beech replied, "I'd be quite willing to encourage the thing's wrath if it meant we could prod it into appearing, but, and a significant but at that…what if I carve the tree, our bony friend leaps out and you for some bizarre reason find yourself suddenly unconscious and drop your weapon— then what's to become of my poor rump?"

"I will not faint, Beech, you have my word."

Dover bit his lip fretfully.

"Fine, then, I'll carve the bloody tree!" Purdy snapped.

Beech nodded. "Good, then, though you are the better shot. Nevertheless…keep on your mount, in case the ball doesn't stop it. Perhaps we could outrun it." Beech patted the warm neck of his vehicle. "Right then, positions!"

Purdy drew a deep breath as he edged the horse close to the tree where the heart carving showed. He pulled out a penknife and extended a tremulous arm. Dover raised the longarm, ready.

"Wait!"

Purdy drew the blade back. "Wait, what? Let's have it done with, Dover!"

The plump man lowered his weapon. "I'm not sure about this. I mean, are we in the right here?"

"I'm not sure I follow…"

"We're trespassing on some spirit's home, just as Pleasance and her lover did. It was minding its business. What right have we to come here to banish it? It hasn't harmed anyone this time. It hasn't even carved up any-one's property. Someone saw it running about near some old mines; what harm is there in that? It might've been out enjoying itself."

"Oh, please, Dover, let's not get into a bunch of conscientious rubbish. This thing killed a girl and a young man. Did they deserve to die for carving a bloody heart on a tree? I was rather fond of doing that in my younger days."

"I've no doubt. You're probably responsible for substantial deforestation."

"Oh, come now, Dover, let's just get on with it."

Beech looked at the musket across his lap and sighed. "This was your plan, Fin; I'm no longer sure it's the just thing to do. We've lost sight of our purpose. We document, we study, we sketch, we record and learn about creatures…"

"We came here because the islanders requested our help."

"But we aren't hunters; we're seekers of knowledge."

"Fine. You study it when it pops out—I'm carving!"

With that, Purdy swung out with his knife, dragging a line across the hard pale skin of the tree. He struck again, completing an X. Dover Beech pulled his heavy musket up to fire as Purdy urged his mount away from the birch, but his horse slipped on the wet grass and gravity jerked him to one side. Gasping, Purdy slammed back-first onto the damp ground. He saw a horse's massive head looming in the air above him.

When Purdy opened his eyes, he found himself looking up into the bespectacled face of his friend.

"What happened?"

"You fainted."

"I did no such thing!"

"Well, Fin, you pick the most inopportune times to nap."

"I, I saw a horse head…"

"Right. It was the one I was sitting on."

"What of the Frost Mare?"

"You embarrassed it to death."

Purdy growled. "Just help me up, will you?"

"It was a good theory, Fin, I'll give you that. Perhaps you should bring that Lilly up here and see if you can't stir up some action, seeing as the carving bit failed."

"Just so, it did seem a reasonable course to take. What's next? Should we dig into the hill and see if there isn't something worth finding?"

Beech shrugged. He was damp and tired and wanted nothing more than to sprawl on a soft dry bed after downing a mug of warm buttered ale.

FIVE

Purdy was mumbling in his sleep, unintelligible dream-words sponged by the pillow that covered his head. Beech smiled. He dipped his quill into an ink jar and leaned into his journal. A day had passed since their attempt to conjure the Frost Mare by carving on one of the trees.

Dover wondered how (after all the shovelling he had done that day) he still had the strength and presence of mind to sit documenting their most recent failure.

He wrote:

"I am of the opinion that any further time spent focused on Turtle's Hill would most surely be time squandered. Though it would seem a significant piece of the puzzle, the site has yet to yield anything besides the carving.

"This morning we set out with the picks and shovels in hopes of unburying some morsel of import. I harbored hopeful visions of a queer skeleton bearing a horse's head on a human body. Alas, the long hours spent penetrating that rocky soil revealed no such remains. I wondered, my back a mass of pain and my hands one great throbbing callus, how ages of tinners had managed to harvest anything from Drowning Tin's cruel crust. I doubt even the northlands of Westermead proper are so peppered with stone.

"It occurred to me that Drowning Tin remains cooler than the mainland, this being the month of Sunpeak when the sun is apt to burn with some vigor. Were it not for the merciful temperament of the ocean breeze I fear I'd have collapsed into our exploratory pits and begged old Purdy to bury me over.

"We must have proved a sorry sight when at last we staggered, exhausted and disappointed, into Ghost Oak. Had any throat ever been so parched? Had ale ever tasted better?

"We delighted and menaced the other patrons with tales of past expeditions, of creatures great and ghastly, until the ale was a golden haze in our heads.

"Now I shall blow out this candle and reward myself with well-earned sleep."

❧   ❧   ❧

Certain flowers only bloomed at night. It was a slow unwitnessed ritual. Salt-pale petals like flattened thumbs opened to praise a tallow moon. Their moth perfume blew soft across the moors, calling to the dusky sea. Beneath the waves, where slithering unnamed creatures haunted muddy shadows, the skulls of the drowned looked up and smiled.

Naban Dimridge stirred. Something on the wind. He sat up in the darkness, the warm lump of his wife beside him. He could smell the ghostly fragrance of night blooms, but there was something else; the sound of brighter blooms coughing, brief thunder and smeared screams.

He was up quick and naked at the door. Opening the slab he saw the moonlight on his fields. The sea hissed somewhere behind the hills, undisturbed. Had he been dreaming?

He sniffed the last traces of sulfur. His nose was not dreaming; someone had been shooting. He was set to go back inside when a wisp of sound came from his hayfield. He squinted as the stalks began to flatten and he saw *it*.

❧   ❧   ❧

"Mr. Purdy! Mr. Beech!" Mrs. Fernwing pounded on the door. "It struck! The Frost Mare!"

"Right!" Beech called back. "On our way."

The men were dressed within moments, grabbing their equipment packs and dashing outside where the magistrate stood with a feral-looking young farmer, who also appeared to have dressed with some haste.

"This is Naban Dimridge," Old Fernwing said. "He saw the Mare."

"When? Where?" Beech snapped.

"Just now, at my farm. It did its icy dance in my hay field!"

"Quick, man, take us there."

Heel-inspired horses drummed a dusty parade along the trail from the magistrate's cottage to Naban Dimridge's farm. Moon-slickened fields passed,

84

the uncut hay chirping in insect voices. It was a mere five minutes' ride; a squat stone farmhouse and barn appeared as the horses scaled a ridge.

Panting as if he had run the distance, Naban dismounted, pointing frantically. "Look! Look what it's done! Tore through the grass like lightning."

A chill breeze shot through Dover Beech's limbs. He had not, until that moment witnessed the creature's handiwork. The moon was bright enough to show what appeared to be a crude thirty-foot-wide roughly circular pattern.

Purdy remained in his saddle, for it offered a higher view of the thing. He pulled out his sketch book. Dover scrounged in his back sack for a small jar as he walked out into the field with high stalks hissing against his legs.

Magistrate Fernwing pulled nervously at his puffy beard, squinting. "Careful, Mr. Beech. It might be crouching in the grass."

Dover pushed on, oblivious.

Purdy called over to the farmer, "Mr. Dimridge, where did the thing go?"

"That way," the man pointed.

"What direction would that be?"

"West."

"What's out there?"

"Depends how far one goes. There's another farm 'bout a mile from 'ere, an' after that there's nothin' but moor and old mines."

Dover reached the outer perimeter of the blasted shape. The path the perpetrator's form had made was a good three feet wide, all the grass having been flattened, paved with a glistening skin of ice crystals.

"Amazing," Dover breathed.

The man stooped, reaching down to touch the damage. It was cold; without a doubt, ice. He took a penknife and scraped some of the frosty substance into the jar and cut several pieces of stiff grass to take as well.

Purdy sneered at the progress of his drawing. He could not get a clear view of the shape from that perspective. He looked around, noting the ridge they had crossed to reach the place. He rode over to it and positioned his steed at the highest point. He smiled. From that height, looking down on the field, he could distinguish the design. It was a heart with a winged dagger floating in the center.

"It was dreadful," the farmer whispered, shuddering. "That nasty big head and the skinny body...all glowin' like, as if it were sculpted from moonlight."

Fernwing poured the man a mug of elderberry wine, paused, thought, then poured himself one as well.

Dover had taken control, issuing commands, setting parchment and jars of herbs on the table in the Fernwing kitchen. His pudgy hands moved with surprising speed and grace as they readied things for the tests. He touched a finger to the now mostly melted ice.

"Salty," he noted, tasting. "Sea water? Tears?"

He opened a small wooden box containing delicate rust-red magnetic filings. "These," he explained, "were given to me by a smith in Westsheer. They came from an ancient monument locals called the Lightning Stone. When placed in a creature's blood, or other fluids, they form meaningful symbols."

Beech took a pinch and sprinkled it into the jar of pooling ice. The tiny needles clumped together unceremoniously and sank. The investigator grumbled.

Next, Dover produced a jar of dark powder. "Ground blackfern, known to some as map root. Spellfolk are known to make use of it."

He sprinkled a fine layer of the powdered root onto a bare sheet of parchment and proceeded to tilt the sample jar so that several melted drops pattered out. "Now, in some cases, the liquid used will, at this point, carve a map through the dust layer, illustrating something of significance, such as a creature's lair."

The drops blurred the powder where they struck and soaked into the paper. Dover snarled, crumpled the parchment and tossed it aside. He looked over a shoulder. "Mrs. Fernwing, is that water a-boil yet?"

"It is, Mr. Beech."

"Good, good. Let's try the steam test, shall we?"

Beech loosened the mouth of a small wine-colored sack and poured some albino powder into his palm.

"Chalk?" the magistrate asked.

"Skull dust. The spellwoman at Sweetcandle taught me this trick."

Dover combined the powder with waxy green needles of rosemary, grinding away with mortar and pestle. "Just a wee bit more...that's it. Mrs. Fernwing, the water please..."

The plump woman brought a mid-sized blackened pot from the fireplace and set it on the table.

"Stand back," Beech warned the others. "The results are not always predictable."

The man dumped the mixture of rosemary and bone into the water, then poured a splash of the icy liquid.

A sharp hiss issued as a pillar of dense steam, wide as the vessel, rose several feet. Voices, hushed with awe, filled the room as the steam molded itself into the wavering outline of a man.

"Remarkable," Fernwing muttered.

The vision remained for only a moment before blurring into a shapeless haze and settling back into the hot water.

Mrs. Fernwing realized she was clutching Dover's arm. "What does it mean, Mr. Beech?"

"I'm sorry to say, good lady, that I do not know."

SIX

"I barely slept last night. I sat listening to the Tarnic's rustling black tide and my dozing companion mumbling, "Lilly," from under his pillow. My head was aswarm with questions, and though sleep whispered her sepia song, my mind refused to yield.

"One question which seemed a great concern of Purdy's was: Had we inspired the Frost Mare's appearance (hence its marking the farmer's property) by carving an X on a tree at Turtle's Hill? The answer, as I see it, is no. If we were responsible, wouldn't the raging beast have carved an X, rather than the recurrent heart-and-dagger design? I shouldn't think there is any direct connection between our experiment and this recent activity.

"The second question, which seemed wont to haunt me through the dark hours, was this: What did the misty figure, which appeared from the pot in the Fernwing kitchen, mean? The shape appeared to be a man's. Could it have been the ghost of the young soldier who died twenty years ago? How I wish I knew.

"When at last I fell asleep, my slumber was less than restful and dreams, which remained elusive throughout today, left an unsettling chill in the back of my mind. It was as if some hidden intuitive fragment had glimpsed future events of a tragic nature, and was struggling to warn me. I began, for the first time since undertaking this adventure, to long for the familiar comforts of rooms back home and the company of my beloved dog Chalker.

"It was warm and bright this morning last. Fin and I set off to Naban Dimridge's farm to take our first sunlit view of the crop-markings. I was pleased to feel the old thrill of purpose, and fought to push away the insistent whispers of dread. What a marvel it was, so precisely sliced through the high grass, the massive image of a heart with the winged blade within. I noticed that the dagger was pointing west, toward the old tin mines.

"Farmer Dimridge showed us where he had first seen the creature appear and told how it had made off in a westerly direction, its ghastly whip of a tail undulating behind it. He also told how he had been roused by the stench of gunpowder, and further, claimed to have heard musket-fire and screams.

"At this point he became concerned. In all the commotion, it had failed to occur to him that his nearest neighbors might have come to some harm. He had, after all, heard the dread shrieks and firing just before the appearance of the Mare. Had they, we suddenly fretted, been attacked?

"We made quickly to the neighbor family's farm and were much relieved to find that all was well. The farmer's wife offered that she too had been awakened by shouts and blasts. Her husband, apparently a heavy sleeper, had heard nothing, and insisted she had dreamt the noises. Both Naban Dimridge and the woman felt that the sounds seemed to originate somewhere beyond the hills south of their farms. We decided to have a look.

"The lot of us crossed a number of rocky pastures and cut through a wind-strangled grove of crabapple trees. A series of earthen banks, perhaps a natural formation, perhaps the ramparts of some long forgotten race's fort, separated us from a narrow grey slope of beach. The scene of horror below will, no doubt, return to me for many a year, when my mind is at the mercy of dreams.

"The crew of the Lazy Arrow was sprawled on the glistening pebbles, their clothing soggy with seawater and gore, their bodies gouged where musket balls had struck. The Captain was on his side, arms roped behind his back, his beard caked with rust, which had erupted from the deep slash across his throat. Tiny green crabs scurried across the corpses, ducking into the folds of their clothes, and the damp pink shadows beneath them.

"There were splintered bits of the boat which the tide had tossed alongside fetid manes of dark bladderwrack, and numerous logs of firewood bobbed in the surf. The farmers, when at last they found their tongues, suggested that the boat had been on its way to deliver wood at Squall Perch, one of the two other villages on Drowning Tin.

"Naban Dimridge asked me if I thought the Frost Mare had anything to do with this, to which, I replied, "Not unless it's taken to shooting people."

ॐ ॐ ॐ

The sunset sky was a field of red clover, melting where a seam of mist joined it to the sea. The village of Gull Hill squatted above, her buildings soaking up the expanding shadows. Windows glowed, one by one, warm slabs of light, floating in the salty darkness. Wreaths of raggedy dried seaweed and fishbones were hung upon each door, as was the custom, to indicate death at sea.

A chubby bespectacled man with bristled blond hair sat at a corner table in Ghost Oak along with a dark-haired man and a plump brunette lass. The tavern was busy with chatter, as villagers met to verbally ponder the grim discovery on the southern shore.

Dover Beech shoved his plate of crab meat away, unsettled by the recollections of tiny green crustaceans fumbling across soggy bodies. The bowl of leek soup would suffice. Fin Purdy looked pale and poked sparingly at his meal, as well.

There had been little talk at their table, and the combined voices from the villagers were like a tangible hum crowding the dim ale-aired room. Lilly leaned her head against Purdy's shoulder as he lit up a pipe-full of sage and mint. Dover continued to slurp pensively at his soup.

The white clay pipe protruding from the corner of Purdy's mouth wobbled when he spoke. "Do you suppose, Dover, there was some sort of altercation among the crew members of the Lazy Arrow?"

"You don't mean to suggest a mutiny, do you? Aboard a silly little wood-transport?"

"Well, it is possible, you know. I mean, wherever there's a captain and a crew there can be a mutiny."

"I'm not up for an argument, Fin, if that's your game."

"Merely speculating, old boy. Could it be that one of the crew went mad and killed the others?"

"All things are possible," Dover said blandly.

Lilly tossed in a thought. "I bet it's pirates."

Purdy studied her skeptically. "Pirates raiding a piddly, over-patched, battered wood-transport?"

Lilly frowned. "Well, now you sound like him." She gestured at Beech.

Dover, blinking solemnly, came to the defense of the lass. "It's not an unreasonable idea. The pirates wouldn't have known it was a simple wood-hauler, until they were on board..."

"'Scuse me, Mr. Beech?"

Dover had not seen the slight form standing to his right, shoulders hunched beneath a shawl and hair like a ruptured cocoon. He turned to Mrs. Squill.

"Oh, hello," Dover said, blinking.

"If it's no trouble, I was wonderin' if I might have a word with you in private..."

Dover looked to his companions, who shrugged slightly. He gathered himself, excused himself and followed the frail woman out through the clutter of tables and talk. The air outside was salty-cool as a breeze licked up from the restless Tarnic's darkness. There were a pickle tub and some barrels outside the tavern; Beech flipped the empty tub over so Mrs. Squill could sit.

She stared off across the water for a long, long minute. The moon was a skull, face down in the sky's vast puddle. At length the woman stirred, catching the waiting man's eye. He smiled gently. "Something troubles you, Mrs. Squill?"

"I have an awful secret to tell, Mr. Beech. Ever since you was out at my place, it's been gnawing to get out."

"Well, I'm honored that you feel you can confide in me, good woman."

She smiled sadly. "You seem a likable sort of fellow, an easy one to talk to…and it's been twenty years, I've carried this dreadful thing around."

Mrs. Squill sucked in a deep breath and straightened, as if preparing for a blow. She looked the man square in the face and said, "I think my husband killed the soldier that my Pleasance went to meet that night. And I think he killed her, too."

Dover's little eyes grew wide. "I see."

"My husband was a man with the temper of ten, Mr. Beech, and not at all keen on the idea of his beloved daughter runnin' about with some worldly soldier. I could see him tryin' to keep it in, but the anger was like a flame behind his eyes. That night she sneaked off to meet her young gentleman, well, he went out to find her. He took his flintlock with him."

Beech grunted, nodding, watching as a tear made across a wrinkled cheek.

"After some time he came home, claiming he couldn't find 'em. But the next morning they found the lad, his head a wreck of blood. They found her horse, too, as I've told you before. Not my Pleasance, though."

"Do you suppose he might have buried her, and that might explain why she was never found?"

The woman nodded, quivered, sniffled.

"Mrs. Squill, was it, in fact, a common bit of knowledge that the soldier was shot?"

"It was never a thing of certainty, I gather. We all just knew his head was shattered like, and the rest of 'em, well, they claimed it was the Mare done it, but I had my own thoughts on the matter, Mr. Beech. And now you know my dreadful secret."

Beech folded his arms, frowning in thought. He squinted through his spectacles. "Your husband never spoke of what happened that night?"

"No. He did not. He acted no different from one who thought the Frost Mare had done it. He went to his grave maintaining that he never found her that night."

"If what you suspect is true, then the Frost Mare has never actually killed anyone."

"Correct, Mr. Beech."

The investigator ached for the old woman; how hard it must have been to believe that her own husband had murdered their child, and to carry that thought alone those many long years...

"Mrs. Squill, would you mind very much if I shared this information with my partner? I can assure you that it will go no further than our lips, but he is my dearest friend and I regard him with the highest degree of trust. He plays an important role in this investigation, and it would be difficult and unfair if I were to exclude him from such pertinent information."

"Do as you see best, sir."

"Very good. Thank you, Mrs. Squill. Now, would you happen to recall what type of weapon your husband kept?"

"I should say I do. A blunderbuss. I've got it still, at the house."

"You're sure of that?"

"I am."

"And he had no others?"

"No, sir, Mr. Beech, just the one. A big ugly blunderbuss."

"I see."

Mrs. Squill hung her head down against her chest, shadows seeping up through the wrinkles of her gaunt face, sponging away her features until only two wet eyes shone. Beech gazed off, lost himself in the rasping sea, thinking about the ghostly shape of a man that had risen up from a pot of boiling water.

SEVEN

From a distance, Beech appeared to be cut in half, his chunky torso left balanced upright on the moon-dewed grass of the Sleeping Yard. His nostrils were filled with the dark odor of shovel-violated earth as he stood in the pit he had dug. Worms, embedded in the sides of the trench, writhed like angry tendrils in the shock of chill air as beetles scurried across his boots, glistening in the lamplight.

Purdy peered about at the dim shapes of hunkering granite gravemarkers, clinging to the handle of the lamp as if it were the reins on a speeding horse. He had been startled once already by his own pipe-exhalations drifting ethereally on a sigh of brine breeze.

"Shall I take over for a while, Dover? We can't have you making a ruin of your back, now, can we?"

A shovel full of dirt thumped above the pit, by the grave bearing an etching of a winged dagger. Dover grunted, "Don't bother, my friend, I'm quite close. This was, after all, my idea."

"Do you really suppose Mrs. Squill's husband did what she suspects?"

"Umf! Oh, I can only hope she's wrong. We won't know 'til we see what sort of damage the soldier's remains will show. Ahh, I've just now struck a layer of seashells, a common burial practice in these parts. We're most certainly close."

Beech leaned his shovel against an earthen wall and began removing the shells by hand. To dig with the metal tool at this stage might risk damaging the remains. The dirt was cool and clingy on his hands.

"Eeeew!"

Purdy perked. "What is it?" Dover was no longer visible; he had bent down inside the burial pit. "Dover?"

"More light, man! I've found him."

Purdy peeked over the edge, into the opening, leaning the lamp in. His partner was brushing dirt off a yellowed shroud, the contents of which poked sharply against the material.

"Here, then, help me get him out," Beech ordered.

Purdy had to lie on his belly in his clean white shirt and reach down to take an end of the coiled cloth. Beech supported the other end as they carefully lifted the soldier's remains out of the grave. The parcel was rather light. It was more of a chore to get Beech up onto the grass; Purdy grunted as he tugged at the man's arm.

"All right, then," Beech panted, "let's have a look, shall we?"

He peeled away the clammy wrap until the citrine grin of a skull showed within the folds and shadows. The forehead of the skull showed a neat unnatural hole; on further inspection they found that the back of the head was shattered where something had exited with great impact.

"A single musket ball," Dover concluded.

"Mrs. Squill said her husband had a blunderbuss, did she not?"

"Correct. This clearly is not the work of a blunderbuss. Either she is wrong about the type of weapon her husband owned, or…"

"Or," Purdy carried the thought, "someone other than Mr. Squill killed the young soldier."

Dover sat back with a sigh, that internal voice of impending ugliness hissing like waves on a beach. "One thing appears certain. Something other than the Frost Mare put an end to him."

"If it did not kill the soldier, then what of the girl?" Purdy wondered.

"The creature, quite possibly, hasn't killed anyone, though it did attack some soldiers. If only we could find the remains of Pleasance Squill, and determine how she died…"

"'If only' won't carry us very far, I fear," Purdy said. But Dover had a strange look in his eye, and he was staring off past the graves, to where the moon snaked haunted tentacles through a cracked nest of clouds.

"We have to find her, Fin. Call it intuition if you must, but I know she's at the mines."

꙳ ꙳ ꙳

The clouds had coiled their springs of tears throughout the long summer night. Morning unleashed the rain in grey sheets, sweeping like a great wet broom across the rumpled floor of Drowning Tin. The moors poured like pools of ash, the grass and bloomless heather, the ragged clusters of weeds saturated with liquid shadow.

Two figures on horseback ventured out into the drowning wind, their

94

cloaks weighed with angry water. The dutiful horses pushed on until the moor sloped west and the beaten track became a sliver, thinner and thinner until the earth forgot to show it. There were brooding jumbles of turf-piercing stone, shallows where sedge thrived, hollows where puddles spread like flattened lead.

It was maze-like down amid the mines. There were grassy rises and moss-clotted projections of granite. Gaping mine mouths promised abandoned darkness, the tin-raped depths betrothed to webs and wind.

The men looked to each other with glum faces. They had put this moment off for too long. The mines would not wait any longer. They tethered their mounts and with lanterns and drawn pistols, entered the first stone maw.

The air was musty and damp, like a potter's shop. Jagged walls ran deep, beyond the lantern's reach. Dover clung to the weight of his wheel-lock, the polished walnut grip smooth and familiar, the steel ball at the butt glinting softly. He set down his light briefly, reached into his pocket and touched the sad little straw horse luck charm Mrs. Squill had given him, the one that had belonged to Pleasance.

The tunnels snaked deep, the tin-robbed walls yawning with rough hollows where picks had chewed. The wind was muffled, a faint trickle of sound. Here and there anemic snakes of rain ran down the walls, having squirmed through the earthen roof.

"Doesn't appear promising," Beech said.

Purdy nodded, his fear-plump eyes gawking. "Not yet. But look there...a light!"

The shaft branched ahead, the left path showing a faint smear of luminosity along the wall. The sound of rain grew louder as they edged gun-first around a corner. They stood before another opening which looked out upon a steep embankment. Beech thought he saw a set of legs, as if a figure were sprawled on the soggy grass.

"What's this?"

As Dover went to duck through the exit-way, Purdy heard something move behind him. Had he really heard a metallic click or was it rain dripping on stone?

95

Beech stared in horror at the eight dead bodies lined up on the grassy slope. They were scruffy-looking men, chalk-pale, their clothing saturated with rainwater and blurred splotches of dark blood. He felt something cold and hard press into the back of his neck, from above. Two figures leaped down from the roof of the mine, men in long grey coats and helmets, their muskets trained.

Purdy spun around and a soldier jammed a pistol into his face. He heard the pounding of hooves, hooves splashing outside the mine. "Don't move," a voice hissed.

Dover looked up into the mounted captain's chilling smile. "That's far enough, Porky," the officer warned.

The investigators did not resist as their weapons were snatched away and they were thrown to the wet ground. The naked foot of one of the corpses was inches away from Dover's face.

"I take it you're the leaders," the captain said.

"I beg your pardon, but what's this all about?"

"You tell me, you lump of lard, or you'll end up like your friends here."

Beech raised his head, glanced at the row of ruined bodies. "Friends? I don't know these men. They look like sailors."

"Pirates," the captain spat. "It didn't take us long to figure out you were holing up in these mines. By the way, we've found your boat and your stores of stolen goods."

"I'm afraid you're mistaking us, sir. I am Dover Beech and my friend is Fin Purdy. We are compiling a bestiary. We were summoned here by Magistrate Fernwing of Gull Hill to investigate the Frost Mare."

The captain chuckled. "My, my, that's a clever tale. You're obviously the ringleader; you've got quite a crafty mind—I'll give you that."

"Sir, I am in earnest. Do we look like pirates?"

Purdy blubbered, "He's telling the truth!"

"Tie their wrists," the officer ordered. More footmen closed about them, a moat of long grey coats. The two prisoners were bound and searched and made to stand.

"You are now," the helmeted horseman snarled, "under arrest in the name of the King and Kingdom law. You must answer for the ruthless attack on Lazy Arrow."

"We are not pirates," Beech insisted behind mud-flecked spectacles. "Send one of your men to Gull Hill and bring the magistrate. He will verify my words."

The captain urged his horse over to the man. "You are an arrogant blot of flesh, aren't you?"

Beech felt a boot slam into his belly. He doubled over and sank to the wet ground, his spectacles dropping off. Purdy strained against his binds and growled, "You bastard!"

The captain looked down, his handsome face smiling menacingly. He swung his boot out, cracking Purdy across the side of his face. Fin thudded on his back beside his friend and lay dazed, looking up at the sky. The tastes of blood and rain mingled in his mouth.

EIGHT

"Gun powder in my veins, that's what my mother always said," Captain Mallot Scry explained, smiling apologetically. His cobalt blue eyes crinkled with warmth and charm. He clapped Dover on the back. Dover nearly spilled the mug of ale that had been thrust upon him.

"It's something of a curse," the officer said, pacing the dark confines of his camp's command post, a hastily assembled rectangle of tin sheets, which stood amid a cluster of tents on a rise looking out over the Tarnic. "Some men are born with poor eyes, some are born with a limp. I was born with a phenomenal temper. It's my greatest weakness, but it keeps me humble."

Purdy smirked, his swollen cheek stinging.

"I've been informed that I was rather prone to tantrums as a tot. I can still recall a number of occasions when I, in a state of rage, would smash my own beloved toys," Captain Scry said poignantly. He stopped pacing long enough to gaze off, his eyes exuding theatrical despair. "I remember looking down at my poor shattered toys and crying over what I had done."

"How tragic," Beech muttered.

"I fear I've shamed myself with my rash treatment of you goodly fellows. But, gentlemen, I beg you to sympathize in some little way with my predicament. My men and I had spent the hours previous to our untimely meeting tracing down a savage horde of men who had ruthlessly slain the innocent crew of the Lazy Arrow. When you popped out of that mine, directly in the network of tunnels where the scoundrels had been hiding, well, it seemed that you were of their lot."

"It's not unreasonable, I'll give you that," Dover admitted.

"Then perhaps you'll find it within yourselves to forgive me?"

Even as Beech nodded, ever so hesitantly, he was aware of the man's manipulative skill. The phrasing of the question, and the rhetoric before it, had been spun with the calculating efficiency of a spider casting webs.

Captain Scry offered Purdy an expression one might see on a repentant boy after a scolding for naughtiness.

"You're forgiven," Purdy heard himself say.

"Ahh, splendid!" The officer clapped his hands together and once more became the tall, handsome warrior, swirling his golden cloak of confidence. He was lion-proud in his vest-like leather brigandine, his sunny curls tumbling about wide shoulders, a hand on his saber grip as if it were a rudder. He seemed younger than his forty years.

Magistrate Fernwing, who had been summoned by some of Scry's men, sat on a wooden stool drinking up the military officer's charisma, perhaps even envying it.

"Captain," the older Kingdom official said, "how long have you been stationed out here? I hadn't the faintest notion a military expedition had been launched."

"We've been here a good two months. A clandestine mission. Pirate raids have been on the increase, relative to the increased number of trade ships venturing to and from the mainland."

"I see."

"I must say, old Drowning Tin hasn't changed in the slightest since I was here last. That was a good twenty years ago, I think. I was a mere foot-gunner back then."

Dover leaned forward on his seat. "You were in the seventh cavalry, then?"

Captain Scry smiled. "I was indeed. A good outfit. There was quite the nasty bunch of pirates about these parts then, I tell you. We tore them up nicely, though. Every last one of 'em."

The captain scooped a pewter pitcher off a table and refilled the magistrate's mug.

"There's some talk, among the higher ranks, of setting a permanent fort hereabout. Nothing too fancy, mind you, but a manned station, to keep an eye on the trade route."

Fernwing seemed enthusiastic. "A fine idea, I say. What's the world coming to when a simple cargo ship bringing wood gets sunk?"

Scry approached Purdy and Beech, carrying the pitcher of ale. "More drink, gentlemen!"

He filled Fin's cup, then turned to Dover. The bespectacled man with the quiet, intelligent face stared at the captain's wrist. At first, the faded, bluish mark had looked like a bruise, but when the soldier got close enough to pour, Dover saw it was an old tattoo in the shape of a heart.

Scry flashed his disarming smile, noticing Dover's stare. "Ahh, a dueling scar," he joked, pondering the heart outline, "from when I was young and foolish, as they say."

Dover smiled thinly.

"Well, then, gents…drink up!"

Dover tilted his mug. The ale went down like bile.

❧ ❧ ❧

"Fin and I were in no condition to do more than sit about old Fernwing's cottage and brood. It was too dark to return to explore the mines and we were exhausted, having been pummeled by wind and rain and that lout Captain Scry as well. Such a despicable man. I was ever so happy to get out of that camp.

"I think, however, that I should like to return and chat further with the good captain and see if he might offer some recollections which could prove helpful to our investigation. After all, he had been stationed on the island during the first bout of Frost Mare activity and the soldier lover of Pleasance Squill had belonged to his regiment."

❦ ❦ ❦

Beech and Purdy were, once more, awakened by someone banging urgently on the door of their bedchamber. Mrs. Fernwing's voice followed, shrill and breathless, "Mr. Beech, Mr. Purdy, it's happened again! The Mare..."

An icy force had raged through a farm field on the outskirts of Gull Hill. The design was the same as before; a heart enclosing a dagger. The two men prodded and sketched and pondered. All the while, the wisp of a voice snaked uneasily through the back of Dover's mind. Danger.

"I still think the answer lies in the mines," Beech said, staring westward, the direction the crop-dagger pointed to.

By the time they had crossed the moor and entered the shallow where mine mouths yawned, daylight was failing. The sun was dragged beneath the Tarnic's uncharted currents, where it drowned in a forest of shipwreck masts.

NINE

Night came on wings of soot and tar, swooping stealthily over the moors. It drooled and flooded, a spreading scorch from a fireless blaze, draining the colors that day had embraced. It was a greedy murk, a moist promise of sallow grass and grim stone. The knolls and boulders and weed-tattered hollows formed one great resinous mass and the cool scent of nightflowers stained the air. Night like a slow dark wave rolled across the wastes of Drowning Tin.

Eight hooves drummed where no path led, to a rise over a glen where the darkness was pocked darker with the mouths of mines. Two horsemen sat sharing the summer-flavored blackness and that pensive anticipatory silence they often experienced when on the brink of adventure. They gazed upon the vague shapes of stone and mounded earth, night's cloaked sky pecked with a million stars.

"Perhaps we should have waited until daylight," Purdy said softly.

"Perhaps," Dover said. He smiled and nudged his horse onward.

🌀 🌀 🌀

They moved into the cavern, a pistol leading, a serpent head, slow and staring. Lantern glow washed warmly over the wall and floor, etching harsh shadows into the craggy surfaces. Small frightened things scrabbled in the darkness and pebbles creaked beneath the men's boots.

Purdy could feel his heart licking against snarling ribs as he followed the shadowy bulk of his friend. He had to crouch to dodge the webs, the husks of moths dangling.

"Nothing in here," Beech concluded.

The next mine was even deeper, more narrow, the air crowded and dank. Coppery light in a sweeping puddle; pistols like dowsing rods. Dover squinted as webs smeared across his glasses.

In one of the little side chambers they found a flattened piece of tin crudely cut in the shape of an egg; a tinner's offering to the mine for a fertile yield.

"Next?" Purdy sighed as they stood out in the tepid air.

Dover reached into his gabardine pocket for a reassuring touch of the small straw-woven horse. He surveyed the dim surroundings. "That one."

The stones around the opening were freckled with lichen like fossilized moths. Dead grass hung like dirty bangs. The air inside was clammy; it felt grey in the lungs, as if they were breathing mushrooms.

Dover led the way through the narrow chamber.

🌀 🌀 🌀

"Fin, will you have a look at that? Footprints."

Purdy knelt with his lantern, poking a finger into one of the depressions. A man's boots had made them.

"Dover, these are fresh. There's dew in them." On closer inspection he saw a similar trail of prints headed back out of the mine.

Beech cocked his head and sniffed at the air. "Do you smell it?"

101

Purdy stood, clinging to his pistol. "Yes, but what is it?"

"Flowers."

Dover turned and headed into the recesses of the granite throat, following the ghostly perfume of night blooms. His eyes were so busy tracing the boot tracks that he did not notice the slender birch-like leg of Pleasance Squill until it crunched beneath his step. He gasped.

"What?" Purdy jolted.

"It's her," Dover whispered sadly.

They crouched beside the web-strewn tangle of bone. The dust-colored fragments of her dress were crumbling softly about the yellowed frame. The skull faced the ceiling, the mouth ajar, a cruel crater like a third eye socket in the center of the forehead. A fresh bunch of pale blue flowers had been laid at her feet.

"Poor Pleasance," Dover said, placing his lantern on the earth. He eyed the bunch of flowers, then looked back up at Purdy. "Apparently someone else knows she's here."

"Apparently so. We must have just missed whoever left the posy."

Dover nodded, absorbed in thought.

"Mrs. Squill will be relieved to hear she no longer has to wonder whether her husband was a murderer," Purdy said. "That wound in the head is from a musket ball, not a blunderbuss. Whoever killed the young soldier, did her as well."

Dover nodded again. He placed his hand on the cool spikes of Pleasance's fingers, looked up and said, "Let's get back to the village and fetch a wagon. Twenty years in this wretched mine is long enough. She shan't spend another night..."

They had turned and started back toward the portal when a soft hissing sound caused them to turn. Was it only the weak light playing on webs, or dust swirling from their mournfully scuffing boots? Was it a luminous vine of mist rising up from the hole in the skull's forehead?

Purdy grabbed his friend's arm. "Dover!"

"Yes, man, I see it!"

The sinuous emission gathered itself into a restless cloud, expanding as more pale light fed out of the musket wound. It began to mold itself, the top elongating into a bony snout, hollow eyes forming behind that. A watery horse skull smiled and a shrill wailing voice poured forth from it, flooding the mine shaft.

"The Frost Mare!" Purdy shrieked. He dropped his lantern and bolted.

Beech spun and also dashed for the doorway. The sound of pounding followed him out.

"Run, just run!" Dover panted.

The men charged up the slope that led onto the moor, the dark air flushing past, the dizzy stars aswirl like snow. The dark wastes spread wide, the scrubby brush rasping against urgent boots.

Dover could hear the swift-striding creature drum-running like an echo of his maddened heart. His lungs worked like drowning wings, his pudgy legs pumping.

Uneven earth offered no cover, the moor flying quickly past. There on the right, a blur of boulders loomed. If only they could reach those rocks they might have a chance to hide, or at least a bit of shelter from which to fight. The yards pounded beneath their feet, but the Mare was faster.

Beech resisted his better judgment and glanced back. The horrifying vision of the Frost Mare dashed over the moor, the great horse skull thrusting ahead of the scrawny white body, the serpent tail thrashing behind. There was a faint glow to the thing, as if it had been steeped in moonlight.

Gravity tugged at Dover's straining bulk. He saw Purdy push ahead, into the dark before them as the Mare bridged the dark behind. The sounds of its hooves, or whatever it had, were now as loud as his heart, and the air grew colder the closer it got.

The blow was like a great chunk of ice slamming against Dover's back. The sound of his grunt caused Purdy to wheel around and watch, helplessly. The Mare pinned the bespectacled man to the moor.

"No!" Purdy yelled.

Dover felt his body being flipped over—he stared up; the teeth grinned down, the head swam above. The long neck stretched as the head shot at his torso, the cold teeth burning as they tore a chunk out of his clothing. They stopped short of breaking the man's flesh and then withdrew, the ripped pocket yielding the small straw luck charm.

The panting man swooned as the milky figure of the Mare drew back. It held the miniature horse in its teeth and seemed to slowly fold against the earth, icy liquid pouring from empty eye sockets. It pressed against the moor until its mass was like a smudged chalk drawing. Closer and closer, it pressed to the ground. Closer…until the last misty echoes soaked into the grass and it was gone.

Dover lay panting until his limbs recovered the strength to work. He staggered a few paces to where the chilled gush of tears had fallen. There was nothing to see but an icy patch, there in the grass; the sprawled outline of a girl. There was no sign of the charm.

Beech looked around in the darkness, trembling. "Fin? Finny?"

He saw a dark heap several yards to his left and rushed over. It was Fin Purdy, face down on the ground, like a doll thrown by a child in rage.

"Finny?" Dover touched his still friend's shoulder.

"Ohhh, my head," Purdy moaned. He sat up, blinking. "What happened?"

"You fainted."

"Fainted? I did no such thing. I, I tripped on a rock!"

"As you wish," Dover chuckled weakly.

"What of the Mare?"

"It's over."

Purdy craned his neck to see the frosty shape in the grass. "The Mare…was it…?"

Dover nodded. "Yes. It was Pleasance Squill."

"Lilly, Lilly…" Purdy's voice struggled from under his pillow.

Dover Beech sat up in bed, leaning into his parchment, a gull-quill rasping across the candle-blond surface.

He wrote:

"Tomorrow the remains of the Squill girl will be buried in Sleeping Yard. Perhaps she and her mother can now take their rest.

"Fin and I are eager to return home to our beloved pets and familiar haunts. There is much work to do on the bestiary, which of course shall include our most recent adventure.

"My partner has put forth the proposition that his friend Lilly return with us and that we might furnish her with some duties at our offices in Bellingtower, seeing as our present cleaning woman, the ceaselessly crotchety Mrs. Lustbladder, is nigh due for retirement. I informed him I would consider the situation. No doubt this good-hearted author will concede.

"As for the case of the Frost Mare, there is but one final chapter that must be written, before the book is closed, as they say."

TEN

The fog covered Drowning Tin like a caul. It started as an opalescent moat encircling the shore, then spread, up across the snarling cliffs, slow across the pebble-blackened beaches, inland where it erased the cowering little villages. Soon the pastures and the wild rolling moors were submerged in the soft writhing mist. Were one to look down on the island from above, it would have seemed an ethereal moon floating on the Tarnic's blackness.

The shape that floated toward the tin mine might have been a man formed of steam. The wraith-colored air was clammy and thick against his face; it obscured the horse he had tethered just yards away. Even the sounds of his boots seemed muffled by the dense vapor.

A jaundiced cone of lantern glare led him into the mine. The chamber filled with the scent of the bunched night flowers which he held in his left hand. He walked to the back of the chamber and stopped.

Captain Scry stepped out into the fog and stood puzzled, his lamp bleeding amber into the froth. Two slow shapes moved toward him out of the mist, taking the form of Purdy and Beech.

"Good evening, Captain," Dover said, a thin knowing smile on his lips. "I dare say, you look rather confused."

The captain let the flowers drop. "Ahh, hello, Mr. Beech, Mr. Purdy. I see you two are taking the air. I was just roaming about, having a peek in the mines, lest there remain some overlooked pirates."

"Oh," Beech said, his voice a chilly thing on the fog, "I thought you were looking for Pleasance."

The handsome officer's face darkened. "Pleasance?"

"Mm. Tell me, did you know she was the Frost Mare?"

"I, I'm not sure what you mean."

Beech drew closer, the lantern glow on his spectacles like magma coins. The captain looked down at the long pointing pistol that weighed in the man's hand.

"Isn't it curious that the Mare waited twenty years, until you returned, to roam again? To scribe the symbol of your old cavalry into fields? To scribe the shape of a heart, like the one tattooed on your arm like the one cut onto a tree where you killed her at Turtle's Heap? I find it rather telling, myself, don't you, Purdy?"

"Yes, Dover. Enlightening."

The captain scowled, the harsh of his face a contrast to the lush gold of his tumbling locks.

"Do tell, Captain, who is that young soldier that lies buried at Gull Hill's Sleeping Yard? A rival for the poor fisherman's daughter you courted that summer?"

Scry chuckled. "Oh, you are a clever one, Mr. Beech. You impress me with that keen mind of yours." The officer's face filled with the bitterness that had steeped inside for twenty years. "Right then, I'll tell it all. Yes, I loved Pleasance Squill, with a love like a madness. She was the fairest thing, the sweetest, a summer's soft dream. I was a hungry young buck, still growing into his uniform when I met her."

Scry looked out across the shrouded land, a ghost of that glorious summer when the drunken blood of youth pounded in his veins. "We would meet at Turtle's Heap. She would steal from her house when her parents slept and I would steal from my camp. I have always been a man cursed with temper and jealousy the likes of which no man should know. That night I rode up to our spot only to find her standing there with one of the other men from the seventh cavalry. I'd never felt such rage, like a blinding white heat inside my fool head. How, I despaired, could she meet with someone else, and at our beloved hill? The lad claimed he was out on his patrol when he happened across Pleasance waiting for me. He spoke the truth, I now sadly admit, but I would hear none of it then. The heat in my head was louder than their protests, so I shot them both. I shot them each in the head. She was standing near her white mare and her blood splashed upon it."

The officer ran a trembling hand through his hair and wagged his skull. "As she lay there I saw a stream of mist rise out from the wound in her head and it became a cloud on the breeze…it blew toward her mare. It passed through the horse and when it came out the other side, it was in the shape of a ghastly creature. I watched it run off across the dark fields."

Dover's voice came softer on the mist, "So you knew she was the Frost Mare. Were you not afraid coming here, knowing the creature once more roamed the island?"

"No, I was not, Mr. Beech. Not so long as I had this…"

The man produced a small, worn straw-woven ram.

"It was a charm she made me to protect me from danger. Besides, she loved me…she wouldn't cause me harm."

Purdy spoke up, "Perhaps not directly, but it seems she wanted justice. Why else would she carve the heart and dagger into those fields? She was attempting to tell the world what you had done."

The captain growled, "No. She, she would not do anything to cause me harm."

"The dead seek justice, Captain," Purdy persisted.

"But I loved her! She loved me. I bring her flowers…"

Tears like melting amber ran lamp-warm down the man's grimacing face.

Dover moved closer. "Captain, may I have your side arm, please?"

Scry lifted his matchlock from its holster and tossed it into the grass at Beech's feet. When Dover bent to pick it up, Scry swung his lantern up into the man's face. The glass cracked and Dover flopped onto his back.

The captain moved with menacing speed, scooping up his weapon, straddling Beech and jamming the pistol barrel under the stunned man's jaw.

Boom!

Blood scrawled like trembling ivy, dark against the misted air. Scry gasped, dropped his gun and pitched over, a gory wound soaking his side. Purdy stood helpless, his single shot spent as the captain scooped up Beech's wheel-lock and placed the snout to his own temple.

Boom!

ELEVEN

"The boat, you simpleton," Beech said, "not 'the goat.'"

Purdy grinned. "Pardon me, good man, but I could've sworn I heard you say 'the goat will be docking within the hour.'"

"Obviously, all that musket fire damaged your hearing."

They lugged their baggage out into the sunlight, and with many a grunt and groan, loaded it onto old Fernwing's cart. The magistrate was suffering a convenient spell of the creak and declined to offer a hand, opting instead to rub at his knees and make pained expressions. They had already fetched Lilly's belongings from her room over the tavern.

"Well," Beech said, drumming his fingers on his belly, "that should do. All this lifting has inspired my appetite; we've still time for a bite, eh, Mr. Purdy?"

"I'm sure, Mr. Beech."

Dover regarded Lilly, "How about you, good woman, you up for a bite? Some steaming sausage perhaps?" He wiggled his brows.

Lilly giggled. "Oh, I could manage a bite, I s'pose, Mr. Beech."

"Jolly good! Then let's be off for Ghost Oak. Fin will need something to cough up once the sea-sick sets in."

A shrill voice came from the path that led away from the village, toward the westerly farm properties. It was Mrs. Fernwing, running, waving her arms.

"Mr. Purdy! Mr. Beech!"

"Easy, Mrs. Fernwing," Dover warned, "Let's not get our horsies in a trot. What seems to be the trouble, dear lady?"

The woman panted, "There's something you should see, out at Mrs. Squill's farm…"

❧ ❧ ❧

The summer air was salt and warmth and the sweet boastings of bee-tickled blooms. Mrs. Squill was standing outside her humble farmhouse when the two mounted men came drumming along the road. They were barely within speaking distance, but then, no words were needed. The smiling old woman pointed out into the nearest field.

"Remarkable," Dover breathed.

Mrs. Squill hobbled over, wagging her head and laughing. "They weren't there yesterday, Mr. Beech, but come morning I looked out and seen 'em."

Dover and Purdy dismounted and walked out into the field where rearing snow-white flowers blazed up from the grass in the shape of a giant heart. They walked into the center through a moat of perfume and dew.

"It's beautiful," Purdy whispered, smiling.

"Beautiful," Dover muttered, breathing deeply. He glanced down at the grass where a tiny tattered straw-woven horse had been left. He picked it up and smiled, then slipped it into his pocket.

Purdy looked over at his friend. "Ahh, what's this? You're crying!"

Dover rubbed a finger under his spectacles. "I beg your pardon—'tis just a bit of dust in my eyes."

Rare Creatures of Westermead

The following are excerpts from a bestiary, a chronicle of mysterious beasts and entities as reported by Dover Beech and Fin Purdy.

The Laughing Tree

Elders in the village of Thistle Keep in the Midlands tell of a curious little tree, which, standing alone in a field, would shake convulsively and emit maniacal laughter. A local innkeeper by the name of Trundle Blackbucket chopped the thing down and proceeded to burn its wood in the public room of his establishment. The bits of wood moaned piteously as the flame took them and a terrible cloud rose from the flame. Some twenty or so patrons were present at the time, and of that number, half were stricken blind and half were rendered mad.

The Floating Woman

We conducted interviews with a number of sailors who witnessed a curious event while serving aboard the trade ship Cullen's Hope. On a clear day in the month of Oakbrown, just ten miles off shore, heading south along a spice route, the ship encountered the corpse of a gigantic woman. The body, three times the size of the cargo vessel, was without clothing, tremendously obese, and drifting belly up. The crew observed the body closely for several minutes before it sank into the sea.

Twenty Hungry Fingers

A swift, chill-watered stream cuts south for a distance of two and a half miles between the western villages of Cold Dance and Cairnwater. Locals claim that four creatures, which appear to be human arms, squirm eel-like through the water and snatch unfortunate animals from the banks.

We gathered a number of folk tales concerning vanishing children who had made the foolhardy mistake of fishing the stream. Several sheep strayed from a field while we were investigating the location and were discovered dead, floating in the water.

The Tear Thieves

The inhabitants of Westermead's rocky north are plagued by nasty little beings known as tear thieves. These malicious nocturnal parasites have form much as humans do, though they are spindly and no bigger than squirrels. They steal into barn stalls and straddle the snouts of horses, sheep and cattle, then lick the livestock's eyes, drinking their souls. The animals grow sickly thereafter and die.

Certain herbs are employed to repel the pests in combinations which vary from town to town. In Whistlestone the villagers use rage-thorn and heather fashioned in swags to be hung in stalls. We armed ourselves with brooms of said herbs and set up vigil in a barn. When at last the creatures came creeping in, we gave pursuit. Though the thieves attempted to hide in the hay and a milk pail, we swatted them with our brooms. The creatures burst into sparkling dust and left hideous shrieks in the air, in a six-foot radius, which lasted audibly for several hours before dissipating.

The Sleeping Tree of Brinker's Down

The horizontal corpse of a great oak tree hovers above a pond in the eastern hamlet of Brinker's Down. The ridiculously brave and insatiably curious may experience visions of their own demise by kissing the bark of the floating tree.

Hollow Meg

The ghastly sight of Hollow Meg has been seen by many over the years. We spotted the beast one misty evening on a moor just west of Milk Treading. It seemed, at first, to be a sickly mare, chewing away at thorny briars. It was pale, emaciated but for a distended belly, and it did not blink.

When the beast turned about, we saw that its belly on one side was cavernously open and a withered child-like creature with bony limbs and blank eyes sat scrunched inside the gap. The boy pulled at the horse's intestines as if reins and the mare jogged off into the mist.

The Solstice Moth

There remains to this day a quaint, archaic ritual, which locals in a number of northern villages perpetuate. At midwinter eve, when the days have shrunk and night rules the calendar, natives leave hot coals on their doorsteps so that a great snowy moth with a wizened man's face might swoop down and carry their offerings off beyond the horizon to relight the sun.

The Black Poppet

Kendrick Heron was a reclusive sort who lived in the hills above Candleberry. He dug up the bones of a hundred dead children (for unknown arcane reasons) and sewed them into a man-sized poppet of black cloth. The clattery, lumpy thing, so it's told, was wont to wander through the village on stormy nights, looking for its master, who was hanged for the murder of a young girl. It would pound insistently at the doors of local homes, wailing in a hundred child voices.

The Powder Men

She was a lovely thing with a dove-pale face and cidery ringlets dangling down from her bonnet. Willy looked up at her through the steam of his punch as she walked into a dark corner of the pub. It made him a bit squeamish, thinking of this refined lady, so vulnerable in her high-living finery, walking about in the slums of Longdoud.

He could plainly see, by her determined manner, that she was not someone lost in the city and seeking directions, but rather someone about some business of personal import. Yes, there was a peculiar, purposeful look in her eyes. She walked straight to a table where the two men sat, cleared her throat and said, "I'm looking for a Mister Mullen Pyke."

One of the men, slouched back to the left, holding up the shadowy wall with his back, grumbled, "I'm Pyke."

The lady said, "I am Pentreece Blackery. I'm told that you are the finest Powder Man money can buy."

Pyke gave his usual dark-sounding snicker. "I'm afraid you're wrong about that, Miss. I'm the best Powder Man money can *rent*," he said.

"Pardon my choice of words," the lady said, then: "I have a problem of the utmost seriousness which will require a man of your ability... Could we go somewhere to discuss this?"

"Here's just fine," Pyke croaked. "This is my partner, Willy."

The second fellow gave her his squinty-eyed, white-bearded grin and offered her a seat. She sat down, though she looked a bit uncomfortable placing her silky green skirt on that rickety old chair, and her pretty hands on the grimy table. Willy felt uncomfortable for her.

"Will you be havin' a glass?" Willy asked. She shook her head, and Pyke proceeded to inquire as to what this was all about.

She just stared at Pyke for the longest minute, though it was doubtful she could see him well. He was slumped back against the wall, his face nearly lost in the shadows, and those unruly lamb chop sideburns, and that big upturned collar of his coat. His eyes were there, but they were dark as well and might've been missed were it not for the glints of lamp light.

She said, "It concerns my husband, I…"

ℰ ℰ ℰ

A year previous…

Coastgrove was the private game reserve of young Prince Roogan. It was a spacious maze of shadow and leaves where an untamed brook wove cool through mossy stones and beds of fern. There were tree-colored hollows where stags feasted on acorns, and briar-crowned hills astir with fox and hare. At its most westerly point, this otherwise darkness-inclined forest gave way to a cliff of jagged rock, which overlooked the vast ocean's agitated grey.

The wood was drowsy with mist that morning as Denner set out on patrol. His musket rested in its sheath alongside the saddle, and his looking-glass and flask of water were on the opposite side. Keen eyes swept the familiar lay of land—his place of employ, which he swore he loved more than its royal owner ever could. The horse moved slowly through moist tunnels of branches and the rider glanced down at where two human skulls were mounted on sticks marking the spot where he had killed poachers the year previous. Somewhere off in the trees ahead an owlcat howled its eerie call.

Denner was a fearsome-looking man—large of build with a ruddy face and wide forehead. His eyes were a stern blue, his mouth of a serious set. His hair was long, a lion's mane, his mustache and beard blond as well. Though his voice could boom out deep and loud it was rarely spent on rage. It was, however, common for him to project his rich vocal tones in gentle songs of love and nature, thus betraying his true temperament.

The game warden continued east through corridors of green. He spied a doe, her inquisitive nostrils brushing through the grass of a slight clearing—as if drinking from the shimmery pools of honeyed sunlight which dripped through the gaps in the leafy roof. The subtle electricity of her poise belied placidity and caution.

Further along, Denner paused to drink from his flask. Brief forms, dark and darting, passed ahead, against a smudge of distant hills. He finished off the flask's contents, then rode on through the thinning mist. Shortly he would reach the brook where the flask could be refilled.

He was just within sight of the water—the horse's steady hooves stirring foresty scents—when he thought he heard a voice. He listened hard and scanned the region, but heard only birds, saw only dense woods.

"Curious," he said, then continued on.

The brook was a fine run of water and it divided the plush acreage of Coastgrove. It maneuvered through the knurly lay of stones and plants without losing its sinuous integrity. The water was a near-luminous blend of gurgles and sunlight as it strayed beneath the morning mist. The light, enthused, trembled sensuously upon its swift surface.

A voice as soft as the faltering haze came ghostly from the brook. "Help!"

Denner reined still his mount and looked up and down the water's length. He could see no one, though that was no surprise, for there were plenty of trees and shrubs to serve as obstacles. The voice, came pleading again, high and strained...

"Help!"

Denner dismounted and adjusted the pistol he wore at his belt. For a man of such mass, he moved with great stealth through the bank's dense greenery. Up ahead, the brook dipped across a jumble of moss-splotched stones—it was there that he spotted something—a rubbery dagger in spasm.

"Help! Oh, help!—I'm caught!"

He drew closer, his hand on his gun. The silvery thing fluttered ineffectually, lodged there amidst the slick heap of stones.

"A fish! A fish that talks!" Denner exclaimed.

He rushed closer, his eyes squinting, perplexed. It was indeed a fish, flashing and thin, though not a trout, nor salmon, but a strange breed the likes of which he'd never seen. Its coppery eyes implored and the mouth gaped as the high song-like voice poured free, "Help!"

Denner was so intrigued with the situation that he remained unaware of the large things which were approaching the brook from behind him. He stepped onto the stones where the fish was trapped and knelt.

"What might you be?" he asked.

"I am akin to the soul of this brook," the fish responded. "It is my charge, as the forest is yours, good man."

"Then how can you have become snared in your own body, if you are the soul of this water?"

"Even souls aren't perfect, my friend. I was waiting for a chance to speak to you, and in my desperation to seek your attention, I leapt on these stones. It was not my intention, however, to be trapped as such."

"Here," Denner said, reaching out, "let me help you."

"Wait! They're coming!" The round-eyed stare of the fish seemed to widen; it strained to raise its head toward the woods behind.

"Who is coming?"

"You must listen, forestry man—my brook is endangered. You're aware that a guest from the island of Gullbride is visiting the Prince..."

"Yes. Lord Chelton Brimsted."

"Yes, yes, him! You must kill him!"

Denner leaned back. "Kill him? Why?'

"He's not a man, I tell you. He's a thing of greed and hostility. He's come to steal me, and thus cause ruin to my brook."

"I can't kill Lord Brimsted. You must be mistaken; he's a man of power and respect."

"Please, you must stop him. He's a horror in guise."

Denner reached out and lifted the fish from the stones which trapped it. It was then that he heard the horses coming up from behind, and he turned. Three men towered in their saddles. Lord Brimsted was in the lead—stiff and dignified with his grey hair slicked away from the thinness of his snide face. A dark cloak poured down behind him. On his right rode his son, whose face matched his own for regal arrogance, his dark hair gathered into a pony tail. An ominous bodyguard with a musket resting across his thigh stayed several paces behind.

"Ahhh, good morning," the Lord said, smiling. "You are the game warden, yes?"

"I am…"

"And what have you there? A fish that speaks?"

Denner did not reply readily. He studied the fish, which now began to squirm in his grasp. He looked back up at the Lord, pondering. He answered reluctantly, "Yes."

Lord Brimsted climbed down from his saddle and pushed through the ferns crowding the bank of the brook. His high black boots gleamed and the buttons on his purple jacket winked. He extended a long-fingered hand as he approached.

"May I see that fish for a moment?"

Denner glanced over at the man's son, who seemed to perk, his eyes like slashes of anticipation. The fish wriggled more furiously, its mouth wide as it called out, "Noooo! Throw me in! Throw me in the brook!"

"Wait!" the Lord barked. "Give me the fish!"

"Please," the fish cried, "throw me, quick!"

Denner looked up into the ravenous eyes of the Lord, then turned and dropped the fish with a splash.

"Fool!" the Lord cried. He slashed the back of his hand across Denner's face, knocking him backward into the water, then lunged at the fish as it tried to speed away.

"No!" the fish shrieked, as those long fingers found it. Lord Brimsted yanked it out of the water, which suddenly, with a great sigh of mist, was gone.

Denner found himself sprawled only in mud and stones, and struggled to pull himself upright. "What have you done?" He watched as the fish, clamped helplessly in the Lord's hands, convulsed, crying, its scales flaking off and clinking onto the ground as silver coins.

"It's mine!" the Lord gloated loudly. "Mine!"

Denner rose, his face red-flushed in rage. He yanked the pistol from his belt and shoved it at the Lord. One loud clap—the spew of smoke—the Lord tossed back, gouged and red, the fish reduced to a rain of coins through the falling man's fingers.

Another blast broke the morning air as the bodyguard's musket blazed.

Denner jolted as the heavy ball tore through his powerful chest. He tumbled back into the muddy furrow where the brook had been and lay shaking like a fish out of water.

Lord Brimsted's son rushed to his father's side. A geiser of small black bird-like things came sprouting from the dead man's slack mouth. And when they all had fluttered off through the trees, the son drew a saber and went to where the game warden lay trembling.

"Death's too good for you!" he sneered as he lopped off Denner's head. He held it up by the muddy mane then wrapped it in his cloak.

"I want you to kill him."

Pyke emerged from the shadows, leering, leaning across the table now so that his massive skull and brutish face were close to Pentreece Blackery. His breath was warm with whiskey. "Who, might I inquire, is your husband?"

The woman did not hide her dispassion—it was as if the name she uttered rendered pain to her tongue. "Summon Brimsted."

Pyke smirked. "The son of the late Lord Chelton Brimsted?"

"Yes. The reasons why I want him dead are no concern of yours, but I will admit that I am rather like you in ways. I am mercenary—my motivation for marrying him was not love, but merely to access things that he possessed. Things that I stole from him."

"A pity that such a lovely bit of woman as yourself harbors so much deceit and cruelty." Pyke was smug and amused.

"I did not say I was cruel, Mr. Pyke, and in so far as deceit goes, what wrong is there in deceiving the evil?"

"You think Summon Brimsted is evil?"

"I know so. I am his wife, after all."

Pyke nodded. He turned to his companion and mumbled, "More drink."

The older man left the table. The woman told Pyke how much gold she was willing to pay him for his services. His eyes sparkled hungrily.

"A price as handsome as that," Pyke noted, "would set me for life."

"I should imagine. Ah—but I've neglected to tell all—in order for you to acquire the amount I have offered, you will need to do something more, other than merely killing my husband."

"What's that?"

Pentreece stood. "Come out to my coach; I have to show you…"

Willy had returned with more drink. Mullen Pyke rose towering from his seat, stepping from the shadows, his movements measured and ominous. He gestured for Willy to follow.

It was drizzling outside of the pub. The alley was dark and slick, fetid to the nose and clammy to the skin. An expensive two-horse coach waited there, the patient driver scrunched under a wide-brimmed hat.

Pyke slid one of his great paws inside his coat, the fingers resting on the handle of a pistol. Willy remained several paces behind, one of his hands similarly occupied, for they had, due to the nature of their work, accumulated some number of enemies over the years. For all they knew the pretty woman with the bonnet was leading them out to be ambushed.

Pyke positioned himself to one side of the coach door. "Mrs. Blackery — why do you call yourself that? You don't use your husband's name, Brimsted?" Pyke asked.

Pentreece's smile was a flash of personal spite and triumph, "Only within earshot of him and his cronies. Blackery is my previous name."

"Hm."

The woman opened the door of the coach, reached in and pulled out two sacks. "In a week Lord Brimsted will be going on a visit to Prince Roogan's estate. He will be hunting in the Coastgrove game preserve. I want you to go in there, for you will need to in order to complete your duties, that is, if you accept this job."

"What's this other thing you wish me to do?"

"You are to take these two sacks — one contains powder, one contains coins — and toss them into the Cove of Womb-brine, at the western edge of the wood."

Pyke studied her. "Why?"

"Because you're being paid to."

"What will happen when I toss them in?" he persisted.

"Something wonderful."

She handed him the cloth sacks. Willy tightened his grasp on his firearm, lest one of the things burst into flame, or some small horrid creature erupt forth.

"I realize this is a strange request. I'll tell you this much—there is some magic involved. That simple sack in your right hand contains a limited amount of silver coins. In my hands it is equally limited, but in the hands of Lord Brimsted the number of coins are infinite. He can reach in repeatedly— endlessly, and pull out fresh handfuls of silver. He, and his father before him, acquired their riches by securing such treasures as this."

Pyke eyed the sack greedily.

"I know what you're thinking, Mr. Pyke, but it doesn't work unless you're like him, like his father was...though you're welcome to try."

"What do you mean?"

"They aren't human."

Pyke nodded. He had forgotten—drink was taking a toll on his memory as of late.

"Before you accept or refuse my offer, I must inform you of the remaining stipulations," Mrs. Blackery said. "Coastgrove is well guarded by wardens to the Prince. You are to steal into the forest without killing any of them. I insist quite firmly on that. Also, more importantly, you are to guard these two sacks with your life—it is imperative they be delivered safely to the Cove of Womb-brine. And, whatever you do, don't open that one."

Pyke looked down at the plump sack of powder. It weighed several pounds and seemed to generate a mild degree of heat. Strange, but it almost felt as if the sandy contents were shifting about of their own accord.

"Should you accept," the woman spoke, squinting into the drizzle, "I will pay you half now, and half when you return, provided you have done as I've instructed. That's not unreasonable of me, is it, Mr. Pyke?"

He snickered. "You're a precise one, you are. Unswerving, right?"

"It's important to me—I apologize if my demands cause you insult; none is intended."

"I suppose," he grumbled, "it ain't so unreasonable, seeing as you're offering such a great amount of payment." Though Pyke was puzzled by the woman's mysterious requests, and somewhat challenged by her demanding air, he had to admit to himself that he felt some respect for her. She was smart, or was it sly? She was brave as well—coming to these parts, approaching a man like himself, and now admitting to him that there was a massive amount of gold in her carriage. He glanced up at the driver, perched in his cloak and hat, no doubt armed beneath the dark cloth of his garment. Yes, there had to be a blunderbuss, or something—this Pentreece Blackery was no fool.

"I'll take on the job, Mrs. 'Blackery,'" Pyke whispered darkly, tucking the two sacks under his coat.

❧ ❧ ❧

A week passed. Pyke and his partner Willy tended to the last minute preparations before settling about a jug of ale at an inn, mere hours from their destination. The room was cramped and dark, the walls leaning in toward the singular light of a sputtering candle.

A new crossbow and bolts had been purchased for the mission. Pyke figured a silent weapon would be more practical than their noisy guns, considering they were to try evading the forest wardens. Of course, the guns would be used, if needed. They had also used some of their advance pay to buy telescoping spy glasses. Willy had sought out a spell merchant and bought a small amount of a substance of cobweb consistency which, reputedly, when stuffed in the ears, gave one an extremely heightened sense of hearing. That could prove helpful in hearing others in the forest before others heard or spotted them.

"This is the big job," Willy said, grinning, "It'll be dusty corners for our guns after this one. Our horses will grow fat, and we too. No more thin blankets on cold nights, no more rooms with leaky roofs. We'll be rolling in fancy beds with fancy whores, and drownin' in drink."

Pyke was indifferent; having finished carving a crude image of a fish in the table top with one of the crossbow bolts, he leaned back in his chair and crossed his thick arms. "Sounds bloody boring to me," he grumbled. "Dusty guns…"

121

Pyke took pride in being a renegade, apart from the life of an honest fool. He was a Powder Man at heart—one who earned his pay by spending gunpowder. For years he had hoped for a great amount of wealth, enough to retire with. Now that the dream of settling down was within reach, he was not so sure that the dream would make a satisfactory reality.

Willy probed him with a squint. "One day, when you're my age, you'll change. I've had my fill of the chase and hunt. The fight as well. I'm getting too old for it, Mull. I'm not so mean any more."

Pyke nodded. He understood. "So we part, after this one."

Willy smiled sadly. They clinked glasses.

ℭ ℭ ℭ

They stole into the Coastgrove game preserve as dawn misted golden through the birch-ribbed hills. They came from the east, ale-brown mares wading across a shallow pond. The water was scummy, stretched out like some vast verdigris shield, and the horses carved rippling striations as they lumbered through it.

Stealth was vital, for the wardens who tended this place were renowned for their keen senses and accuracy with firearms. There were poachers with scars to prove it, and tales to tell, and others whose death-silence was testimony aplenty. Mullen Pyke was not afraid, however.

"Remember," Willy said, as they reached the bank with the forest dark beyond, "we're not to kill any of the wardens, or we forfeit the rest of our gold."

"I remember," Mullen sneered.

They moved on through delirious ramparts of weeds, up through murky mazes of fir and oak. The air was peppered with lazy schools of tiny itch-flies that set the horses' tails to flailing.

"Pssst!"

Willy glanced over at Pyke. "What?"

"Watch out for those," he said, pointing.

Willy looked down to where a number of inconspicuous grey toadstools squatted against the forest floor. They were shock hounds, apt to erupt loudly with a sound much like the startled bark of a dog if trod upon.

"It's best if we go single file from here on," Pyke suggested, allowing Willy to fall behind.

The wood grew thicker. There were wild paths steeped in summer's jugular warmth. At the center of the preserve they encountered a great winding scar where a brook once delighted. It remained barren, and even the vegetation along its banks seemed feeble and strained.

A sudden muffled moan startled Pyke. He threw a look to his right, expecting to see a human source. Strangely, there was none. It came again, deep, louder—it came from his saddle bag.

"What's this, then?" he growled. He reached in and felt the sack of coins, then the mysterious sack of powder. It was warm to the touch, and again the mournful sound came. His hand recoiled. He would be glad to be free of the blasted thing. The thought of it hanging so near to him put ants in his veins.

"Are you ill?" Willy asked.

"It's not me—it's that bag of dust!"

"You don't mean to say—"

"Yes, yes, the bloody thing's groaning!"

Several hours passed. The air grew hotter, making the forest claustrophobic. Twice they were forced to hide from roaming wardens. The tangled trails were choked with humidity, singed with shadow. The powder men, dressed in olive-colored garb, blended well with their surroundings.

The elevated hearing spell was starting to tax Willy's nerves. Each twig snap and hoof fall sounded as if it came from within his own skull. His own heartbeat crashed like waves against some poor boat's hull. The sounds of the wood closed in from all sides until he swore he could hear ants scratching across tree bark and snake bellies hissing river-loud through the grass. Flies droned unbearably and bird shrieks sent quills of ice burning through his spine.

Pyke noticed the agitated look in his companion's eyes, the profuse sheen of sweat on his face, the way he twitched and looked this way and that. "What's wrong?" Pyke seemed more annoyed than concerned.

Willy gasped—that bag of powder moaned—a deep rumbling that threatened to explode his head. He had never been so eager to have a job done with. "It's the ear spell," he answered Pyke's inquiry.

"Dig the blasted stuff out, then."

"Right, right, but can't we dump that awful groany bag at the Cove of Womb-brine first, then come for Lord Brimsted? It's giving me jitters."

"No," Pyke hissed, "we take Brimsted first. Clean your ears if you must."

Willy set to removing the web-like material with quivering fingers. He was able to dislodge most of it. The deafening sounds of the forest faded to normalcy.

Pyke's steely self-control allowed him to master the exaggerated loudness. It soon proved advantageous…

ᘓ ᘓ ᘓ

Thunder!

A mad crashing of branches, the desperate rasping of strained breathing coming quickly closer. Pyke pulled out his looking-glass, opened it to full length and followed the sound, which Willy, apparently, had not even heard.

He spotted motion, off to the east, a dark form. He focused—it was a buck, wide-eyed, air-gulping, smashing through the forest in pain and disorientation. Wind-bent reeds of blood arced out from its wounded side. He watched it slow to a stagger and collapse.

"Dismount!" Pyke spat. He tied his horse to a tree, slung a stout musket over his shoulder and grabbed the crossbow. Willy struggled to catch up with him.

Pyke positioned himself behind the great moss-coated corpse of a fallen oak. The deer lay at the base of a slight slope in a pool of blood and shadow, within shooting range. It was still alive; he could hear it wheezing, and considered ending its agony with a silent bolt from the crossbow, but what if the hunters saw the bolt protruding?

The hunt party arrived, their horses swift over the crest of the hill, then down the tree-dense slope to view the prey. Pyke's brutish face flushed with malevolence. "Blast!" he cursed, "The bloody Prince is with him!"

There were six of them: the dapper Prince Roogan, his three bodyguards and Summon Brimsted (arrogant as ever) along with his personal guardian. A smug grin crossed Brimsted's face as he sat proudly in his saddle dressed in a bright white shirt with puffed sleeves, his forehead agleam, dark hair pulled back into a tail.

"A fine shot, Summon," the Prince said.

"Certainly not my best, dear Prince—the bugger still had some run left in him."

They climbed down to inspect the beast.

"Oh—he's not quite dead yet," the Prince noted.

Willy nudged Pyke.

"What?"

"The Prince is with him."

"Yes, I can see that."

"All those guards…"

Pyke turned to eye him. "I know; I don't like it, but we're here, right?"

"Maybe if we wait, we can catch him alone. Maybe tomorrow he'll hunt without the Prince. He does that, you know."

"Bah! These aren't game wardens, she didn't say we couldn't kill body-guards, did she, mate? No, she didn't. We'll take 'em. Just be careful not to hit the Prince."

"I don't know about this…"

"We're Powder Men, remember? We're the best."

Willy nodded. "Right, Mull, you're right."

Pyke cocked the crossbow, his jaw clenched. He leaned his musket against the tree and placed two pistols, both ready to fire, on the ground beside him. He rose to a half-crouch, staring along the crossbow.

Lord Brimsted seemed irritated that the deer was still not dead. A faint trace of pity flicked on the Prince's face as he offered his friend a dagger.

"Would you care to finish it?" the Prince asked.

Brimsted scowled. "I think it's about done, thank you." He bent over the creature and abruptly staggered back, his eyes wide. He grasped at the end of the bolt which was submerged deeply in his chest. He howled and collapsed.

Boom! One of the guards was flung from his horse. The Prince was too stunned to move. He watched as a large man with unruly dark hair lurched up over a fallen tree, a long pistol stabbing out from each hand.

Boom! Boom! Two more guards went sprawling from their mounts. Willy poked up, his musket shouldered. White smoke sprawled through the air as the forest shook with the blast. The last guard was blown out of his saddle before he could cock his pistol.

Silence. Pyke dropped his empty weapons and pulled a third from his belt. It was a stout thing—he extended it at the Prince. "Throw down your musket, Prince."

The Prince was pale and shaken. He let his weapon fall and stepped back. "P-please..."

Pyke bore a sardonic grin. "No reason to worry, we shan't harm you." He turned. "Willy, tie 'im up!"

Pyke stood over the body of Lord Summon Brimsted who lay on his back, his limbs flung wide. A strange clicking noise issued from his throat and his belly worked like a spastic bellows. His jaw fell open and a fluttering flock of small black creatures came tripping out into the air. As they flew off through the trees, one struck a branch and broke into sparks.

"My word!" the Prince gasped.

Pyke chuckled. He moved over to the deer and inspected it. "A messy shot. But it's dead now."

The Prince gawked at Brimsted, shaking his head. "What were those things?"

Pyke's voice was dark. "Queer thing about those Brimsteds. Not quite human."

Prince Roogan was tied to a tree where the forest wardens would eventually discover him. He watched as the men collected their weapons and headed off to the west. Strange, but the younger of the two looked terribly familiar.

ও ও ও

The plush wood of Coastgrove yielded to the great jagged snout of stone which projected over the ocean's grey turbulence. The Powder Men anchored their horses to a stump and started down the treacherous path that led to the Cove of Womb-brine.

Gulls swam above, voices cast in salty shrieks. Far below the cliff, a circular lip of stone pouted up from the restless waves. The water inside of this was contrastingly still.

Pebbles clattered down ahead of them. The sack of powder moaned loudly as Pyke carried it. Willy was several yards behind, carrying the sack of silver coins. The trail curled lower along the steep side of the cliff.

"They say it's a magic place, good for restoring one's health, or something like that," Willy noted, gesturing to the enclosed pool below.

Click...

Pyke recognized the sound of a gun hammer being cocked and reached for one of his pistols. He turned too quickly, though, and the slanted pebble-cluttered path caused his balance to falter. He fell against the cliff, slamming his back on the wall of stone before landing on his side.

Willy yanked free his pistol and spun around. He found himself staring at a forestry warden, dressed in green, a long flint-gun in hand.

"Halt!" the warden barked.

Willy hesitated.

"Willy—shoot!" Pyke yelled.

Boom!

Willy jerked back, trembling spires of gore casting up from his head. The sack of coins spilled on the path as he toppled over, into the surf below.

Pyke thrust his gun out and fired. The warden slapped red against the cliff, doubled over, and flopped off the path, feeding the sea with the splash of his weight.

"Bastard!" Pyke snarled. "Miserable bloody bastard!"

He picked himself up and stared down into the waves for a while before collecting the coins that had spilled from the bag of silver. He climbed down to the circular rim of the cove and tossed in the two sacks.

"There, Mrs. Blackery," he said, "it's done."

A great rumbling of thunder came from the woods above and beyond the overhanging cliff. Pyke could only listen as a snaking mass of lightning surge-danced through the woods along the barren bed of the vanished brook. The water of the brook was returned.

Another sound caught his ear—the displacement of water. The ripples in the cove, where the bags had gone in, peeled back like lips as a shape came rising from the water's dark throat.

It was as big as a man, a bony scaly thing with bulbous eyes like a fish, though the rest of the face was human in form. In fact, it was familiar—it was the face of the forestry man he had shot back when he was the body-guard of Lord Chelton Brimsted.

The creature sprang up onto the rocky ledge and lashed its long arms at the Powder Man. Its hands flashed silvery like a vice on his head and his skull quick-reduced to pain, pulp and shards.

In the villages that skirted the acreage of Coastgrove, there were tales of a creature that prowled through the woods. They called it Old Scale, both in fondness and fear, and claimed it was guarding the forest it loved. Over the years, there were numerous instances where poachers were found with their heads crushed to pulp. The deaths were attributed to the lore-beast. Eventually the poaching stopped.

There were several rumors as to the origin of Old Scale. One such story maintained that there was some connection between Old Scale and a forestry warden who had been killed years before, a man by the name of Denner Blackery. When his widow Pentreece heard tell of such, she was quick to say, "That couldn't be." Then she would smile to herself.

The Thatcher's Cat

ONE

The stone house stood on a hill in the tiny village of Kilmnook. From this vantage point three stories up, the thatcher could see all of the encircling orchard—the wreath of trees having gone from pink to peak to pounding at the earth with souring red. Summer's end with that one high roof to go, then on to the next town.

Best never to stay too long in one place; that was Norbin's reasoning. Dust of the road in his blood. No shame in that, he thought; there'd be no webs, nor rust on him. Not to say that he was without sentimentality, for he did have his regrets about leaving. Still, he was a craftsman and if he were to make his fortune he would have to go where he could ply his trade, and all the other roofs in Kilmnook were done.

The villagers would be sad to see the young man go, having grown so accustomed to seeing him up his ladder with that slim grey cat perched on his shoulder. Some would recall his first day, how they had thought he was a hunchback—it had been cool, early summer, Norbin had worn a loose tunic over his white shirt, and there had been an abnormal bulge over the left shoulder blade. The spectators had burst into laughter when the bump suddenly shifted and a cat poked its grey head free from the tunic's neckline.

Some of the girls had become quite fond of the lanky fellow. He was not of greatly handsome stock, in the conventional sense, yet his features were not without their boyish charm. His grin was fast and impish, his laughter ripe with mischief. His eyes, for all their youthful blue, were capable of a knowing gaze and his longish hair was the very blond of the straw he wielded so well.

They took delight in watching him at work—his athletic grace, the deft hands fast as pale birds, the glinting smile of the pruning knife. Occasionally he would take a break and play an airy tune or two on the tin whistle, tapping one foot on the ladder, the cat beaming from his back.

They would toss him pears to snack and giggle amongst themselves. Norbin would miss that. He liked the way their eyes felt on him; he liked looking down into their sunny faces.

Norbin and Claylor, a local lad the thatcher had hired to assist him during his stay in Kilmnook, set to work. The boy's duties consisted mainly of passing the materials up to Norbin. The first days spent at the large stone building had been the most strenuous as they had laid a layer of grass sod over the timbers of the roof. Such duties were the domain of earthy odors—musty rolls of sod weighing on sweaty shoulders, the scratchy scent of the thin rope used to sew the unfurled slabs on.

Next the thatcher busied himself with the setting out of flax. Norbin, with ladder leaning against the high house, shook straw loose from bundles and spread it neatly across the sod. He worked steadily, fastening each section by placing a thin length of willow across, pinning that with others, which were bent to form staples. The ash-colored cat, like a stole slung across the back of the man's neck, remained complacent even as the pins were knocked in with the loud whacks of a mallet. The next layer was placed higher up so that it hung down to hide the securing device of the area below; this continued until the peak of the roof was reached.

"Another bundle, my good man," Norbin called down to Claylor, who stood in the back of a long flat-bed wagon which was heaped in amber stalks. The request was swiftly met.

Norbin turned to his small feline passenger and whispered, "Are you comfortable, little Smoke?"

Whiskers rubbed against his cheek and a purr hummed close.

"How 'bout a tune to lighten our labor, would you like that?"

He felt the cat's hind rise, the tail shooting up.

"Ahhh, I thought you might…"

He sang with ease, his hands unhindered in their speed and precision, "Wheat on roofs most common, rye lasts past twelve years. Rushes on the mountain homes sit five before rain tears."

The curved blade of a knife slashed, trimming a new-laid edge.

"Reeds are fine where lakes provide, barley barely used. Flax, the least to catch the flame, the finest I would choose."

They continued on into the afternoon, the blond dust thick in the Gusstar sun. The smell of the flax was heavy in their hair and clothes as it challenged the tart wafting of the enclosing orchard.

Moving the ladder from the right to the left as he progressed, Norbin had completed most of one side of the high building's roof by the time the magistrate's carriage came clattering up the hill.

The passenger who disengaged himself from the coach was a barrel of a man, his dark hair slicked back and tied in a short pony tail. His face was like a plump mushroom, the features pinched in the pallor. He walked back and forth, assessing the situation, his thumbs hooked in a wide black belt.

Norbin grinned down. "Afternoon, sir!"

"Good afternoon. I see that you have accomplished much. Come, take a break for yourself."

"Thank you, sir." Norbin set down the small hand rake he'd been smoothing the thatch with and descended the ladder. Smoke dug her talons into his loose white shirt, but was careful not to cause injury.

The older man clapped the thatcher on the shoulder. "A splendid job, lad. Splendid indeed."

Harton Barth, in his fine silk shirt and black breeches, was the Kingdom official of the village. He represented the hierarchy's loose grip on this outer settlement, and bore well the resentment that came with such duties. Norbin tolerated him with his usual jovial manner.

"So, Norbin, tell me, how does one apply such skill while a parasite clings to him?" Harton smiled his eyes to squints and planted a boot on the ladder's lowest rung.

Norbin chuckled pleasantly to deflect the man's humor, which was often like a dagger thrust at the spine. "I never cease to be humbled by the affections of another species. She is the best of companions in my history of acquaintances."

Harton smirked and nodded patronizingly. "Hmm, I see."

The cat observed the official with an inscrutable amber gaze.

"I don't have much room in my heart for the lesser beasts," Barth said, "but I have plenty of room for them here!" He clapped his palms on his wide belly and chortled.

Norbin smiled.

"Well," Harton groaned, "you take your rest and I'll set about my business. I'm still not decided on what rooms will be used for what purposes. I enjoy strolling about inside and letting the possibilities play in my mind."

"Right. Like a fork in a road, each with a promise of its own."

"Something to that effect."

Harton Barth took pause to produce a slim circular tin. He flipped it open and with two wide fingers as a scoop swabbed his lips and cheeks with an oily jaundice-tinted substance.

"Blasted stuff stinks like a rodent's bile," he remarked. "Keeps my lips smooth, though. Every Gusstar I break into boils—damn pollen wreaks havoc..."

Harton shoved the fingers under the nose of the cat.

"Here, kitty, do we like that?"

Smoke recoiled squinting.

Harton let go a hearty laugh. "I thought not."

Norbin fought to feign a smile.

"You'll excuse me," Barth said with a wave, lumbering off into the vast stone structure which he would soon inhabit.

🙲 🙲 🙲

"So there I was up in that tree with the cold wind blasting and the mother cat yowling..." Norbin bent forward, Claylor and his younger brothers hunched in close, their eyes like golden coins in the firelight.

"The Nast had the kitten by the scruff and something silvery in its free hand—a knife it stole from a kitchen, or perhaps it was a miniature sword."

"A sword?"

Norbin nodded. He continued in a quick hush, "I had all I could do to keep from being blown down—all those wind-maddened branches scratching at me. The horrid little thing took no mind of the wind and scurried higher and higher."

"You could see it?" Claylor asked, awed.

"That I could."

"What did it look like?"

A sly grin flashed on Norbin's face. "Ohhh, it was an awful thing. Just the size of a full grown cat, but spidery—like a man's shape in ways. It was dark in color with the face of an owl, a spray of white hair trailing from its head. And it had a beard like a goat."

The fire snapped—the boys flinched.

"I reckoned the mother cat had disturbed the Nast when she skulked into the tavern's cellar to have her young. Anyway—there I was climbing up after, the cat below crying and the kitten above calling piteously. That wily Nast set to dropping branches down on me! Not twigs mind ya, but branches it hacked loose with its weapon."

"What did you do?" the youngest lad asked.

"Well, what could I do? I ducked and dodged as best I could. Now, I reached a point where I was quite high and the bare branches thinned. The Nast, being so light, continued on to the peak, but I could not. As it so happened I had a length of my thatching rope on my belt, so, working as fast as my hands allowed, I unwound it and tied this to one end."

Norbin reached into his shirt and pulled out a small, green cloth bag attached to a thong.

"What's that?"

"A charm to ward off mischievous domestic spirits like Nasts. One never knows what they'll find up on a roof, you know."

"Oh. What's in it?"

Norbin looked from side to side. "I'll tell, but ya must promise to keep it to yourselves."

Claylor said, "We promise."

"Yes, yes, we do!" the others echoed.

"All right then." In a whisper: "Three fox tears, a crow's sharp beak and the ashes of a lightning-dried oak—just a pinch."

133

There were collective "oowws."

"Well, that old Nast was in a bit of a predicament. He could not climb any higher—I was situated below him—and the branches he rained down at me were the tree's uppermost, and not at all a threat. I swung the rope with the charm and looped it near where he perched…"

Norbin clapped his hands and yelped. "Ah, such a shriek the bastard gave! He let go the kitten and sprang from the tree, falling far below. I caught the poor babe beast and saw a cough of light where the Nast struck the ground."

"Was it dead?"

Norbin sighed. "Well, when I climbed down there was no body to be seen, only a scorch mark on the earth, just at the spot where the Nast fell."

Smoke was curled in Norbin's lap, her head resting on his thigh. He stroked her warm coat absently.

"And that's how you met her?"

"Right. But I didn't take her right away. Over the time I stayed in that village I came to know the mother cat and her younglings. Smoke and I grew fond of each other and have been inseparable ever since."

They were on the edge of the orchard, at the base of the hill where the tall house stood, dusk folding in about their small fire. The Gusstar breeze was the warm breath of apples as it soothed from the west. Norbin observed as through the small-paned windows of the estate a lamp light described Harton Barth's room to room movements.

"I can't imagine why one would desire so large a house," Norbin said.

The light vanished and the heavy wooden door opened.

Claylor offered, "He needs space to keep his offices, rooms for records of tax and the like, and a hearing room as well, for disputes of a legal nature. Servants' quarters too."

"Here he comes," one of the younger boys noted, "we'd best be getting home."

Norbin said his goodbyes to them and headed up the hill, Smoke padding along beside him. Barth stood with his hands on his hips, smiling yellow lips and cheeks.

"A handsome bit of work you've done, Norbin."

"Tomorrow we begin the other side."

"A shame it doesn't keep that color. Gold. My favorite color, if you get my meaning, hah!" He clapped Norbin on the arm.

"Yes, sir."

"I'll be off. You rest well."

"I shall, I'm sure, Mr. Barth."

"And you too, kitty—"

Barth bent down to Smoke who stood at Norbin's side, her tail stirring the air. The man grabbed this and gave a tug, yanking her hind off the ground. Smoke let go a hiss and struck suddenly with her claws.

"Argh!" Barth pulled his hand back and measured the damage.

Norbin didn't know how to react, caught between distaste for Barth's roughness and embarrassment at the effect. "I—I'm sorry, Mr. Barth."

"No bother, just a bit of blood." He chuckled. "As I said, I'll be off—my boots hunger for home."

Harton Barth made his way to the carriage where the bored driver waited. He turned once to view the cat—seeds of hate lodging in the soil of his eyes.

❧ ❧ ❧

A stream curled like a sickles' blade around the modest parcel of land where an old thatched cottage stood half-smothered in pink hollyhocks. The earth edged up like steep steps behind it; dew-heavy goldenrod forming a buttery mist in the dawn haze. Down on the banks there was a stirring of birds, and a hare with mint-scented paws peered out from the dense grey and green of a raised herb bed.

Inside the cramped building, Mrs. Krettle blessed the air with the aroma of breakfast.

"To be sure, Mrs. K, I will dearly miss your cooking," Norbin told the old woman who had boarded him throughout the summer. He ogled the spread of food—pewter plates laden with sausage and wedges of sage-freckled cheese, ceramic bowls brimming with steaming apple porridge. The early grain harvest was well represented by a plump loaf of glossy bronze bread.

Inverted heads of bright owl-eye mushrooms had been hollowed out, filled with apricot jam, stuck with cloves and steamed. There was even a pitcher of mint-water to wash it all down.

Mrs. Krettle smiled, pleased to have so appreciative a guest.

"I'll miss you, my lad," she said with her wide semi-toothed smile, eyes of sparkling wrinkles. "And you, my furry one."

Smoke poured her slim grey body around the woman's ankles, head craned up as she meowed. Mrs. Krettle set down a plate of milk, cheese and bits of sausage for her.

Bellies full, Norbin and Smoke set out for the job site. They passed fields where farmers waded through corn and scythes swooped like steel crows. The road took them west past scarlet pools of poppy and abundant spreads of bee-adorned goldenrod. Gusstar was the month of yellows and reds, from strawberries to wheat, from misted dawn-bronzed plains to the arterial splendor of rowan fruit.

By mid-morning the sun was hot. Norbin curled back the sleeves of his loose white shirt and rolled his grey trousers up to the knees. The flax was scratchy as it whisked across his forearms.

Norbin sang as he worked, Smoke sitting nearby monitoring several birds which had momentarily landed on the building. "Barley on a roof won't do, I fear it will not last. It by far is better spent apourin' from a glass. Rye is best if reaped 'fore ripe, I'd seed a special crop. In northern vales the homes all have heaped rushes on the top. Eastern towns by River Sour oat straw the roofs do seal. As above then so inside: they crush it for their meal. Wheat will stand the wind's sharp tooth, and cap those dry beneath that roof. Flax, the gold of maiden's hair, outlasts 'em all, I dare declare."

A pounding sound caught Norbin's ear—he looked down to see Harton Barth running up the hill path. His little eyes strained wide in his large sweaty face and his good silk shirt was dark with dirt.

"Norbin! Norbin!"

In a flash the young thatcher was making his way down the ladder. He glanced back up. "Stay put, Smoke!"

Claylor ran over and caught the magistrate's arm as he sagged, panting.

"What is it, Mr. Barth?" Norbin asked.

"My—the carriage—accident..."

"Your coach crashed?"

Barth could only nod.

"Where? Where?"

Barth pointed through the orchard. "In the grove. My driver, he's pinned!"

"Damn! Come, Claylor!"

Barth folded to his knees, holding the ladder for support as the two laborers sprinted down the hill, along the path through the orchard to the woods beyond. Harton waited, caught his breath then looked up to where the cat sat obediently, watching after her companion.

$$\mathcal{C} \quad \mathcal{C} \quad \mathcal{C}$$

"There!" Claylor pointed.

The vehicle lay on its side; the horse grazed nearby. The driver was sprawled face up in the road, apparently having pulled himself free. Norbin knelt by the man and put a hand on his chest.

"Speak, man, are you well?"

"I think nothin's broke. My head has some hurt to it though."

"Where did it land on ya?"

"Ohhh, here 'bouts." The man pointed ambiguously—Norbin couldn't tell if he meant his side or back. There was no blood.

Claylor went over to the wagon and examined it briefly. There appeared to be no damage. "What caused it to tip?" he called over. "I see no rock or ditch."

Norbin checked the driver for shattered limbs, then joined Claylor. He noticed an indentation in the road alongside the carriage; it appeared as if a pole of sorts had been placed there to lever the craft over.

"It's a bloody hoax!" Without another word Norbin was off and running down the wooded track, his heart enraged. He saw the orchard now—gnarled trees, waxy dark leaves and gravity-tempted produce. Beyond that the high stone house perched upon a hill—there was a man on the roof.

"Barth! Harton Barth!"

"Oh blast!" Barth growled. The cat squirmed in his hands, talons snared in his sleeve. "You little monster—I'll have your life!"

He jerked the beast loose of his garment and made to toss it over the edge. Smoke twisted violently and broke free, darting swiftly across the thatch. Barth scrabbled after her.

A furious beating of feet carried Norbin up the hill—to the ladder at last! By the time Claylor arrived, and the driver behind him, Norbin was on the roof, a cat-like figure himself in a fierce lanky pose. Barth had chased Smoke to the corner of the roof where there was no refuge.

"Barth, if you touch that animal I will kill you," Norbin hissed.

"Restrain yourself, boy, I am an officer of the Kingdom; I am the law in this fetid little village. You risk much by threatening me."

"Get away from her, then."

"I'll not move till you back down."

Norbin's teeth were gritted, his breathing fast. "Right then, I'll back off, but you must move from there."

"As you wish."

Barth grinned with yellow lips. He started over, carefully.

Norbin took a step back. Another. Barth came within a few yards, then stood at arm's length from the thatcher.

"Keep going, Norbin..."

The ladder was just behind the young man. When he turned away to look down, so as to step onto it, Barth lunged at him, grabbing his throat with one hand. Norbin fought for balance and his charm tore from his neck, falling.

"Threaten me, will you? I'll show you!" Barth bellowed. His other hand swung glinting with the thatching knife.

The ladder kicked out from under Norbin's foot and he slid half off the slanted roof. He grasped at the layer of sod, fingers digging in until he had a grip on the securing ropes. The swipe of the knife passed over his head. One leg swung up, the foot grabbing, and Norbin propelled himself into Barth's bulk. The knife dropped—Norbin scooped it up and lunged, planting the blade in Barth's great belly.

Both men gasped. Norbin looked down to see the warm spread of melted poppies running across his hand. Harton Barth wobbled, his face a yellow grimace, before pitching off the roof—landing with a thud three stories below.

❧ ❧ ❧

Numbed with horror at what had transpired, Norbin sat on the edge of the straw-heaped wagon staring blankly at the ground. Smoke was curled in his lap, her chin propped on a trembling knee. Norbin never did consider fleeing. He had murdered. Barth's driver summoned the constables of the Town Guard, who arrived shortly.

Norbin stood dutifully as they approached. Smoke watched the strangers with wide eyes and looped her paws about the man's neck. The two burly men in long grey cloaks, with pistols and swords on their belts, inspected the scene. One confirmed that the body of Harton Barth was indeed lifeless while the other yanked Smoke away from Norbin and stuffed her into Claylor's arms. They saw to it that the thatcher's quick hands were securely bound behind his back.

As the guardsmen rode off with the prisoner shackled to the saddle of a spare mount, Smoke let out a mournful howl. The cry lodged in Norbin's heart like a wind trapped in a barrow.

❧ ❧ ❧

It was a small cluster of girls, their shawls heavy and wet on their heads. Cold rain drummed down from a low sky of Noovum shale. Through the gnarled orchard, its waste-fruit squishing like mud, up the hill they went. The large stone house leered down from the peak.

"There—" one girl cried, "it sits there still!"

They stood at the base of the new magistrate's home looking up at the small cat that sat on the flax roof like an effigy in wire and fur.

One of the girls, Claylor's sister, flipped open a wicker hamper that hung from an arm and pulled out several clumps of cheese. She took a few paces back and flung one up. The cheese smacked the wall of the house and splashed in a puddle below.

"Higher, higher!" a companion urged.

The girl squinted up determinedly into the rain and hurled another. This one landed on the roof but rolled off. The next attempt, executed with a grunt, was successful. Smoke glanced disinterestedly at the gift—she continued to gaze off into the misted distance. The girls tossed up several chunks of bread and watched a while longer.

"It's no use," the leader said at last.

They set off down the hill, looking back at the lone wet figure as it shrank distant.

It was like this each time. Claylor and some of the village girls had pledged to tend to the beast, had even attempted keeping her in their homes, but she always slipped away only to reappear on that roof. They never saw her take their food offerings and could only imagine that she lived off the birds and mice that made homes in the thatch. She never played, nor strayed from that spot. She simply sat there looking sadly out across the orchard, waiting.

It was a grey frost-haunted Noovum morning when they found Smoke lying on her side on the thatch, stiff, her bedraggled grey fur infested with ice. Eyes of dull amber faced the west. Claylor buried her in the orchard.

Word of the cat's death spread through the village, for its vigil had not gone unnoticed. For months they had seen her. The locals were so taken, never before having witnessed such loyalty in a cat, that they felt compelled to commemorate it in some fashion. The village metalsmith was called upon to make a weathervane. The magistrate who replaced Harton Barth, being a man of softer spirit, agreed to let them erect the memorial. It was not long before the stories began.

The weathervane spun twice through the textured chase of the seasons. Local lore maintained that Smoke's soul had remained up on that roof, within the black metal image of a leaping cat. They claimed that passersby could hear mournful wails echoing out through the orchard when the weathervane turned to the west...

TWO

It was decided—the challenge would be met. The girl lay down her basket
of bramble goods and gathered high the white of her skirt. With careful steps,
like a fawn on ice, she entered the moat of the fortweed's vines.

Lorice had followed the brambled lane south, down to where the River
Grynn toiled over moss-heavied stones and wound through the cool green
shade of the wild wood. She had wandered along the banks, deep into the
closing flora.

The smell was noticed first—a sweet whisper of a scent; she followed it
down a ferned embankment, under low oak boughs and into a small glade. The
fortweed stood in the center, its great green bloom atop a high thorn-fanged
spire. Gnarled green capillaries spilled away from the base of the stalk, the
thickest of these curving upwards like tusks and capped with plum-like fruit.

Lorice took extreme care in maneuvering through the encircling vines,
for those sporadic bulbs could burst if nudged, spewing clouds of an
iodine-dark substance known to sting horribly and stain clothing; the reek
of its vile odor could last days. But that one green blossom was worth a bit
of risk, for the petals were a treat beyond compare—whether boiled into a
tea, candied and stored or eaten fresh—the flower of the fortweed was a
true Gusstar treasure.

Lorice was a creature of grace, going through her slow movements as if
enacting a solemn ritual dance. Her fine neck moved this way and that as
though the dark sliding hair adjusted her balance. Her brown eyes were
calm, her concentration deep. Her charms were wasted on the surrounding
trees—the bare legs reaching out from under the bunched skirt, the breasts
pouting up from a tight violet corset.

She was a strange blend of things—her face almost too refined for a
country girl, the eyes somewhat exotic, wide-spaced and almond-long. Her
lips were full and bowed, the nose less sophisticated in cast. The overall
shape of the face was elegant, the hair swept back from her forehead—
smooth across bare shoulders, deep brown and glossy as horse chestnut.

The smell of recently burst guard-fruit came to Lorice as she got nearer the tall woody stalk. It was the stench of vinegar and death. Perhaps some unfortunate groveling badger or a bird had triggered one of the things.

A dark tendril hissed beneath the sprawl of globes and vines—Lorice froze, one pale foot trapped in mid-air, the other planted between two of the ominous spheres. She held her breath, nearly dropping her long skirt, for instinct urged her to fling out her arms for balance. She looked down and saw the dark squirm of an adder slipping off through the tangles and grass.

The succulent green flower beckoned with its glad perfume. A few more steps. Well placed feet, steady breath. One hand let the skirt lower some then extended toward the prize. Lorice smiled.

"You are mine!" she gasped, plucking the thing.

Lorice pressed her nose into the petals and inhaled before tucking the tail of the bloom in her cleavage and scanning the wide pool of vines. There appeared, from this angle, to be a quicker route out than that which she had taken in. She made her way around the bare stalk, moving toward a dense bed of ferns. The smell of the ruptured fruit grew thick.

Lorice screamed as a dark hand rose out of the ferns and groped at her ankles. She jerked away, bumping one of the bulbs, which hit the ground with a pop, the dark ink breaking across the vines.

The hand retreated. Lorice had not, until this instant, noticed the dark thing lying half in the ferns, half in the fortweed vines. A low groan issued from the wavering bracken.

Were it not for the treacherous expanse of vegetation behind her, Lorice might have hastened away at that moment, never to hear the voice of the man.

"Help…"

The girl eyed the dark mass more carefully, saw the legs outstretched, an arm, long dirty hair and a face made horrid with blood and the ink of the fortweed.

"Please, help me. I am blind."

Lorice was doubly cautious in approaching, mindful of the possibility that this man might mean to trick her. "Who are you?"

The man's voice was weak and strained with pain. "I am a traveler. I have suffered a wretched accident in my carriage. My sight is now gone."

"Oh my, how dreadful!" Lorice reached him. She knelt and put a hand on his shoulder. "Lie still. I'll summon my father."

His face, hands and clothes reeked darkly with the dreaded juice—his face was bloated from the stinging properties. There were cuts both fresh and dried about his face. His eyes were raw-looking cups. Somehow he managed to smile.

☿ ☿ ☿

The injured man was taken to the inn which Lorice's father operated. He was washed up and dressed in a clean-smelling sleeping shirt. A tangy poultice was applied to the scratches on his face and limbs. The deep-voiced father saw to it that the servant woman and his own eager-tongued daughter did not hammer the "poor fellow" with questions until he was comfortably roomed and fed.

The man, having devoured the two plates-full of offered food, now sat pillow-propped in a bed as the innkeeper and Lorice knocked and entered.

"How do you feel, young man?" the father asked, sitting in a chair close by.

"Immeasurably better. I am much obliged by your kindness."

"Good, good. I am Carlton, my daughter Lorice is here as well."

"Ahhh—I am ever so grateful to you, miss. I might've lain there forever had you not found me."

Lorice smiled. "A fortunate accident." She leaned close to examine his face—he caught a whiff of the perfume the fortweed flower had left on her bosom. "The swelling from the plant-spew seems to have gone down quite a bit."

Carlton said, "Tell us your unfortunate tale, sir, and I've yet to catch your name..."

The man gave an ironic smile. "I'd like to accommodate your wish with exactness, yet I fear I am deeply confused by my ordeal and can scarce recall my own title. I am Kamb, I know that much, but my second name, and much more, are sadly lost."

"You have had a poor time of it, haven't you?"

143

The man sighed. "True."

"You say you lost your eyes in a carriage misfortune, yet they look to be rather, well, long-healed."

"Yes. I failed to mention that this wreck was not so terribly recent—I can not say for sure, again due to the jumbling of my thoughts, how long I have been wandering sightlessly in that wood. It could have been days ago, or even weeks. It's not clear to me."

"Were there others in the vehicle, Kamb?"

"I think not. I was traveling to see a distant relation, I faintly recall, and the horse spooked…there was a great rocky drop—the carriage smashed, my eyes with it. I wandered, eating berries, lost, until Lorice came upon me."

Lorice's voice was close and soft. "A horrid ordeal."

"I'm fortunate I did not fare worse. I wish I could tell you more, kindly hosts, but my head is in haze."

Carlton patted his arm. "Don't concern yourself. You're safe now. Perhaps this relation of yours will be searching these parts for you. You may stay here and heal. No doubt some relaxation will bring you out of this state of forgetfulness."

"I hope so. How may I thank you? I am a lucky one to have been happened upon by people of good heart. Thank you."

Carlton stood. "Come, Lorice, we'll let Kamb rest."

"Right. Goodnight, Kamb, sleep well."

"I shall, I'm sure."

He waited until he heard them fade down the hall. He felt the darkness of the room. Slowly he rose from the bed, following summer-night scents to the window. He leaned out, listening. It came faintly on the western wind— the mournful wail of a distant cat.

Lorice followed the sound to the door of the blind man's room. It was a country dance tune, a whimsically trotting piece, flawlessly delivered on a tin whistle. She knocked.

"Come."

She peeked in. "Good morning, Kamb. I heard you playing—it was lovely."

He bowed. He sat in a stiff wooden chair by the window. His hair, having been cleaned, hung wavy and straw-hued. His face, she realized now, but for the scary spaces where eyes once dwelt, had a good deal of charm to it.

"Come in and lend me your company."

"All right, but briefly, for I have tasks to do about the inn."

"I must ask you something."

"What?"

"Is this town Kilmnook?"

"No, this is Shropegrove; Kilmnook is across the river, some miles North."

"I see." The lightness swept from his face and he seemed to be in thought, though it was difficult to tell with no eyes to read.

"Why do you ask? Was Kilmnook your destination?"

"Oh, no, no—I thought I heard someone say something about Kilmnook. I have been there before, I'm almost certain. A pleasant enough place."

"Owww!"

"Careful," Lorice cautioned.

Kamb sucked at the pricked finger.

They were standing at a tall drystone wall, its solemn grey festooned with a vigorous webbing of prickly brambles. Plump berries yielded to their juice-bruised fingers. A wicker hamper grew heavy.

"I smell wheat," Kamb said.

"There's a field very close to here. Your nose is keen."

"It gets plenty of exercise."

She chuckled. "You gather well, considering."

"Do I? Such a clever fellow I am." He laughed.

"Oh, you are that, I've no doubt. Perhaps you're some fancy Kingdom-man of wealth and you don't remember."

"You tease me."

"Yes." Giggles. "Would you prefer I pity you? Treat you like a pathetic thing?"

"No. I'm pleased that you don't patronize me. You're a spirited one. Saucy at times, I dare say."

He knew she was smiling now.

"Saucy? Fine. You call me Saucy and I'll call you Cleverman—how's that?"

"Hmmm. Though I'm not sure I am worthy of so dignified a title, I'll accept, out of respect for you, of course."

Lorice stood with hands on hips, the lush brown of her hair falling sun-warm down bare shoulders. She held her fine breast high, challenging the grip of her corset—this out of instinct. Then it occurred to her that her charms were a waste on this one; the practiced coy of her eyes, the mirror-perfected smile and swoosh of hips all lost to his blackness.

"Lorice?"

"Yes?"

"I think we should make it formal—our new titles. There must be some ceremony of sorts. Come closer."

Lorice flushed. She hesitated. She approached, hands clasped behind her back, swinging her shoulders back and forth. "All right…"

"Are you facing me?"

She nodded. "Yes."

Kamb reached out and mashed a handful of blackberries in her face.

"Oh! You wretch!" She fell back, doubling in laughter. Upon recovering she made good her revenge—Kamb, quite happily, accepted his punishment. He had no choice of course, not being able to dodge the pelting fruit.

"I dub you Cleverman!"

The parlor at the inn was warm of wood and shadow-cozy. Ponderous roof-beams, steeped in the steam of many a hot meal, lent comfort to the nose. A cloaked woman sat by the great yawning fireplace, hunched over a harp, her flaming briar hair hanging where a face ought to have been. Pale spider hands spun tunes rich and ambery, and crisp as ice.

Carlton, his daughter and the blind man were tucked around a corner table over a meal of cider-baked ham and hot buttered goldies. There was talk and ale and laughter. Kamb wore a black wrap of cloth across his eyesockets, at Lorice's suggestion. He sensed her eyes on him more and more often.

Carlton's strong voice came. "Kamb, you grow morose…"

The young man flashed a smile. "Sorry, I was taken by a sadness."

"A memory? Your past returns to you, then?"

"Not so much in detail as in mood. It was a sadness without definition, more a feeling than an incident."

"Ahhh. What a shame to have lost your past."

"There are no strangers to the taste of loss. You've had your fill, no doubt."

"Aye. My missus. Gone just these three years. The Goat Plague got her."

"A plague? That should ring familiar to me."

Carlton sighed. "A terrible thing, lad."

Kamb heard the older man lean close, the voice lower.

"It's something of a mystery still. Happened east of here, not far from the coast. Seems there was this thin little boat goin' up river—not a soul on board, and no means of propulsion to be seen—"

"Against the current, you say?"

"Aye, without oars or sail. It was an eerie sight from what I've heard. There was a pile of hay on it, all stuck with gnarly branches, and three poles poking up from it, each with a goat skull on top."

Kamb ran his fingers absently over the surface of the table, which was nicked rough by forks and knives.

"The boat reached an inlet at Brinker's Down. Some fishermen watched it floatin' along through the mist until it came to the shore. They dragged it up and went digging in the pile of hay. All they found was a bloated, blackened corpse, laid out there with those three poles stuck in his belly, and them grinning goat skulls atop."

Lorice stared into her ale.

"They buried the dead man and burned the boat. A few days later, though, the fishermen took ill—from fever to fits to frothing like the mad.

They'd caught something from that boat—the body. Then they suffered a horrible swelling, and their flesh went black. In the end they got too stiff to move from their beds, that is until the full moon night. Then, much to every-one's surprise, they rose up and danced wildly until—"

Carlton smacked his palms together.

"They popped!"

Lorice flinched. "Father, please..."

"Popped?" Kamb acted horrified.

"They burst. Exploded. I saw it myself, many a time. The plague spread far, across the whole of the Kingdom. My poor dear wife, she went that way." Carlton gulped ale. "Then it just stopped; the plague was done."

"I'm sorry to have inspired this talk, sir," Kamb said.

"Bah! Spare yourself the guilt, lad. The Plague did its dirty business, that's a fact. Our speaking of it makes no difference."

"But I've stirred painful memories—"

Lorice spoke up. "Kamb, your loss of memory may be a blessing, as well as a curse; the painful things in your past need not be retained. You are spared the ache of missing someone."

Kamb was silent for a moment. "But I have likely lost beautiful things, as well."

"No doubt. Still, it is as if you have a second chance, to start a new life of happiness—"

"A life in darkness. Already I forget what things look like."

Lorice nodded.

A generous spread of shade offered refuge from the afternoon sun. They sat in high grass, propped against trees on the banks of the River Grynn. Such picnics were becoming a weekly tradition for Lorice and Kamb. There was plump cheese, raisin-flecked honey cakes, loud apples, tart wine, and the drowning giggles of the water behind them.

Having eaten their fill, they were content to stretch out in the grass and listen to the birds. There was the hum of fat bees daring the spines of thistle.

The river gurgled rhythmically over mossy stones.

After a time Kamb rose and poked about with his walking stick. He stepped cautiously onto the stones which formed a broken bridge across the rushing water.

"Kamb! Be careful!"

"Whoa! You'll make a damp one of me for sure, startling me like that, wench!" the man scolded good humouredly.

"Get back here then, you frighten me."

"This river goes north, you told me, yes?"

"Yes, north. Get back here!"

"Toward Kilmnook. Kilmnook being across the river and north. Right?"

"Yes, yes—what's it matter? Kamb, please, you'll fall in."

"Nonsense." With admirable grace he traversed several of the stepping stones, feigning a wobble on the last. "Wooooo!"

"Kamb!"

He hopped onto the shore. "Ahh, there we are!"

"Oh, aren't we the clever one?"

"Cleverman, at your service." He bowed.

"Don't try that again—the Grynn is not so tame as it seems. The water is deep and fast."

"No need to fret, Lorice, I'm not so helpless as you think."

"I know you're not helpless. Come, sit with me and have some more wine."

The contents of the bottle, like the sun, dropped lower. They were shoulder to shoulder at the base of a well-spread oak. Breezes soft and heather-warm made swiftly through the wood.

"Kamb, are you fond of me?"

He chuckled. "Of course."

"How so?"

"Well, there's such vigor to your sprit, how could I not be fond of you?"

"That's strange—I've never heard a man speak of my spirit."

"Your spirit is all I can see. I dare say it's lovely."

Lorice laughed. "But am I not barbed—my father says my mouth is filled with thorns."

149

"Thorns aren't proof of malice—thorns guard flowers. Your heart is good."

"Then it doesn't matter how I look? I might be hideous for all you know."

"Correct. But you're not, are you? You're as lovely as you sound. I've heard them at the inn, admiring you."

"I wish you could see me."

"It's not so important. Many an ugly soul bears a beautiful mask. I can't be fooled by masks now."

Kamb heard the hiss of a skirt across grass as Lorice stood up.

"Leaving?"

"No. I have a divining charm."

Lorice had several twigs from an apple tree clenched in her left hand. She spun three times sunwise, saying, "Four sprigs to the west—tell the one that I'll love best!"

She tossed the twigs over her shoulder then turned to see what initial they spelled. She frowned. The sprigs lay in the shape of an N.

"Well, what does it say?" Kamb asked.

"It's a K."

"Is it? How intriguing." Kamb grinned.

He heard rustling again and he could tell she was near him. She knelt and her breath was wine. Her voice a warm breeze in his ear...

"Kamb, you can't see me, but there are other things. There's taste and smell, and touch. You may feel me if you like. Hold out your hands."

Slow fingers bridged the air between them, closing softly on the offering. They were plump and soft as mushrooms—thermal—capped with pliant acorns. Kamb's hands slid gently across her smooth terrain, relishing the belly's warm curve, drinking the heat of her throat, up to cup her face, to trace the fullness of her lips. He leaned forward and tasted these.

Lorice leaned him back against the tree and lifted her leg over his thighs so that she rested upon his lap. She unfastened his shirt and pressed her torso to his chest. His hands played through her thick hair and followed the pour of her back—down to the small—out across the flare of hips—behind to where resilient mounds spread across his thighs.

The River Grynn chuckled at their oblivious delight—the dying sun's cider glaze moist on their desperate rhythms. Their bellies clapped, their breath entwined and their sweat shone like dew on the grass.

THREE

It was a profound hush which fell over the inn parlor—as if the air itself was sucked from the room. Three sturdy men of impressive height strode in, black boots loud on the worn wood floor, their long grey capes asway. They all wore grey uniforms, and swords; the leader had a long pistol on his hip, and one of the others carried a cruel-looking blunderbuss. They made for a center table and sat.

Carlton watched from the bar. Lorice stood close and whispered, "What's this?"

"Wardens."

The captain was a serious man with strong features, combed-back blond hair, trim mustache and beard. The rifleman was wide and less refined, hot-eyed, his scowl beset with the wildest, reddest of beards. The third officer was the youngest, his manner calm, yet alert. He motioned to the bar.

Carlton approached. "Good evening, gentlemen, what might you be havin'?"

"A pitcher of mead to soothe our dusty tongues," the young one said.

"Very good. Right fast." Carlton nodded and was off. He came back momentarily with a crowded tray and passed out pewter mugs.

The captain motioned at a spare seat. "Join us, sir, drink."

Carlton smiled. "Thank you." He turned to the bar and gestured for another mug.

The captain wore a silvery chestplate beneath his cloak, the others wore thick leather vests, thonged tight in front. The two of lesser rank had wide-brimmed grey hats.

"I can see from your arms that you are about some serious business," Carlton said. "Fine weapons."

"Indeed." The captain seemed proud. He pulled his wheel-lock pistol free and displayed it. The barrel was thick, octagonal, the stock-handle made of smooth pearwood. The mechanism was iron; the other side bore the ivory inlay of a sprinting vixen.

"A handsome gun," Carlton remarked, truly impressed.

"I am Captain Bromly of Naughtford Prison. Perhaps you could help us."

Lorice floated past and went about cleaning the mess from a nearby table. She was within earshot and prolonged her work so as to hear their conversation. The rest of the rooms' occupants returned to talking softly amongst themselves.

"We are searching the villages in this vicinity for an escaped murderer named Norbin Millson. He escaped six weeks ago. This is your inn?"

"Yes…"

"Then you must encounter many a traveler; perhaps you have seen him. He is young, blondish, clean-shaved, and, most notably, blind."

Carlton all but choked on his mead. He gulped, cleared his voice. "What did this fellow do?"

"Two years ago he killed a man named Harton Barth who was the magistrate of Kilmnook."

"Ahhh, yes, I remember that."

"Witnesses claimed he was defending himself, so he was spared the rope—still, his eyes were put out and he was jailed for life—until his escape."

"How could one without eyes escape a place so, so well attended as Naughtford Prison?"

The man with the blunderbuss chuckled. "He's like a fox, he is. A clever one."

The captain's pride wavered briefly. "He probably had help from inside. Regardless, he is roving about these parts and we are out to fetch him."

Carlton nodded thoughtfully. He had taken no notice of Lorice's swift departure.

Lorice pounded up the stairs, her heart thrashing like wings of ice. She slapped a palm against his door and hissed, "Kamb!"

When no answer came she threw the door wide. The room was dark. A sweet smell radiated from the bed; she groped toward it until her fingers took up the soft green blossom of a fortweed plant. He was gone.

ৎ   ৎ   ৎ

Such a forlorn sound that rode the wind. That lonely call which had urged him from his cell. How it had beckoned, haunted the empty barrow-chambers of his heart all those long months. Little Smoke was waiting for him still.

Norbin pushed panting through the clawing branches, tripping where roots writhed high, snapping twigs, stumbling on rocks. His face was clawed, as when Lorice had found him.

Heartache swelled and tears blurred in the blood upon his cheeks. The night before, when Lorice lay against him, curled warm in his bed, he had decided it was time to go. Too much time had passed, he had let himself fall in love. He feared that if he did not leave soon he would never do so, and Smoke would be left on that roof, waiting forever.

"I'm coming, Smoke," he said, "don't cry—please!"

Guilt knotted his guts. How he had lied to them—the story about the carriage crash, pretending not to recall his past. But what else could he have done, told them he was an escaped killer? What then? If only he could have left Lorice a note of explanation and apology. He wished he had at least said goodbye, and considered returning to do so. No—he had to get to Smoke.

ৎ   ৎ   ৎ

A leathery carcass of a man hobbled over to the table where the three wardens sat. He reeked of drink, and gripped the table to support his precarious bones.

"'Scuse me, lads, but I overheard ya talkin' there."

"Yes?" The captain eyed him.

"That dastardly man you speak of? I jest seen a man, meets that 'scription you give."

"Where?"

"On the road headed, ohhh, north it was, yes, north, toward River Grynn."

153

The table rocked as the three tall wardens shot up.

"The Grynn leads to Kilmnook," the youngest of the three noted, "perhaps he is headed there, having stashed money before his arrest."

"Right. You go on ahead there. We'll check these parts."

The burly red-head snatched up his awful blunderbuss and they whisked out the door.

Lorice stepped from the shadows. What was she to do? Surely Kamb was no monster. She thought she must find him and warn him. She knew short cuts, she would head off the wardens.

She rushed outside as they were mounting their solemn steeds and ran off down the road, clutching the green flower to her chest.

Carlton came out into the street and waved to the men.

"Captain Bromly!"

The officer navigated his beast over. "Quickly, sir, we must be off."

"I know the man you speak of—he has been staying here! He claimed he was injured, that he had nearly no recollection of his past—but it must be him, it must be!"

Bromly dismounted. He pulled his pistol out once more. "My man here will ride on toward the river. I shall search the premises, the stable as well."

His legs grew tired, his palms were numb-stung from catching his falls. Norbin could hear the water now, the river was close. The gurgling sound drowned out the windy cries of the cat. He paused. Had he heard something snapping through the wood behind him?

The man with the wide brimmed hat and the mad red beard bounced in his saddle as his horse cantered along the dusky road. The wood spread deep before him, down the trail through the dense smell of ferns. The gaping mouth of the blunderbuss pointed ahead and he swatted low-hanging branches aside with the thing.

Hooves pounded, crunching acorns like tiny skulls. The horse's eyes were wide, like its rider's its breath untamed. The warden reined the horse in and turned in his saddle, bringing the gun up to aim.

There! Motion beyond those trees! Something white flitted, but the shadows were deep and the dusk had settled and he could not be sure. He heard the crack of branch under foot. Yes—there, he saw it now, a person heading down a steep brush-dense embankment.

"Halt!" the warden shouted.

Lorice shrieked, "Don't fire! Wait!"

The man gasped, startled at how close he had come to shooting an innocent girl. He lowered the awful gun.

   ℭ   ℭ   ℭ

Dawn spread mistily through the stillness of the orchard. The young warden urged his horse up the hill toward the high stone house with the thatched roof and the curious cat-shaped weathervane. He had been through most of Kilmnook before reaching here, and as yet had not found anyone who had seen Norbin Millson.

He was a good twenty yards from the magistrate's house when he heard a woman screaming. He heeled his horse to action and as he approached, observed a young woman in servant garb as she burst out the front door.

His sword was drawn before his boots hit earth. He ran to her.

"What is it, miss?"

"A strange man has invaded the house!"

Metal squeaked, the warden glanced up as the weathervane turned.

"And me all alone, the magistrate off on a visit, and that terrible blind man…" the woman babbled.

"Blind man? With straw-colored hair?"

"Yes! Yes—he's in there now! He came to the door asking for water, so I opened it. He pushed in, right by me and made up the stairs. He's locked himself in the uppermost chamber!"

"Show me the room."

The woman shook violently as she led the warden through a hall and up the flights of stairs to the third floor. She pointed to a door.

"There—he's locked himself in there!"

"Sshhh. Stand away…"

The man held his blade at ready and gave the door a healthy kick. The wood swung in, the man leaping sword first.

The room was filled with morning light which spilled warmly through an open window. There was no man to be seen.

"I fear you are mistaken, miss. Perhaps he has moved to another room."

"That can't be—the door was bolted from inside."

The warden looked at the door, the bolt mount torn half off by his charge. He nodded slowly.

They proceeded to search the rest of the large building, but there was no sign of Norbin Millson, or any other sightless fellow, for that matter. It was not until they headed back outside and stood in front of the house that he was to be seen.

Two horses rode up the hill, the first carrying Captain Bromly and a dark-haired girl in a white dress. The other horse had the blunderbuss-toting warden in its saddle and a limp man draped behind that, his clothing and hair soaking wet.

"That's him! That's the man I told you broke into the place!" the histrionic servant raved. "That's the very same man!

The horses stopped. Captain Bromly dismounted and helped his weeping passenger down. He addressed the young officer.

"What goes on here?"

"This woman claims a blind man forced his way into the house and caused some havoc."

The woman knelt to look at the slumped man's face. "Yes, I'm sure, it's he!"

"Impossible," the captain stated frankly, "this man has been dead for hours. Apparently he drowned while trying to cross the river."

Lorice heard something creak up on the roof and turned to look. The cat-shaped weathervane was gone.

Radley Birchcroft's Decapitation

One night Radley Birchcroft, his belly full of pub-cheer, staggered across the farm fields toward home. He was a stout, unattractive fellow, hard working by day, hard drinking by night. The cabbages he had labored so to rear now proved treacherous obstacles, stretching off in erratic rows like leafy skulls.

By some nasty whim of gravity and timing, the man tripped over a head of cabbage and fell neck-first on the scythe he had carelessly left lying in the field the previous afternoon. Radley's head was cut off.

"Oh, that's bloody lovely," the head remarked sourly. It lay amongst the cabbages and the smell of dewed earth. "I'm dead."

A soft voice came, as if a breeze, to the ears of the severed head. It whispered, "Not quite dead, Radley…you're dying."

"Dying? I'm bloody dead! Can't you see me bleedin' cork's been popped?"

"These are your final seconds, my friend; your perceptions are altered because you are near the edge. The final seconds seem much longer," the voice said in a mild, almost soothing tone.

Radley's head squinted up at the stranger, who had come within visual range. He was a mournful-looking boy, naked, gaunt, with damp black hair and skin as grey as slate. Two blood-red rose blossoms filled the ghastly hollows where there should have been eyes. He sat down atop a plump cabbage.

"Who are you?" Radley asked.

"Death."

"Argh!"

"Don't be frightened."

"I'm not," Radley snapped, "a blasted beetle just crawled up me nose!"

The boy grinned.

"Oh, sit there and smirk. I'm to spend me last long seconds with some scratchy pest in me snout and you're amused!"

"Sorry," Death said.

"Oh, I'm sure! I bet you're just bushel-full of remorse."

"There's no cause to be coarse, friend. I'm not such a bad sort."

Radley's eyes widened. "Oh, no? You're Death!"

"I'm merely doing my job."

"Well, you're not doing it quick enough—this bug in me nose is—"

Radley sneezed.

"There! Take that!" the head said triumphantly.

"Really, Radley, I'm not such a nasty fellow," the boy said. "A garden must be weeded, you know."

Radley tried to nod.

"Garden, right! And speakin' of gardens, would it be possible to, er, work out some sort of deal? I mean, the poor old woman what employs me, she'll be lost without 'er old Radley to tend the fields an' all..."

The slender grey figure of the boy rose, walked over and squatted by the head. He stroked the cooling cheek. "Strange how much compassion desperation can inspire," the boy noted.

"What would you be meaning by that?"

"You're suddenly concerned about a woman you usually refer to in terms that are most colorful, in an unpleasant sort of way."

"Oh come now, I love the old hag."

Death chuckled. "Well then, seeing as we're both in a generous mood, perhaps we could come to some form of arrangement."

Radley smiled. Death thought a moment before speaking again.

"I've got it!" Death announced, the rose petals in his skull fluttering gently, a red strata of blinking lids. "You know of Everblossom Larchstaff who lives across the fields?"

"I do," Radley replied distastefully. "The blind spinster. A lucky thing she's blind too, if you don't mind me sayin', for she'd off herself for sure if ever she saw a mirror. Poor creature has a face makes a cow's hind end look pretty."

"Well," the boy said, "I came dreadfully close to paying her a visit just recently. It seems she did try to put an end to herself...but the rope broke."

"Oh. I didn't know that. What, if you don't mind me askin', was her reason?"

Death sighed. "She can hardly go on living, never having known a man's touch."

"I can't see what man would want to touch the likes of her. What man would want a blind, ugly, goat-breathed ox-bodied woman like that?"

Death looked down at Radley and wiggled his eyebrows.

Radley grimaced. "Ohhh, no!"

"Now, Radley…"

"Let me die."

"Come now, Radley, just once?"

"Eternal sleep, please."

"Radley?"

"Have pity. Is there nothing else I can do?"

Death loosed a long sigh. "Your time is running out, Radley."

"What do you care about her anyway?"

"Just because I am Death doesn't mean I'm heartless. I'll feel rather guilty if she swings herself from a rafter. I'll let you in on a bit of a secret. Do you recall when you were a young boy and you were stomped by that horse?"

"Mm hm…"

"Well, I let you off that time. I felt bad for you."

Radley squinted. "You did?"

Death nodded, staring down with his dew-teared blooms.

Radley mumbled, "Just once, you say? I don't have to marry her? Just a tumble?"

"Just a tumble, Radley, so that the poor thing doesn't have to go to her grave a virgin."

"All right, then, I'll do it, but I get to live, right?"

Death smiled. "Right."

With that the boy rose and strode half a field away, his slim grey body fading into the black night air.

Radley called after the figure, "Wait! Death! *What about my body?* You forgot to put me back on me body!"

❧ ❧ ❧

Having donned a change of crisp unbloodied garb, Radley set out across the fields to the home of the blind spinster, his head tucked under his right arm and a basket full of cabbage swinging from his left. Everblossom Larchstaff dwelt in a modest cottage, a lonely thing of stone behind its crippled fence. Herbs grew in a scented moat that spoke to the dark with fennel and sage and mint.

Radley, with hesitant steps, passed through the fence and the herbs and stood outside the wooden door. The windows of the house were black as soot—no candle glowed within, though night was young. The man put down his basket and mustered the courage to knock.

There were sounds behind the door and a stench when it opened as the owner's breath fumed its fetid greeting.

"Hallo? Who knocks?"

"'Tis I, Miss Larchstaff, Radley Birchcroft…"

"Ahh, Widow Crumpton's field-man! And what brings you here?"

"The widow sent me to give you a basket of cabbage."

"How very nice! Will you come in? It's not often I have visitors, you know, and the summer grows old and the night has a dampness—you might catch your death!"

"The thought's crossed me mind," Radley muttered.

"What's that?"

"I said, you're terribly kind."

It was dark inside, but the widow found an old rushlight and lit it and urged Radley to build a fire that they might have warmth. The man's head rested on a chair as his body layered the logs and kindling. Soon there was flame and the spinster brought fennel seed tea. Radley's body sat, head in lap, the head making slurping noises so that the woman would think he was drinking, though he dared not try, lest the liquid pour out his neck.

"Were you always blind?" Radley asked.

"Oh, no, I had sight as a girl," Everblossom said, half-sadly, half-smiling,

160

her eyes like smoke. "I caused the blindness."

"On purpose?"

"Oh, no, no! Through foolhardiness. I was an ugly thing as a girl, truth be told, and eager for anything that might correct the situation. Well, my cousin told me there was a rare type of spider, in a wood beyond the fields, which, if eaten, could turn the ugliest face beautiful. Well, didn't I go to the wood and seek the spider. But, as fate would have it, I could not quite recall if I was to find the black spider with the white spots, or the white spider with the black spots..."

"You ate the wrong one?"

"I did. Gobbled it down and trotted home to bed, hoping to wake with a face that men would fight for. As I lay in my sleep I was visited by an awful specter...a creature in a grey robe with a hollow hood, with silver bars in the hood, like the bars of a cell and three round eyes floating in the darkness behind them."

Radley shivered.

"It bent over me and I felt its cold breath snuff the very sight from my eyes."

Thump!

"Oww!"

The spinster cocked her head. "Radley?"

The head, which had slipped from its body's lap, spoke from the floor. "No cause for alarm. I stubbed me toe, is all."

"Ahh."

When the body bent to retrieve the head, its foot sent the thing rolling under the spinster's chair.

"Oh, it's so very nice to have company. I scarce recall the last time anyone came to visit. Was it Mrs. Drunning, or my cousin Neestin? I'm not sure, it's been so terribly long. Or was it the peddler selling mouse traps, or that traveler with the wooden leg?"

Radley had not noticed the dog before. It was a grizzly brindled hound, curled behind the woman's chair, watching him with one eye open and one eye closed. It growled.

"Here now, Bricker, what's this grumbling all about? That's no way to behave when we have a guest."

The woman reached down behind her and patted Radley on the head.

"That's a good boy."

Radley squinted.

"I so enjoy this, Mr. Birchcroft, sitting about a nice fire, with a good cup of tea and speaking of this and that," the woman chatted on.

The dog crawled closer to the severed head, poked its nose close and then, to Radley's muffled horror, began to lick his face. Radley's nose crinkled and itched and he tried not to sneeze.

"Such a treat this is! Tell me, Mr. Birchcroft, would I be terribly rude if I were to ask to touch your face? It's so rare that I have visitors and I do so enjoy feeling what people's faces are like. Would you mind terribly?"

Radley dared not speak; surely a blind woman would have keen ears and know that his voice was coming from beneath her very seat—where the dog was still drowning him with its tongue.

"Radley?"

"Ahh-chew!"

The spinster shrieked.

"Hah! A trick," Radley said quickly. "I can throw me voice."

The woman began to laugh. "Oh, my! You gave me a fright, but you are terribly clever, Mr. Birchcroft, very clever indeed. I'd have sworn you were just beneath me."

"Here, then, Miss, you sit still and I'll come over and you can have a grope at me face."

The body rose awkwardly and moved clear of the woman, circling behind her and scooping up the head, which it then held out to the elder hostess.

"Here's me mug, Miss—feel away."

The woman's hands trembled slightly, exploring, and Radley grimaced, being so near her foul breath and her face, which was quite ugly.

"A good nose, and strong jaw," the woman remarked favorably.

"Thanks, Miss. I'll just set and finish me tea, then."

Radley sighed and sat. He scrounged for courting words, feeling sick in the belly. "You know," he said, at last, "you're not so ugly a woman."

Silence.

"In fact," Radley said, "I find you a rather handsome woman."

"Oh my, Mr. Birchcroft! However could you say such a thing? I'm ugly something awful!"

"No—no, you're not. Why, I'd envy the man what could look beneath him and see you..." There, he said it!

The spinster blushed at that, and, impossibly, a look of lust flared in her white eyes.

"Why, my good Mr. Birchcroft, you need not envy, for I'd be ever so pleased if you were to...if you would care to lay upon me."

The woman's chair creaked as she stood. She stepped closer, arms out, her breath before her like some ghastly phantasm. Radley caught her by the wrists. He could not stand to be face to face with that stench—he would need to do something...

"Wait! There's one condition."

"Condition? What's that?" Everblossom asked.

"You mustn't touch my face whilst I'm upon you."

"And why is that?"

"Why, because of the rash."

"Rash? I felt no rash before."

"It wasn't there, yet; it only occurs when lust is in me blood. Oh, 'tis a dreadful thing, like coals b'neath the skin, and catchy too. I must cover me head."

The woman groaned a little and stepped back. "All right then, as you wish, Radley."

The man moved quickly. He set his head safely away, across the room on a picnic hamper, a safe distance from the spinster's horrid exhalations. His body took one of the cabbages and fashioned a cloth about it with rope and the rope about his shoulders so that it approximated a head, then he went to the bed where the woman waited, a great pale puddle of flesh.

Radley could hardly watch. The bed creaked, the spinster moaned and awful shadows played across the low ceiling. It seemed to take forever.

Finally the man's body shook and completed its dread task.

The blind woman laughed heartily, rocking with feverish enthusiasm. She pawed at the man's chest, and then reached for the sack that covered the cabbage, which rocked upon the body's shoulders.

"One kiss!" the woman exclaimed. "I must have one kiss!"

"No, no! The rash!" Radley cautioned desperately.

"I'll suffer the rash, for one good kiss!"

"No—wait!"

The spinster would not hear it. She tore away the cloth from the cabbage and pressed her lips to the leafy globe with such vigor that it fell to the floor with a thunk!

The woman's scream squeezed Radley's head like a fist of breaking glass and he watched, numb and helpless, as she gasped a fatal breath and collapsed, dead of fright.

"Nooo! Oh no! Blast it, I've killed her!" Radley wailed. "I'm ruined. I've spoiled it! I'm doomed! Doomed!"

The head closed its eyes and wept and only opened them when the smell of roses filled the room and Death stood before him, grey and gaunt and staring his flowery stare.

"Take me," the head blubbered, "take me, Death, I've killed her!"

"Take you? Why ever should I want to do that?"

"Because, because I failed."

"I beg to differ," Death said softly. "You did your part, Radley. She died knowing a man's touch, which is as much as she wanted, and so our bargain is complete."

Radley sniffled. "Complete, you say?"

"Yes, my friend. You kept your part of the deal, and so I shall keep mine. I give you life."

With that, the boy turned and faded through the wooden door, back into the ash-colored night.

Radley grinned for a moment, then frowned.

"Wait! Death! What about me body? Your forgot to put me back on me body!"

❧Autumn ❧

Seepburn

The cooling year yields skies clear-blue as well as evenings brisk. Blond begins to steal green leaves. Plump geese haunt the mist-calmed lakes. Baskets creak with the weight of apples, and cider presses drool sweet amber. Herbs, magical and culinary, are cut and hung to dry. The fruits of labor can now be held and eaten. The great celebratory rite of Balance-Tide brings villagers closer to each other and the land.

Oakbrown

Sunset echoes the foliage with its chill copper. How the days have shortened! The rushes rasp in ghost-fed breezes as seed-hungry finches chance the thistle's fangs. The bracken has gone gold and brown, the brambles heavy with plump berries. The days, warm as brewed barley, are etched with frost beneath a rusty moon. Eerie effigies are set about to honor the dead, who, as the year decays, are wont to roam the countryside.

Noovum

Time to gather firewood, time to gather peat. Cattle trudge to their slaughter; the winter stores are filled. Collect rushes to make candles, collect nuts and mushrooms too. Tree branches scratch bare against the sky's expanding grey. Pay close attention to those clouds—the first snow must be feared. The Winter Women will swoop down to cull the aged populace. The days weigh cold, so dress well—the nights are colder still.

Memories of Balance-Tide

I won't tell how many years sit between now and that bright Seepburn morn—but you can see, I've no doubt, that there're a good many. But I was not always this feeble-limbed thing, sitting here like a great wrinkled berry. I had my spry girlish days. Ahh, yes, I've retained them clear and well. I've no fierce regrets, and plenty a warm memory to keep me through the chill of a lonely night.

There were plenty of glad times, back in my village of Greenstone, the best of them at the celebrations. The festivals coiled like a chain through the year, linking us with each other and the land. My favorite of these was Balance-Tide, the time in mid-autumn when there was equal daylight and equal night. It was a time of merriment, for the fields were thick with corn and the gardens crowded with plump vegetables, the brambles mad with berries and birds. There were thanks to be given for the harvest.

But we were wary as well, for that day marked a change. After Balance-Tide the days would shrink to the lengthening nights. It would not be so long before the first teeth of frost bit, and after that would follow the long cold of winter. Provisions had to be made for the troubles ahead, be they the dreaded Winter Women or blizzards. Yes, it was a time to acknowledge both the bright and the dark.

My fondest recollections hearken back to such a time when I was just the age of eight. I can almost feel the air of that bright morn—something special about it. I shared a bed with my younger sisters, Breesil and Celly, who happened to be twins. We would lie there, whispering shared excitement, listening to our mother, who was already busy in the kitchen below. She had been up before the dawn, what with so much to do.

Brant, my brother, who was the eldest of the lot, poked in the door and taunted, "Up you lazies! There's baskets to fill!" We needed little prompting. We washed up, dressed quickly and were down the stairs.

Mother was bustling about, her warm voice humming, her apron like a blurred map of her tasks to that point. Her strong hands were pale with flour and her cheeks pouted plump when she smiled. "There's my girls," she said, "all bright and ready."

There was little time for a bulky breakfast—not that my eager innards would have carried it well—we placated ourselves with those small dark biscuits we knew as "treacle paws," smeared thick with amber apricot jam. Then we made off with our empty baskets swinging.

We spent the morning gathering nuts and butter-bright owl-eye mushrooms, and berries—such berries! The bramble vines were jeweled in red and purple, and they'd spurt at a pinch. Already the leaves along the hedge-runs were going blond. Behind us Grey Drown Pond was blurred gold with heather pollen, and the slopes beyond gorse-gold as well. At one point, it seemed, a squirrel was going to brave our acquaintance. But Celly, delighted by its quirky dance, laughed loudly and the poor fellow shot off.

The gathering, of course, was among the final preparations for our rural revels—the work had gone on for days. We had collected wildflowers, and bright leaves from which we fashioned wreaths. We knotted swags of fir with orange ribbon. Acorns had been strung, pine cones as well. The bounty of nature was to enrich our eyes, as well as our bellies.

Several days previous, my father and Brant had ridden into Westsheer to pay visit to the spiceman. They had returned with baskets creaking with exotic treasures like oranges and gory twigs of red root. There was strange ginger root, like great pale slugs—the meat of which was tart and alien. There were other spices as well, which had traveled the sea to reach our humble table—hard sweet licorice root and sticks of cinnamon. Such a feast of rich scents!

Midday found us home and in the kitchen. My uncle Mullum and his sons had arrived. The boys were out with Brant loading branches into the wagon while Father and Uncle Mull told bawdy jokes until Mother chased them out, clapping on their backs with her broom. She had kept her laughter in until it spilled loose as tears.

"Enough silliness," she said to herself and us, "there are still chores to do!"

Indeed there were, though I doubt "chore" was the appropriate choice of words. We enjoyed decking the place in leaves and flowers, and fragrant sticky pine branches. Breesil refused to handle the skulls, though. I placed a fine set of antlers over the parlor mantle and coiled it in ivy vines, singing away in my carefree youth.

The east side of the house was decorated with flowers and greens, chains of chestnuts and apples, to represent the warm half of the year. The western half of the house was all bare branches, animal skulls and chains of bone, autumn leaves to speak the cold and dark. All was joined at Balance-Tide.

Plates of nibble-foods were put out, also separated by their respective meanings. The berries and warm "goldies" cakes in the east, plates of nuts and pungent cheeses in the west.

Uncle Mull stole back in to sample the goods and lend us advice on the placement of our wreaths and things. He lifted Breesil up so that she could hang a goat horn over the parlor doorway. His great belly jostled when he laughed at her, for she held the horn to her head and mocked the voice of a goat. Breesil was fond of silly behavior, as was Uncle Mull, for that.

Father was about a business most serious, that being the creating of the Warm Keep. Each village has its own recipe for the stuff, and often it varied a bit, home to home. Balance-Tide was nothing without it. A great silver bowl, ringed with a garland of pine cones, was to be filled with a steaming punch of hearty ale and other rich ingredients—this as a precautionary potation meant to keep the blood warm through the coming cold months.

"The fruits of autumn, hot and steeped, through the winter warm you keep," was the toast most often used by those quaffing the brew.

Uncle Mullum joined Father to observe the process. Several quarts of cider and ale were simmered over pear logs in the parlor fire. Apples and sweet owl-eye mushrooms, speckled with cloves, were added, as were raisins, the flesh of an orange, almond dust, licorice shavings, ginger, nutmeg, cinnamon and twisty twigs of red root. Needless to say, the room was shortly filled with an ambrosial steam.

A spike, inside the center of the bowl, received one end of a log of sweet tree so that it stood, poking a foot or so out of the amber liquid. This added flavor, of course—and unbeknownst to myself, at that early age—represented something more, along the lines of fertility, if you catch my meaning.

Many of our festivals had meanings which were lost on our innocence and joy. What did we know, beyond revelry? Ahh, it didn't matter, I'll tell you. Balance-Tide was the first of the festivities that lead us through winter. It was proper that we had our rowdy spells to urge our spirits through the dark, bleak and cold, to sustain us, and distract us, if you will. They were lively times amidst the barren, strung with glad greenery, rich with drink, music, dance, song and laughter, frivolity and feasting. The feast was of great importance, for as Uncle Mull would declare, "If the stomach does not link one to the land, than nothing does."

The kitchen, it seemed, was the womb of such activities. A palace of goodly scents, from golden loaves of bread to the garden magic of beam-hung herbs. Heavy kettles crowded the wide fireplace, hanging from blackened trammels. We carried in potatoes and weighty chains of braided onion from the storehouse, while Mother set to stuffing the goose with apple bits and seasoned crumbs. The table was a clutter of utensils and foodstuffs. Occasionally she would pause, look about at all the mess, sigh, and sip from a glass of mulled ale.

Breesil stood by the fire stirring the apple stew, while Celly and I worked at the spiced pears. We greedily eyed the pies and cakes that were cooling off to one side.

We were all as hungry as one can be by the time the table was cleared and then again covered—this time with the feast proper! Our eyes were great and glassy things in the candlelight (Father had purchased expensive beeswax tapers for the occasion, to replace those smelly, smoky rush-lights). Mother ceremoniously presented the roasted goose, brimming with pride. Father remarked on the crisp brown of the skin and Uncle Mull was reduced to sighs. A knife cut slowly through its tender dark meat. Next came a plate loaded with pink slabs of clove-freckled boar-ham. There were sausages plump and slick and pigeon pie, its crust with a sheen like bronze. We consumed cheeses, berries, goat cakes, boiled vegetables— you've never seen such gluttony and indulgence! The family, gathered about that great splay of plenty, is a memory that warms me still.

Having filled our bellies, it was next expected that we extinguish all the lights and wait for the arrival of the spellwoman. The fires were left going, though, for it was common for the night of Balance-Tide to be chilly. A new anticipation took us. Uncle Mull grumbled his impatience, eager to try that aromatic Warm Keep. I heard him grunt at the urging of my mother's elbow.

Finally, as we sat there, wide-eyed in the darkness, we heard the jingling of bells from outside. It was the spellwoman! Four knocks at the door—Father let her and several children enter. The children were covered in strange costumes, one all fir branches from head to foot, one all crisp leaves, one in sheaths of straw. The spellwoman carried a torch and wore goldenrod strands and barley stalks in her long pour of treacle hair. Half her face was floured white; half was shadowed with ash. She went to the bowl of Warm Keep, said her ancient words and lit a candle that we'd placed upon the top of the sweet tree log which stood up from the liquid. The drink had been blessed.

The children accompanying the woman left us pieces of candied fruit from sacks that they carried, then they made off to their bell-strung mounts to head for the next house.

All gathered about the brimming silver bowl, and Father ladled his prized punch into mugs. It was a glorious brew!

It was well into the night by the time we rode our wagon into the village. A great wreath of branches had been erected. It stood as high as I did then, and its span was that of a small pond. We unloaded our contribution of collected boughs from the wagon. Half of the thing was all gnarled and bare of leaf, the other was the fullness of evergreen limbs. There were poles marking eight points; one held a stag skull, one was wreathed in flowers, others dangled fruit and crimson clusters of leaves.

A bonfire rose from the center of the branchy moat, itself ringed in stones. A team of musicians played merrily, the bubbly frolics of a sack-pipe blending with the fancy work of a bearded fiddler who bobbed about and tapped his feet. A woman played high and fast on a tin whistle and another pounded on a half-drum. There was singing and drinking. Men and boys propped spears on end and tossed apples at the tips, while girls tossed nuts in the fire, and made wishes. Then we all danced around the great circle, marking the turn of the seasons at the great celebration of Balance-Tide.

Ahh, such a time it was, those many years ago. Now here I sit, in my wrinkly raisin skin, too round to frolic, too tired for all that. And winter all too soon will come to nag within my bones. But I've got these memories still, you see, these memories to keep me warm, through the lonely night.

Recipes for Warm Keep

For the country folk of Westermead, the traditional protective punch known as Warm Keep is a vital part of the Balance-Tide holiday. The practice itself dates back to ancient times, or as an old southern-district song notes, "For as long as the gulls have had wings." Different localities have their own versions of the potent mixture, in terms of contents and ritual.

The journal of a spell man, written before the Kingdom established its rule over the tribal clans, recalls the Warm Keep as a deeply mystical potation. Though mainly comprised of warm fermented honey-mead and bits of roasted apple, some magical ingredients were added. These included rare stones, fox skulls and four drops each of blood from a virgin maiden and an old dead man.

Most villages use a silver bowl to hold the drink, while some use a large wooden bowl, or even a cooking cauldron. Ingredients vary in different parts of the island; often individual households add their own distinctive touches—some families are quite secretive about their recipes.

Whether you find yourself in Neebotten or Clyngsbrand, at the time of Balance-Tide, you will surely be treated to some of the brew that is drunk to keep the blood warm through the cruel cold of winter. In some parts it is appropriately referred to as "the good drink."

Recipe from Barrowloam

In a six-quart container mix:
One quart red wine
One quart cider
One palm's worth raisins
Four cored apples, stuck with cloves
One stick cinnamon

One cup sugar
Four pieces candied ginger root
One spoon powdered sweet bark
One cup heather honey

Mix all but sugar; warm over flame. Remove from heat; let it grow still. Stir in sugar. Drink!

Recipe from Shropegrove

Mix good ale and fresh-pressed cider in a large bowl, the proportions to preference. To this add:
Scraps of orange skin
Dust of the nutmeg
Pinch of powdered fortweed bloom
Four cinnamon sticks
Sugar in desired amount
Small pour of the treacle
Apricot pulp

Heat, but do not boil—let it steep and simmer. For luck, add a stone from an east-running stream. Drink!

While partaking of the Warm Keep, remember to use this toast: "The fruits of Autumn, hot and steeped, through the winter warm-blood keep!"

Spider Hill

Mr. Flax puffs on a pipe carved from the long yellow bone of a bull. He tips his cap to Widow Purdy as she sweeps dust out her door, coughing through the long hair that hangs across her face, hair the color of stone or wool. She grins at the old man, leans on her broom and looks him up and down.

"Headed to the village, then, and what may I ask for, dear old Mr. Flax?"

"I aim to get drunk, missus. It's what I do best."

The woman snorts and goes back to sweeping—ghosts of dust away from the broom.

"Good day then," says Flax, back on the dry autumn road.

"Mind the spiders," the widow calls.

Mr. Flax turns and squints. "Spiders!"

Again the broom rests. "Yes, spiders. Have you not noticed them?"

"Noticed 'em? Didn't I wake this very day to a plump black spider just a sitting on my nose and lookin' me up and down—much as you've been known to do."

The widow huffs and the hair over her face flutters like a cobweb.

"Good day," the man says.

🕷 🕷 🕷

Ciderbrook boasts the finest orchards in all of Westermead's Midlands, and this day the air drapes cool blue amongst the trees that rank crooked and dark, fruited, and waxy green where leaves spread shade. Gravity came in the night, like a ghostly old man, testing the twigs and the first fruit fell. Nags amongst the trees rejoice and bees bob about the soft, browning fruit. The air is sweet decay, drifting to the old man hobbling on the road.

"My," says Mr. Flax, stopping beneath a tree. "Such a spell of beauty you cast this day, dear lady."

Smoke goes up from his pipe like lies.

"Your eyes so dark, like chestnuts, and your hair fine as harvest corn. Were I but twenty years younger I would ride you all the day."

The horse looks up, blinks, bends back to its apple-munching.

"Good day," he chirps and hobbles on.

Old stones shape the tavern. The roof is steep thatch and phantoms drool from the chimney. Inside there's no one but the master's wife with her breasts like ten packed into two. Old man gravity threatens to drag down her bodice. A young man's heart flits once through Flax's chest and is gone as he squints at the round pallor of her flesh through the smoke of his bull-bone pipe.

"I'm parched from the dusty road, my dear," Flax says and smiles.

Mrs. Scrimly smiles—she's pretty but for the teeth, her hair a dream of summer breeze and furze.

"Good Mr. Flax, come sit and rest and I'll fetch you something nice."

Flax at a round table worn by warm elbows, stained by dark brews. "Surprise me, love," the man says.

The woman and her breasts are back and she pours from a pewter pitcher.

"A secret recipe," she whispers.

Mr. Flax makes short work of the drink—a spiced night-colored ale, a mystery of hops and cloves. Another please!

Half past afternoon. The crows have found their voices, the breeze has found the leaves, and Flax has found another drink—it stares up at him, glinting and brown like the eye of a horse. He sips, his eyes bulge, he spits out a mouthful of spider and ale.

"Bah!"

The drunken spider wobbles halfway across the table before Flax slaps a hand down on it.

"Ivy Scrimly!" Flax calls and the tavern mistress comes bouncing.

"Another so soon, Mr. Flax?"

"Another nevermore, I should think. Whilst I appreciate your adding this or that to these secret recipes of yours, I'm not so thirsty that I'll drink spiders!"

Red faced and apprehensively smiling bad teeth, the woman apologizes. "I'm terribly sorry, my good Mr. Flax. It's three times today they've been in my brew."

The woman swipes a hand through her hair; a spider drops and scurries across the table. She shrieks, leaps back and her floury breasts leap out of her bodice like great jiggling eyes.

Fate, or worse yet, some mischievous force with sly fingers that puppet the world, brings Mr. Scrimly in at this moment. He's a squarish man with large limbs, coarse features and slightly wintered hair. His eyes are too close, like a stoat's. His bulk moves faster than it should and before anyone can blink, or say, "bodice," he has Flax's throat in one hand and Ivy's in the other.

"Flax, you skinny rapscallion—I'll have your blood! And you, wench, have ya no shame?"

Mrs. Scrimly hastily stuffs herself back into her garment and rasps, "It's not what you think, Goordie…"

Fate, or better yet, some merciful puppeteer with strange threads to the world and its ways, sends a fourth figure bounding into the tavern. The blacksmith's son, breathless, with wide eyes the color of treacle-colored ale, stutters and mutters and stamps like a trick horse, pointing out the open door.

Goordie Scrimly barks, "What is it, boy?"

"Spiders," the boy manages, "up on Hag Hill…"

Scrimly releases his wife and the skinny old Flax, who goes to his drink like a finch to thistle seeds.

ᒉ   ᒉ   ᒉ

All rush out from the tavern's gloom, to the sunny road and down it. Others from the heart of Ciderbrook proper have heard the news and join the procession. Through orchard shade, beneath the early moon like the ghost of a scythe on the cool blue air. Flax's pipe leads the way, its smoke snatched by breezes and smashed like ghosts. They come to a bridge that spans a brook where gravity floats apples, its waters a hushed ribbon of drowsy colors.

From the bridge they see the round green belly of Hag's Hill, plump beneath the clear blue sky and that whispered tusk of moon. There's a story to tell when a hill has a name, and this is no exception.

🌀   🌀   🌀

They say a hag came to Ciderbrook one winter while the orchards slept in pewter light and frost. Shaggy Red took up in a soggy cottage behind a swollen hill. Once, at night, a drunken fellow staggering home saw the shape of the hag, up on the barren mound, with a sack of children's heads and she was planting them in the snow.

Queer as it seems, there were trees there, come spring. They were brittle-looking things, crooked and black, crippled spider-leg trees. Leafless through summer, the trees reared in the wind, a broken crown on the head of the hill. Autumn came, its ferns like hammered brass, its foxes fast like rusted whispers through tall golden grass.

Ahh, but such apples! Fat red apples on every leafless bough! Gallon upon gallon of unborn cider hung from those sickly-looking trees. But it was something worse than envy that drove the other orchard masters to kill the hag.

There was a curse, a blight, its dangling evidence of shriveled, ash-colored apples in every orchard, but for the hag's. The villagers plotted her death in hushed ale voices by rush lights with smoke going up like spectral lengths of wrack.

"At night she climbs naked into the trees and sucks every drop of life from the fruit."

"She dances naked around the trees and mutters queer words."

"The hag lays naked in a field and coughs out strange small birds that flit shrieking amongst our trees."

One had simply to gather two or more villagers about a table at the tavern and, quick as you can say "naked" a new tale of wickedness was revealed.

Curse or no curse, there was another rumor as well…

"She has a great sum of gold hidden somewhere in her cottage."

As if the curse weren't reason enough to do away with the hag, the gold was an added incentive, and why not? Wasn't it true that her purse was growing fat while their crop hung rotting from its branches?

One morning (for the hag slept in the day and did her evil by night) a group of men went to her cottage and stuck her with knives. What of the gold? Well, they searched the walls and under the floor and up in the dank brownish thatch. No treasure was ever found.

That night, with the moon a pale mumble of light behind a shroud of unawakened rain, the dead hag rose from her spattered bed and went to her orchard hill. She was naked, on fire, and she ran screaming through the trees, brushing their skinny limbs with dead burning hands. The trees, in turn, danced in flame and when morning came there was nothing left of the hag and her orchard but a spider-shaped stain of ash. The hill has stood empty since.

❧ ❧ ❧

"Tie my danglings in a knot!" exclaims Flax, when he looks upon Hag Hill. Under less extraordinary circumstances, Widow Purdy would be after him with an angry broom for such an improper (in her view of things) utterance. But she, having joined the others flocking to the spectacle, stands numb, her broom clenched like a musket.

They have crowded together at the little bridge with the dull brook beneath, and all of them with their jaws on their chests. Not a soul speaks. Flax feels Ivy Scrimly mashed against his back and a boy behind her, safe in a forest of legs, gives her a pinch. Ivy's laugh is loud in Flax's ear, laughter like a windy summer skirt.

All the black spiders on the vast isle of Westermead have come to Hag's Hill, their armor amassed in great curvilinear patterns against the green slope. Giant shapes of spider ink.

"I think they're words," Grundle Longweed, the blacksmith says.

Indeed. A sentence, in fact, but none in the village can read, but for one…

Mr. Flax takes a step forward and squints through his smoke.

"What's it say, Flax?" demands Goordie Scrimly in his barrel voice.

Flax clears his throat and recites, "The heart of an apple—a fine golden key—the color of cider—a treasure from thee."

Now the air is thick with murmurs as the town folk huddle and buzz.

The popular question… "What does it mean?"

At the center of this fidgeting swarm, Goordie Scrimly, thumbs hooked in a fine wide belt, announces, "I have the answer to this mystery, my friends… It's twenty years since we tended to that old wretch Shaggy Red. 'Tis a message from that hag, says I."

"What does it mean?"

"Hah! Plain enough; she seeks to be redeemed so that her spirit might know peace."

"Redeemed?" One orchard master asks.

"Yes, you silly snot! From casting the blight that crippled our orchards and made us all poor."

In the twenty years following Shaggy Red's demise, the crop of Ciderbrook has suffered. The apples come, timely enough, but they are small and tart (like early season cider) and less than abundant. This year, however, boasts a bounteous crop—the finest the village has ever seen. The trees ache with their round sanguine gems, fruit swollen with the promise of cider, misted in powdery bloom.

"I know!" shouts Ivy, "A key—there's a key in an apple!"

"And a treasure!" her husband booms.

"Yes, that's it. A key to a treasure."

The villagers hum like a hive.

Ivy thrusts her ribs out triumphantly, heavy flesh menacing her bodice. "There is a gold key in an apple somewhere in Ciderbrook; a key to great treasure!"

Squeals fly up and the clot of villagers breaks apart, scattering for the orchards. A great drumming of feet over the bridge, then this way and that until Mr. Flax stands alone, puffing away. His eyes are to the hill where the huge black letters begin to crumble. A grit of spiders trickles from the fragmenting words, down the pout of Hag's Hill.

Flax sighs and slowly wheels away.

Dusk, cool as stone, stitches the shadows of trees together; they shape sticky pools of black cider. Everywhere is apple murder, the sound of fruit dropping a delirious heartbeat against the grass. A boy tugs on an apple clenched in a nag's square teeth, Widow Purdy swipes her broom through leafy boughs, gets knocked on the nose. Apples to the slaughter.

Apples break like skulls, mash beneath boot and rock, their pale, sweet, ripening innards exposed by knife, scythe and a terrible assortment of bladed and blunt implements. Thick red skin cracks and splits, seeds peer out like the eyes of rats. Apples to the slaughter!

Villagers on their knees in pomace, their hands slick with cider gloves. Well into the night they rampage, their torches bobbing in the dark, across the autumn fields, from orchard to orchard, pillaging, shrieking, plucking and hunting. No apple is safe. Apples to the slaughter!

🍏 🍏 🍏

Midnight comes and goes; the moon—the neck of a swan, long since retired. Stars like ghosts of apple seeds speckle the high black sky above Lennit Noose's orchard. It is the last orchard and the villagers are weary and cold, tired, flecked with pulp, their peasant garments soggy with juice. Still, there is no sign of the golden key.

Ivy Scrimly sighs, sits in damp grass and leans her back against a tree. Her lovely hair is not lovely now and gooseflesh textures the smooth of her bosom. A breeze has come in from the north and it rocks a small round something that hangs on a twig beneath a canopy of black leaves.

"I'm hungry, " she mutters, to no one in particular, plucking the apple.

Deficient teeth clamp and crunch and strike the cold metal heart of the fruit.

"Ooowww!"

She spits the key in her hand. Strange how the gold gleams in the dark. She stuffs it between her breasts, shivers. Ivy rises and rushes off in the direction of Hag Hill.

The other villagers, hunched shapes in a dark of sickly sweetness, see her and hiss with whispers like a barrel of snakes.

She hears the brook before she sees the hill. It is the damp voice of autumn with its breath of rotting leaves. From the bridge the distant hill waits—a ghost. A drowned cricket glints by in the current. The hill comes closer, rising, naked. Ivy's heart itches like a spider and she fumbles free the key.

To the base of the hill with soft steady steps. Soon she will be rich and the thrill is in her blood, sweet as the taste of apple on her lips until…

"Ivy!"

The shout hits like lightning—her meager history skips girl bones through her.

The others have followed, their torches over their heads like crowns. Goordie Scrimly moves out from the throng and points to her.

"Give me the key, woman!"

Ivy steps back. "It's mine!"

Closer still, her husband offers a large hand. "It's ours, love," he softens falsely.

Ivy knows better than to resist as Goordie plucks the key from her palm, pushing past.

Halfway up the hill and the smirking brute stops. He hears it with his feet…a tremor from the hill. Again, the stone shoes of a giant, hard on the green grass, vibrate up through the bones of his legs. Something large is coming, something heavy and large. His heart shrinks to the size of a crabapple and his lungs whisper prayers to each other.

Up over the opposite slope of the hill rises a great black spider of painted wood. Its legs creak, its flat face stares. Up the hill; the hill quakes, stars glint on its painted hide like the tears of moths.

Goordie is frozen, his heart an ice fist until he sees the door on the face of the thing. A door with a gold keyhole.

A grin warms Goordie's face and his heart too rejoices in heat, dashing along the summer roads of his veins, dancing around and around his bones. The spider stops, a cow-length away, its inky weight creaking on long, spindly, ash tree beams, creaking under the weight of the golden treasure he believes waits in the belly of the thing!

The flocked villagers hum and Ivy hovers behind Goordie's shoulder, smiling her odious teeth, her drying hair a vapor of honey. The key glints its cidery gold and clicks as it twists in the lock.

The spider's wooden face squeals open and from the darkness spring thin, grey, headless children.

Ⓒ   Ⓒ   Ⓒ

A whisper of apricot light pierces the dusty little cottage. Mr. Flax stirs in his bed, mumbles and squints. His bones feel heavy, grey where gravity slept, and he rises with a groan, pulls a tattered curtain aside, invites the sun.

Alone these many years, the old fellow has developed his hearthside skills. The only thing he does better than cooking is drinking. There are oat cakes and fenberry scones and pear porridge with its autumn-haunted steam. He fills his dusty belly and goes about the morning chores.

Midday and the roads to the village are dry. A bull-bone pipe dowses toward the tavern; its smoke hints of cherry. Curious, Flax thinks — where is Widow Purdy? Her door is closed up and there's no sign of her broom.

Quiet at the inn.

Quiet in the village.

Quiet in the orchards, but for the crows.

Well, there's just one more place to go, isn't there?

Mr. Flax stands on the bridge and stares at Hag Hill. His pipe drops from his mouth. The hill is bare but for a cider press, like a monument, all red with gore and the villagers, flung like poppets, are heaped at the base of the mound. They have no heads.

Beneath the bridge, the brook slithers, a melted serpent of gurgling red.

"I never cared much for gold," Flax says… "or apples."

He picks up his pipe and heads back home.

The Soldier and the Cryptie

ONE

The moor was bleak and drear-grey; as for motion—only rain. Hills rose to the west, like islands in the sedge and mist. On these, as nipples capping breasts, stood thimble-shaped mounds as high as a man's hip, their crude skull-like features flickering orange. "Muddies," the locals called them. They were an eerie sight for a stranger to encounter, especially on a rain-bleared moor.

Timb, having wandered from his patrol partner, trudged up one of the hills. The weight of weapons and the slick grass made the climb something of a task. He sighed upon reaching the summit and looked around. So much sky, so much open ground; it unsettled him. There was comfort in clustered buildings, he thought—damn that sea of rain!

A voice came from the other side of the mound. "Blast!"

Timb had to chuckle as his partner Brelton hiked up, using his musket as a walking stick. He was mud from helmet to boots, his beard like a dark batter.

Timb jeered, "Ho there, man, you didn't slide up like a snake on your belly, did you?"

"Bloody slippery," Brelton sneered.

"Aye, as a summer whore."

Brelton smiled and clapped his friend's shoulder. He took in the vast and barren view. "Ahh, a beauty of a day! How do those bleedin' Northies find the time to build their ghoulish heads without drowning? I swear on the Queen's plump breasts, I haven't seen two dry days the whole war through."

Timb shrugged. He gazed solemnly at the strange creation. An under-structure of stones showed through where the rain had washed away some of the mud flesh. The eyes were skull-like, the mouth a dour slot. A bowl of

184

burning animal fat sat inside, lighting the hollow features. The muddies ushered in the month of Oakbrown, when the dead were wont to wander.

Brelton insisted on forcing his cheer upon his companion. "Say, lad, what say we take a crack at one of 'em? Have a bit o' fun? A spot of sport to brighten our day? Eh?"

Timb frowned as Brelt took up his long musket and aimed at a distant hill. "Don't go and do that. These things mean something."

Brelton lowered his weapon and studied his friend. "Their own bloody skulls mean somethin' to them, too, but you've no compunctions about blastin' those!"

"An enemy is an enemy. These are like graves, or something of the sort. It doesn't seem right to wreck 'em."

Brelton wrapped his knuckles on Timb's helmet. "You're a bit young to be getting soft, lad. I'm off—if I stand in one place too long, I fear I'll drown. Besides, I don't look at this so much as patrollin', but as strolling about on the lovely moor. You can stand here and guard this muddie."

Timb felt foolish as Brelton turned and started back down the hillside, leaving him standing there. The slick dome of Brelt's helmet sank from view.

"Good," Timb mumbled, "Go."

He gazed out across the moor, at those staring muddies, those blank wind-blinked eyes. So this was the soldier's life...a far cry from the glory and adventure that had fired a boy's mind, not so long ago. Sure, he could have stayed snug in the city, worked at his father's butcher shop peddling meat, but discontent had stirred like a wind in his belly.

After seventeen years of ease and banality, he had joined the King's forces. The world awaited with open air, eager to fill his restless sails. How could he have sat at home while there were men traveling wide waters on great ships—patrolling the spice-routes for pirates? While proud fighters assembled in the Kingdom's name—saber sure, tall in their uniforms, with confident guns across their shoulders? At seventeen and some-odd weeks, he had taken his place among them.

The North War came. Generations of northern district folk had resisted the occupation of Kingdom forces. A bloody rebellion ensued, bringing the hier-

archy's wrath. It was to be expected; those Northies were the most independ-
ent of all Westermead's folk. The army was sent in to "suppress" the revolt.

How fast Timb's fancy dreams had faltered. Glory, adventure—bah!
None of that! There was horror to spare. He had seen it, he had done it. It
blackened him on the inside, like the walls around a kitchen fire.

He'd crawled on his belly through fields strewn with shale-complected
corpses, their bodies red with gaping mouths where musket balls had bitten.
He'd tripped on stray limbs, tasted the mist of a friend's brain. He'd smelled
thatch aflame, heard close the pain-crazed cries of the maimed, had his ears
drummed numb by cannon thunder. And he had killed. He had killed plenty.

How the open space haunted him now. The country with its lonely
expansiveness made him ache for the city's noise and clutter. What glory was
there in standing on some bloody hill in the rain, stationed up in "the bleaks?"

🜨 🜨 🜨

The man was face down, the dog flat on its side. Both were leathery-looking,
wrinkling…blackening in upon themselves. In fact they looked as though
they were natural formations of the forest floor, lying there all decay-webbed
amid wet leaves, moss and shattered bits of shed bark. The autumn woods
were rich with the scents and sights of decomposition.

"It's Fryly Bramber and his dog," Kynn noted stiffly.

The other boy knelt and poked his stick at the vividly defined ribs of the
dog. A chunky hole described the exit of a musket ball. "Bleedin' Flints done
'em for sure."

"And him mindin' his own, out for a hunt, no doubt. I'd s'pected that's
what had become of 'im." Kynn held the muddy rifle that had rested beside
the old man's corpse. "Least he got a shot off. I hope he killed one of the
bastards."

Delt looked over at his friend, his face all rain-damp freckles. His wide
green eyes brimmed hot. "I'd like to have at the ones that did this. I'd teach
them how to die."

Kynn rocked back on his heels, still clenching the old gun. "You haven't
the stuff for all that. You wouldn't pluck a scale from a snake."

Delt was defensive. "I could do it! I've nothing against the spilling of blood, so long as it spills from a body that deserves it."

Kynn Stagwood grinned, his face like a fox's. "Back your words with proof."

Delt swallowed, glancing at the back of the dead man's head—brown oak leaves encircling it like a splash of solidified screams. He turned back to his blond friend, who was also just twelve years of age, and his tongue went numb.

Kynn snickered. "As I thought—your courage is confined to words. And now you can't even muster those."

"Untrue! I've enough courage, if need be, but what am I to do—join militia? They'd laugh. Besides, there's much to do at my parents' farm, and I'm needed there."

"The militia's ranks have been mowed like hay, scarce groups remain to fight. I bid you not to join them in full-fledged battle, but to steal a sliver of revenge for what these Flints have done to us."

Delt worried the rain-glossed shaft of his walking stick, hunched there in the ochre cover of his cloak. "What do you mean, Kynn?"

Kynn shot up, swinging the dead man's grime-saddened gun, his eyes fierce, his smile enraged. "We can kill! You and I!"

Delt's posture faltered, he cast a hand back for balance, briefly grabbing a cold branch for support—or was it the dead man's leg?

"Boom! Boom!" Kynn pretended to fire, his body rocking with mock recoil as he aimed at imagined foes. "Boom!"

It was an unnerving sight for the other boy, and yet that same rage squirmed within him as well. The war had gone on for a year now. He had seen the destruction the King's army had brought with their flint-locks and cannons. Homes reduced to ash-thatched rubble, the gory heaps of gallant men cast dead on their native soil. The lonely wet places which were the eyes of widows and their children.

Kynn knelt now, his face close, his eyes fever-glass. "The Flints can be found, often enough, in piddly groups of two or three, patrolling about like they own our beloved land. If we were to get hold of some good muskets, and situate ourselves in a right safe way, then we could blast a couple of the bastards! Yes, think of it, Delt. Wouldn't it feel good to know you'd made 'em pay? Well?"

Delt cringed. "Yes, but—"

"Ah! Yes—yes is all I need to hear, mate. Then we'll do it, right? We'll paint the scoundrels red, we will! We'll be regular warriors!"

No one in the village of Broodmoor had ever seen Stoat Murmur's face, and it was speculated that it was best they hadn't. For wasn't it possible that the features contained within the tan hood which he constantly wore were as ravaged as his rasping voice? The shape and movements of the hood also hinted at unnatural contents.

The hood was pointed at the top and it contained two sets of eye holes. One pair of these was cut where one would expect eyes to be; the other, smaller pair was close to the peak of the thing. Now one might have assumed that the poor fellow was born with a pointed head and extra eyes, but that explanation would not account for the occasional movement or swelling of material in this or that direction, which would suggest the limbs of a small creature. It was possible that some form of trained animal or semi-ethereal beast lived on his head, but if that were the case, then poor Stoat Murmur's head must have been grossly abbreviated to accommodate it, for those little limb movements would occur just above the normally placed eyes. Most villagers were in agreement that the mystery of just what lived under that pointy garment was better left unsolved.

Kynn and Delt, having traveled some hours' worth of tracks across the rugged landscape of the northern district, encountered the tall figure of the hooded man. He had just completed building a hollow cairn version of a muddie and was lighting it.

"Hello, Stoat Murmur," Kynn said. Delt stood several paces behind them.

The hooded thing rose and looked down—the blink and glint of vague eyes showing through four holes. "Good afternoon."

"We've come for some trading, if that's all right with you."

Stoat glanced at the hampers each boy carried and nodded. He motioned for them to follow.

The man moved slowly on his long spidery legs. A thin trench of a path cut through banks dense with jaundiced clumps of high rain-pummeled grass. They came to a misty hollow where a stone cabin stood beneath a thatch of soggy rushes.

Only four trees stood in the vicinity of Stoat's home, these being great and wild-limbed oaks. Delt noticed that these had been decorated for the Oakbrown season, for here and there, peering out from amidst the darkening leaves, he could spy a dangling human skull. Closer to the house, the visitors encountered a fierce-faced muddie with branch antlers, the exterior seemingly scaled, for countless pebbles had been patiently pressed into the mud. A nearby wooden sign on a post asked in crude faded letters: Do ghosts of yeast haunt ovens?

Inside, surrounded by a shadowy clutter of tools, bins, barrels and objects one might be hard-pressed to identify, the trio sat at a table. A lone lamp was before them, the glass flecked with dried food spatters.

"What can I do for you lads?" a voice hissed behind the hood.

Kynn did the talking. "We understand that you have guns. We'd be most interested in acquirin' some."

Stoat choked out a laugh. "Guns? Boys want guns? For what?"

"What's it matter, eh?"

"I dare say it's an uncommon request. Most uncommon for boys to even come out so far to pay visit, let alone for guns."

"They're for hunting," Delt offered. He tried to keep his eyes trained on the hood's lower holes, though he could not help glancing up to meet the tiny ones in the hood's peak.

"Hunting what?"

Kynn grew impatient. "Flints, all right, we want to hunt some bleedin' Flints!"

A horrible rasping chuckle issued from Stoat Murmur. "Didn't I know it? I could tell, I could smell it. The thirst for copper-stenched gore, it's heavy on you, lad."

Kynn was flustered. "Do you have guns or not? We didn't hike this far to chat, I'll have ya know."

"Ah, you are a bold one. No curse in that, of course, if you got some sense to keep you balanced. You're a might young to be fightin' the Flints, I fear. Killing isn't a game, you know."

"I know. I'm not some blasted half-wit."

"You fancy yourself a hero, perhaps."

Kynn shoved his stool back and stood, as if he were going to storm out. Something in the hood twitched.

"We'll take our business elsewhere, if you don't mind, then, Murmur. It's too bloody bad you won't be tastin' all the fine pastries and mulled ale we brought."

Murmur eyed the hampers. "Pastries?"

"That's right. Goat cakes, fruit pies, goldies and treacle hooves."

"And ale?"

"As I said—brewed with the finest spices..."

"Sit, lad, let's not be rash."

Kynn flashed Delt a confident smile.

"I just happen," Stoat rasped, "to have a few fine weapons I picked off some Kingdom men I found by the Groaning Rock. They were a mess, but the guns..."

The tall man rose and went poking through his amassed goods until he uncovered two long muskets. He brought them over and laid them across the table. One was a flint-lock with a four-foot brass barrel and rich walnut wood. The other was a snap-lock on which a cocking mechanism with tiny jaws was used to hold a piece of flint, which, upon the working of the trigger, would strike a steel plate, causing sparks to fall into the powder pan, firing the charge.

Kynn lifted one of the heavy things and smiled. "They're beauties!"

Stoat greedily gathered the two baskets of food and took them off into an adjacent room. When he returned a moment later, he had a small glass jar with him. He set it in front of the boys.

"What's this, an empty jar?" Kynn asked, smirking.

"No, not empty," wheezed the hood. "The killing toys are yours, but allow me one more chance to discourage your reckless hunger."

"Reckless? Bah! I don't need any bloody discouraging, thanks."

Delt spoke up reluctantly. "What's in the jar?"

The hood leaned across the table, four pale eyes staring. Stoat rasped, "The whispers of a dead man. You want to hear—you'll change inside. If you ache to know of death, open the jar and listen..."

Stoat slid the jar across the table. Delt stared at the cold gleaming glass. He leaned away.

"How about you, angry lad? You'd rather hear a musket's bellow to know the voice of death? Give listen to the jar, let your ears drink well of sorrow and pain."

"I'll not entertain you any longer, Stoat Murmur. What do you know of anything? I came only to trade, not to stomach your silly lessons. Come, Delt, let's be off."

Stoat watched as they took the muskets and whisked out the door. He contemplated the jar, which sat so still in the lamp glow. He thumbed the smooth glass and something under the hood muttered, "Heroes are the ghosts of fools."

TWO

A small bridge of mortarless packed stones led across the brackish flow. The stream sulked around the base of a grassy hump where three great slabs of stone stood taunting the sky. Ghostly slivers of fish darted here and there, the water gurgling as if drowning in itself.

Timb and Brelton made their way through the drizzle, across the crude stone structure, and climbed the slope of the hill. The megaliths towered twice their height, the bases choked in clumps of bronze bracken. Crows foraging amongst the ferns took up noisily at the intrusion. Timb shielded his face from the beating wings.

From this height the soldiers could see much of the western "Bleaks." It was a rough lay of land, void of friendly features—all hills and hollows, mist and mud. There were stones of all sizes and shapes, like bones peeking through the skin of sallow grass.

Timb looked up at the towering grey trio. He had encountered numerous sites where such mysterious ancient monuments remained. Markers? Graves? Magical instruments? He touched the coolness.

Brelton, the older, more brawny of the two, rested his back against one. He leaned his musket against the wall, pulled a flask out of his long flint-colored coat and took a swig. He held it out to Timb who was too absorbed to notice.

"The Spears of Bridgemouth," Brelton noted.

"What's that?"

"That's what the locals call this place. They say that a thing known as Skinny Brimm runs along this way, from these stones here to a tomb across the bleaks, withering the souls of all he meets."

Timb gave his partner a curious look. "Who?"

"Skinny Brimm, who, so they say, is a nasty critter. He's nothin' but a stag skull atop a body of long twined-together sticks that sprints along with a lantern held out. Too bad the Northies can't enlist him to their ranks, hm? He'd be a hard target for our musket shot, being made of sticks." Brelton snickered and indulged in his drink.

"I wouldn't laugh, Brelton. There may be more to Skinny Brimm than legend—I lost an aunt to the Winter Women."

Brelton began to choke, whiskey spilling into his beard. He dropped the flask, grabbed his rifle, fumbled for the trigger and fired. Timb flinched at the blast as a great clap of white smoke erupted. The shot hit one of the three megaliths at the base, bounced off that, hit one of the others, deflected off that and hit the third before whining off.

Timb hadn't had time to crouch. He stood, ears ringing, pale. "What are you, mad?"

Brelton was trembling, pointing, his eyes wide. "It was there!"

Timb looked, saw only the chipped base of the stone. "What was there?"

"Some, some blasted thing...I saw it!"

"There's nothing, you fool. Look!"

192

Brelton wagged his head. "It was like a crab, but, but the shell was like the top half of a skull, and it had little skeleton arms sticking out like a crab has claws! It was scurryin' there in the ferns, I swear."

"You've had enough of that whiskey, Brelton. You could've shot us up good with that one. And if there's Northies about, they know we're here."

"I'm telling ya, I saw it!"

☙ ☙ ☙

The following morning, after a breakfast of porridge and oat cakes, Timb set out on patrol. He resented leaving the camp (where any free time was greedily spent) and today he was doubly agitated by venturing into the open spaces. Several Kingdom troops had been ambushed by Northies the day before; two were wounded, one was dead. The native fighters were a crafty lot, experts at camouflaging themselves into the landscape. Timb felt naked, hiking about, wondering if the surrounding hills were loaded with watchful foes.

Though the morning, thus far, was rainless, the ground seemed mossy-damp and the sky was all far-flung clouds abrim with wet promise. Clouds like a sea of drowning mountains. A murder of crows spilled low with mocking voices. They landed by turn to peck at the moor.

Timb kept clear of the worn pathways, mindful of potential snipers. He moved where the earth pouted boulders, so as to have a chance at seeking cover, if necessary. In his grey uniform he might appear to be a stone, if he crouched down.

While rounding the swell of a good-sized hill, he was startled by a blast of sound. He was quick to kneel and level his longarm. He was a good marksman, to be sure, and as soon as the first white shape came up over the pate of the hill he had it locked in sight. The sheep bleated loudly.

The adrenal flush left him momentarily numb. More heads came poking up, strange-eyed, docile, foamy-white, some with black ears, dark snouts. Timb let out a tense laugh. There was quite a brood of the creatures, milling up and over the crest, then down toward him, like a pour of liquid. Then, moving amidst them, as though wading through shifting surf, came a girl with hair of autumn gold.

She started at the sight of the Kingdom soldier, who knelt still, his gun poised as if to fire. She dropped her staff, her hands flew up to hide her face. "No!" she cried.

Timb let the gun down and stood. "Wait, don't fear—look…"

She squinted through her fingers, then hesitantly lowered them. "You won't hurt my sheep, will you?"

"No, no, of course not. I—they startled me. I'm terribly sorry, Miss, really. There's nothing to fear, I assure you."

"What are you doing?"

"I am on patrol. I'm of the King's army."

She moved closer, her blue eyes tense. Her form was robust and her garb bore the faded colors of dye-plants—the full skirt broom-yellow, her shawl woad-blue. The sheep, oblivious to any danger, brushed against her familiar legs, their soft muzzles seeking treats which she fumbled unthinkingly from a sack that hung from her hip.

"You are a soldier? But you are little more than a boy—they send you to fight our northern men?"

Timb's posture stiffened. "Yes. I've done a good deal of fighting, Miss. And I'm not so young; I'm soon to be eighteen."

"You look younger."

Timb was boyish compared to many of the troops; he was lanky, clean-shaven, with a lean face, his dark hair in jagged bangs, wavy across the ears. His eyes were not those of a fierce spirit; there was something sad about them.

"Well," the girl said, daring slowly closer, "you may have seen battles, but you're still a boy."

"If you insist, but many a soldier is merely a boy who has to kill."

The girl scowled. "Kill. I've seen a year of killing. I couldn't kill." She came closer, the tide of sheep moving along, as if she and they were the cells of a single shifting entity. She touched them absently, though caringly, and they were at her free hand, nibbling. He could see her face better; it was pretty, rounded. She was only a year or two older than he.

Timb held his weapon down at his side self-consciously, less than regal in his worn uniform, grey helmet and boots. "Killing is ugly, granted. But I am a soldier, so I must. I chose this path." He sighed. Perhaps he wouldn't have, he thought, had he known better.

The outer edge of the girl's sheep moat was against him now, their full coats thick with the scent of lanolin.

"This was a good place before the Kingdom men came. I could roam and let my flock graze without fear. I've had my animals shot by your kind—for no cause but cruel amusement. 'Tis a wonder I've not met a similar fate."

"I would never do such a thing—harm defenseless animals, let alone a woman."

She gazed at him, his war-wearied face. "No, you wouldn't. Still, you would kill those who defend this land..."

Timb looked away.

"Yet, you say it is ugly to kill."

He nodded. He felt foolish, standing there with gun and saber.

"Where are you from?" the girl asked.

"Bellingtower, the city."

"Ahhh."

He saw in her eyes as she ran through her thoughts of what a city was. An awful loud place, choked in people and motion.

"I doubt I'd like the city," she said. "I like where I am. But I am a simple girl, content to wander these hills and tend my friends here. You should be bored by a life like that, I would imagine."

"Probably."

She smiled. Her eyes crinkled blue, her cheeks rounded in blushes of heather. It stunned him—how could she smile at him; he was the enemy! His innards clenched.

"I'll be on my way now," she said.

Timb stood mute, filled with his own emptiness. He looked into the fidgety cloud of sheep. "Right," he mumbled, "Good day, Miss."

He wanted to apologize, not just for frightening her, but for standing there in her people's territory, for the things he'd done in battle. His tongue slumbered.

She brushed past him, her sheep bleating along, down the hill. She looked back once and called out, "Soldier! If you find killing so dreadful, lay down your weapons and go home. You don't belong here."

Timb made no reply; he stood sagging and thin, watching her wavy flax as it fluttered behind her. Inside he felt much like the landscape—bleak and windswept.

❧   ❧   ❧

The Flints came on horses. There were at least twenty of them, stiff and grey in their saddles, their helmeted heads skull-smooth. Delt, his two little sisters and his friend Kynn Stagwood had been playing among the aisles of bundled hay when they heard the drumming of hooves.

Kynn poked his head out from behind one of the stacks and hissed, "Bastards!"

One of the little girls ran blubbering into Delt's arms, the other took off for the house. Kynn saw the glint of distant weapons—guns moving to monitor the motion. His guts slammed up into his ribs as he saw the small girl trip, for a split second imagining she'd been shot down. The girl cried louder, picked herself up and ran into her mother's safe apron.

Delt's father, a paunchy grey-haired man, stood in front of their humble cottage, his arms clenched nervously across his chest. An officer rode up to him on a black horse, the breast of his uniform coat studded with silver rank beads. He was stern-faced, with dense lamb chop sideburns framing his scowl. His squint was arrogant.

"Good day," the officer said, "I am Captain Burnclay of the King's North Brigade. Last evening several of my men were fired upon in a field not far from here. The assailants were disguised as bundled hay, such as you have here. By the authority granted me by the Kingdom, I have ordered a search of this and the surrounding properties."

The farmer laughed nervously. "For what do you search, Captain? There is nothing here."

"Hidden militia men, weapons. What have you." He turned to his stoic troops and flashed a signal with his hand. They responded, some dismounting, others pounding off on their steeds, into the ranks of trussed hay. Those on horseback rode along, jabbing their muskets' bayonets into the raspy golden pillars.

Kynn scurried over to where Delt was hiding, still clutching the little girl to muffle her frightful sobs. "Delt—your gun, where is it?"

"Under my bed."

"Blast! They'll find the bloody thing."

"So—they won't know it was us."

Kynn angered. "Well, they might bloody well think it was us, or your father, for that matter. We have ta get it out of there. You and Trilly step out, slowly so as not to startle the trigger-hungry swine. Slowly, hear? You move fast and you'll have a swarm of hot balls comin' at your skull. I'll steal to the house and get the musket. Right?"

Delt nodded. Kynn was off, spry as a fox, dodging, crunching through the army of straw. The cottage was ever closer, the men on horseback behind him, probing along with cruel tips of steel.

"You're wasting your time," the farmer's wife spoke up, glaring at the Captain. "See how you frighten my poor child!"

The man sat back in his saddle, his fingers drumming on his metal powder flask. He smirked. "Madam, one of my men was killed. He'll not get over that, whereas your child will forget this moment duly, unless of course we find something…"

"There are no militia fighters here. You've killed off all our young men," the woman spoke in trembling anger.

"You may look at it that way; I see it differently. Those who chose to go against our forces were merely committing an act of self-destruction…romantic, yes, but most impractical."

"Oh, you are a smug one, you bleeding Flint!"

The Captain's smile turned upside down and he lashed the woman on the jaw with his boot. She spun and dropped to the ground, the child clinging to her waist tumbling as well.

The farmer roared and moved to pounce at the Captain but there was a blur of motion—he was grabbed by two foot soldiers, thrown on his back and held down with bayonets at his breast.

"Be still!" spat the officer.

"No!" Delt yelled, dashing out from the rows of hay, small sister stumbling behind. Their sudden motion brought muskets swiveling...

One of the soldiers called, "Do not fire!"

Kynn took advantage of the commotion. He ducked behind the house, entered a rear window and made his way to Delt's bed. His hands trembled; even so, he readied the weapon with a charge and a ball. His rage was like a surge of serpents through his blood. The night before he had taken his first taste...he wanted more.

Outside, the farmer lay humiliated beside his unconscious wife, tears of frustration running as his pounding chest felt the prod of poised bayonets.

"This is my home, my land, how can you do this?"

"Pardon me," the Captain corrected him, "this country belongs to the Kingdom. We are the law."

The two little girls were bent over their mother, shaking her, crying. "Mother, Mother!"

Delt had been grabbed by the back of his shirt and was held rigid by one of the footmen. "My mother—you've killed her!"

Captain Burnclay scoffed, "Bah! She's not dead. See, the sow still breathes."

Inside the cottage, Kynn had the rifle ready. He sneaked into the front of the building and peered out along the brassy barrel. The weapon clicked ready. He aimed carefully at the chest of the Captain, breathing softly though his heart ran wild. One little pull...

"Is this your entire family? Have you any older sons?"

"No," grunted the farmer. "There is only us."

"Search the cottage," the Captain snapped.

Kynn watched through the small panes. One brief tug and that proud Captain would be splayed like a wind-ravaged corn-dolly, his haughty chest all gore. One tiny squeeze would do it. But what then? The others would be aswarm around the house, outnumbering him, and fast on their mounts. Was he ready to die? Several of the soldiers were heading toward the house!

Kynn moved quickly. He rushed to the window through which he had entered, climbed out and rasp-dashed through scattered leaves. There was an autumn-flaked stand of trees behind the stone building. He hastily buried the musket in leaves of maple and oak. He stood and started away.

"You—halt!"

Kynn looked back. Two Flints sat on their stable mounts, heavy guns trained. "Ha!" One laughed. "It's only a boy!"

The other chuckled. Kynn Stagwood straightened. He smirked at them, his eyes keen and cold. Only a boy, he thought? Hadn't he been something more the night before when he and Delt had opened up on that patrol? He smiled back at them, as adrenaline laughed hotly through his blood.

THREE

The second time Timb saw the girl, she passed with her blathering flock and eyed him silently. He nodded to her. He had situated himself where he had previously encountered her, at the same approximate time. The next day he did the same, and this time she nodded back, reluctantly, or so it seemed.

The following morning he again set out, eager to see her. While nearing that hill with the standing stones, he spotted a figure whom he thought was the girl, but she was without her sheep, and her hair looked more white than blond. She crested the hill afore him and was not to be seen anywhere when he reached the summit. The dead of Oakbrown aroam?

Later, as he stood in the chill, he spotted her. She was talking to her blatting brood, touching them as they passed, her long skirt and blond mane happy in the breeze. He felt an ache inside.

She noticed him and this time she smiled. It puzzled him, how anyone could look upon his saturnine face and react so. It did not occur to him to return the expression, though something inside of him leapt like an eager pup.

She approached him, grinning, her blue eyes squinting as she studied him.

"Hello, boy soldier," she said, somewhat mockingly.

"Ahh," he said, "you exhibit the Northern sass."

"We're a fiery lot, so they say. The southern folk think us crude. Don't you?"

Timb shrugged. "I don't know."

"You like this spot? I see you here each day."

"I—I am on patrol."

She pouted. "Oh." She looked bashful at that moment, like her lambs. "I was under the impression—and forgive me if I am bold beyond proper manners—that you were coming here to watch me."

Timb's face bleached, his throat constricted. He fumbled out a sentence. "I, perhaps so... There's not much else to see here in the bleaks. Nothing of interest. But now I am bold to admit."

She laughed sudden and light. "Oh, how you pinken!"

Timb looked away, smiling foolishly.

"Come with me, soldier, I'll show a place of interest."

She strutted past, her faithful ewes in blurting tow. She led him down a path a ways, then cut sharply across a stretch of brambled field where small creatures winged and otherwise were berry-busied. They came to a spot near the center of the expanse and stopped.

The girl pointed to the ground. "The Fallen's Field, we call it," she explained.

There in the grass were the outlines of six human figures, like shadows sprawled, or fetal in death. No stalks grew within these eerie shapes.

"You made these?"

"No. This is where the war began. This is where the first of our dead fell—just as you see."

"Someone maintains these then, cuts the grass to mark these places?"

"No. They appeared on their own. They are here all year, in summer when the grass is high, and I've come here in winter when the snow was piled a foot and there they were, deep and bare. Are you intrigued?"

Timb nodded.

Next she took him to an adjacent area where hills heaved themselves up from sedge and swampy streams. On one of these rises stood a single tree, its leaves a fluttery cluster of amber and bronze.

"That," the shepherdess said, pointing, "is the Face Tree. Do you see, the eyes, the mouth? Even a nose, like a skull's."

Timb looked for a moment before it struck him. "Yes! There is a face. How strange."

The features were indented in the leaves, crudely, but easily distinguishable.

"Is this a creation or a natural formation?"

"Why, natural, of course. Each year it's here. At night the leaves glow, and they have healing properties when placed across the chest. We collect them when they fall."

Timb near shuddered at the thought of coming upon that big plume of a face aglow at night. These northern parts were rich with strange beliefs and occurrences.

"So, you see, we do have our items of interest."

Yes, thought Timb—but he had seen none that were pretty, like her.

"I fear I must head home—it grows late and my family will wonder what's become of me. I must help my brother with the chopping of wood."

"Right. Thank you for showing me these places."

She flashed that smile again; it tugged his stomach like reins. "You're not a bad sort, for a Flint."

Timb did not return directly to the camp, even after the hours of his patrol had been spent. The afternoon sun had actually broken through the clouds! Amidst all the rain of the autumn season that one burst of light stirred him to wander dreamily, or was it something more than the sun on the bleaks?

He strolled humming into the camp, his musket swinging from one hand. There was a cluster of men over by the medic tent, a commotion of sorts. He headed over out of curiosity, still humming softly. Several men ran by. A wagon stood close, a figure lying in the back moaning.

"They were boys!" the wounded soldier cried.

Timb sobered, picked up his pace. He looked at the man in the wagon, a clump of soggy red bandages where a hand had been. His jacket was cracked by jagged streaks of red.

Timb pushed his way through those who had gathered. Another body was laid out on a stretcher on the ground. It was Brelton, his eyes clouded and mouth slack. His uniform was runny and ripped where heavy balls had nested.

"Brelt! Oh, blast it, man!"

Timb sagged, nauseated.

"They sniped him," a med-man said bitterly, "some boys with muskets, up near the Spears of Bridgemouth."

    ℭ   ℭ   ℭ

"Good morning to you, soldier."

Timb gave her a sullen smile. "Hello, Miss."

"'Patrolling' again?"

"Yes."

"Why don't they supply you with a horse? You must tire of hiking about so."

"I'm of a low rank. And I'm closer to our station than many of the patrol-men who need horses more."

"Ahh, I see."

The flock was about her as usual, all blab and blat and blurt. She fed them treats. Timb reached out and stroked one as it nudged him shyly with its snout. The girl observed this and grinned approvingly.

"They like you."

"Oh?"

"Yes."

    ℭ   ℭ   ℭ

The walls yawned mouths where cannonballs had hit. Chunks of mossy stone were splayed about the ruin of the cottage. Vines now claimed the wearied stones, webs choking the shadowy interior.

"There were thirty of our men hiding out here. The place was something of a wreck even before the battle," the girl explained.

Timb looked at the stillness of the place, trying to imagine the violence it had seen.

"There were over two hundred Kingdom fighters. I've heard that they were moved by the bravery of our lads, even as they mowed 'em down."

The girl fingered a pockmark left by a musket blast.

"It's a sad place," noted Timb.

She nodded. She scrutinized him. "They were fierce, even though they were so terribly outnumbered. You're not fierce. You have no reason to be, though, whereas they did. They were fighting to protect their land. You fight because you're told to."

Timb nodded.

"I like you not fierce."

They went inside where the air was damp and shadow-drowned. Rotten shards of furniture were scattered like abandoned ghosts' toys. A spider had made use of one of the impromptu windows left by a cannon ball and sat content in her fine weave of misty strings.

"Oh, listen," the girl said.

A faint high hum came from the web, shifting melodically.

"It's a spin-bard."

They knelt close to listen, both smiling as the tiny beast in the breeze-rocked web sang. They turned to each other. Timb saw the whole of her spirit flush pinkly into her face, brimming, eyes like fiery glass. He felt his own being surge hotly into his face, a great teetering energy. Some warm gravity drew their lips together. They kissed tenderly in that ruin of war.

            ❧   ❧   ❧

In the days that followed, they went to sit and listen to the spider as she wove her airy tunes. They would stand in awkward anticipation, walking quietly about each other until some point when they would embrace and the tension of hunger became the intensity of communion. Inevitably they made love, as the spider sang and rain dripped from the old beams and traced cool fingers on their newly mapped flesh.

            ❧   ❧   ❧

"No flock today?" Timb smiled. He smiled just looking at her now, filled with the secret of their sharing, which in that lonely grey world was theirs alone. A secret burst of internal sunlight after so many clouds, and so many rains.

"In this downpour? Don't be silly. They're home and dry."

Her name, he had finally learned, was Mercy. Mercy Apple Stagwood. He told her his.

They went to their place, at the war-wrecked cottage. They rushed in laughing, drenched. Timb's helmet kept his head dry, but her mane faired less well under the shawl she had fashioned cowl-like. There was a bit of roof left in the corner where they had made love, and the hole with the spider web was there. But after several minutes they realized that the only sound was the rain.

Mercy bent down and peered at the web. "She's gone. Oh, Timb, she's gone."

Timb knelt beside her, put an arm about her. She shivered cold.

"Timb, what do you suppose happened to her?"

"Perhaps a bird got her."

"Oh, no!"

He tried to ease her worry. "She probably just moved to a safer place. It has been quite chill these last few nights. I should think she's well."

"No," Mercy muttered, "I fear not."

Timb watched her profile as a tear started down the slope of her soft cheek, then as her jaw exploded in a cloud of blood and shattered bone where the musket ball struck. He heard the blast, felt stinging bits of her, wet warmth on his coat. Mercy collapsed against him, gurgling, her eyes wide with horror, her tongue squirming ineffectually.

"No! No!"

Timb turned, saw a figure blur away from a window on the other side. His heart thrashed as he gathered Mercy up and stumbled out into the rain. He had not brought his musket, but he had his pistol, which he managed to unholster. He could see no one, only rain, and miles to cross.

Mercy moaned, her body heavy and wet against him. He hoisted her onto his shoulder, the blood and rain smearing across his jacket. He tried to run, the field mashing wetly under his boots.

From the rooftop behind the soldier Kynn took aim. He trembled, hot with rage at his traitorous sister.

"Hold on, Mercy, please! It's not fatal, I'll get ya help. I promise!"

Boom!

Mercy jerked as the ball hit. A gout of gore covered the side of Timb's face. Mercy slumped off and sprawled in the mud, jawless, eyes wide, a ragged hole in her chest. She wheezed, shuddered and was dead.

Timb howled piteously. He squinted through the rain-pour, saw one figure slide down from the roof of the ruin, saw another running at him, musket leveled.

"Shoot him!" Kynn shouted. "Shoot, Delt!"

The musket coughed out a thunderous clot of smoke, the recoil knocking the boy back a step. He had missed—the soldier kept running at him, his face emerging through the rain—a fierce and horrid mask.

Delt froze. What had he done? He should have been home with his parents, playing, sitting warm and safe with his little sisters, gathered about the hearth. He didn't want this! It was one thing to feel anger and the hunger to kill, but it was entirely different to actually do it. He was not sure if he had killed any of the others they had ambushed, but even if he had, it was better to shoot at Flints than a native lass. Panic overwhelmed him.

The Kingdom soldier maintained his maddened pace. He thrust his long pistol out, like an animal charging with horns. He came within yards...Delt dropped his own weapon and threw up his hands, eyes wide.

"Die!" Timb roared. He fired—the clap loud, burnt powder black on his hand. The ball struck, making a red ruin of Delt's face. The boy flopped back in the wet grass. Timb kept moving, running across the corpse, pulling his saber free. When he reached the building, there was no sign of the other sniper.

He collapsed in the grass, choking, crying. Rain riddled his back, drummed his helmet. He lay there sobbing for long wet minutes. Then he heard, faintly through the rain, the ghostly hum of the spin-bard spider, coming from somewhere inside the ruined cottage.

FOUR

The blanched stubble of the fields spread wide beneath the gangrenous sky.

Hills like misty blastemas sloped up, here and there, off in the distant north. There were crows of scornful screech and swoop, brown thrushes to peck the earth. Small birds to puddles like feathered storms. The tomb was like a massive grassed belly, the voices of those inside grumbling hungrily.

The northern folk entombed their dead in hills, marking each body with a flat circle of inscribed slate. A "full" hill took on a scaled look, with all the markers in place. This particular mound had been ingeniously modified— the deceased occupants independently (and not without reverence) dug up and moved to unmarked graves. The insides of the hill were then hollowed out and a support structure of stone and wood was constructed. There were several such transformed crypt-hills scattered about the area, harboring the men of the northern militia.

Kynn stood blond and small amid the solemn-eyed warriors gathered there in the slim comfort of lanterns and ale. They leaned on their guns and rubbed at their chins as they listened, mumbling bitterly, to the boy's dread tale.

"She was minding her own, just out on a stroll, as she was oft pleased to do. And I heard the terrible din of a gun, and saw as the ball hit her here," he pointed to his face, "smack on the chin."

The rebel leader nodded, his brown eyes a-brood.

"What was I to do, a mere unarmed lad? Well, I tried to carry her, best I could. But those bleedin' Flints were not done—no. They opened up again, and finished her good with a shot right through."

Kynn fell silent a moment in his feigned grief.

"Then they shot Delt, went right up to him and did it. I ran as they reloaded, and managed to take cover in a ditch until they were gone. And that's how it went, just as I say. The Flints killed my sister, and my finest friend too."

The rebel leader groaned. "The shameless bastards—how they'll pay. I promise you, lad, they'll hurt smartly for this crime. Isn't it enough they take sport in killing our livestock? Now they kill our boys and defenseless women?"

Another man spoke up, his red beard like bristly briar and flame. "It's time for the great move. We've waited long enough—they think we've been crushed. We can surprise 'em, as we do so well. I say it's time."

There was a deep chorus of agreement. The rebel leader clapped a hand on Kynn's shoulder. "Yes, then, we'll do it!"

Kynn tried not to grin. "I wish to fight along with you, if I may. I am a crack shot, you know."

The leader nodded. "Yes, small man—you may join us." He turned and gave an order, "Get Kynn a gun."

       ☙   ☙   ☙

The great open spaces no longer unsettled Timb; he was too numb for that. The bland Oakbrown expanses reflected the great void that he felt inside. Dear, dear Mercy—the lone spark of light which he had encountered in that dread place—was stolen from him, shattered.

He wandered, himself like a ghost, finding it curious that he could muster the strength to rise each day, to eat and breathe beneath that smothering weight of grief. He could scarcely stir the passion of rage, or the urge to wreak vengeance. How unfair it seemed…the projectiles that were meant for him, had taken her instead!

He went to where he had seen her first, walking with her loving clan of beasts. He remembered her first smile—how it squeezed her eyes to squints and pink-puffed her healthy cheeks. And her kisses—but never again! She was dead, cold, coiled in shroud and tucked in earth. Only the worms would kiss her now.

       ☙   ☙   ☙

The cook, Jarter, had spent part of his childhood in the bleaks before moving east, then south. He had lived in the city for a time. He told Timb that he had joined the military out of boredom, and presently, at fifty-six years of age, was the oldest man in camp. Everyone liked him.

Timb sat in the corner of the cook shack, on the floor, his knees drawn up. His eyes were red. A bottle of wine (provided by Jarter) stood beside him. The room was warm with cooking. Jarter bustled about, all apron grease and jiggling belly, his steam-crazed grey hair sticking this way and that.

Timb was drunk.

"I loved her, you know," he mumbled.

"Course ya did, laddie."

Timb sobbed, his head on his knees. Jarter took pause from his bustling and bent to hug the young man. "That's right, Timb, have a good bawl o'er it. It'll do ya no good to pack that all in. Rain it all out—you'll sleep well."

Timb's face twitched, his nose poured. "It isn't fair, Jart. It should have been me."

"Don't be blamin' yourself."

Jarter thought for a moment. He leaned close and spoke in a hush. "Listen, Timb, there may be a way to rectify this whole thing. You hear me?"

Timb looked up and nodded.

"There's many a strange and mysterious occurrence in these parts, and ways that the dead can be conjured back. When I was a child there was a young boy who died. His parents did a thing to bring him back, and blast— he did. He came back, not a ghost, mind ya, but body an' all. He was just as alive as you or I, though, cool to touch and grey in complexion. And I never saw him age a day. There's a certain way to conjure 'em back…"

"What is it?"

"That I couldn't tell ya—but I know someone who could."

The wind droned morosely through the scraggly branches of silhouette-trees. The wayfarers sat high in the leaf-haunted breeze, atop their trudging mounts. The road shrank and snaked through brittle, rasping vegetation, puddles scattered like deep black holes, or the hoof prints of some great beast. All along the way they had seen, at varying distances, the glaring, glowing features of muddies, some black against the moon-illumined clouds, others, much closer, scaled in acorns, or fleshed with moss.

Stoat Murmur's stone cabin sat in a grassy hollow with four great oaks around it. The stripped branches dangled skulls, and a muddie grinned an ominous welcome. The wind snaked hissing through brittle reeds, and leaves cried crisply under the weight of hooves. A dark figure moved past a lit window, long arms gesturing, as if the figure were having an emphatic conversation.

Timb looked over at Jarter as they sat outside before dismounting.

"You're sure you want to do this, lad?"

Timb nodded. They climbed down, gathered their sacks of edible goodies and approached the door.

"What if he knows we're Kingdom men?" Timb asked. They were not in uniform.

"Stoat don't care. Long as we've got food."

Their knocks were readily answered by a tall, thin figure with a high pointed hood. Four eye holes observed them impassively. His voice was like that of one choking on broken glass.

"Visitors roaming on such a night? You've come to visit Stoat, I see. Come sit among my treasures, gentlemen."

The door closed. The room was crowded with objects—tools, barrels, animal hides, branches, heaps of straw, and other less defined things, all steeped in shadow. A grimy lantern made a warm puddle of the central table where the men seated themselves.

Something howled outside, something else scraped across the outer walls, the lamp flickered, the surrounding walls of mad detail flung distorted shadowy waves. Stoat chuckled. "The wind is quite active this night."

Jarter emptied his cloth sack on the table. There were plump golden loaves of bread, biscuits, fruit, candied peel and strips of sweet bark. He eyed the hood. Stoat gasped, something between the upper and lower eye holes twitched against the confining material.

The cook spoke. "We've come to seek a favor."

Murmur's long bony hands hovered over the food, as if he were warming them over a source of heat. "Such lovely goods," he whispered. "What do you need, gentlemen? I am at your service."

"We understand that you know much about the dead."

The upper eyes squinted in the lamp light. "The dead, you say? We are acquainted. You wish to hear them?"

"No. My friend here has lost his dearest, and they say you know how to call the dead back."

209

Stoat stiffened in his seat. His silence was long and ambiguous. Timb grew impatient. Though Jarter had told him to save his food bundle for bargaining strategy, he plopped it on the table.

"Here," Timb said, "more treats!"

"No," Stoat hissed, "I can take only one."

Jarter was stunned at this. "You'll not help us, then?"

"Ahhh, I will try, friends, but you tread on risky turf. I can offer you a method, though the outcome is a gamble."

Timb said, "What do you mean?"

"The dead can be made to return, but the nature of their ways may not be what it was in life. Your love may come back whole and sweet, or dark with spite and ghastly needs. The choice is yours to risk…"

"Tell me, I'll take the chance!"

Stoat gave a nod. "Right then. But I'll take just one bag of payment. If she comes back fine, then bring me the other. If not…then you may not be back at all."

Timb leaned close across the table, his eyes sponging the lantern's flame. "Tell now—what must I do?"

"You must kill a sheep, take its intestines and fill them with warm water. Then wrap them about yourself when you lie down to sleep. Call your lover six times, then twice more. She will come to you."

"That's all?"

Stoat rose, moved away and fumbled through his collected trinkets. He came back with a glass jar, half full with a mossy paste. He handed it to the young soldier.

"You may need this."

"What do I do with it?"

"If you hear your name in the night, like a horrible wind, stuff this in your ears. Do not go to your door."

Timb could not kill the sheep. He thought of Mercy walking with her flock. Jarter readied the intestines for him. It was late. He thanked the kindly cook and headed to his cabin.

The camp was like a little village, there on a grassy plateau, moated with mist. The tents and crude huts stretched in ragged rows, now silent. An occasional guard paced.

Timb bolted his cabin door, lit a smoky candle, stripped and coiled himself in the floppy bloated stole of guts. It was squishy warm as he lay down on his blankets. He thought of her smile, her robust flesh, her beaming smile.

"Mercy," he said, "Mercy, Mercy, Mercy, Mercy, Mercy."

The wind dragged its brittle tongue along the rattling walls.

"Mercy, Mercy…"

FIVE

"A Cryptie!" Repeatedly throughout the following morning, the word was whispered amongst the inhabitants of Broodmoor. Someone had seen the ghastly thing standing outside a cottage door—naked and haggard, its eyes just pools of mournful shade, the hair all mired, streaky long. She had stood, calling, calling.

Wreaths of protective herbs were quickly fastened to doors, so that the occupants would not meet the fate of the man they had found. He was a farmer named Cliven Bordly. He had died in his bed in a fit of sweat and frothy throes. That was the way one died, when a Cryptie came to call. No one was safe, for a Cryptie cared little about whom it summoned, though they often paid visit to particular individuals, namely those who had summoned them.

Night came and went. Timb waited. Had he fouled the strange ritual in some way? Where was his beloved? After his patrol he borrowed a horse and rode out to where her family had buried her.

The hill was a brooding thing plated with discs of slate. The yellowed grass was scabbed with leaves from a nearby oak. He climbed halfway up and knelt by her stone. The name was crisply spelled out on the new marker, whereas others were blurred and moss-choked. The air at that spot was heavy with bothered soil. He used his saber to pry the stone free.

Trembling in a sheath of sweat, Timb rolled the heavy grey disc aside and peered into the dank earthen throat. No pallid feet, no shrouded bundle. No rotting stench. Mercy was gone.

❧ ❧ ❧

That night Timb lay awake on his stiff little cot. He watched the door, waiting for a knock that never came. The rain drummed him to sleep.

In the morning they found Jarter. He was on the floor of his cabin, his hands pressed to his ears, his eyes locked in a numb gaze. One of the guard men on duty had seen a naked girl near his shack. She had made off into the rain, eluding his pursuit.

❧ ❧ ❧

"What have I done?" Timb wondered as he sat looking across the bleaks. Clouds gathered themselves in foamy knots against the jaundice sunset. The moor moaned its wind, which licked chill across his sullen brow.

"Death upon death. I've tired of it all. Guns and gore, ghouls and graves. Blast you, northern bleaks!"

The clouds rolled closer in mocking tones of white and grey. They formed a massive rolling shroud, rolling—rolling over the splay of the hills.

❧ ❧ ❧

The blanket was coiled in his fist and damp with dream-spent tears when Timb awoke. He looked about the darkness of the tiny shack. His belly gurgled—his digestion had been agitated as of late. All was still.

A slight breeze whispered outside. He pulled on his uniform, boots and all, and went out to cool his head in the night air. He wandered about the encampment for a while, pausing to speak with two of the men on guard duty. They were looking down the slope into a valley that bordered their small village.

"Sheep," one noted.

Timb perked. He heard the distant bleating and half expected to see a blond girl walking amongst the white shapes. He watched for a moment before heading back to his bed.

Ϭ Ϭ Ϭ

An hour or so had passed.

"*Timb?*"

It was a soft voice that came stealing through the dark, a voice like moonlight on mist. He stirred.

"*Timmmmb…*"

He bolted upright. "Mercy!"

"*Timmmmmmmmmmmb! Timmmmmmmb!*"

"No, Mercy, no!"

Tears broke on his cheeks. She had come to kill him.

"*Timb…*" The voice seared into him like winter wind.

It was right outside his door. He reached into the pocket of his long coat for the jar Stoat Murmur had given him.

"*Timb…*" Her voice moaned deeply, wrapped like great dark hair around his lungs. He felt them being squeezed.

"*Timb…*"

There! He had the jar, uncorked it!

"*Timb!*"

He coughed; his innards fluttered. He stuffed the paste deep into his ears. He stuffed his pistol under his belt, went to the door and threw it open.

She stood rigid, hair dark and drooling. Her stare was like two musket barrels, her jawless gape dark-wide. Her body was bare, all pallid slate, her ribs like clenched teeth, her once plump breasts sagging. The cheeks that once smiled round and pink were haggard muddy trenches.

"*Timmmb!*" she moaned.

"Mercy! It's me! I'm here!"

"*Timb…*"

"Please don't do this! Remember, you said you couldn't kill? Remember?"

He grabbed her clammy shoulders. The vacant face was close, her grave-breath gusting ice.

"*Timb…*"

"Mercy—hear me, if you can! I'm sorry! I'm sorry I caused you to die! I'm sorry I called you back. You're meant to rest now—go back and sleep! Don't kill any more, please."

She was silent, her eye sockets staring like two toothless mouths.

Timb reached out and touched her cheek. "I love you, Mercy."

"*Timb…I love you.*"

He fainted.

*   *

"Here now, Timb, that's no place to sleep, lad." One of the guardsmen was bent over him.

He sat up. "Where is she?"

"Who?"

"Mercy. A girl."

"What girl? You've been tippin' the jar a bit much, I reckon, Timb. I've seen no girl."

The man helped him to his feet and started moving toward his cabin. Another guard jogged over, grinning. "Ho—either of you lads have any fleece shears? Lookie this!"

He pointed down the side of the grassy plateau where the dense flock of sheep had climbed up, grazing. Bleating tones came from the other side of the camp, as well.

Timb watched as several of the sheep stood suddenly upright, the woolly hides flopping free. Muskets rose and belched. One of the guards went down with a grunt, his chest fractured red.

The militia men roared in battle-charge, discarding their disguises, pushing through the frightened beasts that had accompanied them. They poured up the hill, blazing.

"Northies!" went the cry.

Timb slammed into his cabin. The structure shook as balls punched through. He grabbed his heavy longarm, his powder flask, saber and pouch.

There was havoc, hate and madness—every man sprang to the test. The noise was one long-throbbing lightning crash. The fleeing sheep, the clouds of smoke, the screams, the horrid screams—one horrid soup of motion on that hill!

The sleeping tents were shattered, men ran bleeding and aflame. A cannon, disguised as a sheep, mowed down many like a wave. The air was hot and thick with balls, dense swarms of metal flew. Men broke and tumbled, their limbs like foolish toys. They heaped and splayed on reddened grass.

Timb saw Captain Burnclay with a saber through his ribs. He staggered through the smoky gore-damp air. He gibbered orders as he fell, then twitched in violent death, his teeth in final fierceness bared.

The dark figures were amassed on either side and closing fast. They knelt, fired, then fell back. Replacement gunners took their places and hammered off their blasts. It was dizzying and deafening, their mighty muskets flashed!

A stray arm flung past Timb's face as a ball bit through his coat. It clipped the handle squarely from his blade. All about was run and stagger, gallant cursing and despair. Heads like eggs to angry balls, the wails of the impaled. The crying of the wounded ones in red.

The ground soon was stacked and carpeted with fallen squishing forms. The rancor raged, unmindful of their plight. The spitting balls came showering—such confusion was at hand. Timb aimed into their ranks and fired back.

The lead whizzed past, men toppled. Some Kingdom men in nightshirts ran with bayonets aglare. One examined a fresh orifice with indignant disbelief. He cursed and ran headlong into their blows. It was a feast of death, as some had never tasted.

Kynn was there, broad-smiling as he charged quick up the hill, heroic juices surging like a hot voice in his brain. He spun to let his weapon speak, a Flint went squealing back. Kynn laughed and sneered and ran ahead for more.

The rebels were outnumbered, though their anger was the best. They rolled like dark waves upon the foe. Sabers swung in eager arcs, their batteries aflash, battle cries resounding through the smoke.

Timb ducked behind a cabin, which was nibbled and gore-stained. A sliver of protection, where he might reload! He jammed a bullet which was wrapped in greased cloth (for a snug fit) down his weapon's throat, but had not time to finish before a rebel came pounding toward him.

He saw the flash, the smoke so white—even in the dark. The blast was close upon his poor stunned ears. The pain was like a flood of flame, his balance was destroyed. He looked before he fell—his left leg gone beneath the knee!

The rebel stood above him, with gloating grin and eyes. He took his time in pulling free his sword. How small he looked, to be playing this game, thought Timb within his swoon. Something familiar crawling through his mind.

"Ahh, it's you!" Kynn said, surprised. "Well, now we meet again. I did not introduce myself before. Allow me to be proper now, you worthless Flinty swine. I am Kynn Stagwood. I believe you knew my sister. Now I'll do to you what I so merrily did to her..."

Timb raised his pistol up; it jolted in his hand. The boy stood frozen in his tracks. Quick reeds of gore came sprouting as his fingers grabbed his throat—he choked upon his hero blood.

"Drink, bastard, drink!" Timb cried.

The boy fell slowly back.

When morning came, the plateau was one squirming mass of red; raised arms like twisty branches growing from the grass. It was as if some half-formed organism, semi-puddle, semi-mass, was being born, or dying perhaps.

There were moans and there was sobbing, from the floor of slaughter-drench. Muddy men, pale men, bloody men clutching their wounds like medals to their chests. The mist came like a ghost of the sulfur-smoke which earlier had stank, but the mist was not dense enough to hide the terrible scene. Timb lay among them, his head on a damp pillow-torso thinking about the boy he'd been, a boy with dreams of glory and valor. That was before they sent him to the bleaks.

So this was the soldier's life, he thought...a soldier's death.

❧   ❧   ❧

The village of Wheelcairn was a quaint place, located in the eastern district of Westermead. It was on the outer edge of a vast forest of oak and beech and birch. There were farms scattered across the cool green valley, and rich briars where the birds grew plump on sun-fattened berries. It was a sunny place in the spring.

An old woman was out hanging clothes in the warm flower-scented air when she spotted the man with the crutch. "Morning!" she said, as she did each day.

The man's face was sullen. "Good morning, Mrs. Crunder."

"I hear we crushed the last of 'em. The northern resistance, as they call it."

He nodded. "Mm."

"A good thing, too. I bet you'd 'ave liked to been there for that."

Timb smiled an ironic smile. "Actually, no." He really did not care to pursue the matter, though Mrs. Crunder gave him an inquisitive look.

"Now, if you'll excuse me, ma'am, I must get my flock home."

She watched him hobble off, his left stump dangling as he waded into his clustered sheep. They closed in about him, nudging affectionately as he stroked their heads and passed them treats from the sack he wore where a saber once rode.

The Mask of Black Tears

ONE

The whore watched the acorn as it hovered lazily above the head of the sleeping man. Her finger absently traced patterns on his chest, avoiding the long-healed white of scars, as if touching them would disturb his deep slumber. A single window looked out across the roofs of the port town and the dark sea beyond; a salty breeze tilted the flame of the lone bedside candle— the floating acorn's shadow bobbed ghost-like on the wall above the bed.

The woman studied him. His face, even in sleep, was like a mask of cool wax struggling silently to contain a molten core. At least now she was spared his icy gaze of penetrating blue. His grey hair swept back over his ears and away from his forehead; his face was clean-shaven, sneer-lines running from the sides of his nose down past his mouth.

Although she saw many men, stationed as she was in a busy port, the whore remembered Mullein Wick. He had rented her twice the previous year. She did not remember him solely for his brooding intensity—it was hard to forget a man with one arm and an acorn that followed him like a wasp. But there had been two acorns the other times…

The woman gasped and jerked her legs up. The blanket at the bottom of the bed fluttered briefly, then flattened. Wick sat up, shot his arm out and grabbed his pistol from the table. "What is it?"

The woman scowled. "Blasted ghost!"

Wick squinted into the room's dark. "I see nothing."

The whore peeled the blanket back and rubbed at her ankle. There were dark suction bruises, like those some sailors left on her throat in feeble gestures of territorialism. There were several on her foot as well.

"Every Oakbrown he comes back, the little bastard!"

Wick sighed and rested his back against the headboard, lowering his weapon to his lap. "A past patron, perhaps?" he wondered softly.

"No—I don't know what he is, or was. I've seen him…looks like a teenaged lad; just sits there on the edge of the bed all grey and glowing like the blooms of a mothcandle—but only when I'm, you know, earning my pay."

Wick smirked.

"Oh, you find it amusing? It's not good for business, I'll have ya know, mister pirate. It's a ghastly sight if ever there was one. The thing's face fades to nothing above the mouth, and it just sits there watching…" She shivered.

"How can it be watching if it has no eyes?"

"I can tell. I can feel it watching." The whore pouted defensively and worried her splotched ankle. "It spoke once—just once. It was very matter-of-fact in tone; it said, 'I like the heat.'"

Wick closed his eyes. He had seen worse things—years spent at sea raiding the spice routes. The sea was full of ghosts—he had added to them. He listened to the ocean's distant hiss.

"Every Oakbrown he comes back," the whore mumbled.

They sat there in the dark, quiet for a time. Wick put his gun back by the lone candle and reached over to stroke the arch of the woman's back with his brine-rough fingers. A cool breeze came from the open window.

"Listen," the whore whispered.

Wick heard nothing; his ears had been dulled by musket fire. "What now?"

"Scratching. I believe it's coming from out—"

A small animal leapt in through the window and landed on the table. It looked like a cat, thin and black with moon-colored eyes. It poised cautiously and looked up at the acorn suspended above Wick's head.

The whore waved at the thing. "Here now, off with you!"

The creature turned deliberately to the candle and poked its snout into the flame, whereupon it burst like a flash of gunpowder. The beast was reduced to hot-glowing beads, which scattered across the floor, hissing as they rolled. Wick jolted upright and witnessed the tiny lights extinguishing themselves harmlessly.

"I've had enough," the whore exclaimed, "I'll not stay here another night!"

Wick examined the wide pine floor planks before placing his bare feet down. He stood, paced, studied the bizarre burnt patterns created by the rolling lights. The whore took notice as a strange look came over his face.

"What's wrong?" she asked.

"These marks mean something."

Wick shoved furniture aside to make better sense of the lines. He backed several paces and wagged his head, mumbling something under his breath.

"Well, what is it, Wick?"

"It can't be…"

"What's wrong? Does it say something?"

His eyes remained riveted on the scorched floorboards. "It says, 'Mydell alive, south.'"

"What's it mean?"

Wick looked up. "My sister, Mydell—I was told she died two years ago…"

The whore clapped a palm to her forehead and blurted, "Every Oakbrown the whole blasted world goes mad!"

Brammon Kinridge made his morning rounds, his head still heavy with mist conjured by the previous night's carousing. He made sure that his hired men had arrived, as there was much work to be done in the fleeting weeks before winter arrived. Then he trod up a slope with cane in hand, his ale-wearied guts feeling heavy and dark. A wooden fence followed the path, a clutter of sunflowers leaning against it, their impassive black faces drooping. They looked like how he felt.

The gate posts in front of the barn were worn smooth where warm cows had brushed against them. The soil was packed hard by bovine bulk, the flagstone scuffed, its creases dark with field mud and cud drippings. The air was hay and dung as he entered the old stone structure and stood with as much authoritative rigidity as he could muster.

Two servant women were crouched over wooden buckets, rhythmically working the teats of bored-looking cows. They looked up as the man observed them, tapping impatiently with his cane.

"Be quick about it," Brammon snapped. "There's much to be done today."

The young master went back outside; looking north along the road which bisected one of his fields, he spotted a horseman. The figure was but a wobble of shadow against the mistily stippled hills of maple flames.

"Who might this be?" he wondered. "A traveling merchant?"

The rider neared, passing great spiky wheels of straw. Brammon walked back down the slope and waited in front of his house of timber and brick until the traveler came into focus. He shuddered.

"Why, Uncle," Brammon burst in feigned enthusiasm, "I must say this is an unexpected pleasure. What brings you to these parts? Here, let's tend to your beast."

Brammon took the horse by the bridle as Mullein Wick dismounted. The young, smartly dressed blond tethered the horse to the fence as his uncle looked on inscrutably.

"Come inside, dear Uncle, for the morn is chill and the sun tepid. We'll pour you full of warm hazelnut tea."

Wick limped along without a word, his long rust-colored coat flapping about the backs of his calves, the left sleeve hanging empty. A single acorn bobbed in the air about him.

It was warm in the house; a fire crackled. A servant girl looked shyly at the tall stern-faced stranger.

"Tea for our guest," Brammon demanded. "Here, Uncle, sit."

Wick placed a hand on the back of the chair but remained standing. "Looks like you've done well for yourself," he noted with a voice like hemlock-laced chocolate.

"That I have! I'm a regular gentleman of business, with servants and hirelings to work my fields. Yes, I've done quite well."

Wick nodded solemnly as his one remaining hand moved to open his coat, exposing the smooth curve of a pistol handle. "Where is your mother, Brammon?"

"Dead—I wrote you—dead these two years now."

"You lie, but that's all you've ever been good at, isn't it?"

"No, I swear, she died!"

Wick's paw flashed between them and clamped around the young man's throat with a clap. "Where is my sister, Brammon?"

"All right, all right, she's alive," Brammon gurgled. Wick released him.

"Why did you tell me she was dead?"

"To keep you away."

Wick scowled, his blue eyes raging. "Why?"

"I, I knew you'd be angry if you knew what became of her...if you thought she were dead there'd have been no reason for you to come back—you never would have found out what happened."

"Explain."

Brammon looked away. "We were in great debt, the farm was a ruin from drought and pests, so I secured her a position with a wealthy landowner in Weedtower..."

"What of all the gold I sent?"

Brammon shook his head. "I gambled it away."

"Where is she?" Wick growled. He hated to see the resemblance of his sister in this wiry young man's face. It was as if someone had taken her gentle features and stretched them out, weasel-sharp.

"Well," Brammon stuttered, "as I said, I, I fixed her a position working as a servant for this Mr. Culling fellow. She was carrying firewood one day when she slipped and dropped some of the logs into his favorite flowerbed. He was enraged, terribly enraged. He..." Brammon was trembling, his snide face wraith-pale, "he sentenced her to work a year without pay for each flower crushed."

Wick squinted. "That's bloody mad. How many flowers?"

"Twenty or so. I tried to retrieve her, I swear, but he has guards and guns..."

Wick nodded, looked down at the floor for a moment, then pulled the pistol from his belt, jabbed it into Brammon's stomach and fired. The servant girl shrieked; the smoky blast slapped the room. Brammon crashed back against the table, his shirt a torn stain of black powder and gore. He flopped down at his Uncle's feet. Brammon was still thrashing, still gurgling as Wick limped out the door.

TWO

Wick rode until dusk squeezed the sky small. Leaf-heavy boughs closed about the road in raspy clots of shadow as geese stitched honking toward the east. The bird voices drifted off as they slipped from view, small and insignificant, swallowed by the swollen purple above the horizon. Wick hated the inland; already he missed the sea. He could not understand how people could want to anchor themselves to stagnant parcels of earth. To be settled was to be chained—the sea was where true freedom lay—no possessions to carry about, no spouse to tend or young to rear. There was no love to lose when a man lived on the sea; the only tears were the spray of waves. Indeed, there was nothing to love but a ship, and one's own stark existence.

There had been love in his life, he thought, reaching to stroke the silky neck of the horse he'd purchased for this journey, like the pup he had as a boy that would sit with patient head on his knee as he fished the rocks off Skully Point. There had also been his grandmother, who took him walking along the shore in search of tide treasures. They would tempt the waves by drawing in the damp sand, then picnic on treacle paws and spice-cider, watching as their art dissolved.

There had been lovers as well. How they had lured him with wild windy hair, and giggles like flowers tickling the ears. He had clung to their soft bodies as if to submerge himself and leave the world and its ways. He had gazed into brown eyes, green and blue—as if seeking an acceptable reflection of himself, free of scorn. The hunger for approval always led to fears of loss; embraces all too soon became strangle holds of possession. He remembered lying in the dark, feeling so distant, though pressed against the warmth of another; two boats floating close, but never sharing a dock. He would hear the ocean off in the night, whispering to him. Romantic love was a dark place, mysterious and reef-haunted, inevitably cursed by disconnectedness. Fits of the heart…

The person closest to him in his youth had been his older sister Mydell. She was an elusive creature, much as he was. She was more fond of animals than humans, and the village folk scorned her for this preference. But she was simple like a beast, sweet like a dog, self-absorbed as a cat, meek as a ewe. She had a way with the creatures as well—it was as if they sensed the goodness of her heart and kindredness of her spirit.

Mydell married a farmer and Mullein followed his roaring blood to sea, as if his body were a boat caught in the red rapids of his own spirit. Off to adventure and rootlessness, his twenty-four hovering acorns like a flock of restless bees. She raised sheep and cattle and he rode the stormy grey on a pirate ship called Noovum's Sting. She gave birth to a son, he sent men to watery graves. It was as if Mullein and Mydell were a broken whole, in need of balancing their halves of light and dark.

Mydell's husband died when he fell in a poacher's trap; Mullein lost his arm when a man on a spice vessel opened up with a blunderbuss. In his mind he could still see the arm as it sank down into the water, trailing a ghostly plume of red...the hand still clenching a saber.

The road south took Wick deeper into the dark, the strange dusky light having resigned, leaving night to establish itself. Leaves tumbled, a breeze-slanted rain clicking softly as they hit branches, or settled raspily on the road. Wick could see only a fraction of them, the close ones spinning slowly past, or brushing the snout of his mare. They pelted him, their feeble weight like the touch of some unseen, barely corporeal entity.

Off to his right, Wick noticed the vague remains of a stone structure visible through the trees. It was ancient, a lumpy shamble of mortarless blocks with several half-grown oak trees groping up between its rotten roof timbers. A fire winked through bramble snares, its light in a trembling wash across one of the precarious walls.

The silhouette of a spidery man flitted about the flames.

The horse stopped abruptly, giving a startled snort. Wick instinctively reached for his pistol and was aiming even before he could discern what the figure standing off the road up ahead was. He smirked, relaxing, lowered the heavy weapon.

It was a birch-woman, one of the traditional effigy types set out at Oakbrown to mark the season of the roaming dead. She was a skeletal tangle of birch branches laced together with dried lengths of corn. This one's head was a large swollen-colored turnip cut with skull-deep sockets from which two silver coins glinted out. Her hair was a rattling mess of twisted straw and grain heads. Red berries had been scattered around her base, for birch-women were placed only where a female had been murdered.

"Not to worry, good creature," Wick whispered to the horse, "'tis only a scare-figure."

Leaves crunched to the right and again the pirate had his gun drawn and leveled.

A voice hissed, "Wait, rider—don't fire!"

It was the spindly man he'd seen at the ruin.

"What do you want?" Wick grumbled.

"Your horse won't pass here; they never do. This spot, I mean. See there, a small path circles off the main road, rejoinin' it up ahead."

Wick looked. It was as the stranger said; there was a worn detour curving around several trees. He glanced over at the birch woman.

"Yes, you see, don't you? Horses can sense such things—like the unspeakable act that happened at this very site," the wiry little stranger said.

"To what act do you refer?"

"Ahhh, a dread thing, sir. A young lass was passing this way not three years ago, pickin' berries as it were, and the terrible Masked Lady got her. Surely you've heard of her..."

"I have not."

"Ahhh, she's a frightful creature—dwells just south of Weedtower. The only time she can leave her lair is in Oakbrown when she wanders the countryside seeking to do her nasty business." The man looked about to the fields and hills that lay beyond the bordering trees. "She might be out and about this very night."

Wick listened as the breeze stole crisply through dry leaves.

"Why don't you come rest by the fire? My brother can tell you of the Lady better than I, for he's known her horrid kiss..."

❧ ❧ ❧

The man's twin was stretched out on a sheep skin by the fire, his face and head coiled in yellow bandages, and though the night was chill, his bony chest was bare—streaked with several black parallel lines.

The spindly dark-haired stranger supplied Wick with a mug of heated ale. The pirate leaned against one of the shattered structure's walls and watched as his host, whose name he learned was Bendrin, unbuttoned a ragged shirt, revealing the bluish tattoo of a face on the front of his right shoulder. The face looked to be that of the very man wearing the tattoo; it had the same gaunt features, the deep-set eyes.

"I had this done by a spellwoman after Milt's run-in with that monster," Bendrin explained, his eyes in the firelight like two silvery fish darting in and out of the murky shadow-waters.

Wick squinted over the brim of his tankard and slurped the warming contents.

"Milt, tell my friend here about the Masked Lady." Bendrin leaned his ear toward the tattoo-face as the body of the recumbent twin trembled for several moments. Wick thought he heard a whispering sound—perhaps the breeze through the oak leaves above.

"He says, '*I was headed back to the barn at the farm where we were working. Each autumn we hire out to farms about here which might be needing help with the harvesting. It was late, and I'd been at the tavern indulging the barley when suddenly I became aware of a presence. I turned and saw this figure gliding up to me, real quiet, like a rippling cone in her long black hooded garment. I thought her face was lost in the hood until I saw that she wore a black mask. It was a lovely serene face—I saw it flip open, as if hinged on the side—then there was horrible pain, and my eyes were on fire—I fell to the ground in a faint.*'"

Wick looked over at Milt, who lay wheezing through his bandages.

"That was last year," Bendrin explained. Turning to his brother, he said, "Tell the man how you feel now, Milt."

Again the healthy man listened to his tattoo, again Milt twitched.

"He says, '*A year has passed since that dread night and still my face boils with agony…and these scorches on my chest, where her tongues licked, are like bars imprisoning the pain within me. I am joyless—I shall never be free of this suffering.*'"

THREE

Colorful entropic Autumn tucked about the village of Weedtower in hues that ranged from pastel to the luminous. The buildings were close at the center, the cobbled streets thin and shadow-squeezed. The morning air was steamy and hot by the blacksmith's clangy den, sweet where lads dumped buckets of apples into the hopper of a cider-press, feeding them down with a club while a rusty wheel was cranked—the pomace yielded its thick bronze slush. Wick rode through this maze of narrow alleys with dry leaves skittering past.

The air was heavy and metallic with blood by the butcher's shop, soft and inviting by the bakery where the aroma of bramble-berry pies and maple-sauce cakes wafted. An old man sat astride a wooden cooper's mare amidst the scented shavings of teak, working a stave with a knife. Several completed metal-hooped butter churns sat off to one side. He looked out the open wall of his shop as the one-armed stranger passed, two wrinkly squints above a great jutting beard. Three bulky grey women sat outside a tall angular building weaving baskets of rushes. They looked up and smiled at Wick, who nodded politely in response.

At last, he reached the tavern. Inside it was warm and dark, the air close with food and mead. Wick had tucked his little floating companion into a pocket of his long rust coat so as not to draw attention. He ate alone, occasionally eyeing one of the serving maids. She had an uncouthly thick mane of vixen-red hair and the skin of her neck and upper chest was smooth and pale. Her bosom squeezed round above the tight green of her corset, threatening to slide free like plump white shellfish. She jostled maddeningly as she bent over the tables to pick up plates or put down mugs.

Wick stared down into his plate, his hunger for food draining away. He felt the acorn straining to free itself from his pocket. He shoved the plate aside and guzzled his mead.

The chatter about him was a mindless drone. He sneered in distaste. Farmers were slow-witted beasts, he thought. He was cunning and quick, they were like languid cows—in mud to their knees. Yet, looking about at them, he sensed that they were content with their situations. Perhaps, he reasoned, he resented them for this. They with their safe settled lives seemed to be more at peace with themselves and the world than he—though he lived the windy exotic life of a seafarer.

He looked back at the serving lass with her eyes of green smiles and her quick grin and her breasts molding to gravity's whims as she moved this way and that. There would never be enough time, he thought, to be like these people. His blood was crashing surf, the reckless tide behind his stony face. No time to play those silly love games again. No time to settle and seed. All that mattered now was releasing Mydell. He left several gold coins on his table and limped out. The red-haired serving maid had never received such a handsome tip.

❧ ❧ ❧

On his way back through town, Wick noticed something that caused him to pause outside the blacksmith shop—he studied the young dark-haired fellow, whom, he assumed, was an apprentice. The man had three black smears slanting across his face, and several on his right forearm. The other arm bore a fresh injury, no doubt caused by the spattering of molten metal—the flesh was a raw fever-pink, white where hideous hieroglyphics of pus had bubbled underneath.

"You there," Wick addressed the man.

"You mean me, sir?"

"That's right."

The young man hobbled over, stepping around a clutter of tools and scrap. Steam billowed behind as hammer-blows rang. He looked up at the one-armed stranger.

"What can I do for you, sir?"

"Those marks, you got them from the Masked Lady?"

"Aye, I did at that, brave fool that I am. Last Churn, in fact, sir. I went to challenge her." He gave a crooked half-proud grin. "Many men have challenged that wretched thing. I'm lucky to have got off as intact as ya see me standin' now."

"You challenged her?"

"Aye. She's quick, though—those black tears of hers are like lightning..."

Wick squinted. "Why would a man confront so deadly a foe?"

"Greed, I'd venture to say. Yes, I'll admit to that—'twas greed compelled me, sir. You see, there's much to gain if a man can get past her—the most fertile fields in all Westermead rest beyond her lair."

"So men challenge her? For trivial bits of earth?"

"For wealth and power. Land is wealth and wealth is power about these parts, mister. Nothin' wrong with a bit of power, though, eh?"

"That depends on how it's used."

The young man nodded. "Yes, yes, I suppose. But I think it's something more than the land that makes 'em go an' confront the Lady. It's a sort of dark sport, it is, to test oneself in danger's face, as it might be. Ahhh, but she has no face behind that lovely mask of hers—only those poison tears of black."

A shadowy figure moved in the thick steam behind the apprentice, and a voice like steel issued, "Come now, lad, there's work to be done. Don't spend all your strength on the jaw!"

The apprentice grinned guiltily, bending the dark slats on his face. He held up his wrist to display his bracelets of burns. "The poison scorches, sir. Oddest sensation I e'er experienced. After it hit me there was a numbness, but then the burning began, and it's not stopped since. But I've learned my lesson, sir, that I can assure. I'll not do such a foolish thing as that again. I've mellowed in my ways."

Wick gave him a hint of a smile. "You'd best get back to your work."

"Aye, sir. Good day to you then, sir."

Wick headed away but stopped to turn when the apprentice called out.

"'Scuse, me, sir!"

"Yes?"

"What brings you to Weedtower? I've not seen you hereabouts…"

"I've business to settle with a Mr. Culling."

"Culling," the young man sneered, "he's a bastard if ever there was one!"

"So I've heard."

FOUR

Wick rode beyond the edge of the village proper, the road slicing south through a whispering sea of millet. The shadow of the hovering acorn danced ahead of his horse, as if taunting the beast to follow. He passed a team of harvesters, their wagon creaking beneath the hulking weight of hay. The men looked weary, having spent the morning wielding pitchforks and sickles.

Here and there, along his way, Wick encountered other groups of reapers. They were tattered creatures, women, men, even children. Unlike the farmers on the northern side of Weedtower, they did not own the fields in which they worked—they were hirelings to wealthy landowners whose sprawling homes perched boldly behind bramble-seamed moats of stone. A ghost of guilt stirred in the pirate when he looked upon these people, for they slaved so hard for their meager wages while he made his fortune stealing.

An occasional grove broke the monotony of open space. Beech pods popped beneath the ponderous weight of his mare as they traveled through the tangled russet. A long covered bridge stretched across a leaf-colored brook; the beast's hooves tamped hollowly down the cool wooden throat.

A spindly harvest figure of sticks and straw had been spiked to a wall by the far opening. Its head was a plump turnip, now wrinkling and bruise-colored, the crude carved features abstracting hideously. Small flies played across the scowling lips.

Exiting the bridge, Wick could see the stone tower of the Culling manor rising beyond the trees. Shortly he came to a high stone wall where two gruff men with muskets guarded a hinged metal gate. They inquired as to his business.

"I've come to see Mr. Culling concerning a relation of mine who is under his employ," he explained calmly.

Before allowing him on the grounds, the guards took his pistol and the saber that hung from his horse.

࿔ ࿔ ࿔

Wick waited in a cobbled courtyard, encircled by high walls and beds of flowers. The thirty-foot round tower rose as the central point of interest, and, he observed, it was not attached to the massive stone manor house. Two servants stood precariously atop ladders, scrubbing the stones and washing the multi-paned windows that faced out from the small room at its peak.

Eventually a jaunty man in a lacy white shirt and green velvet britches came bounding out of the manor. He looked to be in his late thirties, his blond hair tousled and long, almost too pretty for a male's head. He smiled pleasantly at the stranger, his face shaven and handsome, his eyes pale.

"Tremendously sorry to have kept you waiting—one of the stable boys made such a mess of my prize horse's mane, it was an absolute must that I administer a taste of the cane." He glanced down into his open palms. "Oh, I fear I worked up a sweat! But he got the worst of it." Burch Culling winked.

Wick eyed the man dispassionately, the feign of a smile blinking across his lips.

"I'm sure you get a great deal of practice!"

"Ahhh, discipline is of extreme importance, I'm sure you'd agree, mister..."

"Mullein Wick."

"Wick, right. I am a busy man with much property to maintain and many workers to govern. I expect discipline of myself, as well as my laborers. Which reminds me—I'm told you wish to speak to me regarding one of them?"

Wick yearned to reach out his hand and sink his fingers into this man's lily throat, to rip his snide voice out of him and see blood wash across his fine white blouse.

"Yes. My late nephew informed me that my sister is here. Her name is Mydell."

The two armed guards remained within view, eyeing the tall grey-haired man with the long rust-colored coat and one arm. They muttered to each other.

"Mydell, oh, yes, the name is familiar," Culling said. "I have so many servants, it's difficult at times to recall their names. She's older, yes?"

"Fifty-three years."

"Right." Culling leaned a hand against the base of the tower and looked up at one of the servants, his face taking on a snappish mood. He didn't care for the way the woman was leaning her weight against the small diamond-shaped panes she was washing. He hurried over to her ladder and gave it a sharp kick. "You there!"

The startled woman flinched, nearly losing her balance. She looked down. "Yes, Master Culling?" her voice trembled.

"Don't press so on the glass!"

"Sorry, sir, very sorry…"

Culling snorted with contempt. "Imbecile," he mumbled.

The landowner took Wick by the arm and led him beyond the wooden door of the tower. "Come," he said, "I'll show you my property."

They climbed a spiral staircase to the small circular room in the tower's skull. After waving the servants out of the way, Culling swept a hand across the expansive view, grinning proudly. "All mine," he sighed.

Wick found it revolting that this man felt thoroughly important for imagining that part of the earth actually belonged to him. Men who made their home at sea had no such delusions.

"You must agree it's a lovely view," Culling said.

Wick grew impatient. "I'd like to discuss my sister."

Culling gave a sneer and looked this raggedy stranger up and down. "Well, what of her?"

"I've come to take her away. You have many servants; surely you can do without her."

Culling struck a pensive pose. "Hmmm. You said her name is Mydell?"

"Correct."

"Well, I'm dreadfully sorry, but I can't release her. She's obligated to serve me for some years to come. It's sort of a disciplinary action, a trade of services to redeem herself for damages done to my property." Culling smirked smugly.

Wick glowered down and growled, "You have no right to enslave a woman, especially for crushing some of your bloody flowers!"

"Don't meddle, Mr. Wick. If you find yourself displeased with the situation, might I suggest you take it up with the village magistrate—my brother. I'm sure he would be most understanding."

Wick trembled, fought to keep down the rage that yearned to erupt in flames of bile. His hand hovered in front of Culling's face, the finger aiming pistol-like. "I will water your precious flowers with your blood if you do not release my sister immediately," he seethed.

Culling laughed sharp and high. "Hah! You don't think you'll make off these grounds without my gunners taking you down, do you, Mr. Wick? You won't harm me."

"Duel with me. Pistol, sword—the choice is yours."

"Ahh, I've no need for such silly activities as those. You'd win, I'm sure. However, there is a challenge I can offer you, if dueling is your sport. In fact, if you succeed in doing what I have in mind, I will release your dear sister Mydell on the spot. I will give you my word, and my word is the best!"

Wick squinted. "Explain yourself."

"You've no doubt heard of the Masked Lady?"

Wick gave a disgusted sigh. "You want me to kill her?"

"Yes! Kill her and you buy your sister's freedom."

"You have everything to gain, don't you, Culling? If she kills me you don't have to worry about me trying to kill you. If I kill her, you gain more still—you will have access to the land she guards..."

"The most fertile fields in all of Westermead." Culling smiled broadly. "I do hope you can defeat her. Well, Wick, what shall it be? You could hurl me out the window right now, I suppose, but then you'd be shot trying to leave the tower, and how can you win the release of poor Mydell if you're dead?"

"Give me your word."

"You have it. Then we have a bargain of sorts?"

Wick nodded.

"You'll bring me her mask, for I must have proof."

"As you wish. Now, I would like to see my sister."

233

Culling grinned and pointed out the window to where distant harvesters bustled in a golden field. "See—there! She's one of those specks!"

FIVE

Trees spilled black on the copper sky, like twisted coral, and the village buildings silhouetted too. The air was spiced with wood-smoke, chilled enough to show one's breath. Wick moved briskly, limping through the narrow streets of Weedtower, his long coat flapping cloak-like, his saber slapping against one leg. He reached the open-fronted blacksmith shop and motioned to the apprentice, who emerged squinting from the steam.

"You close soon, yes?" Wick seemed insistent, his eyes a molten blue.

"Aye, sir..."

"Meet me at the tavern when you're finished."

"As you like."

Wick spun around and headed off, a hobbling one-armed shadow against the sunset brass.

   * * *

"What is the nature of her attack?" Wick asked.

The apprentice, Nulton Brisk, wiggled his fingers. "The mask opens and these black things, much as if they were the arms of a squid, fire out. Fast as a blink."

Wick brooded into his tankard of spiced ale. No one had ever defeated the Masked Lady; indeed many had died trying. He was not as spry as he used to be, what with his limp, and just one arm, and he wondered if he were up to the task. But then again, those who had battled her before were simple farmers, not a rugged pirate like himself. Their tools were hoes and pitchforks; his were swords and guns. Perhaps she was no match for him.

Wick had not bothered to tell his companion the details of his troubles; it was not like him to share his personal business with others. He had merely disclosed that he was in a situation which forced him to go up against the dreaded Masked Lady.

234

"I must say, Mr. Wick, you really ought to reconsider. I mean, she's a nasty one…"

"Yes, and so am I. Be at your shop first thing in the morning; I'll be needing the smith to construct a special implement…"

Nulton grinned. "You're a stubborn man, Mr. Wick."

The pirate nodded, staring into the drowsy steam of his drink.

Sleep resisted the man. He lay in his bed at the inn, gazing at a lone sputtering candle as it burned down, slow tendrils of wax reaching to grip the tin holder. The night was windy and wet—drops pattered the window, trees rattled their sabers of bark. He thought upon his sister—gentle, kind, her face round and smile-eyed. Winds of pain filled the sail of his heart.

The smith was a lanky wizened thing; he listened frowning as the seaman explained what he wanted. He seemed reluctant to trouble himself with the project until Wick produced a handful of gold.

"I'll send Nulton out to fetch some leather straps for it," the blacksmith said, scowling. "Be back here as noon strikes and I'll have it for ya."

Wick gave a triumphant little smile, nodded over to Nult and left.

Next he paid visit to the gunsmith. The man marveled at his beautiful snap-lock, with its polished walnut running the length of the long barrel and inlaid whale bone on the grip, scrimshaw depicting sea serpents.

He purchased a smaller pistol as a back-up. It was a snap-lock as well (he found these easier than wheel-locks to manipulate with one hand). The gunsmith gazed curiously at the acorn that hung in the air about the stranger's head.

Wick sat patiently as the old woman rambled on about people and places which, in all frankness, were of no concern to him. She ran a small corner shop where one could purchase baskets, wreaths and candles, which, she was quick to say, were the finest in the land. She and her two spinster daughters made everything themselves, fine crafts-women that they were.

An old one-eyed mongrel dog sat wobbling with its head on his knee. It offered him a floppy smile and drooled contentedly as he stroked its head.

Wick watched as the old talk-some woman skillfully fashioned the likeness of a human hand from wax.

Noon. Wick arrived at the metalsmith's accompanied by the local seamstress. Nulton smiled broadly through the painful streaks on his face and pointed to the object that lay completed on a table.

"It was a bastard to make," the old smith grumbled.

Wick examined the man's handiwork. It resembled an arm, comprised of a spiral of thin metal, the coil covered in sharp barbs. There were straps at the upper extreme.

"Fine work," Wick commented, pleased. "Nult, help me put it on."

Wick removed his coat. They used the straps to fasten the thing to his shoulder, then attached the wax hand to the wrist, securing it with wire. In order to fit the long rust-colored coat over the bogus limb, the left sleeve had to be slit along the bottom seam. The seamstress repaired this, once all was in place.

"You're a clever one, Mr. Wick, you are!" Nulton exclaimed, standing back to admire the end product. "Most convincing, if I must say so!"

The day grew tired, and Wick, stewing in his own thoughts, sat leaning against the base of a wide oak. He was preparing himself inside, slowly, silently, methodically, diverting his rage into a steady hum, so that his mind held its reins. He would need to have control.

The afternoon was peaceful. He watched as leaves tumbled in mute death to join the scattered waste-berries which wrinkled in painful purple.

The air was tart with the rotting sweetness of these bramble-discards. One of the other oaks in the small grove was entwined in a scraggly vine known in the north as bird-net, in the south as bird-snare. It was a cruel plant armed with hideous thorns, which drew nourishment from impaled animals. In fall, with its leaves stripped, it was dry, scratchy, the long spikes exposed—as were the twisted skeletons of small birds—rattling in the breeze.

Wick watched the lone acorn that swam languidly in front of him. "Oak tears," his grandmother had called them. Leaves spiraled past it in their slow dance of atrophy, their colors kissed bright by the afternoon sun. The breeze rustled her cool fingers through the trees, and across his solemn face. He squinted resentfully at the acorn, like a clock's pendulum dangling. He half-heartedly picked up a handful of acorns which had fallen from the tree against which he leaned. He tossed them up one by one, and one by one they dropped, refusing to hang in mid-air. Forty-two of the floating sort had followed him out of his mother's womb, forty-two years ago. Now there was one…

SIX

The boards creaked, the hooves thumped, the long plank-bridge stretched far across the marsh. On either side there were wind-trembling figures stabbing up from the water on poles—they were rags and reeds, some without heads, some wearing sheep skulls, some with impaled turnips. There was an army of the things ranked and leaning for as far as Wick could see. Beyond the bridge, beyond the marsh lay the fertile fields that Burch Culling hungered to possess.

Wick reached the mid-way point and looked back from whence he came. Nothing but distance and those scraggly effigies. He urged his beast on, the bridge swaying and moaning beneath the intrusion. At last they reached the other side.

Wick did not know what to expect. He shifted his weight in the saddle, leaning away from the alien weight of his new appendage. He expected a gate, or a fence, some sign that he had arrived at a place of notoriety. There was only open grassy space and the bulbous mound of an ancient burial tomb rising up against the dusk-soaked sky. He stared ahead, into the black maw of the barrow's entry.

A number of small grey moths sputtered up from the deep grass, disturbed by the horse's legs. They danced in agitation, then made off for the tomb, fluttering inside. Wick would have sworn he had heard them whispering amongst themselves in tiny voices.

He dismounted, pulled free his long snap-lock pistol and set forward. The high grass hissed against his coat; his breath came fast and misty. The barrow swelled before him, its dank odor trickling out. Here and there the earth was damp, even squishy beneath him. It gave him an unsteady feeling, as if he might sink.

Through the stone lips lining the doorway—there was a light inside! Wick prodded the darkness with his weapon, squinting through the web-heavy air. So cool inside that moist stone throat, deeper in...a lone candle on the floor, pooling into itself. The flame stuttered, flung rubbery shadows.

A gasp caught in Wick's chest, his body jolting rigid. There she stood— tall, black, void-faced in her long hooded garment. She was like a pillar against the back wall of the ancient burial tunnel. Wick stepped closer. She did not move.

He brought up the gun. How long could her tentacles reach, he wondered; he should have asked Nulton. He moved cautiously, his legs pulsing along with his heart. He turned slightly so that the artificial arm was held forward. A bit closer; still she did not stir.

Boom! The pistol filled the narrow hall with sound and light. The black figure pitched back, clattering against the wall, the garment sliding down, revealing the skeleton of sticks, which had held the effigy up. He'd been tricked!

"Blast!" Wick cursed. He spun around as the Masked Lady floated silently, steadily into the barrow from outside. Her long robe fluttered black and her mask glinted in the blinking candlelight.

Wick dropped his pistol and went to draw his back-up—the side mechanism snagged on his belt! She was barely a yard away, swimming closer. The mask came into view; it was placid, lovely, the face of a woman formed of glistening black metal.

The man stumbled back until the cool wall was against him and the mock woman's sticks cracked beneath his boots. At last he got the pistol free! He shoved it out and fired.

Boom!

The ball struck her square in the chest, or did it pass through? She continued to move closer, unhindered. Wick heard something creak, saw the mask open sideways. What hid behind was a flat shimmering upright pool, which suddenly spat forth a thrashing tangle of long black whips. They scorched across Wick's jaw and neck. He ducked down, throwing himself to one side. He hit the wall, squeezed past the woman and charged out into the night.

She was swift on his heels, black serpent-tongues firing, flicking. The hovering acorn was hit—it fell into the high grass, squishing down beneath Wick's boot as he staggered back. He was choking in panic; he grasped the handle of his saber and hissed it free. The tentacles sucked back into the hood; the face again was a flat pool of obsidian.

Wick leaned his false arm out and purposefully stepped within range. The whips flashed, wrapped around the offering, snaring in the metal thorns hidden by the sleeve.

"There!" Wick roared.

When the tendrils retracted, the spiked arm was torn free; it clanked against the metal rim of the hood, the lengths still tangled, unable to resubmerge or extend. Wick lunged with the saber, plunging deep into the black—deeper, the sword tearing out the back of the hood. A chorus of overlapping screams issued from the monster as it fluttered back, deflating. The robe sagged and folded, and whatever there was under it now spilled out into the grass, liquid black. The tentacles, tangled around the false arm, withered and twitched before reducing to rivulets. The thorned appendage rolled free and the mask lay still on the heaped and empty robe.

Wick stood staring, trembling. He poked at the mask with his sword. She was dead. He bent and gingerly lifted the serene metal face. That strange pool-like black substance remained on the inside, glimmering ominously.

SEVEN

This time, Wick was met by four armed and ugly men at the gate of the Culling grounds. They searched him, confiscating his pistols and sword before escorting him in. They seemed timid about examining the black metal object he carried in a sack.

The morning sky was overcast in grey—Wick could have sworn there was a touch of winter in the air. He was admitted into the wall-enclosed courtyard, where he stood tired, impatient, joyless even in his triumph over the masked monster. His face and neck were on fire where those swift tendrils had brushed.

There seemed to be a commotion on the other side of the massive stone round-tower. He could see the back of a servant girl leaning against the base of a ladder, sobbing. Two of the musket-toting guardians remained a few yards behind him, while the other two crossed the yard to greet Burch Culling as he exited the manor house. There was a brief hushed conference before the cocky young landowner started over.

Wick studied him, noting the furtive glances of the guards. He walked to meet Culling, peeking behind the tower's thick base to where the crying lass stood. There were two other servants on their knees, scrubbing at a puddle of dark red liquid, which lay beneath one of the ladders.

"Mr. Wick," Culling said with a cautious smile, "I understand you've brought me something." He looked down at the sack, which the one-armed man held.

"Yes," Wick said, "I killed her."

"May I see it?"

Wick held up the bag, but did not offer it. "Bring Mydell, then it shall be yours."

Culling pouted. "Well, you're free to take your sister with you, ahh, but there seems to have been a bit of a mishap…"

Wick looked over at the women sponging up the spilled red, then back into Culling's face—he could see the man's mind working through his eyes, formulating tactful phrases. Wick felt his heart rear up and splinter through his body, a storm of adrenal sparks. His guts sank into his feet.

"Where is my sister?"

"She was cleaning the tower windows, poor clumsy thing…she fell…"

Wick brushed past Culling and looked behind the tower, past the servants to where a figure lay beneath a blanket. He felt himself limping over, his mind melting until his skull was filled with white heat. He knelt, flipped back the blanket. Mydell's round, gentle face gaped up.

"Wick, I'll take the mask, please." Culling came up behind him. "Wick—the mask, I want the—"

Wick rose like a wave in his long rust coat, pulling the mask from the bag. He saw two of the gunners swivel their musket mouths his way, sensed the other two behind him. He lunged, slamming the mask onto Culling's scowling face. The strange black residue sank hot acid teeth into the screeching man's skull. Muskets fired.

      *   *   *

They left Mullien and Mydell for the crows. Left them in a rainy field without ritual or stone. Over time animals and the elements mingled the bones together so that one passing might not be able to decipher what part had belonged to who. Miles away, near the barrow where Wick had battled the Masked Lady, where his final acorn had dropped from the air, a tree sprouted…

The seasons passed, oblivious to human pains and joys. Years compiled—the lone oak grew wide and grey by the ancient burial mound. Each fall its great appendages shed a moat of rust-colored leaves, and acorns rained like tears.

Some Famous Hauntings

The Hamper at Thornwound

An old woman, while visiting her daughter in the south, acquired an old wicker picnic hamper from a shop keeper. Once she returned to her cottage in Thornwound, strange things began to occur. Upon trying to move the thing from one room to another, she found that the hamper was heavy, as if filled with stones, yet it proved empty when the lid was opened.

Some nights, she would hear a man's weeping issuing from the hamper, or scrabbling as if an animal with talons were trapped inside. One evening in the cold of winter, the hamper took to shaking violently. The brave old woman went to it, tossed open the top and discovered a tattered old hangman's noose.

Having had her fill of disturbances, the woman threw the hamper into the fireplace. Later she maintained that, as the thing crumpled black, a man's bloated face appeared in the flames, staring out at her with wide eyes and a smile of absolute madness.

The Phantom Fiddler

For many years the people of South-haunt reported the specter of a man merrily dancing about the streets of their village playing a fiddle. He always wore a full-headed goat disguise and a green vest. No one ever discovered who the phantom fiddler had been in life. He was by no means a shy ghost; indeed he seemed to enjoy being observed. Often he appeared in broad daylight when his musical selections were gleeful dance tunes, but at night the villagers would hear the gloomy laments of his fiddle coming from the woods.

The Hanging Tree at Thistle Keep

A well-known haunting from the Midlands of Westermead concerns a man named Shepherd Arrow-wood. He was a temperamental fellow who spent much of his time drunk on ale, when he was most apt to stir up trouble with his neighbors. On several occasions, he stole sheep from those whose land bordered his. He became vengefully angry when one farmer fired a shot at him, during one such attempt. The following night he poisoned most of his neighbor's flock.

Arrow-wood's enemies met and decided they had suffered enough of his antics. They converged on his cottage and dragged him out into his apple orchard where they proceeded to hang him.

Each Autumn since then, every apple on that gnarly tree bears a hideous, shriveled, grimacing likeness of Shepherd Arrow-wood's face.

The Drowning Lady

Those who brave the rocky shoreline at Cold Dance, on Westermead's windy west coast, know of the Drowning Lady. Fishermen have seen her floating slack past their boats, her mournful eyes unblinking, her long black hair wriggling like seaweed.

Occasionally some poor wayfarer spots a body on the beach and climbs down treacherous slopes of stone only to find that the woman in the soggy white dress has vanished. If you should ever find yourself in a tavern in that small wind-taunted hamlet, you'll be sure to find a fisherman or two eager to tell of an eerie encounter with the Drowning Lady.

Three Harvesters

A group of men, out hunting one fine Autumn afternoon in the cornfields of Kilmnook in South Westermead, encountered a startling vision. Having scaled a slight rise, they looked down to see three skeletons, their bones black as if scorched, running wildly through the golden corn, each waving a scythe in the air. One of those in the hunt party opened fire at the apparitions, which promptly ducked down into the rippling grain, never to be seen again.

✳ Winter ✳

Lowdusk

Trappers take to the whitened wood. Prey forages amid the firs. Young girls hoard holly berries for love charms. The land sweeps gently beneath the gathering flakes. There are stories told over mugs of mulled ale, and the spark and chatter of logs afire. The solstice sun pours fragile hope across the sleeping earth.

Icekeep

Blizzards shriek, windows rattle. Sleet turns gnarly trees to glass. The fields are like wind-polished bone as winter's chill hours collect. Game is scarce and the hardiness of all creatures is tested. Familiar lanes vanish beneath the deepening snows. It seems as if there is no end to these frigid hours.

Freezling

The wise have remained well fed and have not exhausted their stocks of food. The days grow in length, and the storms are less malevolent. The temperatures stray higher; there are hints of long-buried roads. Stars festoon the clear Freezling nights like dew-balls aglint on a spider's web. The sun sets pink over pale expanses, yet rises stronger over evergreen spires.

The Winter Women

Fear rustled crisply through the last clinging leaves on that early Noovum afternoon. The herds had been ushered in from their summer grazing fields; the goods of harvest now weighed heavily in baskets and bins—tucked snugly into root cellars. The noisy celebrations, where dancers formed silhouette-moats around bonfires were over. Toasts of mead and drunken song had faded and the cool wind rasped through those stubborn brown oak leaves—yet even they were detaching, one by one, to ride the precarious currents.

Down in the village, one could sense the anticipation and dread. People watched the sky carefully, and whispered amongst themselves. Each year it was like this. The Noovum sky demanded such scrutiny.

Now that the year had tilted irreversibly towards its dark period, it was only a matter of time before the first snow. The Winter Women would arrive within that fall of cold wet dust. Preparations, just short of panic, had to be taken, for though the spirits made but one seasonal appearance, they were sure to lower the village's population.

$$\mathcal{C}\!\!\!/ \quad \mathcal{C}\!\!\!/ \quad \mathcal{C}\!\!\!/$$

Cydree Lum sat at the front of her wagon, hands absently guiding the family workhorse with subtle manipulations of the reins. She was distracted by all the activity. Behind her the open bed of the wagon was heaped with provisions—things from the village shops, purchased with the meager wages she earned as a potter's assistant. Anything that could not be made, grown, or collected in the wilds had to be bought. Heavy wheels of moon-pale cheese, snug in their waxy red rinds, were piled by clay jugs of cider. There was oil for the lamps, and a new shovel from the blacksmith's shop, which would be used to clear snow.

The buildings in the village were wooden things with thatch roofs and wide stone chimneys. Cydree watched as folks scurried up ladders to string clusters of protective herbs around the smoke-gushing turrets. Some had set up skeletal figures comprised of sticks, their chests all interwoven twigs filled with pale toadstools, which were believed to ward off evil. These scare-effigies looked eerie standing alone against the grey sky.

An old man in a tattered cloak rushed over to Cydree's wagon and shoved a toothless face up at her. "Ahh—girl! Are ya ready for the Winter wenches? Can ya smell it? There's snow in the air!"

Cydree smiled nervously. "I hadn't noticed."

The man scuffed alongside the wagon. "They'll come tonight; mark my word, lass. They'll sweep down all blue and cold—right down yer chimney, and smother the very life out of the flames. You'd best sprinkle snake blood and juniper berries all over ya roof, or they'll come down— whoosh—and getcha!"

Cydree urged her horse to move faster. "Yes, thank you, sir, I'll do that..."

Cydree at nineteen was the eldest of three children; her brother Rallen, twelve, and sister Paleen, seven, were back at their cottage on the outskirts of town. Since their parents had been lost to the Goat Plague four years previous, the plump auburn-haired girl had been forced to maintain the family home. Her mother's sister, Lyma, had come to stay with them some six months past, but she was too old and feeble to take on any responsibilities.

The horse thumped along, leaving the old man behind, his warnings fading into the cold grey air. Cydree sniffed, her keen brown eyes flicking suspiciously skywards. Perhaps the foolish old man was right...

The road led out of the village proper; the houses and shops receding into the distance until all that remained of them were feeble capillaries of chimney smoke. Afternoon sloped towards dusk, the stringy woods on either side leaning in to pitch shadows across the dirt path. Oak leaves frolicked oblivious in a crisp chase. Cydree urged her horse to move faster.

The girl's thoughts were so entangled in worry that the appearance of the stranger, walking toward her on the road ahead, startled her.

"Good afternoon, young miss!" He was a tall fellow, lean, with a scythe nose and a long bony chin. His eyes sparkled darkly as he grinned with greasy charm. He wore a battered black top hat and a long coat of velvet red. A saber hung form one hip and he carried a cane from which dangled a fox's tail.

"Hello," Cydree said cautiously.

"Allow me to introduce myself. I am Dooley Sagebrush, traveling merchant." The tall figure bent in a regal bow, removing his hat with a grand swoop. He rose.

Cydree stopped her wagon and the man came closer. He stroked the nose of the horse as he leaned on his cane, smirking up at the plump young female.

Dooley said, "I've just come from the village of Neebotton and am headed for Weendell."

"That is my village; it's just up the road here."

"Ahh, at last. No doubt I'll do good business there, what with the snow coming and all…"

Cydree cocked her head. "If you are a merchant, where are your goods?"

Dooley smiled a reptilian smile and stepped back, whipping open the sides of his knee-length coat. The insides of the garment dangled numerous objects—little cloth bags scrawled with spell-symbols, necklaces of exotic stone beads, brittle lizard tails, tiny bottles of colored liquid, and gnarled white roots known as "crone fingers."

"You see, miss, I am a charm peddler."

CJ CJ CJ

It took the stranger a minimum of time and effort to convince the girl to purchase some of his wares. He played her fear like an instrument, knowing exactly what strings to pluck. Cydree did not require a great deal of manipulating; she was quite aware of what the Winter Women could do.

They would descend with the first snow, slide down the chimneys of peaceful homes and chill silent the crackling logs. Then they would seek out the eldest member of a household and gently soak through the weave of their blankets—into the sleeper's body. There they would reside until season's end, drawing the heat from the victim's heart, bringing death. The deceased's bones would be crushed to powder and added to the winter's final snow.

❧ ❧ ❧

Crack! The axe fell—the log, standing on its side, split. Rallen, face flecked with sweat, looked beyond the neatly stacked wall of wood as his sister came into view.

"Hurry!" Cydree called over, "Help me unload!"

Paleen stood in a drab brown dress, her little arms full of kindling. She trotted over, spilling most of her bundle. Shortly the things which Cydree had bought were stored neatly in their modest cottage, and the workhorse was contentedly chomping straw in the barn. A new snow shovel leaned by the door.

"Busy, busy," Old Aunt Lyma observed as she sat by the large stone fireplace. She was making a wreath out of dried apple slices and the metallic blue bodies of palm-sized willow spiders.

Rallen walked in, having completed the stick-man atop the roof. Cydree and Paleen prepared the nightly meal. There was cider, cheese, boiled cabbage, fresh bread and sweet bark. They sat at a long table beneath pungent manes of drying herbs.

Aunt Lyma peered solemnly into the fireplace. "It smells like snow out there," she said.

"Not to worry," Cydree replied.

❧ ❧ ❧

Night. Cydree stood outside looking up at the scrawny form of the stick man. The sky drooped in suspended heaps of grey porridge...ominously glowing. The warm light of the cottage windows beckoned her back inside.

The room was long, dark, with low beams. The girl knelt at the hearth and gazed into the jiggling orange plasma. Humans, it seemed, were forever wont to recreate (in vain) the safe conditions of the womb—seeking blankets, sheltering walls, heat. The fireplace was like a womb of flame, to keep one safe from the cold winter of life.

The others had retired. Cydree reached into her skirt pocket and withdrew a small bottle of red liquid, and a sack of rancid-smelling herb dust, purchased from Dooley Sagebrush. The contents of these were emptied into the fire.

The flames rippled in agitation, smoke hissed, logs spat disdainfully. Cydree stepped back, flinching. Then it came…half-visible in vague flashes of red. It was like a malformed toddler, the face almost human, frowning in ugly bulldog folds. A spark dog.

The spirit would, according to Dooley Sagebrush, chase off the Winter Women and keep the logs lit. But the spark dog had other ideas. In one of its brief winking appearances it squinted out of the flames and smiled. Cydree knew not what to do when a hot red blur leapt out and sprinted from the hearth, up over the table, dragging scorch marks, before smashing a hole through the heavy bolted door.

Cydree's shrieks brought her siblings running. They charged outside in time to see the barn burst into flame. Rallen fetched a bucket of water. His rescue efforts were futile; the little barn-stall and the horse within it were lost in a writhing fortress of flame. The spark dog sprang out of the heat and scurried off into the woods, cackling.

Cydree fell to her knees and wept into her palms. Now the barn was gone, the horse dead and there was nothing to ward off the Winter Women. Aunt Lyma would be easy prey. She looked up at the spindly stick-man, blurred through the smoke and tears.

Rallen was puzzled to see his sister's lips curl into a smile.

"Rallen," Cydree said evenly, "Go quickly to the village inn. Bring Dooley Sagebrush here."

        ❧   ❧   ❧

He never did remove his battered black excuse for a top hat. Nor his long red overcoat. He sat by the fire, drinking warm cider, with Cydree sitting opposite, tolerating his seemingly endless string of travel tales. Dooley Sagebrush laughed at his own jokes, his face like a distorted sketch, the angles defined harshly by the firelight. At last, he yawned, dark eyes crinkling shut on either side of his hooked snout.

"It's awfully nice of you to invite me into your home, Miss," Dooley said, as he started for the "spare room."

"Well, you seemed like an interesting gent; I thought it might be nice to have your company about for a few days. Surely you could use a rest from the road."

"That I could," Dooley said. Then he winked and was off.

It was after midnight when the first flakes came down. The wind wheezed through the trees. Cydree pressed a face to the window and watched as thousands of drunken white moths tumbled. Soon there was a fine dusting on the ground.

The door creaked open, a head poked out. She stared at the clouds—a sickly glowing gauze. Here and there, wispy blue streaks wove through the flakes, like falling ribbons, long hair trailing. Cydree shivered. One swooped low over the cottage and swam through the wood smoke, a woman formed of ghostly blue translucence. She vanished into the chimney.

Cydree pulled the door shut and leaned her back flat to it. She gawked at the fireplace as a sizzling sound filled the room. The flames twitched in death throes, then were gone. The girl could almost see it, the spirit. It was naked, gaunt of face and thin of limb, melding at the waist into a vaporous tail. A chill permeated the room; Cydree could feel it soaking into the walls, creaking into the floorboards. The cider in the mug on the table turned suddenly to ice. The Winter Woman turned slowly and looked at the girl, considering…no, there was someone older in the building.

Cydree watched the thing slip silently through one of the bedchamber doors before dashing out into the snow. She rushed through the gentle fall of ghost-locust, ducking down into a stone-lined chamber which was built into a small hillside. There in the root cellar, crouched safely in front of a portable tin coal-heater was Aunt Lyma. The old woman smiled.

Back in the cottage, a wispy blue figure floated over to a bed. The Winter Woman smiled as she lowered herself onto the covers…through the covers…into the sleeper. Dooley Sagebrush lay there oblivious, grinning, seemingly safe in the womb of his dreams.

The Woman Who Cried Birds

Snow fell on Westermead, that great old island, misty grey in the tumbling cold. The silver waters were a melted ghost around it, that place of villages, of twisted orchards, of fiddle tunes in warm taverns and ale as gold as a child's dream in autumn. Westermead was my home until the night when a woman cried birds.

The fire never served me better and I was close by it, and the warming pot of cider hanging there. A woolen wrap about me, and a dead Uncle's favorite song humming, I was smug, snug against the bitterest night of the season.

The wind is a mystery of many voices in Westermead and winter knows fear like a man knows his lover's breasts, even in darkness. Drawing first from an arsenal of subtle notes, it sought to unnerve me, but to no avail, for the sheep were safe in the barn, the apples in the cold house, the mead in good supply. I, a man like a speck on the great world, in my fool shelter under thatch, dared to laugh at the wind.

I poured my cider, I stirred my logs, I put spiced cider in my belly. I cheered myself with song as night fell deeper into itself. I cared not how high the snow piled. Friendly dreams awaited me, and a good soft bed.

At times the wind is a wily thing, and on that night it brought a sound that even I—twenty-nine winters into my life—had never heard it make before. A woman's crying. The sound was at my every window, out in the night and its storm. I had never heard anything so mournful, and the cider soured in my guts.

I am not a hard man, nor the softest sort for that matter, though my life amongst gentle creatures had worn the edges of my younger days, when I would fire a musket to quiet the birds whose summer noise would force me to wake before the sun. What I mean to say, is that the more I listened, the less that wailing seemed like wind and the thought of some poor woman out in the cruel night drew me to the door.

253

I unbolted the door and the wind helped me open it. I squinted out into storm and I saw her, rigid as a scare-effigy in autumn, light hair and long white rags blowing. She was fair and frail, pale in every way, crying. Her tears came away from her, snow-like, fluttering, turning into small white birds. They swirled about her then gathered at her feet, the many small black eyes turned up to me. "*Feed us*," they sang in small windy voices as their woman loomed less solid, like a ghost seen through tears.

I made quickly into my cottage and returned with a length of bread. I broke it into small bits which I tossed to the birds, but they did not take them.

Next I tossed crumbs of cheese which the snow swallowed.

I tossed raisins and nuts, chips of apple and seeds. The flock refused them all and the woman faded to flakes.

"What more can I offer?" I asked at last, but the birds only laughed their small laughs and fluttered up, vanishing in the dark and light of a winter storm.

A familiar sound came, an urgent sound—not the wind, not a woman crying, but the rusty creak of my own barn door and the bleating of my flock.

"Blast!" I cursed.

A flitting white woman lead the sheep out and away, single-file, the birds passing through her pretty white hair, their eyes like currants. I shouted after, gave chase, the storm thick and blurring, the snow pulling at my boots. They wove a ghostly parade through the wind and the white and I could scarcely see them, nor hear the beasts for the roaring cold. I ached and panted, I cursed and wept, following. All was white; the fields, the roads, even the sea.

Westermead snow is a swan of magic feathers, a beauty, a curse, a white song, a shattered puzzle of moon-colored lies. It can charm you and fool you, sister to the wind that it might be. I saw the sheep bobbing, sinking in snow, white backs drawn under. I heard the muffled cries, saw the desperate eyes through the twitchy clots of birds that were pecking, yes, eating their heads!

My legs were deep in the snow, but it was not snow. It was the cold waters of the Tarnic Ocean, Westermead's moat that swallowed my sheep leaving small white birds bobbing on its shifting snow-nourished surface. Small birds like foam on the grey sea.

I stood half in the water, miles from shore, upheld and alone. The sheep had rolled under like clumps of ice and were gone. The woman and her birds were gone too and I was left to pace away the watery years on an ocean-road of seasons that circled forever my Westermead.

The Crow Tree

The eyeless skull of the moon climbed east above the wintered moor as a man on a rust-colored horse approached the village of Milk Treading. A light snow had dusted the road and gave strange form to the shadowy tangles of brittle weeds which populated the undulating wastes. The rider, a thirty-year-old man of good features and straight dark hair, bore an expression of considerable concentration. Many an unfortunate wayfarer had stared into the eyes of that face, eyes of determined blue, on similarly lonesome roads. Unfortunates from as far off as Cold Dance and Westsheer, on down to the southern hamlets of Kilmnook and Stonewater, had encountered the highwayman known as The Owl.

While it was largely lore that had the highwayman sweeping down on unsuspecting riders from above, knocking them from their mounts, Doolan was known to crouch on low boughs and pounce out in the path of his prey. Once he had actually landed on top of some poor fellow, but that was decided by a broken branch rather than a tactical forethought. The folktales they attached to him were no bad thing, however, for Doolan came to realize, over the years, that reputation could make one pistol seem like ten. In fact, he rarely had to pull the trigger of his treasured snap-lock, and only once had he fired a weapon with fatal consequences.

"Do you recognize this place, Doolan?" A voice came from out the cold air.

Frowning, Doolan grumbled, "'Course I do."

"Isn't it ironic, considering your reason for coming this way, that we find ourselves here once again?"

"Right. Bloody ironic. What of it?"

The disembodied voice sighed, then in its rather snappish tone went, "You've learned nothing, have you? Ten years I've spent vainly attempting to strike the redemptive chord you apparently lack, or refuse to heed, as the case may be. The blood of one on your hands is not enough?"

Scott Thomas

Speaking through gritted teeth, Doolan countered, "If you'd possessed the slightest bit of sense, you wouldn't have swung that blasted sword at me. It was not my intent to shoot you, Mr. Drumm. Look what it's got you. Not only did you lose your gold but your life as well."

"Here! It was here!" Drumm's voice rose. "If I had conventional form 'twould be acrawl with gooseflesh!"

"I've enough for us both," Doolan admitted sulkily. His head seemed heavy, as he did not look up from the ground where ten years back Drumm, a young, wealthy, soon-to-be-wed landowner, lay bloodied, dying.

"Look, look, look! There's where it ended—all my life's promise pouring out on the road! I hope you're jolly pleased with yourself, Doolan."

"Have I not told you, more times than there are numbers, that I am sorry? Haven't I been punished enough by ten long years of your ceaseless nagging? I wonder I'm not mad! Haunt me no more, Drumm!"

Doolan trembled beneath the grey of his greatcoat, eyes squinting into the cold night where moonlight, snow and moor resembled mist. He heard only a piercing sound and muffled choking.

"What now, are you weeping? Oh, please! Look Drumm, don't be weeping, I've said I'm bloody sorry!"

The voice in the air strained, "Others will weep too, if you insist on carrying out this mission of yours. If you are, in fact, sorry for killing me, then why do you venture to kill again?"

Doolan steadied himself in the saddle, hand on the prized weapon he had bought with the gold lifted from Mr. Drumm a decade previous, hand on the grip as if it were a rudder. The silver face of an owl capped the butt.

"Gold," the highwayman said at last, "more gold than I got from the likes of you. Enough gold to settle with, so I no longer need roam these bleak roads as a menace. This shall be my last folly, then it's north I'll go to settle. I'll retire my dear pistol and let dust collect thick on my riding boots, and The Owl will only swoop in fireside tales."

"One ghost is not enough for you, Doolan? You wish the eternal company of yet another?"

"Can't be worse company than you, I should think," Doolan chuckled bitterly, "why don't you take your long-due rest then, when the time comes? Let a fresh spirit torment me?"

"You know I can not rest, Doolan, until you free me."

"Consider yourself free then. Be gone, I say!"

"Unfortunately it's not quite so simple," Drumm intoned.

"What must I do? After these ten years you still refuse to tell me that, though you thrust your advice on every other little thing."

"I can not tell you. It won't work. The answer is in you," said the ghost.

"Are you quite sure of that?"

A pause, then... "No, I'm sad to say, I am not."

The rust-colored horse had carried the man past the spot where he had killed Drumm. He glanced back once, then fastened his eyes on the lights of the nearing village. Milk Treading was a sleepy thing in the snow, its quiet buildings of stone and timber half-pale with moonlight, half-dark in shadow.

❧ ❧ ❧

It was warm at the inn, where a good hardwood fire blazed and wide boards creaked tales of a hundred years worth of travelers' boots. Doolan took a table in a corner and brooded over a plate of cabbage and boar sausage.

"Here now, Doolan, eat up!" Mr. Drumm spoke.

"Ssshh!"

"Restless innards?"

Doolan nodded, the short tail of hair at the back of his head bobbing. Loose strands hung about his face.

"Might I suggest you do away with that blasted sausage; a goodly bowl of oatmeal will sit lighter in the belly. Sausage so near the sleeping hour is sure to conjure nightmares."

"You're a nightmare, Mr. Drumm." Doolan snickered.

"Oh, aren't we the amusing one? It's not enough you snuffed out my life, now you berate me as well."

A rotund serving woman with a toothless smile came with a pewter pitcher. Her eyes were like two squirming beetles drowning in the excessive flesh. "More ale, sir?"

A voice from the corner replied, "Only if I can lap it from your lovely cleavage…"

The woman blushed, giggled and batted her lashes at Doolan, "Why, sir, that could be arranged…"

Doolan was quick to speak. "Thank you, but I'm weary from the road. Perhaps some other time."

"Very good, sir, as you like." She waddled away, rather befuddled.

Doolan hissed into the shadows, "Drumm, if you were not dead I would kill you!"

The highwayman paced his rented room until the dark fingers of sleep nudged inside. Out went the candles, up went the covers in a soft tide to the throat. The hour was late. He stared into the blackness, waiting for it to fill him.

Something poked Doolan's shoulder. A voice asked, "The Owl can not sleep?"

"No."

Doolan heard his travel-sack rustle and a small tin placed on the table by his prized pistol. A soothing purring sound came when the tin was opened, the source being the seeds from silvercat, a particularly prolific weed which in late summer crowded the local moors with its feathery grey-green foliage. The seeds were coveted for their soft noise, which Doolan found pleasing on restless nights. Abnormally nervous folk were known to fill tiny sacks with the things, to stuff in their ears.

"Thank you, Drumm."

"Mm. Tell me, Doolan, before you drift off into sausage-plagued dreams, do you imagine you might miss me were I to go on to my rest?"

"Good night, Drumm."

"Come now, is it so unreasonable a question?"

"Good night, Drumm!"

As if cursed seeds, the bits of sausage in Doolan's belly hatched, spilling poison memories into his veins. They followed his blood like a road to his mind, where images whispered, and Doolan, captive, watched…

He rode alone on an ash-colored horse, along the white moor with the brown road and the sad sky drowned in grey. It was Low Dusk, the twelfth month, when days passed quickly through the cold light. Doolan was glad for his greatcoat.

A figure moved in the distance, just a dot at first, then bigger, like a sparrow on the brown branch of the road. The sparrow became a man with a horse beneath him. He was whistling a jaunty tune, which floated to Doolan through the grey air.

Doolan found the grip of a stout flint-lock tucked against his belly. He cocked the hammer and the sound took so to the quiet air that he flinched, sure that the other rider, even at such a distance, had heard.

"Whoa!" Doolan brought his horse to a halt and dismounted. He hunched down beside the beast and hissed, "Up, up!"

The animal raised its right front leg at the cue, having mastered this trick, and held it up as if injured. Doolan, with back to the closing stranger, pulled a black hood on, obscuring all but his eyes. He heard the tune, whistling through the breezeless chill, crisp and high, leading the rider along the trail.

The whistling stopped. Hooves thumped the road and Doolan's heart thumped too.

"Hallo!" a voice came from out the cold air.

Doolan hunched as if tending his horse's suspended hoof.

"Hallo, good fellow, is all well?"

Doolan rose, spun and thrust out his pistol; the rider loosed a yelp.

"Do not move!" the hood barked.

The rider, now just yards away, stuck his white gloves in the air. He was a youngish chap, well dressed in green coat and vest with a black tricorn atop tumbling black locks. A saber hung from his thick black belt.

"I am The Owl," the highwayman explained, standing firm, weapon trained. "I shouldn't resist, were I in your place, lest you be prepared to take a ball between your eyes."

"The Owl? Dear me! Please, I beg, do not fire. Take my gold...I'll not resist," the rider blubbered.

Doolan edged closer, squinting through the holes in his hood. "Dismount. Slowly."

The rider obeyed, climbing down from his horse.

"Right, then, where's your purse?" the gunner demanded.

"On my belt."

"Remove it and toss it here."

Pale gloves trembled the leather case free. It thumped at Doolan's feet.

A pebble, which in any other place, at any other moment might have proved innocuous, found itself under Doolan's foot when he stepped to take up the purse. His weight tilted on the tiny stone, one foot then the other coming out from under him so that he pounded back first on the earth.

"Ah!" The standing man blurred in motion, his sword hissing from scabbard, glinting as he lunged at the fallen figure.

A terrible drum sounded once—thunder spilled across the moor. The rich man's eyes bulged and his mouth went wide. He staggered back, blood raging from a hole in his vest. A scrap of shattered whalebone button, still tethered to the garment by a thread, jiggled as if a moth in a web. He was flat on the road by the time Doolan scrambled up and raced over.

Doolan thought he might retch, standing there on fading legs, his heart in his ears, watching as the man twitched and gasped, and stared at the sky, a horrible red road running out from beneath him. Doolan wanted to do something, yet he did not know what. He wished he could comfort the man, but no words came. He stepped back when the blood rushed at his boots.

"I'll fetch help," Doolan stammered at last, but the man's eyes had rolled white and his lips, wet with red foam, quivered their last and he wheezed out a final wispy bloom that faded into the air.

"No..." Doolan muttered. He turned and threw his pistol out into the hoary sedge.

The Owl picked up the money purse and put it in a coat pocket where it weighted heavily. Just then, as he faced away from the dead man, he heard a voice, which seemed to form from the cold air itself. It said,

261

"You've killed me."

Doolan whirled and looked upon his awful work, but the other man lay silent, still as before, the gory trail having expanded and divided itself into the image of a leafless tree.

❧ ❧ ❧

It was two months before The Owl swooped again. Doolan, sheltered in a dusty room above the public house at Shropegrove, paced and slept and sometimes ate. A window showed him bleak and windy fields. The full sky snowed and once hail as big as musket balls beat on the old building with such fury that Doolan thought all the dead in all the world were pounding at the roofs of their graves.

When half the gold was gone, and images of destitution began to work at his brain, Doolan set out to buy a pistol, never having retrieved that which he had tossed to the moor.

❧ ❧ ❧

"It's beautiful," Doolan said, lifting the long, polished snap-lock as if it were some priceless fragile thing. "I have never seen such a gun."

"I done my best with that one, mister," the gunsmith, a portly man with pocked flesh and sullen eyes, said.

The wood was the gold of honey, and the metal, from the barrel to the powder pan, gleamed so as to make one think sunlight had infused itself into the molten brew from which the pieces were formed.

The silver owl face cap on the end of the grip was added at Doolan's request. Though the weapon took up the last of his wealth, he reasoned that it was sure to generate more. He paid the smith and left.

Some few minutes later, astride his ash-grey horse, gazing down the westward highway, Doolan heard a voice come out of the air.

The voice said, "Off to kill and rob, are we, Doolan?"

With a gasp, and a cold hand slapping his heart, Doolan jerked and twisted in his saddle, but could see no speaker. He drew his new pistol and called, "Who's there?"

262

CJ   CJ   CJ

"Who's there?" Doolan shouted, grabbing his snap-lock from the table, knocking the tin off in the process, sending the purring seeds across the floor like startled ants.

He was in a bed, in a dark room, in Milk Treading in the middle of the night. There was nothing to be seen, but the moon in the window, poking like a breast from a gown of lacy clouds.

The darkness had Drumm's voice. "Unpleasant dreams, Doolan?"

Falling back on a damp goose-feathered mattress, Doolan sighed, "Yes...unpleasant dreams."

CJ   CJ   CJ

According to Doolan's employer the chief occupant of the handsome stone house, with its good roof of flax, would customarily take his horse for an afternoon run. So Doolan sat waiting up in the branches of a tree, by a road, with the hours blowing by on a sharp wind.

He chewed on hazelnuts, which bulged a coat pocket, drank from a flask of spiced ale (normally stored in a travel sack attached to his saddle) and whistled a jaunty tune he had heard recently, though he could not say where.

"Drumm," Doolan called to the air, "come nag me...I grow bored."

The air said, "Why, I should be only too happy to oblige. You know, you rather remind me of a squirrel, sitting up here in this wretched tree chomping away on nuts."

Doolan grinned. "A wretched tree, you say? I have a great deal of affection for the things. Trees give us hazelnuts and chairs and doors and shade when it's hot and fires when it's cold."

"Ahh, cold," Drumm said, "now that's something I don't miss. Though I admit the winter appealed to me greatly in my youth. I was terribly fond of sliding down steep snowy hills."

Doolan nodded. "Yes—great sport, that!"

"Did you enjoy games as a lad, Doolan? Did the peasantry in your village have anything better than turnips for toys?"

Doolan chuckled, "'Course we did. My father carved me a wooden horse and a boat once too."

"In my village," Drumm said, "we had basket races each spring. Such a sight to see those many baskets bobbing along the stream! It was as much a ritual of fertility as it was a game. Whatever one desired to increase was put in a basket; barren women put stuffing from their beds, while others put money or wool or seeds. Whoever's basket was first to make down the stream to a particular bridge, was charmed for the year."

"Hmm."

Doolan gazed at the big stone house on its stubbled hill. Still no sign of his prey, who, he hoped, would soon make his way down the steep path, through the dark and naked trees.

"Nothing like basket races in your parts, Doolan? Turnip races perhaps?" Drumm snickered.

Doolan snapped a twig from an overhanging branch. "We used to make kindle cats."

"You made what?"

"There was a grove of trees that grew just outside the village. Queer things! I've never seen the likes of them elsewhere. They were too small to use for anything but kindling, mind you, but in autumn we'd cut some of the twigs off and put them in jars, then bury the jars until spring." Doolan's eyes gleamed. "Over the winter, the twigs merged with one another, forming spidery things, each different from the next, that scrabbled off into the wood once the jars were opened."

"What became of them?" Mr. Drumm asked.

Doolan replied, "It seems they became other kindling trees, for we'd find them growing in the wood where none had been before."

"Most curious."

They were quiet for a time. A hedge sparrow rustled in the reddish scraps of dock beneath the tree, and nudged at a nut Doolan had dropped.

"Where is that bastard?" the highwayman sighed, at last.

"Perhaps making plans for the marriage he'll not live to see..."

"Perhaps he's off on a tryst with some other poor fellow's wife, the swine," Doolan countered. "In keeping with his character."

"I wonder if she's pretty, this lass who'll be tending a burial rather than her wedding," Drumm said with a touch of melancholy. "You never did see my dear Heather, did you?"

"No."

"She was a fetching thing! Who was the handsomest lass you've ever seen, Doolan?"

The man thought briefly before replying. "It's odd, really."

"This doesn't surprise me, Doolan, coming from you. Proceed."

"Well, when I was a boy, my father would take a cart into the city to sell turnips. He took me along, once I was old enough, and I marveled at the great buildings, and all the people, and the market with its smells and colors. Once I saw a girl, a year my junior, I'd venture to say, standing by the tables of produce holding the hand of an old woman.

"She was the prettiest thing I'd ever seen. The girl I mean. A shy thing, soft and golden with rose petals for blood. She was turned in such a way as to just show the left side of her face. Now being a young lad, I had little use for the company of girls, but I stared at her as if spell-struck, with my small heart dizzy in my chest.

"Then the girl turned and I saw the right side of her face and it had a large birth mark on it, like a skull socket in the center of her cheek. I nearly cried out, I think, then I looked down and did not look up again.

"On our way home, I lay in the back of the cart with my ear to the wooden floor. The road was rough and the turnips that father hadn't sold sounded like thunder as they rolled 'cross the boards. I fell asleep and dreamt of the girl. She was a giant, or I was tiny, and the birth mark had become a vast hole. I went falling into the thing, right into her face and climbed on her teeth as if they were massive white stones. She tried to speak, but her voice just rumbled, like turnips rolling on the floor of a cart..."

"She was the prettiest and yet she horrified you?"

Doolan shrugged. "I was a boy. Were I older, I'd have seen the blemish merely for what it was. It couldn't hide her beauty."

"Why Doolan, there is hope for you."

"Hope. I just hope I can get this business done with so I can get my hands on a chest full of gold."

"Allow me to retract that last compliment," Drumm grumbled.

Dusk came across the land like the shadow of some great bird. Doolan started down the tree.

"Where are we off to now?" a voice in the branches asked.

"The Screaming Skull."

Five Bridges, a drab little place wedged between Milk Treading and the banks of the River Grynn, seemed to invite the winter wind. There were few good hills and the spiky trees were scarce and scattered. The moon made a pale patch behind the high clouds, offering just enough light to show the road, and hint at the sepia heath.

While Doolan's face was stiff from squinting into the thorns of an icy wind, his body was damp and hot beneath its garments, and he was certain that the trembling of his limbs had more to do with his mission than the temperature. When he came to a spot where the earth slid down to the water's edge, he stopped, dismounted, fished a cup from one of his travel sacks and got down on his belly so that his reflection shone like a drowning moon. He scooped at the black river and gulped the cold.

"What are you doing?" Doolan asked the ghostly face, hovering there on the current, and his thoughts carried him two weeks back...

Beneath a milk-white sky, with the day half spent, a black coach jiggled behind a team of grey mares, on a muddy stretch of road deep in a southern wood. There were twisty oaks wide as small whales, beech with grey flaking bark and great pained-looking roots, and birches like slashes of chalk on the shadows which the greater trees generated.

The coach stopped when it came to a tree, freshly fallen across the road. The driver, an old stick of a man with a high hat and baggy black coat, climbed down and stood gawking at the predicament, hands on his bony hips.

A spry figure leapt out from nowhere and landed beside the coach, a long pistol in hand and a hood about his head. The driver could only stare, his jaw hanging, such was his surprise.

"I am The Owl," the stranger announced boldly. "If you resist my demands, I shall place a ball between your eyes."

The ancient driver shook violently, and though he glanced up at the coach where a blunderbuss rested beside the seat, Doolan could tell from looking into watery old eyes that the man had neither the courage nor the speed to make an attempt to get at the thing.

"Now, if you'd be so good as to sprawl with your face to the road, I'll conduct my business and be off."

The driver obliged. He resembled a sickly doll, there in the mud.

"Good, good, now be still…"

Doolan moved alongside the coach, his back against it, weapon cocked, hovering. A woman's voice came from inside the thing. "Fig? Whatever is the matter out there?"

Doolan snatched the side door open and poked his snap-lock into the passenger's face. She was an older woman, with a nimbus of lace about her plump face and a bonnet puffed over her hair.

"Do you very much mind, sir?" the woman said, indignant. "How very rude, pointing that awful thing in my face!"

Blue eyes blinked behind the holes in the hood.

Drumm gave a sharp laugh, which seemed to startle the woman more than the appearance of the highwayman.

"Who was that?" the woman asked.

"I heard nothing," Doolan growled. "I am The Owl, and—"

"The Owl? Well, I suppose if one is to be robbed, then it might as well be by a legend…"

"What's that?"

"Oh, I don't mean to make it sound like an honor, mind you."

Doolan motioned with his weapon. "Out of the carriage. Make haste!"

"You don't mean to have me get down on the filthy road, I hope? Oh, goodness, Fig, look at you, you're a mess!"

"Yes, Mrs. Goodbarrow," the driver agreed dutifully.

The woman lowered her bulk out of the cab and studied Doolan. He eyed her expensive brooch and the gem-encrusted pin in her bonnet.

"Remove your jewelry, and be quick about it."

"If you insist, Mr. Owl, but must you point that thing? Are you going to ravish me as well?" she smirked.

Drumm snickered out of the air.

Doolan said, "Doubtful."

"You really shouldn't trouble yourself over these petty embellishments, Mr. Owl. However, if you're interested in procuring a substantial piece of wealth, I may be able to arrange something..."

"I must warn you," Doolan rumbled, "I am neither foolish nor dim-witted, and any attempt to trick me might have grave consequences..."

The woman smiled. "Oh, I'm sure of that. You must understand, I am a very rich woman, a widow, actually. My dear husband made himself quite the fortune with spice imports. If it's gold you really want, and not these odd bits you see on my person, then perhaps you might be willing to consider a bargain..."

Doolan was puzzled. He glanced back at the old driver, still face down, trembling in the mud. "A bargain?"

"Yes. I am cursed with a rather unfortunate situation, you see, and a man of your skill and disposition might be just the person to tidy it up, so to speak. If you are willing to offer your services, I will pay you a chest full of gold."

"What is it that you want me to do?"

"I want you to kill someone," Mrs. Goodbarrow said, smiling a smile too young for her face.

"*What?*" the voice of Drumm exclaimed.

The woman looked around. "Whoever was that?"

"No one," Doolan said. "The wind."

☙ ☙ ☙

They sat by a fire, over a warm pitcher of pungent brew concocted from black currants. The drink made wild sculptures of Doolan's innards, and its darkness bruised his lips.

"My daughter Bethell," Mrs. Goodbarrow said, pointing to the portrait over the mantel. A pretty plump woman with dark flower-wreathed hair peered coyly from the painting.

Doolan grimaced, "You want me to kill your daughter?"

"No, no, you silly!"

"Sorry."

"Bethell is the dearest thing in all the world to me. An overgrown child, really, too innocent for her own good. She's gone and fallen in love with a dreadful man by the name of Twillis Wingle. She met him in Milk Treading while paying visit to my sickly sister. Twillis is the eldest son of a very wealthy man who owns half the land between Five Bridges and Weendell. The bastard set after my girl like a pack hound, and though I tried everything in my power to prevent it, they've arranged to be wed."

Doolan, sipping his drink and gazing at the picture, found the young woman to be pleasant, with a bovine simplicity. "So, I would be correct in assuming you want me to have off with this Twillis Wingle fellow?"

Mrs. Goodbarrow smiled sweetly.

"Tell me, though," Doolan said, "will it not dispose your daughter to great suffering to lose her beloved?"

"For a time, no doubt, but the man is a swine, you see, and I'll be sparing her a life of misery. She'll be better off, trust my word, and free to find herself a gentleman of substance. Twillis, you understand, has a ravenous appetite when it comes to women. He pursues them ceaselessly, wherever and whenever he can. My poor child blinds herself to his ways."

"I must inform you, Mrs. Goodbarrow, I am not so ruthless as a pirate or a powderman. I have killed but once, and with no joy, I assure you..."

"Mr. Owl, you will need three horses to carry the gold I am willing to give you if you tend to this situation."

Drumm, who thus far had remained silent since arriving at the Goodbarrow estate, whispered close in Doolan's ear, "Refuse! Have you not learned your lesson killing me?"

"Three horses, you say?"

"Three *strong* horses." The woman smiled purple lips.

❦ ❦ ❦

"One more folly," Doolan told his reflection, "then north to settle."

He lifted himself up off the hard earth, his pale reflection blurring and slipping into the black water like a diving swan. He marched up the slope to his patient red horse, tucked his cup away and set off on the road toward the village, gripping his treasured pistol as if a rudder. The road was thin between great wings of heathy earth, darkly feathered with furze. Doolan crossed the first bridge, then four more. He looked back once and they were like stone ribs bent across the River Grynn, and the river was a wound of melted crows.

❦ ❦ ❦

The village seemed a nice enough place with its modest homes gold-windowed in the dark, their thatch silvered with frost, the air still whispering of this and that dinner cooked over hale hardwood fires by wives with rough and loving hands. Doolan hoped to retire to just such a place, to sit near a bright fire with a dark ale, with a darker night wrapped about a close house, to forget what needed forgetting.

Doolan did not need the sign to tell him he had found The Screaming Skull, for he could hear the almost-tuned fiddle and voices like pigeons through the wall. But there was the sign, regardless, its colors dull and cracked, squeaking on its chains, rocking like a drunkard in the breeze. On one side of the large structure was a stable with deep hay-scented shadows and a shabby boy waiting to take Doolan's reins and the coin that he flipped.

"Here we are," Doolan muttered, pausing at the door. He looked up at the sign, which showed a skull with holly leaf wings.

"Yes," Mr. Drumm said sadly, "here we are…"

270

❧ ❧ ❧

Faces hung in the dark air of the wide, low-roofed tavern, faces made strange and half-hidden by weak candlelight. When the door went thump behind the grey-coated stranger, a swarm of eyes turned up toward him—up from tables and smeary pewter mugs—candle-gold eyes like bees hovering in the dark.

Doolan kept his face tucked into the collar of his coat and moved quietly to a vacant table against a wall. Could they see the butt of his pistol pressed out against his coat like an amorous thing? He sat and scanned the room with his sharp blue eyes. The natives continued conversing, their voices a low collective mumble, their shapes dim and hunched.

Doolan's chest pounded as if crowded with extra hearts.

There was a fiddler across the room, or a shadow that looked like one, playing a melancholy tune the highwayman recognized as "The Dead Shepherd's Wife." The skull, after which the establishment was named, was an old brown thing, with no bottom jaw, with holly sprigs on either side, sitting on the great stone mantel above an eager fire. There were garlands of dried apple slices and bay leaves strung about the room, along the low rafters, scenting the air.

"As cold an evening as one should want, out there, wouldn't you say, mister?"

Doolan flinched. "Oh…yes. Why, yes it is, at that!" He had not heard the serving woman approach. She was willowy, freckled, with hair like rain-flattened straw.

"Would you be wantin' somethin' warm, then?"

"Just ale."

While the woman was standing at Doolan's table, several men walked past the great fireplace and splashed some of their drink onto the brown skull. The liquid ran through cracks in the mantel and hissed in the fire below.

"For luck," the woman explained, reading the look on Doolan's face.

"Tell me, does the skull scream?"

The woman nodded. "Just one scream a night. You'll hear it soon, if you stay."

"Whose skull is it?"

The woman shrugged and walked away.

There was a commotion across the room. A man in an expensive red coat had dragged a chair in front of the fire and stood upon it. Drunken cheers urged him as he struggled with the front of his trousers.

"Don't fall in the fire and burn off anything valuable, Twillis," one man chided.

"Hah! This will be the luckiest night of my life!" the tall, handsome young man with lush blond hair declared, and he made water on the skull and the fire sounded snakes. Some angry voices were raised, while others laughed and the fiddler squealed a frolicsome, crooked accompaniment.

"There!" the performer exclaimed, his libation spent, readjusting his garments before turning to bow. "But now I am empty, and must have more ale. Drink for everyone!"

Doolan felt his face becoming a terrible thing with cold eyes, restless teeth and hot skin. A hand reached into his coat to know the wood of the pistol's grip. Another heart was added to his chest.

Drumm spoke softly out of the dark. "Not terribly charming, is he?"

"Too charming, I think," Doolan muttered. "He's drunk from being so full of himself, more so than good ale."

Twillis Wingle sauntered back to his table in the middle of the floor. A number of friends and a buxom honey-haired woman sat with him. The woman, clearly not Mrs. Goodbarrow's daughter, hung an arm about Twillis and snickered against him. His eyes were full of predatory charm.

Doolan took note of an old woman seated somewhere between his table and that of his prey. She was staring at him, gripping a mug with hands like dried leaves. Her eyes were steady, dark as bilberries.

"What's with that old hag?" the man muttered.

"Perhaps she fancies young men with murderous eyes," Drumm offered.

Doolan looked back at Twillis, who was dipping dates in a bowl of honey and piling them into his mouth. His large grinning teeth were like sticky gold. A trembly hand tightened around a pistol grip.

The old woman was gawking as the serving lass brought Doolan ale, and after as he sipped. She was like a horrid effigy sculpted of gnarly dried fruit. Could she know, he wondered? Did she have the gift of telling another's thoughts? Had she seen the bulge the snap-lock made, or the way he glared at Twillis Wingle?

A portly man in a top hat, the brim of which was wreathed with holly, stood before the fire and waved his arms. "Right, now," the man called, "it's nearly time…"

The old woman, gazing still, began groping on her table. She found the base of her candle with one set of fingers, then dampened the others in her drink and used them to pinch out the flame.

Doolan grimaced a tense smile. He exhaled, relieved, "She's blind…"

A chant was taken up by the regular patrons, and it squeezed The Owl's heart like a bellows as it grew louder and louder.

"*Silence for the screaming skull, silence for the screaming skull, silence for the screaming skull…*"

The room, at once, was quiet. Even Twillis, stifling a giggle, was forced to comply.

Doolan thought he heard a wistful Drumm sigh, "I tried."

The highwayman began to rise from his table, all his blood falling into his feet, the ale swirling through his head in a damp mist and his heart fluttering like a bird in a cage of ribs.

"*Darkness for the screaming skull,*" the room said, "*darkness for the screaming skull, darkness for the screaming skull…*"

The shadows ran together, like puddles across the ceiling, as one by one the candles were blown out. Two men carried a large sheet of tin across the fireplace to hide its light. The air sighed as Drumm blew out their candle.

Doolan, moving in the blackness, started when an apple garland brushed his cheek. He leaned back against the wall, clinging to his pistol, edging it out from under his belt.

"*Darkness for the screaming skull!*"

Click! The pistol was out and cocked, invisible. Twillis was just two yards to the left; the back of his head, pouring its enviable golden hair across red velvet shoulders, was imprinted in Doolan's mind. One ball in the back of the skull was all that mattered now, Doolan thought, shuddering.

There was darkness and silence except for the muffled sound of fire crinkling behind the sheet of tin.

The skull screamed. It was one long horrible note, so shrill that it made the darkness brittle and filled Doolan's blood with icy briars. It stopped and for several heartbeats there was silence, then more screams, desperate and piercing, filling the dark room.

Doolan took a step away from the wall, gun first, toward the sounds of commotion. Light gushed from the fireplace as the tin sheet was yanked away and Doolan saw that the shrieks were not those of the skull, but those of the blond woman who had been sitting with his prey. Twillis Wingle was, it appeared, the cause of the hysteria. He was half-sprawled on the floor, half-propped in the kneeling woman's lap, clutching at his throat, which was clogged with dates.

"He's choking!" the woman cried, as the man writhed, his eyes wide in his purple face.

Doolan had taken several urgent steps closer before realizing that he had lowered his gun; he found his own thoughts scrabbling to find some way to save the dying man.

A number of patrons closed about Twillis, clapping him on the back before Doolan could recover from his spell of disorientation. He tucked his pistol away and staggered backward, gasping, trembling, unnerved and confused.

It was the old blind woman who, with a firm push to Twillis' midsection, dislodged the culprit dates. Twillis floundered, panting.

❦   ❦   ❦

The stable boy leapt aside as a ruddy horse and its grey-coated rider came pounding out of the stall.

"Wait!" the lad cried, but the horse made swiftly down the road, away from the tavern.

A hundred hearts pushing his blood, Doolan glared into the night, his face hot as if fevered, and angry words leaping from his mouth.

"I must be mad! I was so close! I was so bloody close—I could feel the trigger aching..."

Drumm was in the air, with snow like broken lace. "Doolan?"

"Blast! Why did I falter? Why?"

"Doolan?"

"I was supposed to kill the bastard, yet when I saw him choking, bloody instinct told me to help him!"

"Doolan, don't be harsh with yourself. Rejoice, my friend. You didn't kill! You spared your hands of more blood."

"I'm a fool. I've always been a fool! I'm done with it all, I tell you. It's north I go, to settle and bury this life of stealing and running. Do you hear me, Drumm? The Owl is finished!"

The man rode on through the air's white kisses, over the bridges like stone ribs, drumming the powdery trail which five times crossed the dark of a river. Doolan was so befuddled by his own actions, or reaction, as it were, that he only half-noticed that his horse, despite emphatic urgings, was not as quick as usual, and something in the rhythm of its hooves hinted at unfamiliarity. Perhaps it was only the snow on the road.

A trembling hand reached down for the flask in the travel sack that normally hung from the saddle, but the sack was nowhere to be found. Doolan looked down at the saddle, the reins, the very beast beneath him, and realized that in his haste, he had taken the wrong horse.

"Blast!"

The man reined the horse around and started back toward the village.

"A simple mistake," Drumm offered soothingly. "The animal has a color much like your own..."

Doolan grumbled, squinting, the ale in his belly churning. The snow came with more vigor, stealing the road, painting a ghostly calm upon the passing heath. Beads of orange shone distant—village windows, he thought, yet they seemed to be nearing at a rate inconsistent with that of his mount's speed. It was as if the lights were moving. No, not windows, he concluded, for the lights were indeed coming to meet him.

"Torches?"

Horsemen emerged from the white air, four wide in a wall across the road. They pointed at him with fingers and muskets.

"There he is!"

Twillis Wingle was one of the riders. He pointed. "See there, he's stolen my horse!"

"Halt!" the men called.

Doolan tugged the reins and the animal stopped.

"Surrender or we fire!" the men called.

Doolan, blinking back against the snow, stared into the mouths of several leveled longarms. Slowly, he put his hands in the air.

❧ ❧ ❧

It was only exhaustion that granted Doolan sleep in the small ancient room, in the squat stone building, on a bleak puckered hill, overlooking a stretch of the most barren heathland in all of Westermead. Dawn brought a streaky sky like garnet and cobwebs, then watery pink feigning heat on the single frosty pane that looked out from the cold chamber. Weak light faded the shadows from the cell, and Doolan rose aching from his plank bed and went to the window.

The man saw, through a hoary glaze, a lone tree, silhouetted on the snowy bleaks. An oak, he thought, with wide base and upward tangles of bare branches, majestic and horrible, pained in the bitter sweep of first light. For some reason, Doolan felt a chill in his limbs and hugged a ratty blanket about himself.

"An awful tree," Doolan whispered.

"The Crow Tree," a deep voice, clearly not Drumm's, said through the door of bars.

Doolan turned to view the jailer, a plump fellow of middle age with spectacles pinching a bulbous red nose, eyes like a ferret's, too close together perhaps, a full dark beard to compensate for a barren pate. A leather vest strained to contain the man's belly, and his limbs, though squat and round, looked strong.

"A terrible tree it is at that, lad, as you may know too soon."

"A hanging tree," Doolan assumed.

The man gave a grim smile. "They always know. To see it is to know."

"Then I'm to be hanged?"

The jailer's little eyes looked down; he puffed his bulk and sighed. "Horse thieves swing in these parts."

"But I am not a horse thief. It was a mistake." Doolan moved to the bars. "Why else would I have headed back to the village? I was returning the horse."

"A reasonable tale, I admit, but there's more of a shadow upon you than you know, lad…"

Doolan squinted. "What do you mean?"

"Well, you know what they're saying in the village?"

"Obviously not."

"They thinks you're that highwayman, The Owl."

Doolan grimaced. He heard a sharp hiss of displeasure from Drumm, who thus far had remained silent.

"The Owl, you say?"

"That's the word, lad, on account of that big grey coat of yours, and that black hood and this…"

The man turned to a table behind him and took Doolan's treasured pistol from it. He pointed to the silver owl face on the butt of the grip.

"Yes, that…" Doolan said glumly.

The jailer studied the prisoner and at length inquired, "Are you The Owl, lad?"

"No," Doolan said, "I am not." He walked back to the window and looked upon the tree, stark against the young day. "Why is it called the Crow Tree?"

"In autumn the leaves go black and turn to crows."

"Won't you settle somewhere, Doolan, that pacing makes me dizzy," Drumm said.

"It's not fair, I tell you! I was through with it all. Now I'm to hang!"

"Perhaps you *should* have killed the bastard," Drumm reflected.

"What?"

"Oh, nothing."

Doolan paused by the glass, looked out at the tree, black against the birdless, cloudless, heatless sky.

"That magistrate was a stubborn old sort," Drumm observed pensively.

"Bastard," Doolan growled. "What cruel irony this!"

"Your decision to redeem yourself came too late, I fear. And you're not quite through…"

"What do you mean by that?" Doolan looked up from the window.

"I mean that if things are left unchanged between us, then I am doomed to haunt this world forever more."

The blue burned in Doolan's eyes and a tear came to his cheek. "Tell me then, Drumm, whilst there's still time; tell me how to free you."

"I can not."

Doolan hid his face in his hands and slid down the stones to the floor. "I deserve the rope, for all I've done, it's true, but mostly for what I did to you," he groaned.

"But, I tell you, Drumm, part of me is glad for it, for your haunting me…you have been my only friend all these years."

"I don't need your sentiment, Doolan," Drumm's voice came coolly, "release me."

Drumm did not speak again and Doolan brooded until dusk darkened the room. The jailer was out, and the only light came from the small fire on the other side of the small building, and from the fading window.

The tree was there, when the man stood and stared, dark against the less dark sky, with the snowy earth all about and beyond it. It seemed, in the strange craven light, that faint figures hung down from the branches of the thing, like sacks of mist. And another hazy form, forlorn and lost, as the ghosts of the hanged, stood beneath the oak. It was a sorry looking figure, a man he had not seen in ten years.

"Drumm!"

The door to the jailhouse banged and Doolan leapt to the bars of his cell. The jailer gave him a curious look.

"Tell me," Doolan spoke urgently, "do you still have my pistol?"

"I do..."

Doolan smiled. "You do? Glad I am to hear it! I beg you, as one who shall die come morning, one last favor..."

"What favor is that, lad?" the perplexed jailer asked.

"You must bury the gun."

"What's that? Bury you say? Are you mad? That's the most beautiful pistol I've ever seen!"

"Yes, yes, so it is, good man. But I bought it with blood, for I *am* who they say. I was The Owl, and I killed a man, and I took his gold and I bought that blasted gun. He was never found, for I buried him, and you must return the gun to the earth with him that his restless soul might know release. I beg you, please, take the gun back so that I might wash away this stain. Please!"

The jailer stared at Doolan over his spectacles, puffed his chest, and asked, "Where's the grave?"

❧ ❧ ❧

"It took you long enough," a voice said.

Doolan stood suddenly. "Drumm!"

"Wasn't it obvious, you fool? That cursed gun you embraced so...all this time it was the key."

"Then you will rest?" Doolan asked eagerly, looking up at the cracked ceiling of the cell.

"Yes. The jailer has found my old bones, back on that dreadful moor where you left them. He's a good fellow, the jailer; I find him rather agreeable, if a bit unrefined. Nevertheless, he has located the remains, having put a good deal of effort, might I add, into digging through the frozen turf..."

The room went silent.

"Drumm?"

The room was silent.

"Drumm?"

Silence.

"Good bye, my friend, Drumm."

279

❧ ❧ ❧

A procession moved slowly along the bleached road, across the frozen heath, beneath a sky like an ocean of ash, in the bleak cold month of Icekeep. A drumming boy led the way, pounding like a drunken heart. Behind him marched a number of musketeers, and the tall stiff magistrate, bundled in winter layers and staring his wintry stare. The prisoner sat on a black horse, which was led by the jailer. The few villagers that cared to leave their cozy homes on such a cold morning to witness the event made a broken shuffling line. Twillis Wingle was among them, grinning.

Doolan stared numbly at the Crow Tree as it grew closer, like the shadow of some great invisible monster with wind-haunted limbs and a trunk as wide as the jailhouse where he had spent his final weeks. Every organ in his body seemed to constrict, and though the lone dangling rope was yet to touch his neck, he found it hard to breathe.

At last they reached the tree, and the horse was positioned beneath one of the low boughs, and the jailer fitted the scratchy hemp around Doolan's neck.

"Sorry, lad," the man whispered.

Doolan gave him a quick, wide-eyed glance, swallowed and tried to nod. The jailer stepped back to the front of the horse and held the bridle. The magistrate moved to the rear of the horse and prepared to swing his switch, which would send the horse out from under the captive.

"As the Kingdom Official of this village, Five Bridges, I authorize this execution in the name of King and country," the man said, his words squeezed out in flattened plumes.

Doolan looked up through the tangled branches to the cold clouded sky, at the taut rope. The drum rolled, a heart in spasm, and Doolan's beat wildly, throbbing in his neck, against the grasp of the rope.

The switch came down on the horse's rump and a saber, snatched from one of the musketeers by an unseen hand, flashed between Doolan's head and the bough of the tree, severing the rope. The horse charged forward, kicking snow and neighing.

The startled gunners raised their long arms and went to fire at Doolan's back, but an unseen hand had stolen the flints from their weapons, which clicked ineffectually. They gave chase on foot, but the horse was off across the wastes and gone, a bodiless voice laughing in the cold air.

❧   ❧   ❧

"And that's my story," the old man said to the boy on his knee as they sat by a fire in a small white cottage in the northern climes of Westermead.

"So you never heard Drumm again, Grampa?" the boy asked.

Doolan smiled sadly and shook his head. "Only his laugh as I rode away from the hanging party."

A young man with dark hair, as Doolan's had once been, scooped up the wide-eyed lad.

"Enough adventure for one night, you two," the man said. "It's time you were both off to bed."

Doolan smiled and drank down the last of his ale.

"Goodnight, Grampa," the boy called as his father led him away.

"Sweet dreams, boy."

Doolan sat by the logs a bit longer, gazing into the hearth, holding his empty cup. The candles burned low, and shadows came like cold black dogs to lie by the fire.

"Yes," Doolan said, "time to sleep."

Heading for his bed, Doolan paused by a window. He could hear the snow and the wind blowing down about the cottage, and the wind sounded like a voice. The voice of a friend.

Home to Broomwood

A year had passed since I'd seen that road and the snowy hills like half-sunk ponies. A year to the day, and how that year had seemed like ten. But home was just the track away with only those few cold miles to cross, then my pack could fall and my numb feet feel and my musket attend a dark corner.

I trudged south along the vague and piling path with snow like sawdust swirling the night about my head. I whistled to keep the cold air out, but the wind whistled back, persistent and scratchy, like a face full of hay, and caused me to squint the whole while. This was to be expected. It was, after all, the month of Freezling when the wind wasn't wind unless it was harsh, and hadn't I known it to slice and wheeze and fling hail big as walnuts? It was a welcome wind, regardless, with home on its breath and that was enough for me.

There was nothing for the eyes but the stretch of milky fields and heaped hills like fallen clouds and clouds like a full grey sail. There was nothing for the ears but the blown snow's hush and my boots crunching holes in the road.

My head was full of strange fancies, as a traveler's head is often filled, with unlikely bits of nothings and half-forgotten songs and jokes in stale fragments. There were elusive bird thoughts and scraps of dreams and warm rushing memories to embrace. Some things that surfaced to swim in my head, I admit I would like to have drowned.

Cresting a slow, round hill, I spied the first true hint of home. It was a shallow patch of walled white earth, pierced by irregular slats of stone. The Resting Field. I'd never known my heart to gladden at the sight of that lonely place, but I smiled a chattery smile and I looked to where the snow made all graves one.

"Hello, Mother," I said, "Hello, Father—it's your son, come home."

Twin markers, a sheep's length apart, stood in the mounded cold.

Southward still, creaking along I went, a bundle of fur, grey uniform and

282

snapping cloak, past the Resting Field, along the trail of rounded turns and swelling hills, with snow beating wings in my face and my musket's bayonet poking up like a grey icicle.

Was it so long ago, on a summer's afternoon, that I raced a pony along that very stretch, all the fool that a boy can be, with grass stains and freckles and berry juice bruises? I was chasing a lass, Betony of the next town over, but her pony was quicker and her legs were about the warm kettle of its belly and her hair was a bonfire behind her. She laughed across a shoulder and shaped her hand in taunting gestures and tossed acorns that never reached me. She was all the charm that a girl could be.

Betony lived five miles north in Mullison. Her father was the baker there, and a bulky spectacle he was, as slow and looming as a thundercloud, with wild fiery hair and sideburns like tails from red squirrels. When he wasn't arm-deep in dough, he was up the hills after hare. It never failed to puzzle me, how such an awkward fellow could capture creatures so spry, yet he did. Afterward, he'd sit on the wooden stool in his shop with limp prize dangling and a gutting knife like a little crescent moon in hand. Then he'd cut out the heart and hold it up like a strawberry and toss it to his dog and Betony would moan in protest, and I would pretend to laugh.

The old stone bridge was like the muffled spine of some great beast, abandoned in the drifts. Three hours' worth of frigid lace had tucked between the stones, a mockery of mortar. Beneath the arch, running west to east, was the stream we knew as Broken Snake. It was wide, as streams go, a ragged wound of secretive water, spiked at the edges with frozen weed stalks, and it traced about the bases of hills and squirmed off into the brittle glade beyond. The Snake was always the last to freeze and even then I could see faint lines of motion and drowsy flakes tumbling to their winking deaths in the black current. The edges were jagged with ice, which soon would spread and meet, scarring over to encase the languid flow.

One still summer day, when I, a whole head shorter, stood fishing the stream, I caught the most peculiar thing. I'd had no luck to speak of, leaning my chest against the bridge's wall, pole drooping over, patient line dowsing. I was dreaming into the eastward wetness, half-watching the tiny fish like silver arrowheads and the fat black frogs that made the water gulp, when a flowery scent came drifting on the breeze and a small wicker basket bobbed in the current.

I hooked the thing and pulled it out and found inside a purple and gold bed of wildflower blooms into which was tucked a scroll of parchment, tied with a ribbon of flame-colored hair. I untied and unscrolled and read the words that had been written with the juice of bramble berries. They read: A luck charm. Only with this can you catch me.

I tucked the lock of hair in my pocket along with the lucky musket ball I'd dug from a tree out at Goat King's Grove.

The lad I was went out about his day, turning chores into games, watching clouds like clotted cream skirting the southern peaks. The sun stayed strong and it etched shapes like ginger root on the edges of the clouds and then it sent them away with their threat of rain.

I heard hooves hammering as I was stacking wood and humming a tune of my own making. It was Betony. She sat smiling down from her round pony, eyes smiling a cloudless sunny blue.

"Catch me," she said, "if you can."

I was off for my mount like a cat before dogs, and she was back toward the road, leaving laughter and dust. I heeled my pony faster and the lass threw acorns back at me, which never reached. We made quick along the road, through hills fat and summered with green, and weed flowers, and the hum of thorned bees. I reached in my pocket where a red serpent of hair was coiled close to my loins and I held it out in the air so that it rippled; I held it to my face and it licked against my cheeks and I kissed it for luck.

Having drummed across the bridge over Broken Snake, Betony's pony began to slow. My beast, a stocky peat-colored thing with eyes big as plums, was a sheep's length behind, straining as if I had torn out my boy heart and was dangling it like a strawberry across the hot, moist nostrils. We passed the Resting Field with its graves like soldiers marching. Then I was beside Betony and she was laughing merrily, and she threw an acorn which reached me. I caught it. I leaned to the side, just inches from dropping, one hand full of the red-haired charm and brown mane, and, reaching, I clasped Betony's hand, which was soft and white and fluttery as a small bird in my palm.

"I've got you!" I cried.

"So you do," the girl panted, as if she, and not her pony, had done the hard running.

At last, we were still, and her hand had not left mine and salt burned in my veins and weighed damp on my back. My heart rolled over inside me and did a strange dance.

"Well," Betony said, "seeing as you've caught me, I suppose you must be rewarded."

With that she leaned over and I saw her face come close, her blue eyes closing and her berried lips, like a damp puckered rose, were there and warm-wet on my own.

She pulled back, giggled and was off, the pony thumping away on the dusty track, fast as ever. I sat and watched, clutching the charm and wondering if she had let me catch her. Warm hands of pulsing wool pressed about my heart.

🙶 🙶 🙶

In the cold, in my brains, there crawled, suddenly, the curious sense that something was behind me, walking slow along the snowy road, between the blue-shadowed hills, in my very boot-shaped tracks. I turned my squint and looked, but the wind tossed up plumes and the plumes skirted, hissing over corpse-shaped mounds. Only the wind walked in my tracks.

It wouldn't be long, thought I, turning back, for the first trees were marching past and then there were more, stiff huddles secreted behind the banks, like soldiers aprowl in the night. The best wood in all of Westermead,

285

it was believed, and these unharvested troops were like stilts with bearded boughs. All the trees in the winter storm seemed half-birch.

It was autumn with quick yellows and slow golds and red like wings of blood, when Betony dragged me by the hand, beneath those same gentle trees. There squatted mushrooms soft as baby rumps and others like welts and levitating pears and didn't they all love the moist shadows and spiny cribs of felled pine needles?

There were quick kisses and Betony's taste lingering and her eyes feasting on mine, and private shadows to hold us. But she pulled away, held up a finger and wagged it like a dog's tail.

"Father wants some buttertoads for soup. Widow Milter shall be over for eats…"

I smiled. Buttertoads, or so the spellwomen claimed, would fire the eater with lust.

"Buttertoads, eh?" I'd quipped. "Perhaps we could do with a wee nibble."

She swatted me and whirled away, the peach swirl of her skirt stirring crispy leaves. She'd seen my eyes and felt my eyes, prying at the lacings of her bodice. And once, with drunken stars about us, and the season's last crickets, my hand felt her hind through her skirt.

"Look! There are some!" Betony delighted.

They were plump, yellow, warted and hugging the soft brown soil, peeking from between leaves and the gnarled grey veins of an oak. Enough to fill her basket.

I was backing away from the grand tree when I heard a crunch and a shrill little shriek. I had stepped on a shin-high dome of dried mud and sticks, like a nest of sorts, I thought, pulling free my foot.

"What's this?" Betony asked, bending and peering and poking a finger into the round opening that was no longer round. "A nest, I think," said she, "and something's in it, but I can't quite see…"

It was small and pink and wrinkly with a body like a budding bird and a face like a wizened man's. There were twigs like a tiny crushed chair and the squish of a table and a candle as long as a thumbnail.

"It's hurt," the lass said.

"Take it out," the lad said.

"What if it bites?" the lass asked.

"Then let me," the boy said, and I did and it didn't bite.

Strange it was, for it was in my hand and gone, but for its weight, once the sunlight struck it. I cupped my hand over and it was back. It blinked in and out of sight according to the amount of light upon it, only constant where shadow allowed.

"We must tend it, take it home," Betony said.

So we did. We filled a wicker basket with a rasp of leaves and tried to feed it chips of cheese and pinches of mushroom. We watched it by the hour; it was huddled and sad and blinking eyes like fly wings.

"I'm terribly sorry, sir," I said, and Betony swore it nodded and even tried to smile.

Two days and three more and still it took no bite or sup. It was curled and wrinkled and blinking its own mysterious thoughts. We called it Crink of the Twigs and whispered our strange language of reassurances to it. On day ten, with morning through the window and the first frost on the glass like ghosts of pressed fern, Crink of the Twigs was gone.

We were never to see poor Crink again. I think he died and became invisible, like a soft leaf-flavored wind, and swept out under the door or through a mouse lair to join the autumn air. Betony liked to think that his friends came to spirit him off. We buried the empty wicker basket in the wood and whispered for him to the air and wind and blood-red leaves.

     ℘   ℘   ℘

Was it the cold miles squeezing my brain and too many hours alone, or was there something behind me on the path? The storm painted strange music through that finest of woods and with each turn I took, I felt the wind of some soft unknown at my back. But the nettled wind was in my face, and not behind and my quick glances disclosed nothing.

I sniffed at the air and my mind leapt ahead of me, leaving my worries.

There was wood smoke on the air, wood smoke scented with pine cones. Ah, the village was near. One more hill.

The trees parted and the hill peaked and my heart shook off the cold. Below there sat houses, snow-thatched and close and with lights gold in windows and smoke from chimneys. Around stretched the wreath of dark trees, like a fence for Broomwood and snow on the fence. Broomwood!

I kicked along quicker through the snow and the path poured down, out from the trees, into the sting and clutter of flakes. There was Mergon Blackmump's stable and the blacksmith's crooked cottage and the spell-woman's squat dwelling with ice-fanged thatch and cat prints vanishing and wind chimes of moon-shaped tin and a white-haired broom by the stoop.

I hear her still, on another winter day, scrawled in the snows of memory; the spellwoman's voice close on my ear and her plump gift of something gold and warted and smelling of forest floors and wanton secrets.

"It's time," she'd said, closing my fingers with hers, around the sticky-soft of a buttertoad mushroom.

There was fire-crackle and pinecones snapping their scented deaths amongst the kindling, and Betony's father leaned on a table with three empty jugs and a gaze that didn't see at all. Soon his head was across a pillow of crossed arms and he rumbled like a cloud full of thunder.

"I have something," I whispered to Betony.

"What would that be?" she asked.

"A secret. A secret to eat and swallow. A secret to dream in your belly."

She closed her eyes and I broke off a piece of the yellow mushroom and placed it on her offered tongue. I ate a piece as well. Gold and darkness melted in my mouth and I sat back, closing my eyes.

Snow was at the windows with fingers of wind and the fire shook, brassy, watery, eating its fuel of wood and pinecones. We sneaked off as her father dreamt quick and dead rabbits and the dog by the fire watched us go into the back of the cottage.

With fast hands and slow eyes I fumbled her garments. Her breasts came free from white cloth folds and dangles of leather lacings like ribbons brushing. Her breasts were small and round as quince, fresh off the spice boats. They were warm as spring and ached with buds of pink and I kissed them once and twice and between them for luck.

Winter warped about the cottage and we were about each other in tangled closeness. There were whispers and flesh and faces of joy that looked like pain. Then we were still and different and silent but for our hearts.

Spring came as spring always comes and Broomwood, ringed with trees, was all music and joy and skirts dancing and girls with flowery crowns circling. There was laughter and mead and gifts for luck and I stood with Betony with the spellwoman black against the green hills and marrying words on her old lips.

℧   ℧   ℧

The snow became the shape of my house, and my parents' house before that. I smiled into the wind and my steps were fast, to spite the curdled snow. There was a light warming the window and rime on the glass like fish skeletons. My love was waiting inside. My eyes went up to the scare-figure on the white roof, a ragged thing with arms like outstretched wrack.

℧   ℧   ℧

My thoughts turned one winter back. Father and I were working the wood, and he was never without advice for this newly wedded chap. Old Willden Thorn brought news of war, far in the rocky grey north. We carried axes and saws and sawdust in our lungs. We carved the finest broom-stems in all Westermead, and the first snow fell like ashes and wind shook the hills. The Winter Women came wispy down the long sky and in morning Mother was dead. The wind had knocked the scare-figure off the roof. We packed Mother in shrouds and dried tansy and she waited, quiescent, but for in our dreams, in the Stone House until spring, when they buried her.

I was not there when the earth thumped and the grave went up and tears went down sad faces. I was not there when father passed that summer, nor when they put him below, beside his bride. I was north and warring in the wet rain and the wet blood and trenches and hate, building the worst memories ever. For I had heard the call for men and left my Betony to fight, my glad heart raw with thorns of parting.

❧ ❧ ❧

Home was just steps away and pinecone smoke came up and out the chimney and blew over the white hills and across the hugging trees that loved, as I have loved, Broomwood.

"Who's there?" I asked.

I spun and the musket was in my numb hands, the bayonet thrusting into nothing.

"*Come home*," the wind said.

Then I saw a figure rise from the forming snow, like that figure up north, where the war drummed around me…the shape of a man rose up from the muddy trench with a musket aimed at my head. He fired—the shot missed, but his bayonet did not and I lay in the brown mud with a faded length of fiery hair in my red hand and the smoke came inside my closed eyes.

"I see," I said, "it's you," never having met this boy. I turned once to the window and saw where Betony sat by the fire, with a shawl, hunched over an unscrolled letter, the letter bearing a Kingdom stamp like a broken coin. She cried quietly at the words there and her tears smeared the ink like the juice of bramble berries.

My one tear ran like a moon setting west as I returned my gaze to the naked grey-pale boy with the sad beautiful smile and crimson rose blooms where there were no eyes.

"*Come home*," Death whispered, taking my hand.

I went.

About the Author

Scott Thomas is the author of *Cobwebs and Whispers* and *Shadows of Flesh*, both from Delirium books. His fiction has appeared in a number of anthologies which include: *The Year's Best Fantasy and Horror #15*, *The Year's Best Horror #22*, *Sick: An Anthology of Illness*, *Leviathan 3*, *Of Flesh and Hunger*, *Deathrealms* and *The Ghost in the Gazebo*.

Thomas is fond of old houses, cats and the music of Corelli. He lives in Maine.

CPSIA information can be obtained at www.ICGtesting.com
Printed in the USA
BVOW041651041211

277553BV00003B/1/A